YO-CAZ-582

WOMAN KING

EVETTE DAVIS

First Edition, April 2013

Designed by Leah Hefner.

ISBN: 1483918939
ISBN-13: 978-1483918938

To Alec and Stella, for your patience and understanding, especially on the days when I asked to be excused from a family activity so I could stay home to write. I love you both very much.

Careful now.
We're dealing with a point on a map of
fog; Lemuria is a city unknown.
Like us, it doesn't quite exist.
- **Ambrose Bierce**

PROLOGUE

Most of you are probably familiar with the fact that San Francisco is a foggy city. What few people know is the real reason for the fog. San Francisco's weather, despite what the nightly news might say, is controlled by a powerful spell. This spell conjures up the cool, wet fog to keep people from seeing what is really going on around them. The fog tumbles across the hills and mountains like a great grey-white wave, pressing inward until it erases San Francisco from view. On those days and nights, when most people can barely see more than the hand in front of their face, the city's Others—fairies, witches, vampires and werewolves—can meet and attend to their business. In the darkness of night, the light muted, the air damp, it can be difficult to know if what you are seeing is real.

For the Others, there can be no trace of them or their activities left behind. The fog is their eraser, a privacy screen cast up to shield humans from an unsettling truth: They are not alone in this world, and they are not in control.

Besides its reputation for fog, San Francisco is also known for its colorful population. It's no accident that so many outlandish people live there. The city is home to an enormous population of Others, alive and undead. That the Beat poets, the free-speech movement, the Summer of Love, the sexual revolution, and the gay rights movement originated in San Francisco is no coincidence. Amidst the tattooed, pierced and corseted, the Others are free to live their lives. In San Francisco, it is easy to hide in plain sight.

CHAPTER 1

"Listen," he said. "You're not going to like what I have to say."

He paused to give me time to prepare.

"The board has decided we need someone more, well... *powerful*. I'm afraid we're going to have to let you go. We want to win this contract without having to compete for it."

"That's ridiculous," I said, my voice rising in indignation. "As I've mentioned to you before, this agency requires the contract be put out to bid. You're firing me because you don't like the way the rules work?"

For a moment, I thought I'd saved my job by presenting the truth of the situation.

"It's finished, Olivia. The board has made its decision," he said. "We certainly appreciate your efforts, but we need someone more *dynamic,* because this contract is very important to us."

In the days that passed, I worked hard to put that unfortunate call behind me. Olivia Shepherd Consulting had a full roster of clients. As a private consultant to individuals and companies with specific political problems, I had a number of other projects already on my plate.

In fact, before I could dwell too much on what had happened, I received a call asking me to interview for an opportunity to represent a large foundation based in San Francisco. The organization had an endowment in the billions and supported most of the arts and cultural institutions in the region. Anyone turning on a public broadcasting station has seen the foundation's name roll past with heartfelt thanks for their generosity. The committee planned to interview several candidates, and assigned me a thirty-minute slot to present my credentials.

Truthfully, I felt somewhat annoyed at not being asked outright to represent the group. I'd done work for a number of the beneficiaries of their grants, and felt that the foundation should have known immediately that I was the right person for the job. Still, I spent the requisite time reviewing the organization, its structure, priorities and board of directors.

When the day of my interview arrived, I was prepared, a binder of information and a list of questions to ask tucked into my briefcase. Nevertheless, the weather that day seemed to conspire against me. Rain fell ceaselessly, and by the time I left for the appointment in the afternoon, the streets were flooded. A fierce wind was blowing, rendering my umbrella useless. It was not long before my leather pumps were drenched down to the soles of my feet. The pant legs of my navy suit, which I had picked up from the cleaners the day before, were soaked, weighing down my steps.

As I trudged toward the foundation's door, the appointment was beginning to feel more like an obligation than an opportunity. Yet, despite my misgivings, I managed to get through the first round of interviews, feeling good about my rapport with the committee.

On the day of my second interview, I walked out of the house with no binder, no power point presentation, and no plan at all for how to secure the job. I had convinced myself that the second interview was a formality and that I would easily convince the foundation's executive committee to hire me to represent them.

As it turned out, I was profoundly mistaken. When I walked into the conference room for my appointment, an assistant asked for a copy of my presentation so it could be loaded onto her laptop. I replied somewhat cavalierly that I had no presentation and would be improvising my remarks. From the worried look on her face, I should have known that

I was not taking things in a promising direction.

While I made it through the second interview, it was not a pleasant forty minutes. I'd come to see the committee carrying nothing but my sense of entitlement. The committee clearly had expected something more substantial.

Afterwards, I tried to convince myself that the fact that no one had called me for two weeks didn't mean anything. These are busy times, I reasoned. And although I had other work to keep me busy, something was gnawing at me. In the weeks since that first horrible phone call, I had begun to feel off balance. I seemed to be missing my former connection to my clients. I became argumentative, when I should have been a peacemaker. I was passive, when I should have spoken up. Nothing seemed to satisfy me.

Before me was a shelf full of trophies. I had won dozens of awards for the witty, pithy phrases and ideas I'd dreamt up for my clients. Work that had won me accolades from my colleagues. I was successful. I had the respect of my peers. I had savings stored away in a bank account. But something definitely was not right. I could still hear the words in my head: "We need someone more *powerful*."

It was time to visit my best friend Lily to get some perspective. Lily's office is on the sixth floor of San Francisco's Main Library. She has a view of City Hall from her window. My offices are nearby on Van Ness Street, also close to City Hall, where I conduct a lot of work for my clients.

"What do you think he meant?" I asked, seating myself in her office as she typed away.

"Why are you obsessing about this?" Lily asked, her fingers flying across the keyboard. "People will say anything to get off the phone. Maybe he was nervous. You don't fire someone who for years has been your consultant over the telephone. He had to know that was tacky. He was probably at a loss for words."

Lily Prescott manages San Francisco's library branches. San Francisco is comprised of a rich urban quilt of different neighborhoods that crisscross the hills and valleys of the city. Tucked into each of these distinct villages is a library branch. The branches, some built early in the twentieth century thanks to the generosity of Andrew Carnegie, are teeming with people at all hours of the day and night.

I met Lily a few years ago when we were neighbors in an apartment building near the waterfront on the Embarcadero. I had returned to San Francisco from Washington, where I'd worked as a press secretary to a member of Congress. Lily came from Portland, where she had worked as a children's librarian. We were both living in small studio apartments until we could find more permanent homes. Eventually we both left the building; I moved into a small house in the Inner Sunset District my grandmother left me when she died, and Lily found a condominium in the Mission. Our time on the waterfront was limited, but our friendship stuck.

"I agree that it's tacky to fire someone over the telephone, but he meant the words he used… *powerful, dynamic*," I said, grabbing a few almonds out of a bowl on her desk.

"Olivia, what's done is done. You need to focus on something else. Maybe you'd like a new book to read. Tell me what you would like. I'm sure we have a copy."

"Lily, why is it that the library always seems to have the exact book I want? I must like titles that interest no one else."

"We have a very well-stocked library," she said. "And you seem determined today to find fault with yourself."

"What about the foundation?" I asked, trying to avoid a discussion about me. "That should have been my project. Instead, they hired Stoner Halbert."

Lily shifted uncomfortably in her chair.

"What?"

"I heard that he might also have been hired to… well, to pick up where you left off with your last client."

"You heard that?" I choked. "That's not something you hear. What's the real story?"

Lily stopped typing and looked over at me.

"I saw them together at City Hall. I suspect he had an appointment to see if he could persuade the department to forgo soliciting bids and just award them a sole-source contract."

"And how long were you going to wait before telling me this?"

"Olivia. What does it matter? I didn't want to upset you."

"Too late," I said, and walked out of her office.

CHAPTER 2

Stoner Halbert. Suddenly he was the new star on the rise in San Francisco. Everybody wanted to work with him. People seemed to think he possessed some kind of magic. It was painful to admit, but I was jealous. And a tiny bit worried.

I could count on one hand the number of women who did the work I did. Politics and public affairs are not a landscape women dominate. When we do, we often fall into three categories: ball-busters, bitches or sluts. I had long ago lost track of the number of times I'd been complimented on "taking the bit between my teeth," or been a "real bull dog."

While male consultants can be brilliant, relentless, even sexy or magnetic, those qualities don't seem to exist for women. Women, it seems, can only be compared to racehorses and loyal pets.

Stoner Halbert was a former chief of staff to a prominent member of the California Senate. His wife ran an investment firm. The two had long been the darlings of the political and wealthy elite. Their photos ran in the society pages weekly as they were snapped at various functions, wrapped up tightly in fashion's latest creations.

Then one day, the FBI charged Amber Halbert with insider trading and embezzlement. The ensuing news coverage detailing how she had stolen and defrauded some of the state's biggest names in politics and business became too much for Stoner to bear. He resigned from his post to shield his boss from further embarrassment. Amber pled guilty to avoid a more stringent jail sentence, and the two quietly divorced.

Not long after, Stoner set up his own consulting business. From the moment he opened his doors, the city's elite were enthralled. He was collecting big names and big projects. And now, it seemed, he had added one of my clients to his growing list.

After I left the library, I realized I needed a break and decided to get out of town for the day to see my mother. The magnificent, but overwhelming India Rose Shepherd, a landscape painter of some renown, lives in a house in Bolinas. Bolinas, a small hamlet north of San Francisco in Marin County, shares something in common with my mother: Both are difficult to find unless you know what you are looking for.

Crossing the Golden Gate Bridge in my Audi wagon, I headed north on Highway 101 and exited in Mill Valley. After a thirty-minute drive over the hills and through a winding valley, I passed Stinson Beach As I drove past the lagoon, their silver-blue waters glowing in the dusk, I caught a glimpse of a lone heron standing in the shallow inlet.

I turned off the highway onto a side road, although there are no signs or markings to indicate the nearby town. A half-mile further, I followed a long narrow road that led to my mother's home.

Rose, as she likes to be called, lives in a barn that had been converted into a home in the late 1960's. Since then, it's been renovated and modernized many times. There are also two separate cottages on the property, which look out at the rough-hued green grey of the Pacific Ocean. One is her studio and the other is a guest house where I often spend the night. Although I had packed an overnight bag for my trip, I wasn't sure if I would stay. I can never be sure of anything when it comes to my mother.

I'm the only child of a single mother. Unlike many children in the same situation, I didn't suffer any economic hardship. My mother came from a wealthy family that did not disown her when, unmarried, she became pregnant with me.

On the contrary, they embraced her and pulled us into the family even more closely. My grandfather was a successful dairy farmer who gave my mother the land she lives on today. My mother displayed a talent to paint very early on, and by the time she was in her early teens it was quite obvious she was a prodigy. She was sent to art school and returned a successful artist, whose landscape paintings continue to sell for princely sums.

My mother does not, however, always manage her life successfully. In fact, she has struggled through most of it. Rose carries more than just her skill for painting. She's also an empath. Put simply, she can feel and read another person's emotions.

There is no such thing as a poker face around an empath; they possess X-ray vision into your soul. Rose can read people, feel their nervousness, sense their hesitation to do something, detect their anger or sadness. She refers to it as "picking up on the energy of the universe." My mother, grandmother and her mother before her were all empathic. All of the women on our side of the family carry the skill, including me. They call it the Gift, but I have never seen it that way.

From an early age, what I saw was my mother drinking herself to sleep at night to avoid feeling anything. She swallowed too many pills with her friends in order to maintain a barrier between the energy of the universe and herself. And then, when she did focus on her painting, she would remain sequestered in her studio for weeks, inevitably collapsing in her bed for several days afterwards.

As I grew older, I worried that my mother would kill herself, either through her excesses or through exhaustion. Now, at 32, I understand my mother's moods and simply try to avoid her when she is on the dark side of the universe.

As I pulled to the end of the drive, my mother walked out of her house to greet me, her wavy brown hair trailing in the breeze behind her. This is another trait the women in my family are known for: long, lustrous brown hair streaked with red and gold. I could see from her bright, brown eyes that she was sober and happy, a rare thing in the year since my grandmother had died, leaving her with no other woman beside me to confide in. As I got out of the car and began to walk toward her, she smiled.

"So you've come to bury your anger out here in the country, have you?"

I knew she would read my emotions—she always did—but I had nowhere else to go.

"I have," I said. "But if you could wait a bit to finish reading my mood, I'd like to come in and rest."

Rose nodded and escorted me into the house.

After settling down for a much-needed nap on the couch, I awoke forty minutes later and went to look for my mother. She was not in the house. I slipped on a pair of her shoes that were sitting by the door and walked over to her studio, following a path illuminated by small lights set along the paving stones. Maintaining an old habit I'd been taught as a child, I knocked once before entering.

"Come," she called, and I opened the door. She was sitting in front of a canvas with a brush suspended in her fingers. In front of her was the view from the edge of our property. I had seen the same scene a million times growing up, but somehow in her painting she had made the sea seem alive. The deep green blades featured in the grassy cliff that marks the end of our land appeared to be moving. For a moment, I thought I could hear the crickets in the grass, too.

"It's beautiful, Mom."

"Thank you, my dear," she said in a soft, low voice that was reserved for me. "Now why don't you tell me why you decided to come in the middle of the week for a visit? You haven't done that since gran was alive."

When my grandmother Bella Rose was alive, I often visited during the week. After she died, I stopped coming as frequently, not only because I wanted to escape my mother's grief, but also to avoid my own.

"I'm not sure why I'm here, Mom. I have been feeling a little unsettled lately."

My mother nodded. "I can feel your unease. What's happened? Have you seen Lily? She usually makes you feel better."

"Things are not going as well at work as I would like. I got fired from a job recently, and I managed to blow an interview for a big project that easily should have been mine to win. Honestly, I just don't feel like myself."

My mother abruptly dropped her brush on a tray and turned to face me. "Olivia, you are *not* yourself," she said. "Not really. You haven't been yourself for many, many years. I think maybe it is finally catching up with you."

I should have seen the speech coming. But I was feeling so lousy that I had forgotten where this kind of conversation would lead with my mother. Now, there was no avoiding it.

"Mom, please."

"You're agitated. I don't blame you," she continued. "But you have turned your back on a part of yourself, Olivia Rose. It's like wearing contact lenses when your vision is fine to begin with. You've intentionally turned off your own sixth sense. It's no wonder you don't feel like yourself. How long did you think you could keep this up?"

"For as long as I live," I said, as an image of my mother drinking in our darkened kitchen crept into my mind.

"I don't need to use my skills to sense your anger at me, Olivia, and I understand. I love my gift, but it does overwhelm me at times. Your gran was the only person who knew how to help me keep it in perspective. It's one reason why I never married. I didn't want to have to pretend I could control my emotions."

"So it was OK to be out of control around me?" I snapped back.

"No, but it's not the same thing," she said.

"You could have turned it off, Mom," I said, cutting her off. "I have. You don't need to open yourself up like that."

Rose shook her head. "Look at my paintings, Olivia," she said gesturing toward her easel. "Do you really think they would be so alive if I stopped feeling? I could not function if I closed myself off," she continued. "Every time I place a brush to the canvas, I feel the energy of life though my hand. I cannot turn my back on who I am because it's difficult."

"Difficult? You call boozing your way through life difficult? You call taking drugs and sleeping for days difficult?" I said. "That's not what I call it. I call it chaos. I think this curse from our family is a disability. And you medicate yourself to survive."

My mother leaned back on her painter's stool, looking beleaguered.

I had said too much and regretted my words immediately. I apologized and she forgave me, never having been one to let an emotional outburst offend her.

Soon after our argument, I left her studio and retreated to the guest house to go to bed, but my sleep that night was miserable. I tossed and turned, in the grip of a terrible, unexplained anxiety. At one point, I was plagued by a dream featuring an enormous black panther that seemed to be stalking me. When I woke up in the morning, I decided to head straight back to San Francisco. I felt guilty leaving my mother without saying goodbye, but knew that she would understand.

CHAPTER 3

For several days after returning home I did not sleep well. Though I fell into bed exhausted, I was awakened in the middle of the night by a dream featuring an enormous panther walking beside me. The setting for these walks seemed familiar to me, but I could never tell exactly where we were. A very odd detail in these dreams was that I felt the animal wanted to speak to me. But of course that was ridiculous.

Lack of sleep made me increasingly agitated as the days went on. Indeed, I was in no mood to be gracious when the call came from one of my clients asking for an impromptu meeting at my offices. In my experience, no client ever wants to meet the same day unless they intend to fire you. I agreed to the meeting and spent the better part of the morning trying to keep my already shredded nerves from disintegrating.

At 1 pm inside our office conference room, I greeted my client, a real estate developer who wanted to buy a pair of apartment buildings, tear them down, and build two enormous towers in their place. It would be a difficult project because it involved temporarily relocating hundreds of people, and then offering them a chance to return to the new apartments in the towers, but at the same rent they paid previously. My client also wanted the height of the two buildings to be greater than what the law allows, something that worried city officials, who had never granted such a waiver.

The list of concerns had been mounting, now making it almost a full day's job to respond to the telephone calls and emails regarding the project. I have a small but highly competent staff in the office, yet it was obvious that this project was becoming overwhelming. Generally, I don't believe in being overwhelmed and refuse to allow myself to feel that kind of emotion. The problem, in this case, was that it blinded me to my own limitations.

"Thanks for making time to see me, Olivia," he said with a smile that did not reach his eyes.

"You don't need to thank me, Tom," I said, my lips fixed in a weak grin. "But I am wondering what brought you to my office in the middle of the day instead of calling."

"Listen, um, I have been speaking with my investors and we have decided that we'd like to bring in another consultant to help, err, round out the team."

"Round out the team," I repeated.

Tom looked down at his hands for a moment before he spoke, a sure sign I was going to hear bad news.

"The thing is," he stuttered. "We've been speaking with Stoner Halbert and have asked him to come on board."

There he was again. It seemed we were going to be spending a lot of time together, whether it suited me or not.

"I see," I said calmly. "Have I failed to do something? Are you unhappy with my work?"

Tom shifted in his chair, but again would not meet my gaze.

"Olivia, this is a big project and we absolutely must get approval. The bank has given me a limited time to complete the entitlements, or the loan will evaporate. Lately, well … Look, this is no reflection on you. I think this is a situation where a larger team makes sense. We need some additional firepower."

It was difficult for me to hear him speak because the blood was pounding so loudly in my ears. I had never been superstitious before, but I was beginning to wonder if someone or something had jinxed me.

You know how there are moments that define us as adults? Well, this was one of them for me. I did not want to

15

lose the project. I was already worried about my reputation, having lost one client already to Halbert. Professionally, I could not allow myself to become enraged, so I swallowed my pride. After a lengthy and awkward moment of silence on my part, I put on my game face and smiled.

"Tom, if you think that bringing Stoner on board will help improve our chances, then I am all for it," I said, my voice slightly cracking. "Why don't we set up a meeting next week to get the team together and brief him on the status of things."

Tom smiled, and this time it was a genuine smile.

"I knew this wouldn't be a problem for you, Olivia," he said beaming. "You are one tough cookie. I'll tell Stoner to call you and you two can arrange a meeting."

"Great. OK," I said, beaming right back at him, "I will look out for his call."

We shook hands and I showed Tom out. After he left, I walked back to my office, shut the door, and, for the first time in many years, began to cry.

Halbert must have been on Tom's speed dial, because he called me less than an hour later to arrange a meeting. By the time he called, I had stopped crying and had moved on to brooding.

"Aren't you a good sport," he purred into the phone when I told him I would make the necessary arrangements to merge our teams. "Not many people would be as gracious about having to work with another consultant. What's your secret?" His tone was friendly, but oddly biting and I was anxious to get off the phone.

"The important thing is for this project move forward and for the client to be happy," I said, trying to sound indifferent.

I was, of course, lying.

CHAPTER 4

After everything that had transpired, it seemed like a good day to leave work early. My head ached, the result of a toxic cocktail of sensations swirling within me. I needed to deal with my anxiety, embarrassment and anger. Since when did I need help to complete a project? Why was I suddenly not powerful enough? I had no answers to these questions, but I felt a growing sense of unease.

At home, I tried to work in my garden. Putting my hands into the dirt usually helps to distract me from my troubles. For some reason, the lots in the Inner Sunset are more generous than in other parts of the city, and my yard is larger than most. Slowly, I had been transforming my plot into a Provençal garden, complete with olive trees and lavender. I am an unabashed Francophile, having visited the country many times with my mother over the years to attend her exhibitions.

My introduction to French began in kindergarten, as my mother insisted that I attend a French bilingual school. There, a kindly older woman from Toulouse taught me my earliest words. In addition, I lived in Paris briefly during college through an exchange program, where I expanded my studies to include French grammar. The garden is one way I stay connected to France—right down to the antique wooden park chairs outside on my deck.

This time, however, even the garden didn't help me relax. Though I managed to settle a half-dozen shade plants into the soil on the south side of the garden, I still didn't feel any better than I had before. In fact, I felt worse. I went inside and opened my laptop. I fiddled with my iPod and created a few new playlists. I updated my Facebook status, and then went back to Spotify to look at new music. Finally, after another hour of spinning my wheels, I texted Lily and asked her to join me for drinks. She immediately agreed to meet me.

I dusted off most of the soil from my clothing and went upstairs to shower and change. I pulled out a black cotton dress with ballet sleeves and a pair of leopard-print flats, then rummaged through my closet until I found a slate-grey cashmere cardigan that draped to my knees.

I headed off to the Mission, a part of San Francisco where one should not show up in a suit and tie. The epicenter of fashion and cuisine, the Mission is in constant motion. It's a favorite spot among the young and creative who are drawn to its avant-garde clothing boutiques and stylish restaurants. It also happens to be one of the warmest parts of San Francisco—blessed with less fog than most parts of town.

I was meeting Lily at Foreign Cinema, a popular restaurant where movies are projected onto an enormous wall. On nice evenings, it's heavenly to sit outside on the patio and watch a film while enjoying *steak frites* and a nice glass of Bordeaux.

Lily was waiting in the long hallway that led to the hostess station when I walked in the door. She smiled, a tentative smile, given that the last time we'd seen each other I had left in a funk. But Lily was my best friend, and it wasn't her fault that Stoner Halbert seemed to be stalking my clients.

As we were about to be led to our table, I noted a group of men checking her out. Lily's beauty is such that it can be startling. She is over six feet tall, with straight black hair that falls down to the middle of her back, the blackness accentuating her pale, seemingly glowing, skin. Tonight she looked especially striking in a pair of slim jeans tucked into boots and an amazing vintage military coat, complete with brass buttons. She'd fashioned her hair into two long braids on either side of her head and, as a result, a small tattoo at the back of her neck was visible. The tattoo was a tiny bit of writing in a language I did not recognize.

"What's the tattoo?" I asked as we walked into the dining room, leaving Lily's admirers behind.

Lily smiled and rubbed her fingers over the images. "It's nothing. It's a design a friend made when I was in college. It's gibberish, really. Sometimes I forget it's even there."

"What does it say?" I asked, intrigued by her reticence.

"It's written in an old language," she said. "It means peace and order."

"Peace and order," I repeated. "Sounds nice, where can we find some of that?"

Lily squeezed my hand. "You never know, Olivia, it might be right around the corner."

We were seated at a table outside in the courtyard. The movie was starting early, before sunset, because it was *Lord of the Rings*, the first part of the trilogy.

"Oh, I love that movie," Lily said picking up a menu.

"We could do with a bit of make-believe," I said, scanning the dinner specials. "It's no fun to be in the real world at the moment."

"It was no picnic for Middle Earth," Lily said. "After all, they had a war to contend with."

"Yes, but it's make believe," I said, pausing to order a glass of wine with the server. "In the real world, there are no such things as fairies or dwarves. There is no handsome warrior who will come to save civilization and pledge his undying love to the woman of his dreams. That kind of magic only exists in movies."

Lily seemed to be struggling with a thought; she furrowed her brow and appeared to be on the verge of telling me something. But the shadow quickly passed, and she laughed. "Well, thank goodness for movies… and martinis," she added quickly as her drink arrived at the table.

We ordered dinner and sat back in amicable silence to watch the Hobbits. Once our plates arrived, Lily turned her attention back to me.

"How are you doing, Olivia? We haven't spoken since you came to see me at my office."

"I'm not great," I said honestly. "I feel like Stoner is stalking me. He seems to have found a way to get in between me and two of my clients; they all appear to think he's magic, a new, powerful consultant with a set of skills no one has seen before."

This brought the same dark look back to Lily's face. "Do you think someone in your company is helping him?"

"No, I think *I* am helping him. I am not at the top of my game," I said, trying to keep my voice low because of the movie. "I'm not doing my best work, and each time I make a mistake, he seems to be right there. It's beginning to take a toll on me. I haven't slept well in weeks."

Lily leaned over and placed her hand on mine. "You're having trouble sleeping?"

I nodded. " I fall asleep, but then I am plagued with the same confusing dream."

Lily's face took on the same worried look again, "What kind of dream, Olivia? Are in you danger?"

What an odd question to ask, I thought, but I decided to ignore it and describe my dream. "I'm having this dream. It doesn't seem dangerous, but when it happens, I feel like this animal is trying to speak with me."

"What kind of animal?" Lily asked, looking pensive.

"I'm sure it's nothing." I said, feeling the need to reassure her. "It's a black panther and she seems to want to speak with me."

"She?" Lily repeated. "How do you know it's a she?"

"Good question," I said, pausing to take a sip of wine. "I don't know, really. It seems like a she. In my dreams, the panther walks beside me, but she never blocks my way. And when I wake up, it feels like she is still there, trying to help me. Crazy, right?"

Lily shook her head and smiled. "Maybe the panther is trying to tell you something. But it might take a while to figure out what it is."

"Well, let's hope it happens soon," I said, "Before Stoner manages to take over any more of my business."

I went home that evening feeling better. It had felt good to tell Lily about my problems at work and about the dreams. I was hoping that confessing my anxiety would help me finally get some sleep. Instead, I was plagued once again by the dream. This time, however, the panther's purring sounded even louder in my head. It seemed that the animal was trying to get my attention. I woke up in the middle of the night feeling quite unwell. Not only was I was disoriented from a general lack of sleep during the last few days, but also hungover from the wine I'd consumed with Lily. I went downstairs and climbed on the couch in my living room. Wrapping an old wool blanket around my shoulders, I flipped through the channels on my television until dawn trying to relax.

I took the next day off of work, again. I was too tired to go into the office. My trusty iPhone allowed me to scan emails and return a few calls, but I remained in a funk and could not seem to focus on my work. I decided to catch a movie, and then go out again that evening for drinks. This time Lily wasn't free to join me, so I went out on my own.

Throughout the following week, I followed the same pattern. I drank all night and slept all day. As the week progressed, I grew inexplicably more despondent, ignoring my office altogether. Although what I was doing would only make matters worse, I could not seem to help myself. By the fifth night, as I fumbled to open my front door, I felt angry. I don't know how long that emotion had been lurking in my psyche, but by the time I turned the key in the lock, I was more furious than ever.

"What the hell is happening?" I yelled out to no one in particular. I lived alone and had no pets, so I was unconcerned that anyone would hear me. I threw my purse on the floor and stomped into the kitchen. As I stormed through the doorway, I caught my elbow sharply on the frame. Crying out in pain, I slumped to the floor sobbing as I cradled my injured arm.

I was angry that I had bumped my arm. I was angry that I was behaving like my mother, staying drunk for a week to avoid what was bothering me. Then, my thoughts drifted back to what I had been avoiding all week: Stoner Halbert. I had to return to work and face my clients. I had to work with *him*. I could feel the unmistakable sensation of someone *gaining* on me, and I feared soon I would have no business to go back to.

"What did I do to deserve this?" I cried out again into the emptiness of my kitchen. "What I am I supposed to do?"

Still holding my arm. I slid across the floor and propped myself against one of the cabinets. As I sat on the floor of my kitchen crying, the image of the black cat from my dreams popped into my head.

"Why don't you tell me what you want?" I murmured, my head resting against the cabinet, my eyes closed. "Please, speak to me."

Not long after I said those words, I fell asleep on the kitchen floor.

CHAPTER 5

When I awoke the next morning, I felt very cold. Then I realized that I was not in bed. Had I somehow failed to make it home? Slowly, I began to remember the details of the previous evening and I opened one eye. I was sprawled out on the floor of my kitchen. My body was stiff from sleeping on the hard stone floor, and I was chilled to the bone, having slept without the benefit of a coat or blanket. I was about to get up when I heard a voice speak to me.

"Let me help you up," the woman said, her speech revealing a hint of a foreign accent I could not place.

"Lily?" I asked aloud, thinking I was too hung-over to recognize my friend's voice. Maybe I had let her in last night, or maybe I had called her and she had used her key. Either way I was glad that she was there.

"It's not Lily," the voice said. "Open your eyes, Olivia."

I did as I was told and promptly let out a scream as my eyes focused on the figure standing in my kitchen. It was not Lily. I had never seen this woman before.

"Who are you and how did you get into my house?" I asked, wondering if I had managed to leave the door open. Maybe some deranged person had walked in off the street. I did live in a city, after all. I began calculating how quickly I could get to the phone and call the police. But as I glanced at her more closely, I saw that she didn't look homeless. She seemed about my age and was tall, slightly more so than Lily. She also had long black hair, but it seemed almost darker than black, like the color of a raven's wing, or say, maybe, a panther. She was wearing skintight leather pants and a dark sweater. The fingers on her hands were long and slender and adorned with several silver rings. She wore a small silver hoop through one of her eyebrows, which framed green eyes that almost glowed like a cat's. I was beginning to see a pattern that unnerved me.

"Are you the panther?" I asked, shocked at the absurdity of my question.

The woman nodded. "You did invite me here, Olivia. You asked me to come and tell you what I had to say."

Too stunned for words, I began to question whether I was losing my mind. All this time I had worried my mother would be the one to become ill, now it seemed I had it backwards. I sat motionless for a moment and stared.

"This is your problem, Olivia," she said. "I've been watching you for several weeks and you haven't lifted a finger to help yourself. Get up off the floor. Stand up."

The woman offered me her hand. I grabbed it and felt the warm flesh of a human being against my palm.

"How is this possible?" I murmured as I rose. "Are you really here? I'm not hallucinating?"

"I'm real," she said. "As real as Stoner Halbert, only I have come to help you."

"How do you know about him?" I asked. "How do you know about me?"

"Your grandmother sent me," she said. "Bella chose me to watch over you when you were born. When you ran into trouble with Stoner, I expected you to summon me, but you do not practice the old ways of your family. I've been forced to appear in your dreams to get your attention."

"*Summon you.* I have no idea how to do that," I said, my tongue slightly swollen in my mouth. "I had no idea my grandmother could do that sort of thing. I was drunk and angry last night. I didn't know my outburst would result … well, that it would bring *you* here."

The woman laughed. "There is a lot about this world you don't know, Olivia, and that has put you in harm's way."

I walked slowly to a barstool and sat down. It was too

much. Not for the first time that week, my head was pounding and I was exhausted. Now there was a strange woman in my house claiming to be my guardian angel. I couldn't imagine what would happen next. I decided to make an espresso, and find out.

"Do you drink coffee?" I asked and then paused and extended my hand in a way that said *I'd like to call you by a name.*

"It's Elsa," she said. "And tea, please."

"Elsa," I repeated. "I have Earl Grey and green tea."

"Earl Grey," she said, and I began to fix our drinks.

I set two warm mugs on the counter. Elsa took the bar stool across from mine and began to sip her tea. She seemed to savor it more than the normal person would.

"Don't they have tea where you're from?"

"It's been a while since I've been called to your world. I remember now how nice it is to visit."

"What do you mean, my world? Are you dead?"

"No, not dead. Unable to move on," she said without a trace of sarcasm. "As you may have guessed, I'm not from this time. But I do live in your century regularly now."

Perhaps it was the combination of fear and a raging hangover, but I was unable to keep up the light banter and decided to put my questions to her. "Why are you here? What have you been trying to tell me?"

Elsa put down her cup and saucer and turned to face me. "I came because your grandmother feared what would happen if you continued to block your gift. Before her death, she summoned me and told me she had seen a vision in which you were in danger. She asked me to visit you periodically and ensure you remain unharmed. For many months I watched and saw nothing out of the ordinary."

"And now?"

"Now? You're in danger. It may have seemed wise at the time to not use your powers, Olivia, but turning off your instincts has made you vulnerable. You're not even trying to sense when you're in danger. It's why Stoner Halbert's demon picked you."

This remark caused me to drop my coffee mug on the marble counter where it promptly broke into several pieces.

"I'm sorry, did you say *demon*?"

Elsa sighed. "I can see we will have to start at the beginning. Your friend Mr. Halbert has been dabbling in black magic. After his wife ruined him, he sought revenge and became interested in the occult. He has managed to conjure up a minor demon that promises him great wealth. The demon has given him an advantage, a sort of influence…and he is using it against you and others."

"Why me?"

Elsa seemed to pause for a moment. "What's the expression? *You are a sitting duck.* The Others can see that you have intentionally blocked off your senses. It makes you an easy target for their mischief. Halbert's demon has gone in search of the most vulnerable. An empath who refuses to listen her instincts? That is an easy mark."

"Why should I believe any of this is real or true?" I asked, now frightened beyond measure. To cover my feelings, I leaned down to pick up the broken porcelain pieces.

Either I was having a complete mental breakdown, or there was a spirit guide in my kitchen discussing a demon. My grandmother had told me stories when I was a child of the time-walkers who visited her village in Scotland. In her tales, they brought news of loved ones and warned of impending dangers. Free to move between the past and the future, these witches were welcomed cautiously by the villagers and warmly by women like my grandmother, who had their own gifts. I always thought they were part of a charming folklore, the stuff packed into books in the library.

Elsa smiled and set down her teacup. "It's nice to see you get angry, Olivia. It's long overdue, but welcome. Who do you think I am then, if not someone sent here to help you? I could have killed you while you were passed out in your kitchen. And yet, here I am and you're still alive."

"That's my point," I said. "You could be anyone. You could be some con artist off the street. Why should I believe you?"

"How would I know about your gifts if not for your grandmother?" Elsa asked. "You can try to pretend you're not connected to any of this, Olivia, but your grandmother was a great seer. Your mother is extremely receptive. The fact that you have ignored your lineage doesn't erase the connections."

The mention of my mother sent my head spinning. Demons. Spirit guides. It was all too much. I knew Elsa wasn't a vagrant off the street. Her arrival at the moment I asked for her could only be connected to my dreams. But I wasn't ready to face these facts.

"I'm tired. I think you should leave and come back another time when I feel up to a discussion," I said, walking toward my front door and opening it.

Elsa stared at me, a look of fury in her eyes. "Do you really think you can avoid me like you've avoided everything else? You asked me to come!"

I nodded. "I didn't know what I was asking for. I don't know why my grandmother sent you, but I don't need your help. I will get some rest and fix everything tomorrow."

"You cannot fight the demon without my help, Olivia. You need me."

"That's exactly my point," I said as I ushered her to the stoop. "I don't intend to fight."

I shut the door, managed to walk upstairs to my bedroom, and I started to cry.

"God damn it," I screamed as I tossed a pillow across the room. "God *damn* it!" I had asked her to come, but I truly meant it when I said I didn't know what I was asking for. What did I need? An exorcist? A psychiatrist?

My mother and all of her warnings came back to me. I was hunched over on the edge of my bed sobbing, when my phone beeped, signaling a text. I picked up my mobile from my nightstand. There, blinking, was a message from Stoner Halbert. I glanced at his message:

Olivia, where R U?
Client has asked me 2 B project manager.
I'm up three to nothing, and we're only in the second inning.

I threw the phone across the room, feeling sick to my stomach. I managed to make it to my bathroom before I began to vomit. Why, why was this happening to me? In all my life I had never harmed a soul. My only weakness, if you could call it one, was that I had refused to accept my Gift. I had forsaken my emotions for logic, relying on the power of reason to solve my problems. Now though, it seemed that logic could be easily overpowered by magic, for no reason at all.

I leaned against the edge of my toilet wiping a cold cloth across my lips. I hadn't given Halbert my phone number. I had to suppose my ex-client had turned it over. I felt trapped inside my house like a mouse in a cage. Would I find him waiting for me outside one day? Elsa was right. For once, I couldn't fix a problem on my own. I needed help. I knew she would come again if I called her.

"Come back," I said, more quietly than I intended as I walked to my bed to lie down. "Please come back."

I awoke several hours later from a dreamless sleep. I climbed out of bed slowly and grabbed a robe from a chair nearby. I walked into the bathroom to look in the mirror. The face staring back, while worn and puffy, didn't seem any different. I had no marks on my body, no bumps, no bruises or scars.

Whatever Halbert was doing to me, it was all in my mind. I shook my head ruefully. He would drive me crazy if things continued this way. Normally, I was the queen of calm, never showing the world if I had a problem. But this much upheaval was bad for business. I would never be able to keep a poker face in public now.

I began to panic again, thinking about Halbert. I sat down on the edge of the tub to calm myself. It was at that moment, that I heard the sound of the television coming from the living room downstairs. I hoped it was Elsa, or maybe Lily had let herself in. I walked downstairs and found Elsa sitting on the couch, her shoes and socks off, watching a reality TV program that appeared to center on second marriages and Botox.

"You know, that stuff will kill you," I said, relieved that she had returned.

"It's fascinating," Elsa said, looking away from the television screen. "Do people really spend their time watching this stuff?"

"Yes. Quite a few people; these programs are very popular."

Elsa shook her head and clicked off the program. "It's no wonder the Council is worried."

"The Council?"

"Later. It's too complicated. How are you feeling?"

"Better, but I have been thinking about what you said to me. I want to know what's happening to me and I want your help."

"It's the demon," Elsa said rising from the couch. "He is a minor demon of the lowest order. Halbert is not skilled enough yet in the dark arts to conjure a major demon, but this one is still a demon. Their job is to harm their caller's adversaries."

"How?" I asked. "Do they use physical pain?"

Elsa shook her head. "Not this demon. He's not designed to cause physical pain; he's subtler. Have you been acting odd lately? Acting in ways that are unusual for you?"

I nodded. "When I visited my mother recently, I told her I didn't feel like myself."

"What did she say?"

I was about to admit my mother had been right about something and it made me uncomfortable. "She said that as long as I ignored my gift, I wasn't really myself."

"She was right. You have cut yourself off from your true nature and the source of your power. When you do that, it is very easy for an Other to knock you off balance."

"What is an 'Other?' "

"An Other is someone like me, or a vampire or a demon. There are humans, and there are the *Others*."

"What do you mean knock me off balance?"

"You said it... you don't feel like *yourself*. Have you been more argumentative? Have you been over-confident that things will be fine, when in reality they are getting worse?"

Again, I nodded.

"That's the demon."

It was a relief to hear someone tell me I wasn't going crazy, or that the events of the last few weeks were not totally my fault, and yet the joy of reassurance was overshadowed by her explanation. I was being plagued by a demon? To hear it described in such dispassionate tones was unsettling.

"Am I under the control of this demon now?" I asked, afraid to hear the answer.

"Yes and no. There have been moments when the demon cast spells that made you act badly, or he flummoxed you. And he is working spells and charms on your clients. How else do you explain walking away from your work, or that a client asked you to bring Halbert on your team? But he has not tried to possess you physically. Once I began to appear in your dreams, I placed a protective spell on you to limit his manipulations."

"Why just limit things?" I asked. "Can you stop this?"

"It all depends on you, Olivia. You were born with abilities that should make it difficult or impossible for a demon to target you. You would have known that the emotions you experienced were not your own. It's even possible you would have felt the presence of the Other. We won't know until we open your senses and see what kind of gifts you really have."

I shook my head. "I don't want to 'open my senses,' " I said. "I don't want to feel more emotion. I want your help to get rid of this demon and go back to work."

Elsa picked up her shoes and socks and began to put them on.

"This time *I'm* leaving," she said. "It's obvious that you are not prepared to deal with the situation and I can't help someone who won't help herself. This isn't a school project that you can ask your parents to fix. You are a grown woman in trouble—a trouble only you can make disappear. If you won't help yourself, then there is nothing I can do."

"What happens if you go?"

"More of the same, only minus me in your dreams," Elsa said. "Halbert will continue to take what he wants from you until there is nothing left."

She used my pride against me, and it worked. I couldn't stand the idea of losing my business to him that way— stripped to the bone, all my clients and past successes erased.

"OK," I said, swallowing hard at what was unfolding. "What do I have to do?"

Elsa smiled. "I am glad you asked."

CHAPTER 6

Elsa asked me either to close my business or take a leave of absence. Both suggestions seemed too dramatic, so I put her off, saying I would start with a vacation. I informed my remaining clients I would be out again for several weeks. Then I called my staff and apologized profusely for being out of touch, giving them all modest pay raises as encouragement to stay on and manage things while I was away.

My home has three bedrooms. Besides mine, one is an office that I use when I work from home rather than downtown, and the other is a smallish guest room with a double bed. I gave that room to Elsa, complete with a fresh set of sheets and a tutorial on how to use the remote control for the small television perched on a table inside. It was obvious that wherever Elsa normally spent the bulk of her time, cable was not available.

I went to bed that night and slept soundly for the first time in weeks. My peace was short-lived, though, when I was awakened at 6 am the following morning by Elsa, who stood looming above me, a pair of my running shoes in her hands.

"Up!" she said. "It's time to begin your training."

I mumbled something about it being too early and rolled over. This time she pulled the blankets off and let the cold air roll over me. I shot up and tried to pull the blankets back, but Elsa was not budging.

"Up!" she repeated. "You need to get into fighting shape."

"Where are we going?"

"I did a little scouting while you were asleep last night.

There is a place nearby where we can begin our work."

"Are you going to feed me to the lions?" I grumbled.

Elsa snorted. "I am not quite that old, if that is what you were implying. Besides they would not have fed their seer, possibly their local healer, to the lions."

That caught my attention. I didn't know anything about Elsa or where she had come from. For all I knew, she did live when the Romans built their coliseums. She seemed to know I had a few questions on the tip of my tongue because she quickly cut me off. "Later. I will answer your questions when we return."

Not long afterwards, I was staring at a steep set of steps inside Kezar Stadium, an old football stadium located nearby. "You want me to run the stairs? Why?"

"When I was your age I could ride a horse for miles while holding a crossbow," Elsa said, her hands on her hips. "I've fired a rifle from horseback while hunting with my tribe. Can you do that?"

I shook my head, trying not to laugh at the image of me with a crossbow.

"You need to get into fighting shape to protect yourself," Elsa chirped. "After a few weeks with the demon, I fear you've lost some of your energy."

"I have no need to shoot anything from the back of a horse," I barked back. "I can't see how this will help me at all."

"Just run the stairs," Elsa deadpanned. "I will see you at the top."

This was too ridiculous. Hunt. Ride a horse. I was a modern woman. I rode public transportation. It was with that kind of mindset that I prepared to walk away. But where would I go? I had asked Elsa to stay, and more importantly, I hated to abandon a challenge. How hard could it be to run the stairs?

I took off with gusto. The first few steps seemed easy. "Piece of cake," I mused privately. As I climbed higher, however, my legs began to quiver. Then they began to ache, my hamstring muscles burning like a match to the strip on the box. I gasped for air, unsteady as my legs began to wobble. As I was nearing the top of the steps, I tripped and missed breaking my nose on the corner of one of the wooden benches by mere millimeters. I barely managed to pull myself upright, still gasping for air.

As I sat down to collect myself, I watched Elsa, decked out in a pair of my yoga pants, come running up the stairs. She was not out of breath when she reached the top. I hid my face as she approached.

"Don't be embarrassed," she said. "I didn't do that to humiliate you. But I did want to make a point. You need to know your body and know your emotions. The best way to do that is to be physically fit. Being fit also gives you mental endurance, and you will need those skills when you allow your gifts to return."

"I think I might throw up," was my brilliant reply.

"By all means," Elsa said in response, "but when you're finished you need to run the stairs again. We're going to be out here every day until you can do this easily."

"Why?"

"I outlasted my enemies because I rode harder, rode faster and rode farther," Elsa said. "Endurance is everything in war."

"War," I said, a shiver running up my spine. "I'm not at war."

"Do you want your career back? You will have to stand up to the demon and Stoner Halbert to do it. That is not something that can happen without work. Think of it this way. I have been watching television and the men of your era seem to like fit women. It is easy to distract men using physical beauty. It will give you one more skill to use to your advantage."

It was not the motivational speech one would normally hear from a personal trainer, but it worked. And so, my training began, and in those first few days, Elsa and I settled into a comfortable schedule. We exercised for several hours each morning before returning home. The city, it turned out, was a wonderful boot camp, with endless hills to climb, many lined with hidden staircases. We drove to Crissy Field and ran the path to the Golden Gate Bridge. After a few weeks, I was able to run across the bridge as a part of my regimen. My afternoons were left open, and I spent that time running errands, touching base with my office and working in the garden.

Although I was feeling better, I wondered what Elsa had in store for me next. She'd asked me not to tell Lily about her, and so far, I had honored her request. Lily was pretty busy with her own life, but eventually she would want to spend time together. One afternoon as Elsa and I were having tea—she'd banned coffee from my diet—I asked if I could see Lily.

"Not yet," was her reply.

"Why?"

"Because you need to focus," she said in a schoolteacher's voice. "If you bring your friend into this, she will only distract you."

"Distract me from what? It seems as if your work is almost done here," I said, feeling confident. "I am exercising, I feel great."

"We are a long way from being done," Elsa said. "This is simply the conditioning you need to get physically ready. We have yet to unlock your senses and see how they work."

"No," I said. "How can allowing myself to feel more possibly help?"

"You will not help yourself by remaining ignorant," Elsa said. "The reason you feel well is because I'm here, and because you're not in the direct path of the demon. The minute you step back into your office, you will experience the same problems again."

I didn't know what to say. I did feel better and I was growing used to Elsa, although I knew next to nothing about this woman living in my guest room.

"Why are you doing this?" I asked. "I know you said my

grandmother summoned you, but why do you have to stay?"

"I don't *have* to stay," she countered. "But as a spirit guide, my job is to help you escape danger. My work isn't finished yet. And, I have business with the Council that keeps me here."

"So you aren't necessarily staying for me," I said, certain there was something she wasn't telling me.

"Why are you so anxious to see me leave?" Elsa asked. "We have much work to do. I sense you have a great power, Olivia," she said. "I feel the energy in you. But you are in danger as long as you fail to use your instincts to see what is happening around you."

"I'm afraid," I said. "This gift you keep referring to has made my mother's life difficult. I don't want to become like her."

"Mother, father, sister, brother," Elsa said shaking her head. "We cannot escape the bonds of our family, their blood is our blood."

"I don't have any of those except my mother. I never knew my father and my grandparents are dead."

Once again, Elsa paused for a moment as if she were acknowledging something important in my statement. "Your gift is passed through the women in your family, so it matters little about the rest. My mother was a shaman in our village, as was her mother before her. These skills pass through one generation to the next. One day, you will have a daughter."

"Stop," I said, holding out my hand. "I'm not getting married. I'm not having a child. Look at me. My life is out of control. I am having a conversation in my kitchen with a ghost about how to beat the devil at his own game. How on earth can you talk about a future with marriage and children?"

Elsa looked amused, but not in a good way. "Technically, I am not a ghost and I have never seen anyone beat the devil at his own game," she said. "You are nowhere near ready to do that. I am asking that you take responsibility for your own life and use the tools you were given. By all the goddesses of the known world, I have never seen anyone reject her bloodline so readily. This wasn't a choice when I was your age. People in my tribe, in my village, depended on my mother to seek out the spirits to learn about the harvest, to heal the sick and protect our elders."

"What about you?" I asked, angry at her lecture. "What did they depend on you for?"

Elsa turned her head away from me slightly. For the first time since she'd revealed herself to me, I could see hesitation. It seemed that she too had secrets.

"We are alike in many ways Olivia," she continued. "I did not reject my skills when I was your age, but I did not manage them well, either. I wanted to do more than help old men bring in good crops for the village. So I began to dabble in things that were beyond my measure."

Elsa got up from the bar stool and began to pace around the kitchen.

"Eventually, I left my village in search of someone or someplace where I could learn how to gain more power. I was not content to see the future; I wanted to control it. After much searching, I found an old witch who promised to help me gain introduction to a school of magic where I could learn the secrets of casting powerful spells to control things… nature, the weather."

"So you wanted to be a powerful witch?"

"I wanted power," Elsa said. "I had no specific occupation in mind."

"Did you find the school?"

Elsa nodded, but her face was grim. "The *scholomance* was in the mountains of Romania. It was very remote. I began my journey in the fall. It took more than a day to reach the top of the mountain and find the castle."

"And…?"

"The witch was true to her word," Elsa said. "She sent me to the door of a school where all things dark could be learned. I should have been more cautious, but I was eager to begin my lessons. I knocked upon a large wooden door with a raven engraved on the front. After some time, an elderly man dressed as a servant opened the door. He confirmed it was a school, but said they only accepted ten students at a time. At first I thought he was sending me away, but then he said that I had arrived just in time and would be the tenth student. He instructed me to secure my horse in the stables nearby and return to the castle. Excited, I quickly did as I was told. As I walked back toward the school, an angel appeared on the branch of a tree next to me."

I raised an eyebrow, but did not interrupt.

"The angel called out to me by name, and implored me to not enter the castle. He told me it was the house of the devil, and that of the ten students chosen, one would have to stay behind and be sent to hell as payment for the lessons. The angel was certain I would be the one to make good on the debt, and he urged me to reclaim my horse and ride away from the castle that very moment."

"Did you leave?" I asked, caught up in her remarkable tale.

"I was eager to become more powerful, but I did not want to give my soul to the devil. I agreed to leave with the angel. As I turned to retrieve my horse, the door of the castle swung open. The servant I spoke with was there again, but this time, he was dressed in the clothing of a gentleman. I realized I had been conversing with the devil himself the entire time."

At this point I was speechless. The devil? Was she joking with me to make a point?

Elsa sensed my skepticism. "If you decide to continue with your training, you will come to see that there is more to this world than meets the eye. I didn't believe I would ever stand toe-to-toe with the devil until that day, either."

"Go on," I urged.

"The devil asked us both if we would like to come inside for a cup of tea. The angel laughed and said 'you know very well that I will not walk through those doors.'"

"'Then I will come to you,' the devil said. I had seen many evil spirits in my time as a shaman, but I had never felt such evil as I did when he approached us. He was standing as close to me as I am to you. By knocking on his door, he said, I had already offered myself to him. The angel replied that he had been watching the school for more than 100 years and knew very well that until I crossed the threshold, I was not subject to the devil's contract."

I have to admit, she had captured my attention. I motioned rapidly with my hand to continue.

"To my surprise, the devil asked the angel if he would take a walk with him. I did not know at the time, but it seems that the devil enjoys making deals and negotiations. Testing the intellect of his opponents gives him great pleasure.

"The angel agreed to walk with him, but only if they stayed outside the castle. It was dark now, but a full moon glowed, illuminating the grounds. While waiting for them, I leaned against the tree, listening as the mountains came alive with the sounds of creatures in the area, including wolves. I vowed to myself that I would go to the barn and lock the doors if they didn't return quickly.

"After a short while, they returned. But at that moment, I had never been so frightened. I had climbed the mountain to the school full of the energy of an ambitious woman in her thirties, with no idea of the true expense of the knowledge I desired. Exposed at the doorway to the devil and his brood, I now understood that some things are too costly to pursue. And furthermore, I had angered the devil by refusing his wish. If he won the argument, what would become of me once I was inside the castle?"

I had the same question burning in my mind and was beginning to imagine all kinds of torture, images straight out of all the late-night horror movies I had seen.

"The devil seemed to enjoy my apprehension, for he grinned broadly and took his time to speak. 'You are free to leave,' was all he said, and then he disappeared into the darkness."

"Is that it? You walked away?"

Elsa was about to finish her story when my doorbell

rang. We both looked at each other, wondering who it could be. I shrugged my shoulders and got up to find out.

When I opened the door, Lily was standing outside.

"Where have you been?" she asked, pushing past me. "Why are you blowing me off? You won't come out, you don't answer my texts."

She stopped mid-sentence when she saw Elsa standing inside. Both women grabbed me, each trying to tug me to safety. I yanked free and yelled at them both.

"What is the matter with you two?" I asked, gesturing with my hands to make introductions. "Elsa, this is Lily, my best friend. Lily, this is, well, this is Elsa."

Elsa responded by asking me a question. "Your best friend is a fairy?"

Lily, not to be topped, asked, "Why is there a time-walker in your house, Olivia?"

This clearly was not going to be a normal ladies night at home for the three of us. I wasn't sure which one to answer first.

"Elsa is the panther from my dreams. She is here to help me… it's a long story. Why does Elsa think you are a fairy?"

Lily spoke to Elsa, ignoring me. "Who sent you?"

"I could ask you the same thing," Elsa said. "Are you supposed to be guarding her?"

Lily looked slightly defensive as she turned to me to give her reply. "I met Olivia when we were neighbors. I don't usually take humans as close friends, but I could see she was special. I am not officially her guardian, I never asked for permission. We became friends. I have always tried to look out for her. She is flying blind, you know."

"Have you seen the demon?" Elsa asked.

Lily shook her head. "No, but I sensed his presence. I placed a few minor charms around her home to keep him away, but since I am not her guardian, I could not intervene."

This seemed to satisfy Elsa, because she took a step away from me as she nodded in agreement. But I was not happy being an invisible third party.

"Hello," I said, waving my arms at them both. "I am standing right here. Can you two tell me what is going on? Lily, you're a *fairy*?"

Lily smiled. "Yes, but honestly, is that so shocking to you, after seeing Elsa appear? You must know by now that there is another world of creatures beyond what humans can see. When I first met you, I could tell right away that you had extra gifts. I expected you to notice what I was, but you never did. After a while, I realized that you weren't even trying to use your senses."

I was feeling a little embarrassed. Only a few weeks back, I'd sat across from Lily at dinner, staring at the tattoo on her neck, which was clearly some kind of fairy marking, and she did not reveal herself to me. Now, everyone in the room seemed to know more about me than I did.

"So what is this? Are you my friend out of pity? I've been telling you everything that is happening to me—am I some kind of project for you to look after?"

"I'm a fairy, Olivia," Lily said, clearly annoyed. "We don't reveal ourselves to *anyone*. I'm your friend because I want to be. If I pitied you, I would have asked my clan to assign a real guardian to watch over you, someone you would never have seen nor met."

"Is it against the rules to be friends with humans?"

Lily and Elsa looked at each other and laughed. "It's not encouraged," Lily said.

"Why?"

Elsa held her hands up. "I think you've heard enough for the time being, Olivia. Why don't we go into the kitchen and make some dinner."

CHAPTER 7

"Make some dinner" actually meant ordering Chinese food from around the corner. Once the food arrived, I opened an app on my iPhone to listen to a San Francisco Giants baseball game. We sat for a few moments eating pot stickers and listening to the sounds of the local announcers calling the plays.

There are probably plenty of people who wouldn't expect sports to be a family interest in a house primarily full of women, but they would be wrong. My grandfather loved the Giants, and I have fond memories of listening to the play-by-play coming out of every radio, in every room of the house. When we would drive into the city, the sound of the cheering crowd from the car's radio would envelop us as we crossed the Bay.

My mother is not as enthusiastic about baseball as I am. But she does enjoy soccer, a result of her many sojourns to Europe over the years. She calls it football, but few people in the U.S. understand what she means, since that name is reserved for the large, hulking creatures that hurl themselves at one another every Sunday. Soccer, on the other hand, is a sport that involves very thin, agile men (usually very handsome men) running up and down a field for 90 minutes in shorts. Who wouldn't enjoy that? My dinner companions appeared not share my love for baseball or soccer, however.

"Baseball is not a sport," was all Elsa could muster as she sampled another dumpling. "There is no blood involved."

Changing the subject seemed like the best idea. "Tell me about being a fairy, Lily."

Lily put down the container of garlic green beans. "What do you want to know?"

"Why do you work in the library?" was my first question, followed by "Where is your family and what kind of powers do you have?"

"I come from a clan of fairies that has always lived in the human world," Lily said. "We've dedicated our lives to public service. Although we make visits to the Other Side, we mostly stay in this world. I'm one of a long line of librarians. And yes, I have added a little magic to the library system. Who would return to a library if it never had the book you wanted? Having a well-run, popular library system is good for San Francisco."

"Why libraries?"

Lily finished chewing before she spoke again. "Because fairies are voracious readers of books and texts in many languages. Working in a library affords us the luxury of being surrounded by words and information. There is no better way to learn about humans, and the world in general, than to work in a library."

"What does that have to do with public service?" I asked, putting another dumpling on my plate.

"That is easy," Lily said. "Libraries are important for humans. In the human world, being able to read is the key to all of your activities. It's pretty clear that the less people know, the worse their fate is. Allowing people to have access to the same kinds of information for free is important. When people are uneducated it …well, it creates opportunities for others to manipulate the situation."

Elsa snorted. "Humans want to be controlled; they appreciate limited choices."

I decided to ignore Elsa's pointed remark for the moment. "Tell me about the rest of your family."

"Everything you know, the story I've told you, is true. My father and mother are retired, but did work as librarians. They do live in San Jose. My sister really lives in Seattle and my brother really lives in Portland. He's a firefighter, but that's rare; normally we're terribly afraid of fire."

"And your powers? What kinds of things can you do?"

"I'm not a circus act," Lily said, again sounding slightly annoyed. "I don't do tricks."

"I'm sorry, Lily. That came out badly."

Elsa placed herself into the conversation and turned to me. "I think we need to focus our energies on freeing up your gifts."

"And how do you plan to do that?"

"I have to run an errand," she said, "but tomorrow we're going out on an overnight adventure."

"Overnight? Are we camping?" I asked, wondering what destination she had in mind.

"You could say that," she said with a smile. "I need to leave in a few moments to look for some supplies. Assuming I'm successful, we will leave here tomorrow night after sunset."

"Where are you going? And how will you get there?" I asked casually, not expecting the reply I received.

Elsa looked at Lily when she spoke. "I travel using a portal in the park."

"Can I come tomorrow?" Lily asked.

Elsa nodded. "Yes, it will be better if there are two of us."

"What's a portal?" I asked, worried.

Lily and Elsa exchanged knowing glances. "It will be better if we show you," Elsa said.

"OK," I said, feeling relieved to avoid, if temporarily, yet another hidden detail about the world I'd missed. Lily and Elsa left the house in unison and I watched as they walked down the street together into the night's thick fog. One minute I could see them very clearly, and the next, they were gone.

CHAPTER 8

For the first time in many days, I woke up alone in the house. I confess I missed my roommate, or at least I missed the feeling of having someone nearby. I don't have a great track record with men. There have been no great romances in my life. Instead, I have amassed a collection of single-night memories. To be sure, there have been a few multi-week excursions, but they never transformed themselves into repeat engagements.

It would be nice to feel great passion for someone, to feel my body long for another with every fiber of my being. But that has not been a sensation I've experienced. Perhaps watching my mother come unraveled has made me timid. From where I sit, spilling over with emotion looks messy, and if unreciprocated, humiliating. As a result, the only male voice heard emanating from my living room on a regular basis is the baseball radio announcer Jon Miller.

Even without Elsa, I followed my normal schedule, rising early to eat a banana and then heading straight for the park to work out. I entered at Ninth Avenue and ran west toward the coast. I managed to reach the graffiti scarred retaining walls of Ocean Beach in less than an hour.

To cool down, I decided to walk onto the broad beach and stretch on the sand. The fog from the night before had retreated, perching along the edge of the horizon as if it couldn't decide what to do next. The sun was coming up into the sky and the air around me was cool and mild. It felt delicious to be outside. I decided to prolong the feeling by walking over to Judah Street for a cup of coffee at a nearby beach café.

The Java Shack was fairly busy, with other people apparently also working at extending their morning. I managed to find a table outside and picked up a rumpled copy of the *San Francisco Chronicle* someone had left behind. For several minutes I sipped my cappuccino, gazing at the sea, enjoying the first moments of quiet I'd had in days.

As I regarded the foamy waves rolling in and out with the tide, I worried about what was coming next. I was rapidly moving toward a moment when I would have to open myself up again to feel my emotions and those of others, something I had avoided for a long time. I felt like Pink at the moment when the bricks of the Wall are set to come tumbling down. What would I discover, I wondered, when the dust settled?

I pushed aside my worries and settled in to scan the day's news. Within a few minutes I came upon a headline that surprised me, "Internet CEO Seeks Return to Congress." I read with interest a story about my former boss, Levi Barnes, and his decision to run for office again, this time as a congressman representing Silicon Valley. My first job in Washington, D.C. had been with Levi when he was a congressman representing Salt Lake City, Utah. After losing a particularly tough re-election bid, he'd left politics and moved to the Bay Area to become an entrepreneur. It seemed unthinkable that, after losing so badly before, he would give up his privacy and success to reenter national politics. What had changed for him? It had been more than a year since the two of us had spoken, and I made a mental note to call him to catch up. I was also curious to see who he had hired to run his campaign.

The high-pitched squeak of the N-Judah streetcar jarred me out of my thoughts. It was time to head home. Seeing that a train had reached the end of the line, and was turning east again toward downtown, I decided to hop on and ride back to my house.

By mid-afternoon, a few hours later, Elsa had returned. She walked straight into the kitchen and began brewing some kind of concoction that gave off a quite unpleasant aroma. I came into the kitchen just as she was placing small button-shaped fruits into boiling water with what looked like cinnamon sticks and a vanilla bean.

"What are you making?" I asked, trying to breath through my mouth.

"It's going to be a tea," she said. "You're going to drink some tonight before we go out."

"Is it going to taste as bad as it smells?"

"Actually, it's going to taste worse," she said, keeping her back to me as she hunched over the stove brewing her potion. "The trick is to drink quickly and not think about it."

"What does it do?" I asked, thinking that I should know what I was getting myself into.

"It should help you regain your senses," Elsa said. "It's an old recipe that has been used by many women over the years."

"Where did you go last night?"

Elsa kept her back to me. "New Mexico, mostly. I had a few other stops to make."

"You don't seem to have flown on a commercial jet to get there," I said, hoping to provoke a discussion about portals and time-walkers.

For the record, it's not that I find it difficult to imagine that there is more to things than what we see at first glance. And I don't doubt that the world has more complexity to it than we imagine. I've just never wanted to accept it.

What I want from life is something more rational. If I'm going to pay attention and care, then I want to know how the mysteries work. If I can understand the mechanics, then I can manage my fear. After years of living in a very logical fashion, now I'm expected to be Alice in the looking glass, throw caution to the wind and drink my potion so all can be revealed.

"You know I didn't fly on an airplane," Elsa said. "I used a portal. It's a door between places. They are scattered across the city."

"Where do you go when you use them?"

"With a little practice and focus, you can go anywhere," Elsa said.

"Am I going to use one tonight?"

"No. Tonight you're going to work on finding those instincts of yours so we can see what kind of empath you really are. I sense you have great abilities, Olivia, but you have stuffed them so far beneath your skin that only the most drastic efforts will draw them out." She removed the pot from the stove and strained the contents into a ceramic pitcher, which she placed in the refrigerator.

"It will be better chilled."

"I'm scared," I said, admitting the obvious. "What's going to happen to me tonight?"

"Lily and I will be with you," Elsa said. "Whatever happens, and maybe nothing will, you will be with us and we will take care of you."

"This is not a reassuring speech," I said.

"I'm not here to reassure you." Her voice was stern. "I'm here to protect you and to get you to stop living a half-life."

"A half-life," I repeated. "How is running a business and owning a home a half-life?"

"Olivia, you were born with a sixth sense—a set of instincts that allows you to read people before they even know something themselves," she continued. "Instead of using those skills, you have buried them and left yourself vulnerable to all kinds of danger and mischief. At minimum, you might have been able to stop Stoner Halbert's demon from stealing your clients. Do you think a man with eyesight would knowingly blind himself? That's what you've done."

"I haven't blinded myself," I responded, my pride wounded once again. "Did it ever occur to you that maybe I see more clearly than you do?"

Elsa snorted. "After tonight we will see if that's really true. You should go upstairs and rest. You won't get much sleep tonight."

CHAPTER 9

Not long after drinking the tea I began to feel ill. Elsa must have known what was coming because she was at my side, quickly guiding me toward the sink where I began to wretch. Lily was also there, running her hand up and down my back in a soothing motion. They were both murmuring words in my ear to calm me, but I was in no shape to understand. Large sounds filled my head—±vibrations, really—that resonated off my sternum as I grasped the edge of the sink. A great freight train was barreling through me, and I could feel it coming down the tracks through every bone in my body.

"What is happening to me?" I asked, my heart racing inside my chest.

Elsa grasped my shoulder and whispered in my ear, "Don't be afraid. Whatever happens Lily and I will not leave your side. Just remember: Not everything you see tonight will be real."

We must have left the house after Elsa's remarks, but the particulars of our exit are a bit fuzzy. Next, we were walking through a pair of ornate green iron gates that featured delicate-looking vines and leaves. We strode onto a red brick path sheltered by a canopy of trees. Moonlight illuminated the path and suddenly I felt as if I were a bride in a wedding, although what I was about to be joined with remained a mystery. In the middle of the path sat a well-worn sundial perched on a stone pedestal. The metal glowed with a golden light. Fascinated, I reached out to touch the illuminated dial. The moment my skin made contact with the triangle of the dial, I felt a jolt of energy run through my body as a panoply of voices began to pierce my skull. I laughed aloud as if I understood the joke, and tried to listen to the conversation. Before I could lock onto a single word, Elsa removed my hand from the dial. I turned to face her and exhaled suddenly. She was awash in color, shimmering waves of yellow, orange and green pouring from her body.

"Oh my God, oh my God!" I exclaimed, reaching out to touch the light. "You're so beautiful."

"What do you see?" she asked.

"I see colors," I said. "I hear voices and I see colors."

"Good," Elsa said. "Don't worry, you're not crazy. The peyote is working. Let's see what happens next."

I looked up to see billowing strands of moss hanging from a Monterey pine. A cold wind arrived, carrying in a wicked fog bank that was rolling across the park at a furious speed. I should have been cold, but instead my skin burned as the crisp air enveloped me. On fire, I quickly shrugged out of my fleece and flung it to the ground. Again, I lost track of time, and when I refocused, I found that we were standing in the main concourse of Golden Gate Park, where the de Young Museum and Academy of Sciences are located. I swallowed hard, my tongue feeling too large for my mouth.

The park was bursting with noise. Every living being, it seemed, made some kind of sound as it moved. The night was awash in color. I absorbed all of this information and felt it take root as a young tree establishes itself in new ground. I laughed again, feeling an uncanny sense of new knowledge. I was ruminating on the meaning of the sounds I was hearing when my attention was abruptly drawn to a fountain in the center of the concourse.

The bowl of the fountain was illuminated by lights below it, and in the center of its pedestal stood an enormous stone saber-toothed tiger. Trapped between its massive claws was a serpent that was partially coiled around the cat's body. Locked in a fierce battle, the massive, muscled arms of the cat, which looked more human than feline, seemed to be moving, wrestling with the snake.

I sat down on a wooden bench nearby, unable to tear my gaze away from the fountain.

"It's Elsa!" I yelled aloud, surprised at the sound of my voice. "It's Elsa taking on the devil."

Now Elsa laughed. "What do you hear, Olivia?"

Responding to her question, I strained to listen. At first I could not detect any sound coming from the fountain. But as I focused, I began to feel a vibration moving through my body and I stood up, unable to sit still.

"Up," I said. "It's saying, 'Get up and come in.' "

Elsa preened like a proud mother. "Very good. That's exactly what it's saying. One day soon we will go inside, but for now we have to say goodbye to The Guardian."

"The Guardian," I whispered to myself. As I murmured the name, I caught sight of a light coming from a large tower in front of us. I also could feel the intense light. "Bright!" I screamed as the light expanded behind my eyes, momentarily blinding me. I pressed my hands to my eye sockets and bent my head in pain.

"What light, Olivia?" Lily asked. "Where is the light coming from?"

I pointed up toward the tower, which belonged to the de Young Museum.

Elsa turned me so that my back was away from the source of the light. "You must breathe deeply and try to push the light out of your mind, Olivia. Focus on the light and push it away."

The pain from the light roiled my already sensitive stomach. Taking a deep breath, eventually I was able to do what Elsa asked. I inhaled and exhaled, slowly bringing my attention to the center of my forehead where the pain was the strongest.

Meanwhile, Elsa had begun shouting at no one in particular in a language I didn't understand. While Lily stood nearby looking grim, Elsa walked briskly to the fountain, touched the edge of the cement and disappeared.

Hand outstretched, I screamed for her. Lily was at my side immediately, pulling me away. Quickly we grabbed our things and began to run, setting a brisk pace through the wet foggy night. As we passed through the damp, muddy trails of the park's forests, I removed more clothing, dropping items along the way. My body temperature continued to climb, despite the fact that I was now wearing nothing but a running bra and bike shorts.

"I need water, Lily," I said, my throat raw from running in the cold night air.

She opened a backpack and handed me a bottle.

"Drink," she said. "The effects of the tea will start to wear off in a few hours."

"Is Elsa coming back?"

"I'm not sure," Lily said. "She had to go see someone."

"She disappeared," I said, distracted by the buzzing in my ears.

Lily nodded. "Yes. But she will come back."

Very quickly, we found ourselves back in the land of glowing flowers, strolling through an open meadow, dotted with pink and purple foxglove. We crossed a road, climbed a dirt path and after a few minutes of walking, came to stand before Stow Lake, a man-made lake established in Golden Gate Park in the 1800's. Half-dressed and disheveled, I paused on the sidewalk, transfixed by a small island a few hundreds yards inside the enormous lake from where I stood. The island, shrouded in mist and almost completely covered by a fallen tree and overgrown flowering vines, seemed to be calling to my overheated body.

It didn't take much for me to oblige.

"Hot!" I cried out, and waded into the lake.

"Olivia, noooo!" came Lily's frantic cry, as she jumped in after me.

We swam to the island, but never made it out of the water thanks to a ring of thorny blackberry bushes lining the shore. Rebuffed, we made our way back onto dry land. Standing on the sidewalk and dripping wet, Lily removed a small towel from her pack and handed it to me.

"It's not much, but it will help dry you a bit," she said, rubbing the water off of her arms and legs.

I sat down on a nearby bench and began to listen to the world around me. A cacophony of sounds rang in my ears. I could hear the fish swimming below the surface of the water. I detected the faint sound of owls in the trees rustling their wings. Smiling, I took Lily's hand in my own.

"This place is alive," I said with conviction.

Lily smiled and squeezed my hand back. "See what you have been missing," she said gently. "Now, you are really alive, too."

CHAPTER 10

My first sensation was of something cold and hard pressing into my lower back. Then the smell of damp, rotting plants filled my nostrils. I remained motionless, trying to recall what had happened. Where was I? Then I remembered my adventure in the park and the tea Elsa had given me that caused me to hallucinate.

I lay still, testing my body. From one limb to the next I wiggled, waiting for injuries and pain. I moved my head from side to side and slowly opened my eyes. As soon as I focused I recoiled, for there, not an inch from my face, was an egret. The small, white bird was studying me. I smiled at him. "Either you are in the wrong place, or I am sleeping in your bed," I said quietly to the bird.

The egret opened up his wings and flew away as I sat up to survey my surroundings. I was sleeping on a small patch of dirt inside a lily pond near the side entrance of the de Young Museum. Why here, of all places, I wondered, and then I recalled hearing a man's voice at the end of the evening. The voice was insistent, urging me to leave my old life behind to join him. I had followed the voice, getting as far as the museum, but could not find its source.

At some point I must have lost Lily and come back here to fall asleep, choosing to slumber beside a statute of Pan with his lute. Now, as the light of day pressed against my sensitive eyes, the nature of my situation dawned on me. I was a half-dressed woman trespassing on city property, and I needed to get up and leave before someone saw me. The good news is that given the kinds of characters that inhabit

San Francisco, I wasn't too worried about looking odd as I strolled back to my house. I was certain my unkempt nature wouldn't raise so much as an eyebrow.

I wondered what had happened to Elsa. I concentrated for a moment and then, one by one, the images of the night returned. I recalled with clarity that Elsa had disappeared into the fountain. I remembered the bright light and her attempt to shield me from it.

My running shoes were sitting next to me and I reached over to slide them on to my filthy, bare feet. As soon as I climbed out of the pond and hopped onto the sidewalk, I spotted Elsa sitting on a bench nearby. Her eyes shut, and she appeared to be dozing lightly. I walked toward her, intending to gently tap her on the shoulder, but as I approached she opened her eyes with a start.

"Olivia," she said, smiling, "you've returned to this world. How do you feel?"

"I feel great," I said. "My back is a little sore from sleeping on a rock, but other than that, I feel fine." As I stood looking at Elsa, I began to see some of the same colors I had from the night before. Elsa was gently giving off waves of yellow and orange as she stood before me.

"You're giving off colors again," I said.

As soon as the words left my mouth, I felt a rush of warmth invade my body. It was the feeling of pleasure, but the feeling was not my own. It belonged to Elsa. "I can feel your pleasure, too," I said, shaking my head. "Is that what you hoped would happen?" Again, a rush of warmth ran through me. "You're pleased. I can tell."

"I am pleased," she responded, rising from the bench to stretch. "How much more you can do with your gift remains to be seen. We're going to work on it a bit, and then I am going to introduce you to a group of people who are very interested in meeting you. They'd like you to come and work for them."

We walked back to the house in silence, my mind too preoccupied with the show unfurling before me. As I walked past people on the street I could clearly see the outline of their auras and feel their emotions. Unfiltered, it was disorienting, and by the time we got to the front door, my stomach was churning with all of the morning angst I'd picked up as my neighbors headed off to work. I placed my hand against the door jam and closed my eyes for a moment, remembering Elsa's advice from the night before. After a few moments of deep breathing, I regained control of my senses. I nearly had been overwhelmed by other people's emotions, but with some measure of confidence, I realized that I could calm my mind when necessary.

I was about to reach for my hide-a-key, when the front door flew open. Lily was standing in the doorway half awake, wearing one of my bathrobes. Evidently, she'd had the good sense to come home and sleep in a bed.

I watched velvety green light coming off of my best friend and felt her happiness at my safe return deep inside my heart. It was lovely to feel that kind of friendship from another being.

"Thank you," I said. "I am very glad to see you too. What an adventure we had last night. Did you know that your light is as green as that island we swam to?"

Lily giggled. "It worked. You can see my aura. I am green and sometimes a little blue comes through. Most fairies are. If you ever see a red color coming off a fairy, you should run and get away as fast as you can. It means something horrible is about to happen."

I nodded, distracted by my stomach, which began to grumble.

"I'm starving. Let's have some food and we can talk some more."

"I can't stay," Lily said. "I have to go to work. You know the library is open seven days a week."

"Suit yourself," I said. "I am making pancakes."

After I had eaten and taken a shower, I came downstairs to find Elsa sitting on the floor in the living room, meditating. Legs folded, eyes closed, she was chanting softly.

I could see very strong orange and yellow pulses coming from her body as she took in breaths of air. I wondered what colors my body gave off, but when I tried to look after my shower, nothing appeared in the mirror.

"Yellow, orange and a twinge of red," Elsa said. "I can hear your thoughts now, Olivia. Your mind is very powerful. We need to be careful so that you don't telegraph what you are thinking to those who would use the information against you."

I flopped down in a chair and sighed. "You can hear my thoughts. I can feel your emotions. How is this supposed to be better for me? I feel more vulnerable than ever."

"You are more vulnerable... for the moment," Elsa said. "It will pass and you will come to learn how powerful a woman is when she uses her sixth sense."

I sat for a moment contemplating my future. It certainly couldn't get any worse, I reasoned. I now had the power to read people and know their emotions. If I could figure our how to protect myself, maybe I could get back to work and retrieve my clients from Stoner Halbert.

"What about the demon?" I asked. "Will it go away now?"

"Soon you will be able to keep him out of your head and then he will have to move on to someone more vulnerable."

Thinking about being vulnerable reminded me of the horrible light and pain from the night before. "What was that light last night? Why did it hurt my head?"

Elsa paused a long while and then said, "It was someone trying to read your thoughts."

That didn't sound good at all. "Read my thoughts. Why? Who was it?"

Elsa frowned. "He's the head of an organization that's very interested in humans who have extra skills like yours."

"Really, how odd," I said. "He sounds like a freak. How does he know about me?"

Again, Elsa didn't answer immediately.

"I am a member of the Council, it was my responsibility

to tell them that I was leaving my post temporarily to help a human," she explained. "When I told the director about your gifts, he became very interested."

"The Council," I said aloud. "It sounds like a John Grisham novel."

"I don't know who John Grisham is," Elsa said, her stern voice returning. "But I assure you, the Council is very real. Gabriel Laurent is the current director. He's the one who tried to contact you last night."

"Does he always try to blind people to say hello?"

"I told him it was too early to try such a thing," she acknowledged. "I asked him to wait a few days and promised that I would bring you to meet him."

"Is that where you went, when you left? To see him?" I asked. "You touched the fountain and disappeared."

Elsa nodded. "I used the portal to jump to the top of the museum, where the Council keeps its headquarters."

"How did you do that? I mean how do you make sure you get where you want to go?"

"I use my mind. It will guide me to where I want to go."

"And what does *Monsieur* Laurent want with me?"

"It's nothing, really; he wants to speak to you about a job."

I knew right away that Elsa was lying.

· CHAPTER 11

From the moment she began speaking, I knew that Elsa was holding something back. I could feel her hesitation. By now, I also knew her well enough to know I should back off and wait to ask her again later. So I let the matter pass, and dressed and readied myself for my first day of learning how to use my reclaimed skills.

We were headed to the Mission District. Elsa insisted we use the subway to travel downtown. Riding the public trains, she said, would be a good place to practice. As soon as we got on the N-Judah streetcar, Elsa leaned in and whispered my assignment.

"Focus on one person, and try to block out the rest. Find one person and tell me what you see and feel."

I scanned the train looking for my target. A few seats away, I locked on to a well-dressed woman who looked to be about 25. She was tall with long blond hair, held in place by a tortoise shell headband. Her hair, which had been brushed until it shined, cascaded down her back. She looked successful and content—an easy first assignment, I told myself.

When I examined her more closely, though, I began to see a different story. She was encased in a solid red line of fear. She was worried. I could feel it. Her heart also held another emotion: longing. I sat down on a nearby train seat and watched her.

"She's worried," I said to Elsa under my breath. "She's trying to reassure herself about something, maybe not reassure, but I think I can feel her trying to soothe herself."

Elsa pulled me up and walked us to the second car of the train. "Try again."

I was feeling more confident, so I decided to try something more challenging. This time I locked on to a slightly disheveled homeless man, his belongings piled high on the seat next to him. I focused in on his coloring and saw something odd. He gave off a grayish color that looked like smog hovering over the hills. As soon as I tried to read his emotions, he turned around to face me. He knew I was trying to read him. Although he smiled at me, his behavior was anything but friendly. He began to press back, sending some very dark emotions my way. I felt a rush of sadness, and realized that he was trying to drive me to despair. He was persistent, trying to drive negative feelings into my head. Elsa appeared at my side.

"That's a demon, Olivia. Can you feel him trying to drive a wedge through your soul? Block him out."

Once again, I practiced using my breath to lower a blind over my mind's eye and closed off my nervous system. Soon, I began to feel like myself again. The demon turned away from us and looked out the window.

"He gave up very easily," I said.

"He probably knew he had no chance with you," was Elsa's reply. "Demons, in general, are a lazy lot and do not like to work hard. I think he knew better than to test your will."

"Are they always grey?" I asked as we made our way out of the train station.

"Always. You must have a soul, or some connection to humanity, to give off an aura. Remember that. Grey is the absence of color. As servants of the devil, they have no humanity left inside them, and therefore give off no color."

"Wow. That is scary. What would have happened if he'd succeeded?"

"You would have left the train feeling like your life was not worth living," Elsa said ruefully. "Demons are responsible for a lot of the suicides you read about that happen in public—the stories about people who jump into the path of a moving train, or leap from the Golden Gate Bridge. Their deaths are often incomprehensible to the people who know them. Now you know the reason for their actions."

I shuddered slightly as we rode the escalator up from the bowels of the subterranean train station, trying to shake off the gloom of the demon and Elsa's story. Would that have been my fate, too, had Elsa not appeared? Would I have been doomed to toss myself over a bridge when Stoner was done with me? I didn't want to know.

We exited the station at 16th and Mission. From there, we moved west, walking through the crowds on Valencia Street. There were dozens upon dozens of bodies moving through the neighborhood. I held still, allowing myself to feel the energy of the people passing by.

"Don't lock on to it or try to absorb it, let it move past you as if you were browsing titles in a book store," Elsa said.

If I had been in a bookstore, the floor would have been a mess. It felt as if I was bumping into everyone who passed. A jolt here, a jolt there, I was being brushed by anger, anxiety, sexual longing, happiness and true love. Each time someone passed, they tickled my senses. I began to regulate it, as if searching a radio by turning a dial. I concentrated, focusing my mind to pull in from one person but not the next. A rainbow of colors passed behind my eyes, and I was enjoying my newfound skills until something began pressing on my skull again.

I looked up, trying to find the source of the pain and found myself staring into the dark green eyes of a man with long hair and a nose ring, whose piercing gaze seemed to be picking at my head. It was a very specific kind of pressure, but it came with not a trace of emotion.

"Elsa, that man over there is trying to force his way into my head."

"Vampire," was all she said.

"Vampire? In the Mission?"

"Especially in the Mission," she said.

"He is picking at my skull like a woodpecker."

"Make him stop."

I closed my eyes and forcefully shut him out. He smiled, saluting me with two fingers as he passed.

"He doesn't give off any emotion," I said as he passed. "Only that pecking sensation."

Elsa laughed. "Vampires don't feel emotions the way humans do. It has something to do with the absence of a beating heart. If you ever get to know a vampire well, you will learn to read their feelings more closely."

"Wow, a vampire and a demon, all in the last hour in San Francisco," I said, shaking my head. "I never imagined it was possible."

"And now?" Elsa asked.

"I'm not sure," I said honestly. "But I do know that everything I thought I knew has changed."

"That is a good beginning," Elsa said, putting her hand on my arm. "Let's go find a place to meet Lily for dinner."

We settled on Bar Tartine, a quaint bistro on Valencia Street. Lily arrived at about 5:30 looking exhausted. Seeing her made me realize how tired I was, too.

"I don't think this will be a late evening," I said. "We both look like we could use a good night's sleep."

A waiter took our order for three glasses of wine, and a sampling of house-made meats and cheeses. I added on a bowl of warm olives, and Lily asked for some bread. Once our drinks and small plates arrived, I quizzed my magical friends on what really was going on around me.

"You're very lucky to live in San Francisco," Lily said, licking a drop of olive oil off her fingertip. "This city is the most magical of any in the world."

"You don't mean picturesque, do you?"

Lily smiled. "Nope. I mean magical, with a capital M. After a while you will feel it. The land itself is part of it. Very early civilizations knew it, too, the Ohlone Indians, for example."

Lily's comments reminded me of something from my adventure the night before.

"I think I saw them," I burst out, interrupting Lily's sentence. "I saw them at Ocean Beach last night. I ran there after leaving the park. There were hundreds of people chanting, and I saw a woman—their shaman. I thought I was hallucinating."

Both women exchanged glances. "You were having a vision, but it's extraordinary that you saw the Ohlone," Elsa said. "Your abilities are very strong, Olivia. You picked up on a very old memory embedded in the land."

"You were amazing last evening, but I did have a brief scare," Lily said, joining the conversation. "After Elsa left and you began to run towards the lake, I thought at one point that I'd lost you. You seemed to disappear from my line of sight, but then I found you again at the foot of the water. I think my eyes must have been playing tricks on me."

"I was running around like a crazy woman, maybe a tree or a bush blocked me from view," I said as I nibbled. "My memory of specific details about the evening is hazy, but I do remember one thing. I heard a man's voice. He asked me to leave behind my old life and join him. I followed the sound of his voice all the way to the museum, but never located him. I'm guessing it was just a hallucination."

My companions both laughed. "If we ever do this again, I will remember to brew a weaker tea next time," Elsa said lightly.

Elsa shifted in her seat, and just for a minute I felt apprehension coming from her. Then, very quickly, the emotion disappeared from my radar, almost like a shadow that disappears from the corner of your eye when your turn your head to find its source. But it was clear that for the second time in one day, Elsa was hiding something from me.

CHAPTER 12

That night I slept deeply and did not stir from my bed for ten hours. I woke up feeling stiff, but otherwise remarkably well, considering my discovery that I shared my city with fairies, demons and vampires. At dinner, Lily had also briefed me on witches, who seemingly find San Francisco especially welcoming to their lifestyle. *We are not alone*, it turns out. We are all actually walking side-by-side on Valencia Street, although most of us have no idea. Few people realize they are stuffed into the N-Judah streetcar during commute hours with the undead.

What was I to do with this newfound knowledge? Was I supposed to return to my old life, knowing there were two worlds living side-by-side in San Francisco? I was prepared to let those questions percolate at the back of my mind as I got on with my day, but magic, it seemed, was in the air. No sooner had I turned on the Giants game on television, that I noticed that one of the pitchers was a vampire. With his long black hair and pale skin, this starting pitcher had always caught people's attention. It was rare, I realized, that he ever pitched a day game, and now I knew why.

Sure enough, as the sun began to retreat from the plate and the shadows grew longer, his pitches gained in velocity. In the ninth inning, he was relieved and as I stared into the bullpen, I noticed one or two other members of the team were also Others. A vampire and a demon playing for a major league baseball team. It seemed the world I knew was really gone forever.

Elsa had left the house earlier in the day, and did not return until almost dusk. Normally a woman of few words, she had not been in the house ten minutes when she suggested we go out for dinner. "I was thinking The Moss Room," she said.

"The Moss Room," I repeated. "That place is kind of pricey and it can be hard to get a table."

"Actually, we've been invited to dinner," Elsa said, a bright smile on her face. "The director of the Council, Gabriel Laurent, has invited us to join him."

"What's the catch?" I asked. "First he tries to blind me, and now he wants to wine and dine me?"

"No catch," Elsa said. "He wants to meet you and, if there is time, discuss a job. I think we should go. Your old job is going to seem quite boring now, anyway."

"I'm not so sure about that," I said, feeling slightly bullied.

"It's just dinner," Elsa said lightly, but I could sense some uneasiness. She needed me to go to this dinner.

"OK," I said. "What time are we meeting him?"

Elsa looked relieved. "One hour."

"Great. I will go upstairs and change."

The Moss Room is named after the moss that grows on one of the subterranean walls of the restaurant. Tucked underground, below the California Academy of Sciences, guests dine inside a snug room adorned on one side with moss and trickling water, and on the other, brick and glass. It is designed as a terrarium for the culinary set, and guests must descend a long glass stairway that terminates at the broad elbow of a majestic wooden bar to enter the dining room. As we came to the last step, a man seated at the bar turned to face us. Instinctively, I knew this was Gabriel Laurent. Impeccably dressed in a gray cashmere sweater, jeans and a black sport coat, he was the picture of casual French elegance.

"Hello, Elsa," he said, revealing his accent. "This must be Olivia."

"Hello," I said, turning to face him, resisting the urge to show off and *parler*. Eventually, he would come to know that I was fluent. "It's a pleasure to meet you, *monsieur*."

Gabriel stared at me for a moment, but did not speak. He was glowing with a deep blue aura that sparkled like a sapphire.

"You're so blue," I blurted out, before I could stop myself.

I could sense his pleasure at my remark, but like Elsa, he too held something back.

"I can see what they say is true," he said. "You are quite adept...I am anxious to discuss your gifts in greater detail. *Alors*...Let me tell the hostess we are ready. I have reserved a private room."

His last word came out as "O*h-stess*," spurring me on to speak in his native language. "*Comment allez-vous?*"

Gabriel turned around and smiled. "*Bien, merci. Vous parlez très bien, mademoiselle.*"

"Thank you. I've studied French for many years," I replied. "It was a sort of requirement with my mother."

Once again, he stifled some emotion, but I felt a drop. It was curiosity.

"You must tell me about your mother, *eh,* your family sometime," Gabriel said, as a hostess led us to our private quarters. "I am curious to know about your background. There are not many humans with the kind of powers you seem to have."

The private room, it turned out, was a clear box off the main dining area. The small glass-walled salon was soundproof, but transparent to the rest of the diners. It made for interesting theater. We could see everyone as they came and went through the dining room, and they could see us, but they could not hear a word we uttered. I didn't think this was a coincidence at all.

Almost immediately after being seated I began to feel nervous. It took a few moments to realize that the emotions were not my own. Thanks to my training, however preliminary, I knew the difference between my feelings and those of others. They feel too sudden—the emotions—when they belong to someone else. The question now was which one of them was nervous, and why?

Gabriel ordered a bottle of wine and asked that it be decanted as we looked at the menu. Once the wine had been arranged and we'd been sitting for a few moments, Gabriel spoke again.

"You've had quite an eye-opening experience in the last few weeks, Olivia," he said, rotating his wine glass gently between his fingers. "For most of us, the knowledge that the universe is divided between two worlds is introduced gradually by our peers as we grow older. You have had to absorb the entirety of the situation quickly. Do you know why your parents never told you the truth?"

Interesting. Elsa, it seemed, had not told Gabriel about my mother. "I'm afraid you can't blame my family," I said. "The blame, if it must be assigned, is all mine. My mother and grandmother did try to educate me, but I refused."

"Refused? I don't understand."

I snorted. "That seems to be a running theme these days. I didn't want to use my skills. I've watched my mother nearly drink herself to death trying to avoid her feelings. She's a brilliant landscape painter. Her artistic skill, combined with her *gifts*, has made her quite in demand, but it has never made her happy. She has been overwhelmed with her emotions, and everyone else's for a long time."

"And your father?"

"I don't have one, at least that I know about," I said, feeling a rush of anxiety. "My mother told me my father was a man she loved deeply, but could never marry. Beyond that, she has never said a word. I stopped asking after a while, knowing she would say nothing further."

"She never married?"

"No," I said. "She's had a few boyfriends over the years, but she has never had a serious relationship with a man. She often said she'd been in love once and it was enough."

"And your *grand-père?*"

"He's dead. So is my grandmother. I have an uncle, but my mother and I are the last two of our immediate family. I have no siblings."

That brought an odd look to Gabriel's face. "I see," he said, quickly recovering as he poured wine into our glasses. "And now that you have learned more about your skills?"

It was my turn to feel nervous. "I'm not sure. It's remarkable to see people in well, in a different light, but I'm not certain how all of this will affect my life in the future."

"Your honesty is refreshing," Gabriel said. "Most humans would be eager to find a way to use their skills to their advantage. To make money, or gain power."

"Are you human?" I asked, knowing I was being too forward with the Frenchman.

"It's a good question, Olivia. One I will answer in time."

"Why does everything always take time?" I was losing my patience.

"Because when you step out of the human plane, you can see that time is infinite," Gabriel said. "The world is an old place and history is repeated every minute, every second, that humans spend on the planet...in the tiny gestures and major decisions they make every day."

"Those who fail to understand are doomed to repeat...?"

Gabriel nodded. "Exactly. When you are in the stream of time, it is difficult to see all sides to an issue. One advantage the Others have is the gift of perspective. When you have lived a century, you can step back and examine issues differently. War, religious intolerance and famine, they all take on a different significance decades later. But as a human, you are bound by the moment."

I looked over at Elsa, who had remained silent during the discussion. "Do you see humans as such frail creatures?"

She nodded. "Not frail, but blind. They don't make decisions for the long-term, only for what feels good in the moment."

"This is fascinating, but what does it have to do with me? I'm not sure how I fit into this discussion. I am human, living in *this* time, mortal and destined for dust one day. Not long ago, I had a successful business and a nice house with a garden. But now…"

We paused as our meals were brought in. Once we had taken a few bites, Gabriel spoke again.

"You want to know what comes next. It's a good question. You wonder if you can continue doing things the same way, knowing what you know now? The answer is yes and no."

Gabriel turned to Elsa. "Does she know about the work of the Council?"

Elsa shook her head. "No. I was waiting for you to tell her."

"Are you familiar with the United Nations, Olivia?"

"Yes, why?"

"You know that their mission is to promote peace and stability among nations."

"Well, their success is debatable, but yes, I'm familiar with their mission."

Gabriel responded with a grim smile. "As you said, their success is mixed. Why? The governments of the world, in my opinion, are no match for religious intolerance, xenophobia and renegade dictators. Millions of dollars are spent globally, and where are we? Half the world's female population remains uneducated; old wives' tales and superstition still reign. Do you know a person can still be accused of being a witch and stoned to death in some parts of the world?"

This remark caused Elsa to involuntarily flinch. "Have you been hunted?" I asked her.

Elsa nodded. "Small villages are breeding grounds for that kind of hysteria."

Gabriel continued. "Even here in your country, religious zealots would like to dictate who you can marry."

I nodded. "Don't forget banning abortions for women," I added.

Gabriel leaned forward to continue. "Can you imagine how dangerous it would be if the religious extremists were able to take the reins of your government?

"Can you imagine if the president of the United States were a religious fanatic, or perhaps, the men and women in your Congress were?"

"Some days it seems as if that is already happening."

Gabriel glanced at Elsa and I could feel their anticipation as they finally came to the point.

"It could be much worse. Many of us have lived through the days of witch-hunts and Inquisitions. We know the damage one ambitious official can cause when he sows superstition and distrust among the disenfranchised."

"I can't imagine the United States ever being that provincial," I said, feeling a little overwhelmed by their comments. "After all, we were founded to avoid the rule of one man or woman."

Gabriel reached at his side for a small canvas satchel. He unzipped the khaki colored bag and pulled out a few copies of newspaper articles.

"I assembled these in preparation for our meeting," Gabriel said, as he slid the papers toward me.

"Evangelical Voters Courted in Presidential Bid," read one headline.

Another said, "Civics Education Called A National Crisis."

"Your country is intent on electing people who believe in a "God-endowed" policy to control the courts, education," Elsa said. "If they should achieve a majority, it could be disastrous."

"And the remaining population cannot name members of the Supreme Court or the first seven presidents," Gabriel added. "You see, we are forever at a tipping point, where intervention is necessary."

"Intervention?" I asked, once again feeling alarmed. I had the feeling I was being recruited into some kind of battle. "What do you mean?"

EVETTE DAVIS

Finally I was able to connect the nervousness I'd been feeling all evening with its owners. Both of them shared the anxiety equally, but it was Gabriel who spoke first.

"I'm the leader of an organization designed to help with these matters globally. This intervention I spoke of, the Council, is an organization devoted to maintaining stable governments across the globe," Gabriel said. He paused to order a second bottle of wine.

"Do you know the story of The Watchers from the Bible, from the Old Testament? It is the story of a group of angels sent by God to live on the earth and help humans."

"No," I said, shaking my head. "I'm not all that familiar with the Bible."

"I see. Well, we are like them. The world is full of magical beings—Others—as we refer to them. We, *they*, do not want to be visible to the outside world, hunted for religious reasons or perhaps exploited for financial gain or political power. For decades we have lived among humans and co-existed. The equation is simple: The more educated and stable the population, the more insulated Others are from harm and persecution."

"How does it work?" I asked. "Do you have an army, is there fighting?"

Gabriel waved his hands emphatically to dismiss the comments. "Olivia, I am not asking you to fight in a war, or join an army. Here in the U.S. and in Europe, we work the same way as others do: we use the political process. We work to ensure stable, moderate people are elected to every level of government."

"What do you want me to do?"

"I want you to do what you do now and run a campaign," Gabriel said, smiling. "But also to use your new-found skills to help *increase* the odds of success."

"Increase the odds?"

"Yes, of course," he said. "It's much easier to win an election when you know what voters are thinking ahead of time. You can help a candidate correct his messages in a

72

matter of seconds. You can sit in a room with a journalist and sense their intentions before they even begin an interview. It all makes for much better odds."

"Why should I do this for you? I can go back to running my company."

Gabriel nodded. "True, but you never can tell your clients or colleagues about your talents. Who will believe that you can see someone's aura, or read his or her emotions? If your competitors come to believe that, they will try to get you fired or disqualified. Who will you share your gift with? Who will you ask for advice? Elsa can't stay with you forever, she must return to her work.

"I've seen your record," he continued. "You're a talented consultant. Surely you must see the value of using your skills to help make a difference? You can shape the future, help ensure zealots don't run governments."

I set aside his pitch to help save the world for the moment. It was difficult to imagine my contributions amounting to that much, but his other remarks hit home. I couldn't share my secret with other humans. They would think I was crazy. Then again, maybe I didn't have to; maybe I could enjoy my new skills in private.

"I know what you're thinking," Gabriel said. "That you can keep it all a secret and continue on with your life."

I nodded. "Why not? No one has to know."

"True. But don't you think you would be living a half-life, Olivia? You have been given the rare opportunity to see what is behind the wizard's curtain. In your case, there is real magic to be found, not some cheap parlor trick."

"Maybe, but I never asked for these gifts," I said. "All I've ever wanted was to live my life in peace."

"*Mon dieu!* Who doesn't?" Gabriel said, offering a sympathetic smile. "But that is not always what fate has in store."

CHAPTER 13

I woke up the next morning knowing that I needed to clear my head. A bike ride out of town would be just the thing. The red wine and conversation had made my night's sleep less than solid, but I managed to wake up feeling rested enough. Gabriel had closed the evening asking me to consider his offer, but the truth was that I had bigger issues to contemplate.

I knew that Gabriel was right when he said that I would never be able to reveal my skills to my clients or colleagues. But that wasn't the part that bothered me. What I worried about was that I could never share all of what I knew to others. Beyond Lily, who could I tell about this new world of mine? And was there any man out there willing to date a woman who could tell his true colors on the first outing? To see the world so differently and to be so limited in whom I could share it with, well, it didn't sound appealing.

I planned to work through these issues through rigorous exercise and reflection. I left the house on my bicycle and made my way through Golden Gate Park, up into the Presidio and across the Golden Gate Bridge. I continued riding, past the Marin Headlands and on to Mill Valley, stopping in the town's village square for a break before heading back again toward San Francisco. It was a classic San Francisco day, sunny but with a cold, biting wind. I slogged through the tourists in Sausalito and rode my bike up Alexander Avenue, turning right to climb the hill toward the lookout points.

Now, after several hours on my bike, my leg muscles rebelled against the abrupt change in grade as I climbed. I was pressing against fierce, chilling head winds, using the confusion I felt as my energy source. Although my body ached, it felt good to push so hard. The wind wicked the sweat off my torso, and I began to feel the delicious tightness of my skin as it reacted to the frigid air.

My efforts were rewarded when I reached the top of the road and gazed out at the stunning view of the city's skyline, the beautiful twin spires of the bridge across the Golden Gate, and the San Francisco Bay. To one side I could see Baker Beach and to the other the skyline of downtown San Francisco. It was beautiful, and despite being exhausted, my heart felt lighter looking out at the city I called home.

I got off my bike and decided to walk through the old World War II tunnels and examine the view from behind one of the gun turrets. I locked my bike into a rack and began walking toward the opening of the tunnel. As I approached, I heard music coming from inside. As soon as I entered, I saw what looked to be a man in the distance, sitting against one of the walls. I could not see his face, as the bright sunlight shining through the other side of the tunnel made it impossible to see more than an outline of his body.

It was the music, though, that caught my attention. The notes were rolling off the guitar with great sadness and melancholy. Despite the beauty of the music, I hesitated to walk closer. A bit of pressure was building in my head. I took a sip of water from my bottle, thinking that I was dehydrated, before it dawned on me. The pressure was coming from him. I was being pecked at again, which meant that the man I was staring at was actually a guitar-playing vampire. I was in no mood for examination after such a long ride and immediately shut him out.

Out of the shadows I saw him raise his head and laugh, and then he looked away and continued to play his guitar. It was an easy decision to leave, but as I turned to head back toward my bike, the mystery musician spoke.

"Don't worry," he said in a voice that carried a trace of a Southern drawl. "I won't try again. I didn't realize who I was dealing with."

I decided not to answer. I don't normally speak with strangers under any circumstances.

"Don't you want to finish what you started?" he asked, a touch of sarcasm in his voice. "It's worth it to get to the other side."

I wasn't sure what he was saying. The previous evening's discussions had further opened my eyes to the world around me. There were two dimensions to everything. Was he saying I was afraid, or did he mean something else? I wasn't afraid, although I had never been alone with a vampire in a dark tunnel before. Now that I was really focusing, I could detect a very bright green aura surrounding him. He was very calm and I didn't feel threatened in any way. His stance made me curious: who was this mysterious, guitar-playing vampire with the velvet-green aura down at the end of the tunnel? I walked toward him to find out.

Walking briskly, I closed the gap between us, but he made no effort to move or rise to meet me. In fact, as I approached, all I could make out was a cowboy hat, bright red hair and a pair of faded jeans beneath an old acoustic guitar. Whoever he was, it was clear he was not prepared to speak with me again.

I had been raised to never chase boys or men—a policy I amended on the spot to include the undead—so I gave him a feeble wave and he tipped his hat back in acknowledgment. Then I walked through the tunnel and into the clearing. The air was growing colder and I could feel the fog beginning to push its way in. The chill in the air convinced me that it was time to get myself back across the bridge and into a hot bath.

Elsa would want to discuss Gabriel's offer to come and work for the Council when I got home. The fee he had offered me was enormous, certainly more than I made on my own in a year. Although I didn't need the funds, it was intriguing to be offered a king's ransom for doing a job I loved doing. When I finished gazing at the churning sea below, I walked back through the clearing and approached the tunnel, hoping to catch a glimpse of the guitar player again.

When I stepped into the shadows, I discovered I was alone.

By the time I returned home ninety minutes later, I'd decided to accept Gabriel's offer. Whether it was the encounter with the vampire in the tunnel, or Gabriel's remarks, I now knew I had to make some changes. Despite my resolution, I decided to call my mother to gauge her reaction. After all that I had experienced, the visions I'd seen of my grandmother, I felt I needed to talk to her.
We'd parted ways so badly weeks before, and now I was anxious to clear the air.

Within seconds of dialing she picked up her receiver. "Olivia," she said warmly. "You have found your gifts. I can feel the energy pouring out of you."

"Wow," I said. "Even over the phone, Mom?"

"Your energy is very powerful," She said. "How did this happen?"

"I met someone, a woman who's been helping me. Her name is Elsa and she has been a sort of, umm a mentor. She said Grandmother sent her."

There was a pause on the line.

"That is exactly the kind of thing she would think to do. Interesting that she appeared now…well, then…are you OK? It's a lot to understand at your age."

"That's funny. A man I met said something very similar."

Again there was a pause, but then she said, "A man, you mean someone your age?"

"No," I said. "Elsa introduced me to a man, who runs an organization that protects people like us, and others from harm. His name is Gabriel Laurent."

For the third time, my normally verbose mother was silent. "I see," she said finally. "He's French. What did he want?"

"He offered me a job, to work for an organization called the Council. I would run political campaigns here, and maybe in states across the country."

"I don't know, Olivia, this is all very sudden," she said. "Maybe you should take some time off and think about things. Perhaps you would like to take a trip to France? I have an exhibition coming up in Paris, we could travel there together and relax and see the city."

"Mom, I would love that, but I need to work and stay busy," I said. "I feel like I have already been on vacation, the way I have abandoned my company these last few weeks."

My mother sighed into the phone. "It's not as if you need to work, Olivia. Your family has ensured that you have plenty of money. What can it hurt to take things slowly? You don't know anything about this Laurent fellow. Perhaps he does not have your best interests at heart."

I was now able to clearly map the outlines of my mother's state of mind. She was worried, but whether it was for me, or in general, I could not tell. "Don't worry, Mom," I said, wanting to reassure her. "I like Gabriel. He seems very nice. Perhaps it's because of our years in France, but I felt very comfortable around him."

She hesitated for a moment, then spoke. "Very well, honey," she said warmly. "I'll have my assistant send you my travel plans. Perhaps you will come to Paris for a few days and take a break with me."

I was about to say goodbye and thanks when she spoke again. "Honey, remember there is a lot still to come. I hope you will be ready for all that there is to know."

"Please don't worry," I repeated. "Elsa is helping me. I feel better than I have in a long time."

After we hung up, I turned to Elsa who had been listening in the hallway. "Well, what do I do next?"

"We should visit Gabriel at the Council offices," Elsa said. "We can go tomorrow evening. I'll text Gabriel."

"Can't we go tonight?" I asked, anxious to get started now that I had made the decision.

Elsa shook her head. "He's not there. Tomorrow we'll go. The Council convenes after dusk," she said. "It must be dark when we approach their offices. If it's foggy, we can use a portal. If it's not, then we use the main entrance."

"What does fog have to do with it?"

"Come into the living room and sit down, Olivia. If you're going to work for the Council, then I might as well begin your education." Elsa walked toward the couch. "Once you cross the threshold of their doors, there will be no turning back. You will be privy to some of the world's greatest secrets."

"You make it sound dangerous. What happens if I change my mind?"

"That's exactly my point; you can't change your mind. Once you've been exposed to the Council, you are bound by its rules. It is a serious commitment. I know, I have been working for them for many years."

"How did you get started?"

Elsa began to rearrange the pillows on the couch, avoiding my gaze. "I told you the story of how I almost gave my soul to the devil," she said. "But I never told you what happened when I was released."

I nodded. "What happened?"

"After the devil told me I was free to leave, I ran to the stable to get my horse. As I was adjusting my saddle—I planned to ride through the night to get off the mountain—the angel who bargained for me came into the stable. I asked him to tell me how he had won the argument with the devil, but he would not reveal their conversation."

"That's it? He never told you?" I asked.

"He did not, but he did tell me that there would be a price for my foolishness."

"A price?"

Elsa nodded. "Yes. He told me that to repay my rescue from the devil, I would have to pledge myself to helping others for an undetermined period of time. I have been a time-walker, moving through the centuries, helping humans and Others, since then."

"How long do you have to do this?"

Elsa sighed. "For as long as it takes. It's been hundreds of years and I have yet to see the angel again. When he reappears I will know my payment has been made."

"Well that doesn't seem fair," I said. "You've been at this for a long time."

"Yes, but to ask God to save your soul from the devil when you almost willingly gave it away...well, who knows what had to be promised to free me."

I watched Elsa closely. She was beautiful to look at. Sleek and powerful like the cat that appeared in my dreams. Her punishment not only had made her immortal, but it also had frozen her in time. She was not aging. Perhaps when she finished her penance, she would be allowed to grow old.

"Is that how you came to work for the Council?"

Elsa nodded. "I discovered them during my travels. I had no idea how to repair the damage I'd done. It made sense to work for them. They gave me a way to have a purpose and fulfill my obligation."

"Are there others like you inside?"

"If you mean people who travel through time, yes there are. But are there others doing penance? Not that I know of. Yet I can't imagine I am the only person on earth who almost gave their soul away to the devil in the pursuit of power and knowledge."

Elsa's tale reminded me of Stoner Halbert. We all, it seems, have to make our own beds. How did a rising star in politics come to call for the devil? I tried to imagine that much burning hatred or shame; a feeling of despair powerful enough to bypass God and ask for help from the dark side. I couldn't imagine ever wanting that kind of revenge or power.

"Is that what Stoner Halbert has done? Given his soul to the devil? What will happen to him?"

Elsa shrugged. "It's hard to know when these things catch up with you. It can take years for evil to be rebuffed, or it can be immediate. The circumstances are never the same."

"What happens if I decide that I don't want to do this?" I asked, the proposition of my "new life" suddenly weighing more heavily on me

Elsa rose from the couch and began to pace. "I don't know what would happen. No human has ever been allowed to work for the organization. Once you join the Council, it's hard to turn your back. I can't make the choice for you, but I strongly encourage you to take Gabriel's offer. This is your destiny."

"How can you be so sure?"

Elsa hesitated and I experienced a brief sensation of nervousness again.

"Come on, Elsa, tell me what you know."

Then it was gone; she was good at hiding her feelings from empaths like me.

"I'm sure because I have been doing this for a long time, Olivia. Your gifts deserve to be used for greater purposes than building condominiums."

Elsa's words stung a bit. I'd never set out to change the world, but she made my career seem insignificant. We get up, we go to work, we do a good job and we come home. Why does life have to be more complicated than that? And yet, it is. I now had the ability to read people and sense their emotions. I was either going to Las Vegas to make my fortune, or I needed a place to use my skills where I wouldn't frighten people.

"Text Gabriel," I said finally. "I will join the Council."

CHAPTER 14

The next evening as we left my house for the park, we stepped into a dense wall of wet fog. The humid mist on my face jogged my memory.

"I forgot to ask you last night about the fog," I said, as we pulled our collars up around our necks.

San Francisco's fog is legendary. Summer in San Francisco means never seeing the sun, at least in my neighborhood. Sometimes the fog rolls in gently, bringing a quiet, sultry climate to the city. Other nights, the fog rides the heels of a wicked wind that bends trees and howls through the narrow alleys between the row houses.

"The fog is a tool of the Council's," Elsa said as we walked. "San Francisco is enchanted; a coven of witches created a spell to summon the fog in order to protect our kind from prying eyes. When the fog is present, its easier for the Council to operate and for magical creatures to move about the city."

"Seriously?"

"Seriously," she said. "It's the perfect device for maintaining a curtain between our worlds. It can be summoned at any time, especially if the Council has called a general meeting at its headquarters."

What Elsa said made sense. Things that look odd in the shadows are probably easily explained away to humans. The fog obscures light. It muffles sound. I remembered my peyote-induced trek through Golden Gate Park, and how foggy that evening had been. Perfect for hiding a half-dressed woman running toward the sea.

"Huh, it's a brand new world," I said, only half-aware of how true my words were.

Before I knew it we were standing at the foot of the Music Concourse, gazing up at the tower of the de Young Museum. By day, it's the fifth-most visited museum in the country. By night, it is the headquarters of the Council. We looked across the plaza at the building sheathed in copper, gleaming in the evening light. According to Elsa, the fog was not quite thick enough to use the portal so we walked to the side of the museum, passing Pan's Island and lily pond, where I'd spent the night. We continued to walk, bypassing the normal side entrance reserved for museum members. Instead we made our way along a sidewalk partially obscured by ferns. Almost immediately we were facing what looked to be a solid wall of copper. Elsa placed her hand on the door. The area beneath her palm began to glow.

"Fingerprint recognition," Elsa explained matter-of-factly, as the outline of a door appeared, then clicked open slightly to let us pass. Once inside, Elsa turned left toward a bank of elevators. "We're going to the top of the tower," she said, as she pressed the button on the wall.

I scanned the surroundings as we entered; the museum's lobby looked exactly the same as it did in the daylight. The elevator, which was taking us up twelve floors to the observation tower, also looked the same. I wondered whether the museum's iconic top-floor viewing deck would also be unchanged. I was, I realized, slightly disappointed. I'm not sure what I expected. Maybe I'd watched too many Star Trek episodes, but in my mind I had conjured up a different world. I'd imagined a series of rooms with glowing flat panel screens featuring rotating, three-dimensional orbs that depicted faraway destinations and tactical information.

When we arrived at the top of the tower, however, my imagination was rewarded by the sight of a room full of several flat screens mounted to the walls. A dozen men and women were seated at desks, hunched over laptops and iPads, their mobile phones within arm's reach. At first glance, it could be an office anywhere in the world. Except it wasn't.

I looked up to see Gabriel walking across the room toward us.

"*Bonsoir*, Elsa, Olivia," he said as he grasped my hand to shake it.

"It looks so normal," I said, gesturing at the scene before me.

Gabriel nodded. "Modern technology almost makes witchcraft unnecessary at times. We can track people and issues far easier than our predecessors."

"How is this possible? Do you pack up at the end of every evening?" I asked.

Gabriel smiled. "There is not much to put away, and what is on the walls is enchanted. Humans cannot see the panels as they stroll through the deck during the day. The rest is portable. Thanks to wireless technology, our offices transport easily and, for the most part, are paperless."

"Is the museum aware of your presence?" I asked, imagining rumors floating through the city about the de Young's haunted galleries. "What happens when people here work late?"

Elsa and Gabriel exchanged a knowing glance. This is where they begin to bind you with their secrets, I thought to myself, the way they fold you in.

"They know," Elsa said. "The museum knows we are here."

"It's true," Gabriel said, seeing my raised eyebrows. "The museum spent a fortune to build this magnificent copper building. Copper, as you may know, is an ancient metal dating back to the Romans. It is a very important metal in the supernatural world. You are standing inside a building that has the ability to conduct energy back and forth between individuals and the spirit world. It acts as an amplifier for our thoughts, for sending and receiving psychic communications. Can you imagine? No better building could be constructed for our purposes."

"When we learned of the plans to build the museum, we contacted their executive director," Gabriel continued, "Although human, she is quite the diva and has a reputation as a bit of a sorceress herself. She was only too happy to accommodate our request in exchange for a sizable donation."

I nodded. "It all makes frighteningly good sense."

"But," Gabriel said, his head cocked to one side. "There is something on your mind."

"It's nothing. I'm amazed at the business-like way in which this all operates. You have a state-of-the art building, wireless technology. It all seems, well…routine."

"Did you expect us to fly around on broomsticks and play quidditch?" Elsa asked sharply. "That is a children's fantasy."

"What Elsa means," Gabriel interjected diplomatically, "Is that we've adopted today's standards like the rest of the world. We cannot survive if we fail to adapt to our surroundings. But I will take credit for the business-like way in which things run. In my other life, I'm the CEO of a computer graphics firm that makes 3-D images for movies. Our offices are near Marseille. I started my career in the mid 70's at Industrial Light and Magic in Marin."

Before I could think too much about what he'd said, Gabriel grabbed my arm and led me away.

"It's time for your grand tour," he said.

Elsa said she would stay behind in the main arena, as it was called, and monitor things.

Although I remained wary, there was something very comfortable and familiar about Gabriel. I found myself easily being led by him, and before I knew it, we were back in the elevator. We went down one floor and stepped out into what looked like ordinary office space filled with cubicles— complete with more young workers seated, heads down at their desks.

"We use most floors of this tower," he said, gesturing toward the desks. "A director and one deputy manage the

Council. Our positions rotate every five years. You'll meet my deputy, Aidan Burke, in a few minutes; he keeps his office on the floor below. A crafty Irish shape-shifter, he and I have been friends for years. We're in the fourth year of our term; next year the deputies for central and eastern Europe will take control."

"You're not very excited about that," I remarked, feeling a deep sense of ambivalence coming from him.

"Very good, Olivia," he said. "Your skills are becoming second nature to you. But to answer your question, yes, I have reservations. Zoran Mikić is a werewolf. By day, he is the governor of the Croatian National Bank. His deputy, Nikola Pajovic, is a vampire, as well as a wealthy Serbian developer who builds casinos on the Adriatic coast. They have a unique partnership, with Nikola acting as more of the leader. I worry, at times, about their commitment to the mission of The Council."

I could almost say the same thing, feeling at a loss myself to understand what the Council's purpose was. Why did it need deputies and rotating staffs to monitor humans?

"Gabriel, I hope you don't mind my asking, but why is all of this necessary? What exactly is it that you, *we*, do?"

Gabriel nodded. "Yes. Let me explain. As I mentioned, the Council is divided by region, with directors holding positions for North America and Canada, Mexico, Central and South America, western Europe, eastern Europe, Asia, and finally, Africa and the Middle East. Each sector monitors elections and shifts in government. We try, when possible, to intervene in elections to ensure moderate candidates take seats in government.

"Why not every time?"

"That would be a little too obvious," Gabriel said. "We're a clandestine organization, looking to protect the interests of our kind. If we influenced every election, it would draw too much attention to ourselves."

"And why is this necessary?"

Gabriel walked over to a desk and asked for one of the

iPads. He quickly called up a news article and walked over to me.

"Read the headline," he said, gesturing to the text on the screen.

Presidential Candidate Holds Prayer Rally
Oklahoma City (AP)—Thousands of evangelical Christians flocked to the state's capital today to participate in a prayer rally at the invitation of Governor Bob Ferry. Ferry, a devout Christian known for handing Bible verses to his aides, is preparing to run for president.

"This guy is a joke," I said, shaking my head. "Why should you worry about him?"

"It is easy to laugh at him here in San Francisco. He seems very remote from your life. But do you remember the story of the Trojan horse, Olivia? The people of Troy believed the horse to be a gift and therefore let it into their village, only to be destroyed by the Greeks hiding inside. Ferry is a man who prays for rain, and who bans books from his state's libraries because they promote witchcraft. One man like this may be a joke, but when you elect an entire Congress full of them."

"Are you telling me that men like Ferry are a threat?"

"*Exactement.* He carries in his heart the same vision as other zealots: to turn us into true believers. The civilized world is a mile wide and an inch deep. If you create the right settings, religious fanatics could control this country. Already in Europe we see the beginnings of nationalism and xenophobia. Here in the U.S., a congresswoman is shot in the head at point blank range; in Norway, government buildings blown up...Extremism is everywhere. A witch burning doesn't seem so implausible when laws and justice are meted out in God's name."

"Do you really think that the country could be hijacked by people like this?"

Gabriel looked out through the open windows at the darkened sky beyond. "I would rather ensure that it doesn't happen."

"And how do you see me in all of this, again?" I asked.

"I see you running a campaign. Levi Barnes, your old boss, is running for Congress. It's a new seat created by the latest redistricting process, so it's wide open, no incumbent. He's declared, but hasn't picked his campaign staff yet."

"And he's going to hire me...because you asked him to? It's been a decade since we've worked together."

Gabriel smiled. "I know him well because of my work with technology. He invented an application that essentially turns a smart phone into an encrypted credit card. He sold the technology for an enormous sum...an amazing man, really."

"I'm not surprised," I said, "but you still haven't answered my question. Why is he going to hire me?"

"Because you're the best person for the job," Gabriel said. "And because I will strongly suggest that he does."

"Suggest," I repeated. "You mean a spell?"

"If that is what it takes to get him on board, yes."

"Why would you go to the trouble to gain one congressional seat in Silicon Valley?"

Gabriel smiled as he walked us back toward the elevator. "What makes you think it's one seat? I told you it's about the total number of seats held. Our job is to ensure rational, moderate people win seats."

"I should think the hardest part would be to get rational, moderate people to even run for office."

Gabriel nodded. "It is increasingly difficult."

We descended one more floor, walked out of the elevator and stopped outside an office with its door closed. Gabriel knocked and the door was quickly opened by a tall, slim man with dark black hair and bright blue eyes.

"Hello, Aidan," Gabriel said warmly. "This is Olivia, the empath I told you about."

Aidan, whose handsome, dark features were slightly distracting, even for a man easily a decade older than me, gave me more scrutiny than I would have expected. He seemed to be examining me closely, although I could not detect an ounce of emotion coming from him.

"Hello, Olivia," he said cordially, a hint of an Irish accent coming though. "Welcome to the Council. Gabriel has high hopes for you inside this organization."

"You can check out, but you can never leave," I said with a smile. "Oops, I said that out loud, didn't I?"

Aidan tossed back his head and laughed. Now I could feel his warmth bubbling up. "Yes, something like that, I'm afraid. In fact, we need to get you set up for your work. I told Gabriel I would manage that task so he could see to other business."

I said goodbye to Gabriel as Aidan shut the door to his office. For a moment we sat in silence, but then Aidan began to speak, fixing his blue eyes on me.

"I'm a shape-shifter," he said. "In my village in Ireland, every other year one boy is born with the skill to shift. It's considered good luck to be the family whose child is born with the talent. My parents however, were not as thrilled as others might have been. I didn't stay at home for long. I met Gabriel one evening outside Aix-en-Provence. He was walking in the hills under the glow of a full moon and we…ran into each other."

"Is it painful to shift?" I asked, knowing it must sound so utterly human.

"At first, when we're young, yes, but not now."

I could feel genuine friendship coming off of Aidan in waves. I felt a sense of loyalty and duty from him. I wondered why he'd taken such an instant liking to me.

"Why did you volunteer to help me?" I asked. "Don't you have an HR department like all global bureaucracies?"

"Because I wanted to meet you myself," Aidan said. "It's unprecedented for a human to work for the Council. Gabriel is impressed with your skills and hopes you will be able to increase our chances of winning elections."

"I hope I can live up to everyone's expectations," I said. "What happens to people who lose elections?"

Aidan's eyes twinkled. "We send them out with the werewolves."

"I see, my fate will rest with Zoran," I said jokingly.

Aidan's smile disappeared, and I detected a momentary sense of loathing. "Oh, I do hope that is never the case, my dear, I do hope it is never the case," he said. Then quickly he changed the subject by opening a drawer in his desk and pulling out a small device that I did not recognize.

"Is this going to hurt?" I asked.

"No, but it will be weird," Aidan said. "I am going to embed a tracking device in your skin. No matter where you are, in this time or another, we will be able to find you."

"Did you say 'in this time?' "

Aidan smiled. "I did. You know about the portals. It's possible that you will use them to go back in time one day. We all wear them. Well, most of us do, anyway."

I held out my arm as instructed and Aidan used the device to stamp the skin on the underside of my arm, near my wrist. I felt pressure and heard the pop of air, but there was no blood, only a tiny blue dot where the device now sat under my skin. I glanced at my arm and then back at Aidan.

Aidan nodded, seeming to understand my thoughts. "It's semi-permanent, but it can be deactivated if necessary. And it will convert to a homing beacon if you're in trouble."

"How can I get in trouble running an election for a congressional seat?"

"Olivia, you should know better than anybody that politics is a dangerous business."

CHAPTER 15

Before leaving that evening, Aidan gave me several binders with information to read. It was mostly organizational charts of the various Council directors, as well as the Council's mission statement. I gave him a slip of paper with my bank account on it and he promised that funds would be transferred into it almost immediately. Normally, I said, I did some work before I got paid. Aidan laughed and said that Gabriel had wanted to compensate me for the time I had lost in transitioning to my new life.

I knew my mother would be furious if she found out about the funds. It would only confirm for her that there was something strange about a group that was willing to pay me before I'd even been on the workforce a day. But I was happy to take the money. I wasn't convinced that Levi Barnes would hire me. If this new arrangement didn't work out, at least I would have extra funds in my account to support myself until I decided what to do next.

It was decided that first night at the Council's offices that I would keep my firm open and use the same employees. Since I already had a track record running campaigns, it was a perfect cover for my work with the Council. Gabriel had returned to Aidan's office and handed me a binder with information about District 15, the new congressional seat Levi would be running for.

Previously made up of two other districts, the new territory was enormous, encompassing two counties, all of Silicon Valley, part of the state's farm basket near the city of Salinas, as well as the coastline near Santa Cruz. In my opinion, it was political suicide to try to represent such a huge district, the interests of urban, suburban and agricultural voters certain to clash over the years. I couldn't wait to hear why Levi Barnes wanted to return to the House of Representatives.

The last thing Gabriel told me that evening as I prepared to leave was that we were having lunch with Levi the next day at the Four Seasons Hotel on Market Street.

"You work fast," I said in response.

Gabriel smiled and said he would meet me in the dining room.

At home later that night, I read through the materials I had been given. After his defeat, Levi Barnes left Congress and Utah for California. During the following decade, he became a very wealthy man. His most recent invention, enabling smart phones to act as credit cards, had ensured that he, along with his children, would never need to work again.

I wondered how much he had changed in the decade since I had worked for him. We had parted ways on good terms, but had taken different paths. His life had been consumed with entrepreneurial pursuits and mine with politics. He was married with a family. I had started a business in the City. Time had passed quickly. But now, here we were again, being reunited by Gabriel Laurent, a man whose connections and background I was only beginning to grasp.

I arrived at the Four Seasons dining room at 1 pm, as directed. I checked in with the host, and was led to a table where Gabriel and Levi were already seated.

Levi Barnes was aging very gracefully. His short, black hair had grayed somewhat in the decade that had passed, but his blue eyes looked as crisp and aware as ever, and he had managed to keep his tall frame fit and trim over the years. Gabriel, once again impeccably dressed in dark jeans and a white oxford shirt with driving loafers, was almost vibrating with feelings of approval toward me. And while he was holding something back, I was sure of it, there was no hiding that he felt almost proud of me as I strolled to the table.

Both men stood up to greet me. Gabriel gave me the traditional *bisou* on both cheeks and Levi clasped my hand in the two of his.

"Olivia, it's so nice to see you," he said. "I'm embarrassed that it's been so long since we've seen each other."

Right away, I opened myself up to Levi, curious to know what he was feeling. His aura was bright yellow, glowing like the sun on a summer day. This was a good sign, as yellow tends to demonstrate people who are positive, have strong intellect and are imbued with the power to inspire. Those are good skills for elected office. He was feeling a deep sense of curiosity, but was otherwise happy. For someone who had to quickly assemble a team and jump into a congressional race, he struck me as remarkably calm. I wasn't sure if that was his nature—I didn't remember him being that calm before—or maybe it was Gabriel's influence.

We all took a seat as I spoke. "It seems you have been a bit busy."

Levi laughed. "Yes, I guess I have," he said. "The valley is a remarkable place. There are so many ideas to pursue, so many businesses to start…well, it captured my attention."

"And now," I asked, as the waiter came by to bring me a menu. "You're ready to return to Congress?"

Levi nodded. "Utah was unpleasant and I didn't think I would ever return to politics. But a lot of time has passed and I have changed my mind. I have enough money to last a lifetime. My children are grown and living their own lives. I am ready to do something new—or old, I guess, in this case," he said, smiling.

The waiter came and took our order. I was almost too excited to eat and requested a bowl of soup. Gabriel frowned and added a piece of fish to my lunch, saying, "the sole here is too delicious to be missed," and ordered a bottle of Sancerre to go with the meal. It struck me as odd, his desire to feed me, but despite my efforts I could not detect any untoward motives on his part.

If Levi found it odd that a French digital media executive was ordering lunch for me, he didn't show it. Gabriel told Levi that we knew each other because of his interest in building an office tower in San Francisco. "I have toyed with the idea of re-locating some, possibly all of my employees to San Francisco," he told Levi. "France is lovely, but we have no start-up culture and our film industry has less of a need for the kind of 3-D animation we develop. I spend so much of my time coming to California that it makes sense to relocate. Olivia has been kind enough to put up with my half-hearted efforts to look at parcels of land and provide me with a political analysis of my chances."

"This is a great time to build in San Francisco," I said, going along with the charade. "The city has incredible tax credits to offer technology companies willing to relocate here."

Gabriel went on to say that he was too much of a Frenchman to ever move away. "I might rent some space for a satellite office," he said, "but to leave Marseille completely would be *tragique*."

Our plates arrived and we sat in silence for a few minutes, until Gabriel spoke again. "Levi, you've declared your interest to run for Seat Fifteen? Are you certain? If so, you need to assemble a campaign team immediately."

Levi's concern about my role was coming through loud and clear.

"Maybe I can step in here," I said, feeling confident for the first time in weeks that I knew what I was talking about. "Levi, you know me as twenty-something press secretary. I didn't help run your first campaign. But like you, I have been busy since we closed down your office in the Rayburn Building ten years ago. I have been building a very successful business here in San Francisco, including running campaigns."

I had managed to catch Levi's attention, and I could feel his growing interest.

"I represent a number of both national and international corporations, as well as individuals, in their dealings with both the media and government officials," I continued. "I have run a number of campaigns to protect their interests. I have an extensive background in business and development in the Bay Area. I understand the dynamics of election politics. In short, I believe I have the leadership, skills and required relationships to run this congressional campaign for you."

"She is considered one of the best," Gabriel said, pouring more wine into Levi's glass. "And then, there is the fact that you two have already worked with each other."

"You know my work ethic," I said. "I was the first one in the office and often the last one to leave. This will be no different."

Levi was curious, but not sold. "How do you think I win this race?" he asked.

I smiled. "Well, it's not magic," I said, cringing inwardly. "Your money is not enough. Look at Meg Whitman, she spent millions on her campaign for governor, but at the end of the day couldn't connect with voters. Voters support people they like, people who understand their issues. You are the perfect candidate. You came from another state to chase your entrepreneurial dreams, and after years of hard work found success. You've raised a family, nurtured a marriage and now after your success, want to return to a life of public service. You have a background in both business and education; you are exactly what California needs at this tumultuous time in the state's history."

Once again Gabriel vibrated with happiness. He was very pleased with my speech, and, luckily, so was Levi Barnes.

He agreed to hire me right then and there, offering his apartment in San Francisco as a temporary campaign headquarters. We were nowhere near ready to open a campaign office in Silicon Valley, so using his apartment and my office as a base of operations was perfect. I offered to work for free for the first few weeks so that Levi could decide if I was a good fit for the job. I didn't need the funds since Gabriel was paying me, but Levi just laughed and said money was not an issue.

Within a matter of days, he'd paid my first month's salary and deposited $1 million in a campaign account "to get us started."

CHAPTER 16

Aidan was sitting at his desk, deep in thought, when I arrived one evening a week later to brief him on my progress.

"Knock, knock," I said as I walked into his office.

"The intrepid consultant returns," he said, swiveling his chair away from his computer to face me as I took a seat across from his desk. "How are things going?"

"So far, so good. I'm writing a campaign plan and interviewing pollsters," I said. "Most evenings after sundown, I'm here, training with Elsa."

"And the campaign?"

"The campaign seems almost too good to be true," I said. "How often does an open congressional seat appear with few competitors vying for it? It's a district representing a huge portion of the state's population and wealth. Admittedly, not nearly as sexy as San Francisco, it's still home to billions in venture capital and agriculture. So far, press coverage has been sparse. But I think we have days, maybe hours to get this campaign up and running before we're in the spotlight."

"And then what?" he asked.

"I'm certain an opponent will appear, and begin to evaluate their chances. Why not? There's nothing to lose, since it's an open seat." I said. "The big question is whether another Democrat will challenge Levi. I'm going to speak with the head of the Party and see if I can preempt a challenger."

"Do you need someone to come with you to help

persuade him?" Aidan asked. "Gabriel is good at that kind of thing, you know."

"I don't think we need to bewitch Paul Levant, not yet at least," I said. "He's been president of the California Democratic Party for more than 20 years. I know him—he's salty, irascible, but he does have one soft spot: he loves women's rowing. I've already checked the race schedule. There is a regatta coming up in a few weeks at Lake Merced. I'm going to approach him then."

"Do you think you'll be able to read him clearly?"

"Yes. Everyday it gets a little easier," I replied. "Besides, Levant isn't one to hide his emotions. I won't have to work hard to know what's in his heart."

"That's fortunate," Aidan said. "We have had great difficulty in some of our other races trying to get ahead of the opposition. Too much magic is too obvious, so we take baby steps."

"Why can't you just put a spell on an entire town?" I asked, only slightly in jest. "Who would know?"

"We would," he replied. "I'm afraid it's against the rules."

There were, it turned out, a myriad of rules to follow when it came to the Council. Secrecy was reinforced at every opportunity. We were to monitor and possibly intervene on behalf of humans, but without drawing attention to the organization or ourselves. I was never to discuss my skills with anyone, even my family, which in my case seemed like an unnecessary rule since my mother already knew what I could do. We also were forbidden to attract the attention of the police or other authorities. That rule caught my attention.

"That reminds me, I've been meaning to ask you something," I said, changing the subject. "I was reading the rule about not attracting the interest of the police and it got me wondering if there are really Others who break the law."

My question brought an immediate rush of Aidan's anxiety to my solar plexus.

"There are Others involved in every facet of life: Navy

Seals, astronauts and yes, even criminals," he said, a reluctance in his voice.

"Criminals," I repeated, as if it were the first time I'd heard the word.

"You'd be surprised," he said.

I was surprised and I wanted to pry further, but a glance at my watch told me I was now late to my appointment with Elsa, so I nodded and left the room.

Elsa was engaged, face-to-face, with a man in a heated argument. There was a *New York Times* article up on the screen of a computer in front of them, but I could not make out the headline. Watching their body language, it was clear there was little love lost between them.

"Hello," I said, interrupting them. "I don't mean to intrude, but it's time for our appointment, Elsa."

"You must be Olivia," The man said, offering me the sort of bitter smile reserved for competitors and enemies. It took only seconds for me to realize he was a vampire—one who, for some reason, did not like me at all.

"We are, it seems, to have a human in our midst."

"Olivia, this is Nikola," Elsa interjected before I could respond. "He's a member of the eastern European delegation and next in line as deputy to the director."

He was also up to something; his energy was as dark as a lump of coal. Darkness suited him. Tall, lean, and *looming*, Nikola was the perfect embodiment of the menacing undead.

"Hello, Nikola," I said, intentionally ignoring his remark about humans. I returned his gaze, making sure to look him in the eye before I turned my attention to the computer screen to take a closer look at the headline, which announced that a former Serbian army general had been convicted of war crimes at the International Court of Justice at the Hague.

"Were you two talking about this?" I asked, pointing to the screen.

"I'm sure it does not concern you," Nikola said.

"I'm a member of this organization," I replied.

"We can discuss it later," Elsa said, cutting me off again.

"We need to get started on our work. Nikola, if you'll excuse us..."

Before I could ask any questions, I found myself hurled into a private conference room.

"You know," I said, "the first time we came into this building, I didn't notice so many private rooms. Can you make rooms happen to suit your needs?"

In response, Elsa pointed to a piece of paper on a large conference table. It was some kind of map of the city. But not the type normally drawn by the U.S. Geological Survey. Instead of the usual lots and blocks, the map contained numerous vibrant color images including a picture of the windmill at the far west end of Golden Gate Park and a drawing of the archway on Grant Street that marks the entrance to Chinatown. On another part of the map there was a lone dragon floating above a doorway and a statue of Willie Mays in front of AT&T Park. I also recognized the fountain in the music concourse outside the museum depicted among the map's other images.

"It's a map," I said, knowing I was stating the obvious. "What are these images?"

Elsa ran her fingers along the drawings. "These are the locations of the portals hidden across the city. Although you can carry a copy of the map with you, it would be easier if you memorize the locations."

Memorizing was never one of my strong suits. "That doesn't sound easier," I said. "I'd rather have a copy."

"You can't walk around with a paper copy of the map in your hands," Elsa said. "If you choose to have a copy it will have to be imprinted onto your skin with a spell, but..."

"But what?" I asked.

"Well, I don't recommend it," Elsa said. "For one thing, it introduces your body to a powerful form of old magic that is painful, and two, it can be difficult to be on the run and try to conjure the map up onto your skin."

I was trying to decide which part of her remarks to deal with first: the part about it being painful, the fact that that you could use witchcraft to do something like that, or the part about being on the run. "Could you elaborate more on the part about 'being on the run?'" Day by day, the Council was beginning to feel more complicated.

"I'm not trying to frighten you, Olivia, but our situation is different," she said. "Like you, we have a mix of good and bad people, but in the human world you walk away when someone bothers you. In our world, now *your* world, you won't always be able to do that. You will need the portals. They also can be a great shortcut if you are ever running late."

I could tell that Elsa was being honest. She wasn't trying to frighten me, but she was worried about my safety. What she was hiding, I couldn't really say. I wasn't sure if her worries were real, or the result of living centuries on high alert. Our conversation brought me down to earth again. My responsibilities for the campaign were lengthy and serious. I felt the weight, but I welcomed it. I was happy to be involved and pressed to do my best. I knew how to do that.

The Council was something altogether different. I had a tracking device in my arm near the pulse point at my wrist, and as surely as I could feel my heart beat through my skin, so too could these people find me. I had agreed to run a campaign for Levi Barnes, but I really worked for the Council, an organization that sounded lofty in its ideals but had its own fractured political environment. Layer-by-layer, I was starting to realize the complexity of the commitment I'd made.

Elsa in her own way was making sure I understood. It was clear that she did not mean to harm me. She did not even mean to warn me. It was well past the time for that. I was already tagged and ready for duty. Elsa, it seemed, was trying to accomplish what my mother had hoped to do. She was preparing me for my life, my new life. She wasn't my mother, and maybe that made it easier. It wasn't her fault that the things I needed to know were intimidating.

"I'm not all that good at memorization," I said again,

looking her straight in the eye. "If it's all the same to you, I'd rather have the map imprinted on me."

She nodded, her green eyes signaling comprehension. "We will need to find the old witch who lives nearby. Nadia will bind the map to you."

After we finished our discussion about the map, we practiced blocking, another skill Elsa insisted I needed to have. Blocking is the act of keeping people out of your head so they can't read your thoughts or harm you. I thought I had mastered that skill in the first few days after my peyote trip when we had ridden trains around the city. But she was not backing down.

"Didn't I already do this on the train?" I repeated. "What else is there to know?"

Her reply was swift. Elsa pushed against me with her mind with so much force that I almost fell off my chair. As I feebly tried to block her, my nose began to gush blood.

"See what I mean," she said, handing me a tissue. "Blocking is like one of the baseball games you love so much. Energy shifts. One distraction, one error and you can be behind in the count, as you like to say."

My task for the remainder of the evening was to focus and maintain my blocking. No matter how hard Elsa pushed, I was to resist. I had to focus and not divert my attention, for even a moment. That was somewhat easy if I was standing still watching her. But then she insisted we go outside and run. Trying to block while moving was a whole other story. I had to look down to see where I was going and try to keep her locked out of my skull. As I tore though the forest behind the museum, jumping over logs and trying to avoid obstacles in the dark, I could feel her pressing on me.

At first I was too distracted to keep her out and she wasn't even trying very hard. Then my eyes finally adjusted to the darkness and I began to use my senses more efficiently. I calmed my mind as Elsa had instructed and began to imagine a huge force of energy surrounding me. It both protected me and propelled me. I could see the glow in my mind's eye—a sensation Elsa had told me to expect. I was generating a field of energy around my body and my mind. For a short while I was able to run with ease and felt no pressure in my head. Then, for one moment, I got distracted and my mind wandered and just like that…Wham! It felt like Elsa had taken a bat to the back of my head. I went down in the mossy loam of the path and curled up into a ball.

"Why did you stop concentrating?" Elsa asked as she ran up and bent over me.

"Why did you wallop me in the back of my head?" I gurgled from the forest floor.

"I didn't mean to use so much force," she said, trying to help me up. "You were doing so well, you were aglow. I was testing you and then—poof! you stopped blocking…" Elsa stopped mid sentence when I abruptly put my hand to my nose, where I could feel the warm trickle of blood starting up again.

"Let's go inside" she said. "I will help you clean up."

CHAPTER 17

After a couple of weeks avoiding nosebleeds and working what amounted to a double shift, I was ready for a break from my duties. Luckily, my need for a diversion coincided with the arrival of a bluegrass music festival. Planned and paid for through the generosity of a local philanthropist, the annual event is a three-day tribute to the twangs and twinges of guitar, fiddle and banjo. The music is performed in several large meadows and groves in Golden Gate Park where bands play continuously from late morning until dusk. Because it's free, tens of thousands of people stream into town to enjoy the music. I couldn't think of a better way to spend the last days of San Francisco's Indian summer than outside at a concert.

On the first day of the festival, I printed out a map of the five stages and the program of performers. I perused the lineup of bands and plotted a strategy for moving as little as possible while enjoying maximum sun and music. After some quick deliberation, I decided to make camp in an area where local bands would be performing. Most of the big names I wanted to watch like Iron and Wine wouldn't perform until early evening. I knew some people would stake out a place now for those shows, but I didn't have the heart to sit for several hours through music I didn't like.

I had invited Elsa to join me, but she declined, saying she had some work to review with Aidan. Alone, I grabbed my camp chair and a thermos of rum and coke and headed for Golden Gate Park. With little trouble, I found a good spot to sit in an open grassy field, directly in front of one of the smaller performance stages. I opened my chair, put some sunscreen on my face and prepared to enjoy the day.

Technically, you are not allowed to bring alcohol into the park. I say technically because, although the law is very real, it's rarely enforced. In fact, it seemed to me that I'd rarely been in the park at a festival where alcohol and other assorted goodies were not being passed around.

Although I was beginning to think of the park as a gigantic hideout for magical beings, and as the headquarters of the Council, the park was also a human refuge. In a city as dense as San Francisco, with more apartments buildings than single-family homes, the park is a backyard to thousands. It's a place to run, walk, think and get high. Today was clearly one of those days when getting high took precedence over other activities.

As I unscrewed the cap on my thermos and poured a bit of my cocktail into the small plastic cup, I was tapped on the shoulder and handed a joint. When I'm working I usually don't smoke pot. I am paranoid that there will be some kind of campaign emergency and I will be too out of it to solve the problem. It was also true that Elsa would have been less than thrilled at my attempt to dull my mind, which she was working so feverishly to sharpen. But I am human. It was too beautiful a moment not to take a little hit.

Not long after, I was feeling right as rain and leaned back in my chair to enjoy the music. I pulled out my schedule and read the name of the first band: Three Blind Mice. A trio came on stage, a woman carrying a fiddle, a man with a stand-up bass and, a few seconds later, another man sauntered out with an acoustic guitar in his hands.

He was pale, amazingly so, with a slight sprinkling of freckles across the middle of his face. He had fiery red hair that hung straight to his shoulders. Before he began to play, he pulled a hair band out of his pocket and tied the hair back in a ponytail. This made it easier to see a small hoop earring in his left ear and to see his eyes, which were a shade of green similar to the moss on the shady side of a log. He had a long, narrow nose that sat above a set of pale, pink lips. He was moderately tall and slim in a way that appealed to me, as I have never been one for bulky, muscular men.

OK, I'll admit that I was intrigued.

But I couldn't say why he caught my attention. In San Francisco, there is no shortage of tall, gaunt, waifish men to gawk at. I noticed also that he had a fabulous set of tattoos around his wrists and elbows—again, not a rare occurrence. With him, though, there was a certain *je ne sais quoi*. Maybe it was the way his grey shirt and faded jeans hung on his body. Maybe it was the pot. I was trying to put my finger on what it was that caught my attention when the trio began to play. The moment I heard the music, I knew he was the vampire from the tunnel.

The recognition was immediate for us both. When I looked back at the stage, his green eyes were gazing directly into mine and he had a slight smile on his face, as if he also was satisfied to find me. I held his gaze. I sank back in my chair and locked on to him and watched as he moved his fingers up and down the neck of the guitar, fret-to-fret-to fret, hitting every note while never taking his eyes from mine.

In general, romantic fairy tales don't sway me, especially now that I know that fairies can actually be quite evil. But, honestly, I was quite dazzled by the gorgeous musician making eyes at me. Now and then I would look away to chat with someone, or look out at the swelling crowd gathering. He periodically switched instruments, using a banjo instead of a guitar, but the moment I turned my head back to him, he would meet my gaze.

I was enjoying myself, but I realized that I needed to bring our staring contest to an end and leave before the vampire got the idea I was actually interested in getting to know him better. It's been well established (by me) that I don't have boyfriends. I sleep with men occasionally when I feel the urge, usually the kind of men who don't want to be called again. This suits me fine. I'm not interested in romance. I don't believe that people meet, fall in love and get married. There is no such thing as happily ever after. And now, with my newfound powers and a sidekick named Elsa, I am especially not interested in dating.

Of course, this vampire never said he wanted to date me either. I had no evidence that he wanted anything to do with me. Last time we were alone, he'd abruptly stopped talking and disappeared. In fact, I didn't even know if vampires liked humans, let alone dated them. But the biggest black mark against him? He was already dead, which meant he had a lot of free time on his hands. To me this was the fatal flaw. The last thing I needed was a guy with too much time on his hands hanging around.

Having had this entire conversation quickly in my head, I reluctantly packed up as the band was ending its set and abruptly set off, walking into the massive stream of people surging toward the main stages. I was never so relieved to be swallowed by a crowd and I hoped it would help me disappear. I was allowing myself to be pushed along with the general direction of the mob when I felt a whisper of breath against my ear and a set of firm fingers on my shoulder.

"I see you still can't finish what you start," he said, his Southern drawl sounding stronger today.

I turned to face him and was prepared to deny all when I found myself looking into eyes far darker than they had seemed from the stage. I exhaled before I could stop myself. My God he was beautiful. And calm. He was still giving off the calmest waves of energy I had ever felt. I, however, did not feel calm. I was feeling anxious. How had he found me so quickly, and in such an enormous crowd?

"Have we met?" I asked, using my haughtiest voice.

My remarks caused him to throw his head back and laugh. "You spent my entire set ogling me, and now you're going to pretend we don't know each other? That is downright cruel."

"I was not ogling," I said, unable to steel myself against his charm. "I was watching you play. I happen to like bluegrass music."

"Liar," was his reply.

We were at a standstill. As I stood watching him, trying to control my breathing, it occurred to me that he was standing in the mid-day sun.

"Are you going to burst into flames if we stand here?" I asked genuinely not wanting to draw that kind of attention to myself. I mean, how would you explain that to the police?

He smiled. "No, I will not burst into flames, but I would like to get my hat and my guitar and find some shade. Would you care to join me, *ma'am*?"

It was the *ma'am* that got me. It was delivered in a velvety drawl that sent shivers down my spine. I was transported to my imagination's version of the South, with a door being opened at some luncheonette so I could stroll in and order a tall glass of lemonade. And like that, all of my "I don't date," "I don't get involved," disappeared and I walked off with a strange vampire into the middle of a music festival.

We walked back to the stage where his band had performed. He pulled several lanyards with plastic badges from inside his shirt and showed them to a guard, who let us both walk behind a makeshift fence. As we headed toward the back of the stage, I found myself ready to ask questions.

"Do your band mates know?" I asked.

"Know what?"

"You know," I said. "What you are?"

"They know," he said, picking up the same straw cowboy hat he'd been wearing in the tunnel. "They don't much care as long as I show up for our performances."

"They must live in the Mission," I blurted out before I could stop myself.

My Southern man of mystery smiled. "You mean because in the Mission no one would notice a vampire walking around?"

"Exactly," I said, glad he understood what I meant.

"I'm William Ferrell, by the way," he said, extending his hand.

I took his cool hand into mine and for the second time I

could not control a gasp. He was an old soul. I could tell now why he was so calm. He had lived lifetimes; the energy he gave off spoke of conservation and time. I was amazed at what I could feel coming from him. But more than that, I could feel his strong interest in me. He was burning with curiosity about what I was and was clearly letting me read him to see what would happen.

"Why are you letting me do this?" I asked.

"Tell me your name," he said, holding on to my hand.

"Olivia. Olivia Shepherd," I said.

"Well, *Olivia,*" he said, stretching out the syllables out. "I am trying to figure out what you are."

Although we were in a crowded place with people who had been partying for hours, I was leery of saying anything. The Council had been explicit that I was not to discuss my skills or the existence of the Others with regular humans.

"Shhhh," I said, laughing. "You'll scare the humans. Let's get out of here."

William picked up his guitar and we began to walk. We left the festival compound and headed east along the sidewalk until we got to the entrance to Stow Lake. I don't know why I took him there. I guess I thought it would be quiet and it has some nice shady groves where we could talk.

By now it was late afternoon, and the clouds were moving in. The light around the lake was slightly dulled, and the sun had to push through the clouds to be seen. It was still beautiful to look at and I was pleased to see a flock of geese flying across the lake, honking as they came overhead. I led William to the inner ring of the lake, where a dirt path climbs to the top of what locals call Strawberry Hill. I didn't have to worry that he would be out of breath from carrying a guitar as he walked wordlessly next to me. When we got to the top, I gestured to show him the panoramic view of the city. He smiled.

We sat down on a large boulder and looked out at the Pacific Ocean and Marin headlands laid out before us.

"Are we alone?" he asked, knowing the answer. "Can I ask again?"

"I'm not sure what to tell you," I said, feeling apprehensive. "I have only begun to understand myself. I am human, but I come from a long line of women with the ability to read people. I can read their emotions and auras. Sometimes I can read minds. Actually it's closer really to reading *their intentions,* not their actual thoughts. I only recently learned that I can do all of this."

"Recently," he said, sounding surprised. "Where I come from, this kind of talent was passed from mother to daughter. Why didn't your mother tell you?"

Gosh. Was I really going to divulge my family history to a strange vampire, whom I hardly knew, in the middle of the park?

"It's complicated," I said. "My mom did try to tell me. She is an artist who can pick up on people's emotions, but it overwhelms her. She has a major substance abuse problem. Her paintings are these mad, amazing landscapes that display the energy of the land in a way that really captivates people. She is an amazing hostess who loves to entertain. People adore her and we used to have parties at our home that would last until dawn. It's too much for her, though. She can't separate out what belongs to whom. The energy eats her alive. I was raised in Bolinas where she has a house and a studio. She's very wealthy, but very fucked up. I never met my father."

"Anyway," I continued. "I had no desire to be like her. It was scary to watch as a child. She could be so happy, but then..."

"So what have you been doing all these years?" he graciously asked, helping to change the subject.

"I'm a consultant for companies, and sometimes I run political campaigns," I said. "Lately though, I've had some bad luck and some major changes in my life."

"Hmm," William drawled. "Are you getting married, is it something like that?" he said laughing.

I slapped him on the shoulder, shocked at how solid he felt to the touch.

"Don't tease. I am pouring my heart out to a complete stranger with a Southern accent. The least you can do is be sympathetic."

"Darlin, my accent is real," he purred back. "I was born and raised in Tennessee."

"In what year?" I asked, hoping he would tell me.

"All in good time," he said. "Eventually, I'll answer all of your questions."

"Are you really a vampire?" I asked, wanting to firm up the situation.

He turned to look at me and asked, "Are you really a human who can size people up for what they truly are?"

"I am," I said, pleased with his explanation for my gifts.

"I'm glad we got that all sorted out," he said. "Now, what do you mean bad luck? In my experience, there is no such thing as bad luck. There is bad information, bad planning or bad execution. If you have one of those three, then you usually have bad luck."

He did have a point. I suppose when you've been alive for as long as he has, you have the luxury of seeing things more clearly and separating out your own emotions. I guess in a way I did have some or all three of those in my basket. I had failed to use my gifts and missed opportunities in my work.

"I suppose you could say I had a triple whammy. Thanks to a demon unleashed on me by a competitor, I managed to get myself fired from a project. Then I tried to compete for another big campaign. I made a mess of the presentation and lost the work. At that point I got mad at myself and sort of let things go."

William nodded, indicating I should continue.

"I got angry. Then I grew depressed. Around that time I began to have dreams with a great black panther in them. And she seemed to want to speak to me."

"Oooooh, now that is spooky," William said. "Are you

telling ghost stories up here on the mountain top? I feel like I am back home with my kinfolk."

I slapped him again on his very solid, tattooed arm. I was growing to like him and his sense of humor. And there was no denying that he was incredibly sexy. There were worse ways to spend my time.

"Actually, I am telling a ghost story," I said smiling. "I have a sort of ghost of my own. Her name is Elsa and ever since she arrived, she has acted as a kind of mentor and guide. I mentioned this awful night when I broke down. The next morning she was there, standing in my kitchen. Elsa was the panther. It scared the shit out of me. I won't deny it. It's not that I didn't believe in spirits. I really never gave it much thought. Now, of course, I know that the world is really divided into parallel worlds, but it was a bit of a shock to see an ancient time-walker sitting in my home."

I could see this story had actually shocked William, because he was now looking at me with a new appreciation for my situation.

"Where is she now?" William asked, sounding a little worried. "What happened to the demon?"

"The demon," I repeated, realizing I didn't know. "I don't know exactly what happened. When Elsa appeared, everything bad that was happening stopped. Then she gave me this peyote drink and I ran through the woods and saw colors." I was babbling a mile a minute, the same way a child would quickly try to tell a story. "Why do you care? Are you worried she won't like me talking to you?"

William nodded emphatically. "She is here to help you accomplish something important, Olivia. Few humans in the world manage to catch the attention of a time-walker. You have what my dear departed mother would have called a powerful spirit."

I laughed. "I don't think Elsa will care. She…" I was about to say she works with vampires, but I wasn't so sure I should tell William about the Council.

"Did you tell her you were going to go for a walk alone

in the woods with a vampire?"

I shook my head. "I didn't know myself," I said, hoping this wasn't the end of my evening.

"It's none of her business," I added, suddenly worried I would never see William again.

William shook his head to disagree. "This is powerful magic that should not be interrupted."

"I don't want to interrupt," I said, raising my voice, "I am happy to learn what Elsa wants to teach me, but I don't like being told who I can be friends with."

William bent his head down and began to laugh softly. "My dear, sweet Olivia, you have a lot to learn about the world you've entered. Vampires don't make friends," he said. "They take lovers."

And then he leaned in and kissed me. Kissed me until my lips felt like they would blister from the heat. I had no idea how powerful sexual energy could feel until that moment when I opened myself up to it. It was easy to understand now what someone meant by being lost in a kiss. In fact, I was so lost in thought that it took me a few moments to realize I was actually no longer kissing him. At some point he'd disappeared—like he had that day in the tunnel. Once again, I was alone in the dusk light. This was the second time he had managed to disappear on me. I vowed there would not be a third as I grabbed my things and headed for home.

CHAPTER 18

My sleep had been restless, but this time I had the vampire to thank for my insomnia. His kiss had seared my soul, and I'd spent the evening tossing and turning, yearning for him in a way I had never wanted a man before.

The timing of our meeting, I realized, firing up my espresso machine, was horrendous. I was running a multi-million dollar campaign and assuming a new role as a consultant. My window for romance was slim at best, assuming I could even find William Ferrell again.

I must have been daydreaming because I did not hear Elsa come into the kitchen. "How was the concert?" she asked.

"Good, fun," I said. "I met a vampire. His name is William."

"You met a vampire, as in he came up and introduced himself?"

"Yes. Sort of...what I mean is I had been staring at him, err watching him perform. He's in a band," I managed to stutter out, sounding like a teenager.

"And, what happened?" she asked, sounding like my mother, which got my defenses up.

"I am over thirty years old," I said, sounding more like a teenager. "I can take care of myself."

Elsa was shaking her head in a way that oddly reminded me of William. Once again I was going to be lectured on all the things I didn't know. I held my hands out in front of me to indicate I wasn't in the mood.

"Listen, he already told me I didn't know what I was

getting into," I said. "And he told me you would not approve at all."

"He was right," she said. "Vampires are serious creatures, Olivia. They do not *make friends* with humans."

"So I've been told," I said. "Listen. I will probably never see him again, so let's drop it."

Elsa nodded, and I went back to making myself a cappuccino. Once that was out of the way, we discussed how to contact Nadia, the witch versed in old magic who would transfer the map of the portals onto my skin. It would not be hard to locate her, Elsa said; she could be found most days feeding the ducks and geese at Stow Lake. All we had to do is walk over and look for her.

The sun was already high as we climbed to the top of the stairway at the foot of Stow Lake. The trees were lush and green and our surroundings seemed brighter against the brilliant October sky. There were turtles sunning themselves on logs, and ducks resting on the grass as Elsa scanned the perimeter of the lake, looking for Nadia.

"There she is."

'She' turned out to be an elderly woman, who despite the heat, was dressed in multiple layers of clothing: tights, floral dress and a large cardigan sweater. And for good measure she had a floral scarf tied around her head and knotted at her chin. Next to her was a worn red wagon stuffed full of bags of bread pieces and birdseed. Nadia, it seemed, was well stocked for her work.

"That is Nadia?"

Elsa nodded. "You were expecting a pointy hat and a magic wand?"

"When you said old magic, I guess I got an image in my head of someone more scary looking," I said, cringing at how stupid I sounded.

"I said o-l-d magic, not black magic," Elsa said with a laugh. "But don't be fooled. Nadia can be very scary when she needs to be."

Nadia looked up and acknowledged us as we approached. She and Elsa began conversing in a language that sounded vaguely like Russian. The two chatted for a few minutes, each one periodically looking over at me. Finally, Nadia turned to face me completely. "This is going to hurt," she said, sizing me up. "But it will be over quickly."

I glanced around the lake, taking in our surroundings. There were a few other walkers strolling nearby, but for the most part it was empty. I wasn't sure how this old magic was supposed to work, but I was pretty sure we didn't want any witnesses. Nadia picked up on my thoughts and shook her head.

"I will come to you, to your home, in a few days," she said. "In the meantime, I need something of yours, a hair or a fingernail."

I looked over at Elsa at a loss, never having been a party to this kind of request before. In response, she yanked a hair off my head and handed it to Nadia. The elderly witch immediately reached into the pocket of her cardigan and took out a white handkerchief. Carefully, she put the hair inside the cloth and folded it closed. Then she returned the material to her pocket.

"How will I know when to expect you?" I asked, once again exposing my ignorance. But the old woman smiled and patted my arm.

"Don't worry, I will find you."

I wasn't worried. I had read Nadia's intentions while we were standing together and I was certain she meant me no harm. It was hard to tell her age, but she was well over 200 years old, judging by the color of her aura. I was getting good at reading tones and hues, and hers were not the stuff of the modern world. After a few more moments of pleasantries, we said goodbye and parted.

A few days later, I was working on my laptop at home when there was a knock on the door. Lily was over, sitting on the couch reading a book. Elsa was in the living room doing yoga. "It's Nadia," Elsa said from the other room, rising from her mat to open the door.

It seemed rude to stay seated, so Lily and I both got up and walked to the door to greet her. In the dusk light, Nadia looked much younger. She arrived with another colorful headscarf covering her hair, but up close her skin was moist and pale, almost flawless. She caught me scrutinizing her. "Thanks to the old ways, I age more slowly than one might think," she said, looking at me directly.

Before I could ask what her secret was, she urged us to move in to the kitchen. The four of us walked in, and I took a seat at the peninsula. Nadia stood at the counter, unpacking a small bundle she had removed from her sweater pocket. Slowly, she unrolled the cloth to reveal a small brown glass jar filled with a clear liquid, and a paintbrush. The brush was made of a dark wood and was ornately decorated with symbols I could not decipher. The hairs of the brush were stark white and shaped into a point.

"Are you left-handed or right-handed, " Nadia asked, grabbing my attention away from her supplies.

"Right," I said as she placed the jar and brush on the counter.

"OK then. We'll do your left hand because it will be sore for a day or two."

This conversation made me a little uneasy. I had a vision of my left arm blackened and hanging limply from my side. Lily came up behind me and placed her hand on my shoulder. "Don't be scared," she said quietly. "I've seen this kind of old magic before many times. It will feel a little like getting a tattoo. A short sting, and then the next day your skin will feel as if it has been burned."

I washed my left forearm in the sink and dried it. Then, following her directions, I laid my arm on the counter. Nadia removed her heavy cardigan, saying she was warm, and instructed Elsa to bring her a candle and some salt. Elsa brought both items to her and took a step back.

"Dim the lights," Nadia said to no one in particular. Lily got up and turned off most of the lights in the kitchen, leaving a single bulb above the stove for illumination. Then Nadia lit a small white candle and picked up the glass bottle. She ran the flame under the bottle several times and then tilted the candle until it began to drip wax onto the counter.

"North. South," she chanted in her Russian-tinged English. "East. West. These are the directions in which we travel." She continued to drip wax until the face of a compass appeared. When she was done, she asked Lily to slowly sprinkle salt along the wax pattern as she spoke. Nadia ran the flame of the candle under the bottle one more time and then began to murmur the words of a spell under her breath. Slowly she unscrewed the cap on the bottle and handed the candle to Elsa. Then she picked up the paintbrush. Symbols began to glow when she clasped the handle. Nadia dipped the brush into the jar and continued to speak.

"Subnoto. Signum. Terminus."

As soon as the brush touched my arm it began to sting. I had expected her to draw the images on my arm, adding each site I had seen on the map. Instead she was running the brush up and down the length of my arm, much the same way a painter would try to cover a wall. As my arm was coated with the liquid, exact copies of the line drawings I had seen on the map began to appear. I'm not sure how long it took her to complete the process. I was transfixed, watching the map take shape on my arm. The pain was no less and no more than what Nadia and Lily had promised. It stung and my arm burned, but I was almost too distracted by the magic to be uncomfortable.

When Nadia was finished, she asked Lily to put the last of the salt on the wax compass on the counter. Then the old witch placed the brush in the flame of the candle and said *"Termino."* The hairs of the brush glowed, but did not catch fire.

I looked down at my arm. There were a half dozen line drawings sitting at the surface of my skin, all angry red and swollen at the edges.

"Can I touch?" I asked, hoping I could put a cold cloth or some ice on my arm. Nadia nodded and took a small clay jar out of the other pocket of her sweater, which I was beginning to suspect was bewitched to hold anything she needed. She opened the pot and moved it under my nose several times so I could pick up the fragrance.

"Calendula flowers," she said, as I smiled at the scent. "It will help your skin heal." Nadia rubbed the salve on my arm and asked Elsa to bandage it for the night. "In the morning, you can remove the bandage," she added, as she began to pack up her belongings.

"What will it look like tomorrow?" I asked, worried there would be some big, ugly mess on my arm.

"The map will be visible for the next few days, but only to you," she continued. "It will disappear and only return when you request it."

"Request," I repeated, but Nadia shook her head.

"Not out loud. All you need to do is think about the map to see it. The map is bound to you now." I stared at my arm, marveling at how, for the second time in recent weeks, I'd managed to stamp myself with permanent ink.

"There is one more thing," Nadia said, interrupting my thoughts. "The map will change."

This caught everyone's attention.

"How do you mean?" Lily asked.

Nadia fixed a stare on the three of us, much like a schoolteacher dealing with an inept student. "The magic that binds the map is a part of the same spell that creates the portals. If the locations change, or a route is blocked, you will see it."

"And if I leave San Francisco?" I asked, thinking this handy information.

Again, Nadia fixed me with eyes that spoke volumes about my inexperience. "The map will display the portals located in the place where you are. If your arm is blank, it means there is no exit."

That sounded ominous.

"I think it's time for tea," Lily interjected, thankfully.

We made Nadia a cup of tea and the four of us sat in amicable silence for a few minutes. Finally the old woman stood up abruptly and declared that she was tired and wanted to leave.

"I will walk you," Elsa offered, but Nadia declined, saying a walk in the crisp night air would do her some good.

When we reached the door, Nadia asked for my hand and began to examine my palm. She stood quietly for a few moments and then spoke. "You are destined for great things, Olivia. You have a long life line and..." Nadia had stopped speaking.

"And what?" I prodded.

"You have a great adventure ahead," she said, almost squinting at my palm. "I see two great loves will enter your life."

I replied with my own question. "Did I make the right decision joining the Council?"

Nadia squeezed my hand and stepped closer to me to ensure only I could hear her whispered words. "That was not your choice, *miloska*," she said. "Women kings are born and must accept their fate."

"There is no such thing," I said back.

Nadia began to leave. "Oh, but there is," she said nodding. "There is." And then she quickly walked down the stairway, on to the sidewalk and into the night.

I remained in the doorway, unsure of what to think. I decided it was better not to mention too much to Lily or Elsa, who'd stayed in the kitchen. I knew Nadia wasn't crazy, but she was old and maybe a little bit nostalgic for a different time. I walked back into the kitchen to find Elsa tearing a linen dish rage into strips for my arm.

Lily broke the silence. "OK, tell us: Did she read your palm?"

I nodded. "Yes. She said I would live a long life and have two great loves. I assume she meant the two of you," I said, trying to make a joke out of it. But neither Lily nor Elsa was laughing.

"Nadia is a great seer," Lily said. "If she said love, she means it."

I found the entire conversation a little overwhelming after my cartography session. "How will I ever find one love, let alone two, when I've got a campaign to run and you two as my chaperons every evening?"

"Whatever Nadia told you is going to come true, Olivia. So you'd better be prepared," Lily said, undeterred.

CHAPTER 19

Fortunately, I didn't have time to dwell on fortune cookie predictions, or the mysterious old woman who doled them out. My arm, while tender, was healing nicely and, as Nadia had said, the images were invisible to everyone but me. That made my next job easier, as I was off to find the head of the Democratic Party and convince him to not run a candidate against Levi.

The expression "three is a crowd" holds true for both romance and politics. A three-way race is a disaster because it splits the ballots, making it almost impossible to gain a majority of the votes. A three-way race usually results in a run-off.

I was determined to help Levi avoid that fate. I drove over to Lake Merced and found my target. As I expected, Paul Levant was ensconced on a bench, watching a regatta. No one was seated next to him, probably not a coincidence. Throwing caution to the wind, I slid alongside him on the bench. Levant, a small bag of popcorn in his hands, turned to look at me, shook his head and chuckled.

"I figured you would come to see me, sooner or later," he said, popping a kernel into his mouth.

"You must have ESP," I said, watching the women of the University of San Francisco glide across the water.

"Maybe," he said, "Or maybe I read somewhere that you're running Levi Barnes' campaign for District Fifteen. I do try to stay current on my political news."

"I liked it better when I thought you had magical powers," I said, enjoying myself.

Levant handed me the bag of popcorn and smiled. "On second thought, I do have ESP, because I know exactly what you are going to ask me."

"You do?" I asked, feigning ignorance for the sake of our conversation.

"You want to know if the party is going to support someone else for that seat," he said. "The answer is no; no one wants it." Levant was agitated. I wasn't the cause, but there was an undercurrent of worry running through him; it felt old, like it had been with him for a while. "The Republicans are looking for a candidate, Olivia. They want a Tea Party rep for that seat, someone who can appeal to the conservative money in Silicon Valley and the farm belt."

"You think a guy who writes code for Facebook games is going to vote for someone who thinks the world is flat?" I asked tartly.

Levant shook his head. "Don't be so flip. They won't be as obvious as that," he said. "It will be about taxes and regulation. It will be about immigration and education, maybe a tad bit about water rights in the Central Valley. Stuff your guy is not as good at."

"What do you mean, no one wants it?" I asked, not wanting to discuss Levi yet.

"Just what I said," Levant replied, taking back his popcorn bag. "No one wants to take on the Tea Party, or the Republican Party. It's impossible to raise a million dollars in this economy. At this rate, the Democrats will be lucky to keep the seats we currently have in Congress."

Here was my opening. "Fortunately for you, money is no object for Levi Barnes. He's prepared to spend to win. And he's a Democrat."

Levant shook his head. "At this point, I am glad someone is willing to run for the seat. I'm getting too fucking old for this shit. As far as I'm concerned, a Bible's main use is to swear in a candidate, and that's about it. In my day, we didn't let these fights become so personal. Your guy is walking into a shit storm of hard feelings in Washington."

"Paul, don't worry," I said, feeling the need to reassure him. "Levi is a former member of Congress and a successful businessman. He can stay above the fray and he'll be a bright star for the party…you wait and see."

"If he can win, kid. If he can win," Levant said, turning his gaze to the wooden boats on the water.

"Maybe if you use some of the ESP you've got to help us, it will be a sure thing," I said, gathering up my belongings.

"I think I'd rather send you a check," Levant said. "Be in touch with me about your campaign plan; the Party will support you."

I walked to my car, but waited until I was on the road back to my house before I made the call to Levi.

"Levant is backing us," I said, feeling jubilant. "The party will bankroll our efforts."

"I don't need their money Olivia," Levi said. "I'll tell Paul to use it for another race, for someone who needs the help."

"We will take a little help from the party," I said. "For one thing, it will look better if they're seen spending some resources on us. We don't want anyone to think our campaign is operating out there alone."

After I hung up with Levi, I called Gabriel. He didn't pick up, so I left him a message letting him know that I'd secured Levant's backing. I also told him about Levant's funny comment about the Bible, knowing he'd get a kick out of the image.

With Paul Levant's promise in my back pocket, I was free to continue with a research project I'd started a few weeks back. It took patience, but finally one Sunday, as I was reading the entertainment section of the paper, I was rewarded. There, in a small box, was a listing for Three Blind Mice. They were playing later in the week at the Treasure Chest, a nightclub on Divisadero Street. This was my chance to see William again. Now that the campaign was on the right path, I didn't see why anyone would object to me taking a night off. Nadia's pronouncements aside, the truth was that I couldn't stop thinking about him. I wasn't sure what bothered me more, being caught in the horrible cliché of pining for a vampire musician, or my actual yearning for him. Regardless, I was determined to see him again.

When the night of the show arrived, I was pleased Elsa had forced me into such a rigorous exercise regime. I pulled a pair of very slim black jeans out of my closet, along with a beat up pair of brown cowboy boots, and then searched in my drawer for the sexiest bra I could find. I knew I was playing with fire—not to mention being pretty presumptuous, but if there was a make-out session in my future, I wanted to be wearing the most provocative underwear possible. I rummaged around for the black T-shirt I was looking for and grabbed a khaki safari jacket off a hanger. I looked in the mirror and liked what I saw. I was stylish without trying too hard. At the very least, if I missed William, I would no doubt meet someone interesting, and the truth was that I was in the mood for a little night magic.

I called a cab and within ten minutes one arrived at my doorstep. It was approaching 9:30 when the car neared the club. I began to feel nervous. What if I walked in and he was there with another woman? What if he didn't want to speak with me? I was rethinking the whole idea when the car pulled up to the curb, but by that time it was too late. There outside, leaning against the wall in a pair of faded Levi's and his signature cowboy hat, was William. It seemed likely he had picked up on my thoughts and knew I was coming when I got within a few blocks of the club. I sighed, realizing there would be no sneaking up on him.

As I paid the driver and stepped onto the curb, my nervousness returned. I'd never really chased a man before, and now I felt my whole life depended on what I would find when I looked into William's eyes. I glanced up slowly, and was relieved to see he had a wide grin on his face. "Well, now," he said emphasizing his accent. "What do we have here? Have you gone AWOL from your barracks?"

"No, sir," I said. "I gave myself a pass for the evening."

"Allow me to escort you in," he said.

William took my hand in his and gave it a slight squeeze. He was wearing a plaid flannel shirt with the sleeves rolled up to his elbows. The red of the shirt accentuated his tattoos and made his hair seem to shimmer in the club's subdued lighting. I thought that after we got inside the club he would let go of my hand, but he didn't. He continued to hold it as he led me through the nightclub and beyond a door marked with a sign that said, "**STAFF AND BAND MEMBERS ONLY.**"

William greeted a security guard sitting on the other side of the doorway and then guided me along a short hallway to another door. He continued to hold my hand as he led us into a small dressing room. Inside I found his band mates lounging on a couch. They were both smoking; a bottle of Jack Daniel's with three glasses stacked next to it sat on the table in front of them.

"Cat and Jack, this is Olivia," William said, pouring whisky into a glass. His band mates both nodded and said hello as if they had been expecting me to show up at anytime. In fact, I could tell from their emotions that they were not the least bit surprised to see me. I was flattered, but unsure if their feelings meant he wanted to see or me, or knew eventually I'd come looking for him. William passed the bottle to Cat and then took a sip from the glass in his hand. I must have looked surprised, because William turned to me and said, "I can drink alcohol and have been known to eat lightly from time to time."

I nodded, taking the glass from him when he offered. I took a sip of the bourbon and immediately began to cough. I don't usually drink hard alcohol without something mixed in. William laughed.

"A tenderfoot, I see. We'll go find you a girl drink at the bar." He grabbed my hand again and we retraced our steps through the same set of hallways and doors. When we arrived at the bar, William was greeted by name and I soon had a rum and diet coke with lime in my hand. We were standing side-by-side at the bar. He'd ordered another shot of Jack and was slowly sipping his drink while gazing out at the stage.

"I have to go on in a few minutes," he said. "Will you stay until I'm finished?"

I turned and laughed. "I think the better question is, will you? You have a habit of disappearing."

William took my hand and focused his dark green eyes on mine. "I don't plan on disappearing again." And with that, he bowed slightly at the waist, and turned to walk onto the stage. Not long after, Cat and Jack joined him and, gracefully, they launched into a set similar to the one I had heard in the park. This time, though, I really listened to the lyrics.

I was born more than 100 years ago.
I am one of the oldest souls you'll ever come to know.

It turned out that William was also a songwriter. Who knew vampires had so many talents? It was one of the few details I knew about him. He, on the other hand, knew a great deal more about me. I guessed that was probably not an accident. When you live so long, you have to keep yourself hidden from view. At some point people must notice you never grow old, or that you never eat food.

Yet after everything I had seen and done during the last few weeks, I was beginning to realize that most humans noticed very little. As long as their paychecks arrived and their cable television worked, they were happy to live very limited lives. It worried me that I lived in a country full of people who could be made content so easily. I suppose that's why the Council exists, because humans are content with their ignorance.

I managed to drift off, lost in my thoughts. After a few moments I caught myself and when I glanced up, I saw that William was watching me. For the remainder of his set I focused on his performance, appreciating his skill with a guitar. He seemed to be able to make his instrument ache with sadness, and I knew without a doubt that William Ferrell had seen his share of misery. Twenty minutes later, they finished their set and were quickly besieged by friends and fans. I stayed back at the bar, unsure of my place, but it wasn't long before William separated himself from the crowd and walked over to me.

"Don't you want to stay with your friends?" I asked.

He shook his head. "They're not my friends."

"So what should we do now?" I asked, feeling a little like I was back in junior high.

"Now we get out of here," he said, grabbing my hand. We packed up his guitar and banjo and said goodnight to his band. Once again, they did not seem at all surprised to see me leave with him.

"Did you know you would see me again?" I asked, hating myself for needing to know.

"Yes."

"Did you expect me to come find you?"

"Yes."

"Why didn't you come find me?" I asked, feeling like I was doing all the work.

"How do you know I didn't?" he said.

"Did you stay away because of Elsa?"

"I know enough to stay out of her way. Let's put it like that."

"So what changed your mind?"

"Nothing. I am playing with fire, just like you are." He said. "I wanted to make sure you had the courage to try. This life is not for the faint of heart."

We walked outside with his gear and strolled round the block. There, parked on a nearby street, was a brand new black Subaru wagon. I laughed.

"You were expecting a black horse maybe," he said sharply. "I'm not a character in a novel, Olivia. I live in this world, just as you do."

"Ouch," I said, laying my hand over my heart. "I laughed because it seems like such a practical car. I was expecting something more rebellious. Like a motorcycle."

"A motorcycle," he said. "*Darlin*, those things will kill you."

I laughed, once again reminded of how much I liked his sense of humor. He unlocked the car and opened the passenger door so I could climb in. I realized I had no idea where we were going, but I could wait to find out.

Moments later, after passing through the Castro and past Dolores Park, we were pulling into the driveway of a lovely Victorian home on the edge of the Mission. William pressed the button on an opener fastened to the sunshade of his wagon and pulled inside the garage. From there he led me up a set of stairs.

William lived in a very old, well-restored two-story home. As we reached the top of the stairs, we faced a small living room with a fireplace. The room was decorated just the way I would have done it myself: a combination of old and new, a bohemian mix of deer antlers, wooden antique furniture, and a smidgen of modern touches that respected the age of the house.

"Can I have a tour?"

William nodded and walked me from room to room. Next door to the living room was another small room that had been converted into a library. Floor-to-ceiling bookshelves lined the walls. A brilliant red-and-orange antique Afghan carpet covered the wooden floors, which looked to be the home's original planks. In one corner of the library sat a chocolate brown leather chair with a brass library lamp leaning over its arm. The shelves were neatly arranged, but I could see that William had been collecting books for decades.

There were first editions of Hemingway and Fitzgerald. I spied several biographies of Winston Churchill as well as an entire section of poetry by T.S. Elliott. For a reader like myself, it was mesmerizing, and I must have looked intrigued because William broke the silence with an offer to let me borrow anything that interested me.

From there, we toured the rest of the house. There were two bedrooms on the main level, both decorated to look like guest rooms. On the floor above, there was a large loft space with an enormous round bay window in the center of the room, and surprisingly, several skylights had been cut into the ceiling. There were lovely blackout shades made from a rich fabric bolted into the skylights. But for now, because it was evening, the blinds were open, leaving us a clear view of the full moon in the night sky. There was no bed in the room, just an old drafting table that had been converted to a desk. There were more bold rugs on the floor, and a set of leather chairs that looked to be companions to the one in the library.

The most striking aspect of the room was the collection of guitars and banjos on display. He had at least five acoustic guitars sitting on stands in the room, as well as three or four more banjos, also on stands. A brand new Denon turntable on a small table sat next to the instruments. A series of storage racks with hundreds of vinyl albums was nearby. Like his library, William's taste in music looked to be varied and wide-ranging. John Coltrane, Zeppelin, and Willie Nelson were sitting side-by-side, along with Serge Gainsbourg, the Jam, and the Clash. I smiled inwardly at the depth and variety. This was clearly the room where William spent most of his time. The space was full of his calm energy and it was obvious to see from the design that he did everything in his power to create and maintain that sense of peace.

We walked back downstairs and into a kitchen that could have passed muster with any editor at Sunset magazine. The sunken white porcelain sink and 6-burner Wolf range complemented the large stainless steel refrigerator, which most likely would be empty.

"Cook many big meals?" I teased.

"As you know, I am not much of an eater," he drawled back. "I have a small property management business, and over the years, I have acquired a few investment properties in San Francisco and other cities. One day I might sell or rent this house. It will be more valuable with a working kitchen."

"I can't imagine ever wanting to leave here," I said, thinking of the beautiful home my grandmother had given me. "I have a nice old house, too. My grandmother left it to me in her will. I hope to live in it until I ..." I was about to say more, but then I stopped.

"It's OK," William coaxed. "You want to stay in the house until you *die*. You are human, Olivia. You can discuss your life in a normal way."

"I didn't want to seem insensitive. I have no idea how you feel about being a vampire."

"Living forever has many advantages," William remarked thoughtfully. "I have amassed a lot of interesting objects and wealth. But there are moments when time does drag on."

"Are you going to tell me how you became a vampire?" I asked, hoping there was a bottle of wine and a fireplace in my future. I must have pushed that wish out very strongly because William immediately followed up with "red or white?" I chose red, a lovely 2008 Pinot Noir from the Russian River, and we went back to the living room to sit down.

"The fireplace doesn't work," William said. "And now there are so many laws about when you can burn wood that I have not bothered to have it repaired. The last thing I need is someone knocking on my door to cite me for burning wood."

We sat down on a very comfortable chocolate brown leather couch—I was beginning to detect a theme in his tastes—and he poured us both a glass of wine. I was using all of my self-control not to blurt out the long list of questions I had for him: How old are you? Where are you from? How did you come to live in San Francisco?

I was sitting at one end of the couch, using the corner as a sort of brace. I had no idea what to do. Should I sit closer to him? Should I stay away? Was it hard for him to be around a human and not want to drink their blood? My mind, I was beginning to realize, gave off strong signals to those who knew enough to pay attention. I was hoping he would say something before I burst with pent up anticipation.

"My goodness, you are having a go of it over there," he said. "Try to relax, Olivia. I promise to tell you everything you want to know, but first I want something from you. If we're going to do this, share our secrets, then I want something from you in return."

"What do you want?"

"I want a kiss," he said smiling. "You and I, we're making a deal of sorts…and I want a kiss to seal the bargain that we will keep each other's secrets."

A kiss? How dangerous could that be? In my short but intense training in magic 101, I'd never heard of a kiss being any sort of binding contract. If you discounted the fact that I was agreeing to kiss a man who appeared to have been dead for more than a century, while sitting alone in his living room, with no way to get myself out, or drive myself home, then yes, the request seemed rather harmless.

"OK," I said.

"OK?" William replied.

"What do you want me to say?"

He looked slightly wounded. "Madam, I have kissed other women before and usually they have shown a little more enthusiasm."

It turned out that even the undead have egos, but I was more willing to ease his mind. "I have not stopped thinking about you since the moment you kissed me in the park," I said, taking a sip of wine for courage. "It's possible that I am being quite irresponsible, but of course I want to kiss you. I want to do much more than that. But at the same time, I feel that I'm completely out of my depth. You have to admit this is all a little out of the ordinary."

"No, *darlin*. I don't think so," he said. "That's not the way I see it. I am a man who wants to kiss a pretty woman, and that is something that hasn't changed since the dawn of time."

And then in a blink of an eye he was right next to me, kissing me again in that way that made my lips feel like they would catch fire. This time, though, I was prepared and I kissed him back with equal intensity. His lips were cool to the touch, which was initially a bit disconcerting, but as I grew hotter, the coolness was soothing.

As we continued kissing, his hands explored my back and made tentative advances toward the front. I felt more than ready for him to slip his hand under my shirt. I had been exploring his body, marveling it how lean and hard it felt. I was certain he could pick up on my thoughts and I reached to unbutton his flannel shirt.

William pulled back from my advance. "Olivia, you are a handful," he said, making a noise that almost sounded like the exhaling of breath. "There is no rush. I haven't even told you my story yet. There will be plenty of time for us to get to know each other better. Besides, taking a vampire lover is a complicated business, and you may want to know more before you sign up for that responsibility."

Honestly, I would have signed over the deed to my house at that point. I was so aroused, it took a few moments for his words to even register in my brain. I have never much good at delayed gratification; it is one of my weaknesses.

Still, he had a point. I didn't know anything about taking a vampire as a lover, but honest to God, at that moment, nothing sounded better. Then I thought of Elsa and her reaction if she believed I'd slept with William. Reluctantly, I came back to Earth.

"OkK" I said, taking his hand. "You're right. And I do want to hear your story." William poured us both more wine and began to speak.

"You know my name is William Ferrell. My full name is William Aubrey Ferrell. I was born in Tullahoma, Tennessee in 1830. My father was a farmer who left South Carolina and took work with the railroad. I was one of six brothers and sisters. As you can imagine, we were pretty poor. We had some land to grow our food and raise a few chickens, but it was a difficult life. I was born in the house we lived in. When I grew older, I trained as a carpenter and made decent money for the family making furniture and repairing things for the people in our village.

"I started playing music when I was a child," he

continued. "There was a man in town with a guitar and he taught me how to play in the spare moments when I wasn't helping my mother tend to my brothers and sisters. I made my first guitar myself out of some extra wood I was given for a job. I carried that guitar with me everywhere. In fact, it was with me in Louisiana when I died."

Once again I heard William make a noise that sounded similar to breathing. He was occupied with the past now, and I could feel his emotions becoming more intense. "When the war broke out, there was no question whose side I would be on. I served in the nineteenth Tennessee Infantry. By then, I had moved to Knoxville, where there was more work. I joined in the spring of 1861."

While I found his story captivating, I was also doing the math in my head. We were sitting in William's living room in late September of 2011, which meant I was sharing a couch with a 181 year-old vampire. There was no doubt, I mused silently, that I was making the moves on a much older man.

"One year later I was dead," William continued. "I died in Louisiana at the Battle of Baton Rouge."

"You don't have to tell me any more," I said taking his hand in mine. "At least not tonight."

"Actually I'm fine," he said, looking intently at me with his mossy green eyes. "I haven't told anyone the story of my life for a very long time. Truthfully, it's nice that you want to know."

"I do, very much," I said.

"So, we were in Baton Rouge. We had started with 1,000 strong men, but by the time we arrived, there were barely 100 healthy souls remaining in the division. We arrived with no tents and little gear. Many of the men had neither coat nor shoes. Imagine, walking for days on end, your feet bloody and raw. There was no food, and our bellies ached with hunger. Many were ill with dysentery. The filth and disease were overwhelming. The horror of watching your brothers, cousins and friends killed or maimed. I think for some it was probably a blessing to be killed.

"Did you feel that way?"

William shook his head. "No. After all the death and destruction I'd seen, I didn't care much about winning or honor, but I didn't want to die. I wanted to survive and go back home to my family."

"Did you? Survive the war?"

"Sadly, no," William replied. "I remember the day of the battle very clearly. It was very humid and also foggy. The air was heavy and wet and I couldn't make out the landscape beyond my feet. It was a bloodbath; almost five hundred men were killed on the battlefield, out of two thousand, maybe three thousand soldiers. I remember lying on the ground, listening to the screams of the wounded, while civilians from town ran their hands through my pockets looking for valuables. There I was, 32 years old, miles away from my family, and I had never even kissed a girl."

"Wait. What do you mean, you'd never kissed a girl?"

William chuckled. "Women were not quite so *fast* as they are today. And I was too shy to say anything. And then there was the fact that I was too poor to offer for a lady's hand anyway. What would I have given her? I had barely enough money for the roof over my head. In those days there were few women from good families who would have consented to marry me."

It was a shocking story, but did make sense. It also made my kisses all the more intriguing. "I guess you learned to kiss after you became a vampire," I said, hoping for more of his story.

"I did, but I haven't had the wild life you may imagine. Anyway, I was turned right there on the battlefield. I had been lying on the ground for a while, having been shot several times in my leg. It must have hit an artery because I started to bleed out. There was no doctor in the camp and no medics to come and help me. Believe me, as bad as war is today, at least soldiers have the proper tools and support in battle.

"My second father was a Union officer. I mistook him for a priest because he came so close to me. I thought he had come to take my confession. Of course he had something different in mind. He told me that I was minutes away from dying, but that he could save me. He asked if I wanted to see the world, live a life of endless travel and immortality. I felt my limbs growing cold as the blood left my body and I knew I had little time left to live."

"Were you scared?"

"Of course," he said. "I was human like you and as afraid of death as anyone, but I was also intrigued. As a poor man in Tennessee, my life's prospects were limited. What my new father offered was a life beyond what fate had in store."

"So you agreed?"

"I did, and I walked out of Baton Rouge the next day and on to a new life."

"Where did you go?"

"Paris. It was an interesting time to be abroad and my new father was convinced that the United States would never evolve into a civilized country."

"So you speak French?" I asked, feeling odd at the way our lives seemed so neatly connected.

"*Oui, je parle français, et toi?*"

"*Oui. Bien sûr.*"

"*Bon,*" he said. "If you're nice to me, maybe we will visit France together."

I was ready to be very nice to him. I was also very tired. I looked at my watch and realized that it was after midnight. I didn't want to go home, though. I didn't want to leave William. Once again, he was not far behind my thoughts.

"You can sleep here tonight. As you can see, I don't have a bed in my room. I don't normally sleep, but you can use one of the guest rooms."

I suddenly had a vision of being one of many who walked down that path. I must have made a face, because William took my hand.

"I am flattered at how popular you think I am, but the

fact is I've never brought a woman home with me. You're the first."

His confession was my undoing. Baton Rouge, dysentery, never being kissed; I considered that maybe it was all a fabulous lie to seduce me. But I was holding out hope that it wasn't. Regardless, my emotions got the better of me and I burst into tears, overwhelmed. I knew I was in serious danger of falling in love with an old Southern gentleman. OK, an old dead gentleman, but there was no doubt he was different then anyone I'd ever met. I managed to get out an "I'm sorry," before he picked me up and carried me to one of the guest bedrooms. He pulled down the sheets and laid me on the bed. With little difficulty he pulled off my boots and tucked me in.

"You see, Olivia," he said gently. "I told you there is a lot to consider when you bring a vampire into your life." I nodded, but said little else. I was asleep in seconds.

When I opened my eyes the next morning, it took me a few minutes to realize where I was. I was still in my clothing from the night before; everything was buttoned and snapped into place. I glanced at the watch on my wrist, horrified that it was already 9:30 in the morning.

Horribly off schedule, I jumped out of bed and opened the door of the bedroom. I padded down the hall to the bathroom and freshened up. When I came out I heard the sound of guitar coming from upstairs. Slowly, I climbed the steps and walked into the loft. It was a lovely image, and I worked hard to keep my mouth from hanging open.

There, sitting in one of the leather chairs was William, shirtless, a guitar in his lap. His red hair was loose around his shoulders, and as he leaned forward to play his guitar, I could see more of the tattoo work on his back. There was an enormous angel with its wings outstretched across his shoulder blades. It was magnificent work, and I wondered whether the angel was in honor of the man that saved him that day on the battlefield, or for something else.

"Good morning," I said, knowing he was aware of my presence.

"Hello, sleepy head," he drawled. "I was beginning to worry you would snooze the day away."

"It seems I might have. I don't remember sleeping so deeply for a long time."

"You got an earful last night," William said. "I can imagine it was a bit of a shock. How are you feeling?"

"I feel great," I said, and I meant it. I was happy to have found William. I knew it was going to make all of the rest of what I had to do more complicated, but I didn't care.

"Mind if I come over and say hello?" I asked.

William set down his guitar and opened his arms. I came and sat on his lap and lay my head on his shoulder.

"Do you sleep?"

"Not so much," he said, adjusting his body to accommodate me.

I was eager to feel his skin against my body. He smelled delicious, lemony, like a very sweet sugary lozenge, with a hint of rosemary. I sat there for a while not saying anything, sitting in the cocoon of his body. I'm not sure how long we sat in the chair together. Time stopped. We kissed, but it was nothing urgent. After a few moments, we paused to talk, revealing the small details of our lives.

I told him more about my campaign and described Levi and explained how I had worked for him before. I didn't mention the Council. I'm not sure why. I had a feeling that maybe this thing between us was too fragile to be laden down with such complicated issues. In fact, it all felt a little complicated. I'd never spent the night at a man's home before where we didn't have sex. I'd never spent the night at a vampire's house. I wasn't sure what to expect, but I was out of time to wonder. I looked at my watch and thought of the long list of obligations I had pending. I was long overdue at work.

"I have to go," I said. "I don't want to, but I am really running late for what will be a very busy day."

"Can I see you again?" was his reply, which sounded so normal that I laughed.

"Forgive me," I said. "It's just that this sounds like the conversation any man or woman would have. Are you asking me out on a date?"

"I am asking you on a date," he said, crossly. "Please keep in mind, darlin, that I'm not a character in a pulp-fiction novel. I won't be using mind control to lure you to my side."

"Bummer," I said. "What about bats? Will you be flying in my window like Gary Oldman?"

My remark seemed to defuse the moment. I had no desire to offend him and I was relieved when he shook his head and smiled.

"No bats, no flying. I have none of those tricks up my sleeve. I meant what I said last night. I'm simply a man who wants to date a pretty woman."

"You are a man who drinks blood," I said looking him in the eye. "That does seem like a topic worth discussing."

To his credit, William did not break our gaze. "I might take a taste, but I will not *drink* your blood unless you offer it to me, and even then I might refuse."

"How do you survive if you don't drink human blood?"

William turned away slightly from me as he spoke. "I do not need to eat as often as young vampires do."

"Yes, well you are 181 years old," I cut in.

William smiled. "I can see you're good at math. So when you are as old as I am, you do not need to feed daily."

"But when you do feed, what do you drink?" I asked. "And why wouldn't you drink from me if I offered?"

"When I first became a vampire, my hunger was overpowering, but now I can survive for weeks without feeding. When I do need to eat, I drive up into the hills and search for wildlife. Deer are plentiful nearby so I never have much of a problem."

"I saw you drink alcohol last night."

"Interesting, isn't it? All of the myths about vampires and most of them are as untrue as we are undead. Alcohol is something I've grown accustomed to over the years. Newly made vampires require a lot of blood to survive. Alcohol is too disruptive to their nervous system. But later, as you are able to feed less, you can introduce other forms of pleasure back into your life. For me, its whisky, sometimes wine. I like to eat raw fish and meat occasionally. It's good to blend in with people and eating and drinking makes it easier to disappear in a crowd.

"As for you," he continued. "You might offer your blood to me for all of the wrong reasons," he continued. "Drinking your blood would bind you to me, and that, *darlin,* is a permanent thing."

"But if I offered?" I said, a hint of pleading slipping into my voice.

"I would have to be certain," he said. "It's a different life, a complicated life. Unless I was convinced you understood the responsibility, I wouldn't accept. Vampires don't share, Olivia. We don't compromise, and we're not very patient."

I wasn't ready to let him drink, but being stubborn by nature, his lecture was igniting a challenge within me.

"Then why are we doing all of this?" I asked.

"I can see I got your back up a bit," he said. "Don't mistake my intentions. I want to be with you, Olivia. But after 180 years on this earth, I have had my share of heartbreak."

He meant it. I felt his sadness, really, his disappointment. To be alive for almost two hundred years must have meant a few bad relationships. I nodded, and kissed him gently to convey I understood.

William quickly dressed and dropped me at my house. I would have invited him in, but I knew Elsa might be there and I really needed to get to work, so we said our goodbyes. As I walked in the door, he sent me a text asking me if I would join him in two nights for a paddleboat ride at Stow Lake. It was so old-fashioned and romantic, I accepted right away. Unfortunately, my exuberance at being in the midst of a full-blown romance ran straight into a wall of disapproval standing in my kitchen. Elsa was there, decked out in black leather pants with an actual silver dagger stuck in one of her boots. Lily was standing next to her.

"Lily, what are you doing here?" I asked.

"Elsa texted me when you didn't come home last night," she said, looking sheepish. Being a mother hen did not suit her at all. I turned to face my housemother.

"What's this all about, Elsa? What did you think had happened to me?"

Elsa was angry but also relieved. I'm not sure what she thought had happened to me, but she was experiencing real relief that I was home safely. I hadn't told either of them where I was going. I didn't want company, and I had not wanted anyone to try to talk me out of being with William. Looking back, my secrecy was probably impractical.

Elsa didn't reply, so I posed another question. "I suppose you both want to know where I was last night." Two heads nodded in unison.

Elsa spoke first, "Why didn't you leave word where you were going?" Lily looked pensive, as if she knew bad news was coming. She was worried about a conflict between the three of us.

"I should have left a note, or texted one of you," I said. "But can I ask why you were so worried? What did you think happened to me?"

Elsa didn't want to tell me exactly. Her fury was dying down a bit, but she continued to restrain herself. "Olivia, you are the only human agent working at the Council and you've been the target of a demon attack. Gabriel, errr, I mean, you report directly to the director. Anything could have happened to you. There are plenty of people who would be interested in your talents and connections."

It sounded reasonably plausible. I wasn't alone anymore. I was a part of a team. "Look," I said raising my palms up in surrender. "I am sorry. I should have checked in. Next time I will be more considerate."

Lily was relieved. Fairies didn't like conflict. But Elsa

wasn't finished. "Are you going to tell us where you have been?"

"I was with William," I said, my chin up slightly in a defiant pose. Now we were back to two against one. Lily and Elsa were exchanging glances that spoke of serious handwringing.

"You spent the night...with a...*vampire*?" Elsa asked.

"Yes and no," I said, resenting the tawdry emphasis. "I slept at his house, as in a pillow and a blanket, not with, you know, *him*."

Lily was craning her neck to get a good look at mine.

"*No*, he did not drink my blood."

This was met with more raised eyebrows and sideways glances.

"Really. He did not ask, and I did not offer." This caused them both to calm down, but I resented the image they had painted. "I need to take a shower and jump in my car to get down to Palo Alto, but I want to tell you both something before I leave. William isn't the villain you imagine. I scanned the newspaper advertisements every Sunday looking for a listing for his band. I took the taxi, unannounced, to his show. And I am the one who pushed to have sex...and he turned me down. *I chased him*."

This seemed to catch Lily by surprise. "Olivia, honey," she said gently. "Are you sure you want to go for something so complicated for your first serious boyfriend?"

Ouch. Leave it to my best friend to state the obvious. Of course, I hadn't planned on having a boyfriend. I hadn't planned on a century-old vampire catching my heart.

"William is different," I said, sounding like a cliché. "He's not like anyone I've ever known. He is intelligent and funny..."

"He's dead," Elsa said, interrupting me. "He drinks human blood. Can I ask where you see this thing going? Did you tell him about the Council, about your work?" It was clear Elsa didn't like vampires. She didn't seem to trust them. It was a deep-set feeling that I didn't think I could change at the moment. So I didn't try.

"I'm not sure where it's going," I said. "He doesn't know about the Council. Now, if you'll excuse me, I'm off to a campaign meeting."

CHAPTER 20

Once I was in my car, I phoned Levi and Gabriel. Despite being thrown off my regular routine, I managed to check in with them by phone at a time that was still within my normal schedule. It was thrilling to have the first part of my day occupied by a make-out session with my boyfriend, rather than campaign duties. I hoped I wasn't overstating things too much by calling him my boyfriend. Maybe a human man would have said we were dating, but I'd been the first woman to sleep at William's home. I didn't believe a vampire would compromise his privacy for a date, especially one that hadn't involved the removal of clothes.

I quickly put all of my giddiness behind me as I set out on Highway 101. My calls to both men were brief, but important. We were opening a new campaign office in Palo Alto, a wealthy quasi-suburban community that also is home to Stanford University. We were going to open the office with a kick-off party that evening where volunteers could come after work and celebrate with a glass of wine before picking up their supplies. Gabriel and Levi would be arriving at 5:30. The party began at 6 pm

I hung up with both men just as my office called and patched me through to Patrick Wright, the day-to-day manager of the campaign.

"The first shipment of door hangers has arrived," he said.

"What about window signs?" I asked in response, hoping they too had been delivered.

"Yep, they're here," Patrick said. "All 2,000. Now all we need is an army of volunteers to deliver them."

"Amen," I said. "I hear you. I'll be there in thirty minutes and we can go over the rest of this."

As promised, thirty minutes later, I pulled into a parking spot on University Avenue and walked toward the headquarters, which had already been decorated with "Levi Barnes for Congress" and "Barnes for Seat 15" campaign signs. As I got closer, I noticed a man peering in the window, his hands cupped around his eyes to shield out the glare.

"Can I help you?" I asked as I approached the front door. A set of brown eyes focused on me with suspicion. He was human, I detected very quickly, and very curious.

"Is this Levi Barnes's campaign office?" he asked.

I nodded, glancing at the dozen posters in the window. "It is but we don't officially open until tonight," I said. "Can I help you?"

"I'm JP Ellington," he said, grasping my hand tightly. "I'm a reporter with the Silicon Valley News. I'll be covering this race."

I responded in kind. "I'm Olivia Shepherd," I said. "I'll be managing the campaign." I'd had this kind of conversation dozens of times before, but never when I could read a reporter's emotions. JP was surprised, about what I wasn't sure, but I had a few ideas.

"You seem surprised," I said, deciding to see what would happen.

"I am," he said, showing no hesitation. "I guess I expected to see someone I know."

"You mean a man?"

"Yes, ah, I mean you're not from the Valley," he said, sounding a little sheepish.

I ran through my resume and let him know I had been part of Levi's staff previously. He seemed satisfied, or at least a little less skeptical.

"Can you come back at 6:15 tonight?" I asked. "I will make sure to introduce you to Levi right away." I was trying to sound casual, but the truth was that I wanted to begin on a positive note with a reporter who would be covering the campaign. "We're not open yet," I said smiling. "I need a few more hours with my staff to get ready."

JP agreed to return in a few hours. We exchanged business cards and I wrote my cell on the back of mine. We shook hands to seal the deal, but as I turned to leave, he held on to my fingers a second longer than I expected, causing me to look up into his brown eyes. His face was framed by dark, curly brown hair that had been cropped short. He was wearing a blue-green plaid shirt with a navy sweater vest and Levi's.

"OK, so I will see you in a few hours then," I said, pulling my hand away.

JP smiled. "You'll definitely be seeing me again."

True to his word, JP returned and stayed for most of the party, interviewing guests and, of course, Levi. I kept a close eye on him, but could not detect anything but professional intentions when it came to the candidate. Levi, having already been a congressman, needed very little help with the media.

The kick-off party had been a success, the festivities lasting longer than any of us had expected. As I was cleaning up later that evening, I thought for a moment about how things had gone. More than 100 supporters dropped by to celebrate and take home a campaign sign. It may seem odd, the fixation with campaign signs. But for a candidate they're important. To drive or walk through an area or a specific street and see a sign in every window is a powerful visual. It's street-level advertising and it can be quite successful. It also can be intimidating to your opposition, although we didn't know quite yet who that would be.

Pleased, I went to sleep that night happy that things had begun so smoothly.

The success of the evening was one of the topics I was prepared to review with Gabriel and the rest of the team when we held our de-briefing meeting later in the day. Thanks to the end of daylight savings, darkness arrived much earlier, which meant we could begin our meeting sooner.

At the moment, it was early morning and I was stretching in my bedroom, preparing to go for a run in the park. I pulled on my running shoes and slipped a spare front door key into a small pocket in my running tights. By the time I made it out the door, the pink light of dawn was peeking over the edges of the sky from the east, but racing to beat it was a cold, wet fog. I could hear the horns blowing off the coast as I set off on my run, and by the time I made it to the music concourse near the de Young Museum, the fog had made it all the way into the city. I was curious to know if today's wet mess was the result of nature or something else.

I wasn't aware of anything special going on, but it was likely I didn't know everything that went on with the Council. I was only a human consultant for them, after all, and not a full-fledged member. I quickly passed the museum and headed down a side path that cut behind the building and onto another road. By the time I turned the corner to head west and go deeper into the park, the mist was so thick I could not see more than a few steps ahead.

The low pitch of the foghorns could be heard every few seconds now, no doubt warning large cargo ships away from danger out on the bay. I was so distracted listening to the repeating rhythm that it took me a moment to register that there was a man standing on the sidewalk in front of me. I stopped myself abruptly mid-run and waited. Thanks to the fog, he seemed to have appeared out of nowhere. That would have been startling enough, but what was more shocking was his appearance.

Approaching me was a tall man with tight, curly black hair. He wore a garish suit consisting of a bright red velvet blazer, a red shirt and black trousers tucked into cowboy boots. A straw cowboy hat sat perched on his head. He was overdressed for any occasion, but in this situation, his clothing appeared even more absurd. The combination of his attire and physical build gave him the look of a menacing rodeo clown.

But I knew instinctively that there was nothing silly or

good-natured about him and I also knew our meeting was probably not a coincidence. The figure in front of me was a demon. I could feel him trying to trip me, to flood my mind with despair. Maybe if he'd dressed like another runner in the park I would have been caught off guard. But his gaudy costume had alerted me immediately. I stopped directly in front of him, prepared for anything.

"Olivia," the thing purred. "We share a common connection. Stoner Halbert sends his regards." Ah, so this was Stoner's demon, I thought privately, wondering how he managed to stay anonymous with such outlandish taste in fashion.

"I'm not sure you can call it sharing," I said. "But I know Stoner. What does he want?"

The demon smiled, revealing a set of very brown teeth. "He wants you to know that there will be another candidate in the race for Seat 15."

I'm not sure why, but his involvement didn't surprise me. Stoner Halbert was after my life, mostly because he thought it was easy to take. But he didn't know what I'd been up to these last few weeks. He didn't know about the Council. The fact that I was even able to hold this conversation was proof that Elsa had saved my life.

"You tracked me to the park on my run to tell me this?" I asked. "Why not hold a press conference and make an announcement like other candidates?"

It was a little childish of me to spar verbally with a demon—essentially a bag of bones with bad intentions. After my quip, the demon became angry and I felt the full force of him against my skull. I knew I could hold him off for a while, but not indefinitely, and I began to wonder what would happen if I tried to run past him. In the end, I decided to take a different approach, in the hope that I could cut our visit short.

"Listen," I said cordially. "You can tell Stoner that I have received his message and that I said may the best candidate win."

This seemed to take his temperature back down to normal. "OK then," I said, "if you don't mind, I am going to go now."

Once again I was treated to a smile and the demon pivoted his body so that I could pass on the sidewalk. I slipped by the big red one gingerly, thankful that I noticed a path leading up a hill back in the direction of my house. Curtailing my run and heading directly home to avoid any more trouble seemed like the best idea. I ran at a brisk pace toward my house, glad that I had slipped a key in my pocket.

Now that I had managed to put some distance between Halbert's messenger and myself, my adrenaline kicked in, causing my hands to tremble as I put the key in the lock to my front door. I closed the door behind me and leaned against the wood to catch my breath. Elsa was not home. She had been staying away for longer periods of time, and I was beginning to wonder whether my roommate would be moving on shortly.

Staring down a demon is tiring business. Feeling depleted, I went upstairs and took a warm shower to calm my nerves and heat up my bones, which felt hollow and chilled from the encounter.

Once I was dressed, I returned to the kitchen to make myself a cappuccino and plopped some bread into the toaster. While I waited for the toast, I checked my phone for messages. I had several texts from William, reminding me that we were supposed to go out tomorrow night. I smiled and texted him back that he could pick me up at 5 pm I had a second set of texts from JP asking me to call him. I clicked through on the number he'd sent, which looked to be his cell and within a few seconds he picked up the call.

"JP, it's Olivia," I said.

"You got my texts?" he asked.

"That's how I knew to call this number," I said. "So what's up? Are you calling to tell me that Levi has an opponent?" I could feel his disbelief over the telephone. He thought he was going to be the one to surprise me. I liked being able to surprise him; it almost made the visit from the demon cowboy worth it.

"How did you know?" he asked.

"I ran into someone who knows Stoner Halbert," I said. "He let me know there was going to be a opposing candidate. But I don't know who it is."

"Her name is Lacy Smith," JP said. "She's an attorney and a member of the local Tea Party." I was listening to JP and formulating my statement. I knew he wanted a comment, an official one from the campaign.

"I assume you are looking for a quote from the campaign?"

"Yes," he said.

"OK. Here it is," I said. "We welcome Ms. Smith's entrance into the race, and look forward to a spirited debate about the issues as the campaign progresses."

JP snorted into the phone. "That's it? You don't want to comment on her credentials?"

"I'm really not familiar enough to make any further statements," I said, knowing I sounded very much the reticent campaign manager. "So...is that it?"

"Actually I have one more question," he said. I knew before he asked that whatever he was about to say, he felt nervous. "Do you want to have dinner sometime soon?"

His request surprised me. Setting aside William and my already head-over-heels feelings for him, it was a plain old bad idea to date the reporter covering your campaign. It was unprofessional and downright dangerous, since the line between lovers and adversaries can get blurred in a hurry. And let's face it; the press is often a campaign's adversary. I decided a work-related brush-off was my best tactic.

"You know, these days my schedule is pretty jam-packed with work," I said, trying to sound nonchalant. "Why don't you ask me again in a few weeks?"

This elicited an "OK, will do," and we said our goodbyes. I turned the ringer volume up on my phone, expecting similar calls from reporters during the next several hours. I decided to make another espresso and work from home until it was time to meet with Gabriel.

After I hung up with JP, I left a voicemail for Gabriel telling him about Lacy. Then I called Levi and briefed him on both Lacy and the quote I'd given to JP. Levi asked if he should make a statement. I discouraged him. "You can comment when she says or does something that deserves your attention," I said. "In the meantime, let me be the one who speaks."

When I'd finished with Levi, I called Paul Levant, the head of the Democratic Party, to let him know his prediction had come true.

"Shit, that was fast...Love the name though. *Doonesbury* has a character named Lacey, except she is a tough old Democrat; nothing like what you're facing."

"And what am I facing?" I asked, knowing I would enjoy his answer.

"It's like I told you before," he said. "To me, a Bible is something you put your hand on to make a point. With her, it's a manual for living."

"I'm not sure if you know, but Stoner Halbert is running her election," I said, changing the subject.

"Interesting," he said. "That guy seems to pop up everywhere. It should make for a great race; the two of you will both give as good as you get."

CHAPTER 21

A large picture of Lacy Smith was staring down at me from a screen on the wall when I walked into the conference room to start my meeting with Gabriel and other members of the Council. Joining us were Elsa, Aidan Burke and an older woman in her fifties with beautiful, long grey hair, who was introduced to me as Madeline Klein, the Canadian Ambassador to the U.S., as well as a witch and longtime member of the Council.

The meeting began with a briefing about some of the other campaigns the Council was working on in the United States. Political issues in Europe and beyond were not going to be a part of my agenda for the time being.

Aidan opened up his laptop and began reporting on a number of political races—some in California, some in other states. There was a congressional race in Alabama, several contests to retain the seats of incumbent superior court judges in Pennsylvania, Kentucky and Ohio. All told, the Council seemed to be involved in, or monitoring, more than two dozen races.

"Why do these particular fights interest you?" I asked Aidan, as I was getting ready to give my report.

"We're looking for situations where we can make a difference," Aidan said. "But, as you may recall, we have to be careful not to be too obvious."

"Yes," I said. "You scoffed at my request that we just cast a spell on an entire town."

"Exactly," Aidan said, laughing. "But occasionally you do read about candidates that have an amazing comeback from behind. There are moments, you see, when voters can be persuaded to have a change of heart."

"Don't you wish you could win every race?" I asked.

"We're not a political party," Gabriel said, joining the conversation. "We don't want to control the balance of power absolutely."

"Why not? It seems like things would be much easier."

"Be careful. Those words or some facsimile have been spoken by many a dictator," Gabriel said grimly. "We're here to help maintain a balance, not dominate the fate of mankind. There must be some room for humans to make bad decisions and live with the consequences. There must be some opportunity for them to fight for their own causes."

"So you don't care if I win the campaign?"

"*Bien sûr*. I do care." Gabriel said. "I want you to win, but that is not what we were discussing. You asked why we don't just bewitch entire towns and states. We choose races where we know we can make a difference. We identify individuals who we know will go on to play a major role in the advancement of human society. So yes, when we send you in to work, we want you to win. But using magic is not like painting a house. You can't just cover everything up and hope it will endure through the years."

"I understand," I said, feeling slightly humbled by his remarks. "Shall I start my report?"

"Please," Aidan said, offering me a reassuring smile.

I started the discussion by describing my encounter with Halbert's demon in the park earlier in the day. "I really credit Elsa," I said, four pairs of eyes fixed on me as I described the creature's red attire and cowboy hat. "Without my training, I don't know if I would be here now describing all of this to you."

Elsa grimaced. "You were wise to limit your time around him," she said.

"Why do you think he came to find me in the first place?"

"It's a good question," said Aidan. "One we will look

into. We expected Halbert's demon to move on to easier targets, not to go looking for you."

"Maybe someone sent him," Madeline offered, speaking for the first time.

"I would have thought Halbert did," I said.

"As I said," Aidan said. "I will look into it."

"Olivia, " Gabriel said smiling at me. "Perhaps until we get this sorted out you will refrain from running alone in the park? We can't afford to have something happen to you in the middle of the campaign. I would be happy to pay for you to join a fitness club."

"Wow," I said. "Do you treat all of your campaign consultants so well?"

The emotional response was quick, and I felt the communal apprehension at my words immediately. Then, very quickly, it disappeared and everyone in the room was all smiles.

"Olivia, you're helping elect a candidate who is destined for great things," said Madeline. "I come from a long line of witches who predict the future. Levi Barnes could be a great leader for your country; his contributions to peace will be immense, but he must be elected first."

"OK, I will stay out of the park, unless Elsa is with me." With my own security issues out of the way, I circled back to the woman staring down at me from the screen on the wall.

"Lacy Smith is a svelte, forty-something conservative woman who believes that God should control everything, right down to how the government establishes the tax code," I explained. "She's generally regarded as a decent public speaker, but she does have a few on-the-record incidents of making outrageous statements. I'm hoping we'll see some of that during the campaign."

After providing a few more personal details about Lacy, I moved on to give the group an overview of what had been accomplished so far, touching on everything from the need to develop a poll, to the final design of the campaign's logo. I told them about the campaign office in Palo Alto and the success of the kick-off party.

"Good briefing," Aidan said. "We'll expect you to provide another update in a few weeks."

After the meeting ended, Gabriel asked me if I would have dinner with him. I agreed easily, glad for an opportunity to spend a little time alone with the man who had changed my life so greatly. I walked into the main area of the Council's offices chatting with Aidan about the full moon arriving the next evening.

"Will you be going out?" I asked.

"Oh, yes," he said, his delight obvious. "I shall go for a long run in the park."

Suddenly I had an image of myself galloping across the forest the night Elsa had given me peyote. "I highly recommend it," I said giggling. "A good run in the middle of the night can be very satisfying."

After saying goodnight to Aidan, I waited while Gabriel walked away to fetch his coat. As is my habit, I started to scan the area, watching what other people were up to. One corner of the room caught my attention. It was at the far end of the main hall, where Nikola Pajović kept his office. The door to his private quarters was closed, but outside, seated next to the door, was an olive complexioned man vibrating with anxiety. Broadly built, he had the body of a soldier or a bouncer at a nightclub. His hair had been shaved, so only dark black stubble remained. It matched his beard, which was also closely shorn.

A prominent red outline hovered around him. His energy was all wrong: dark and full of anger. He wasn't human, either. Knowing the company Nikola kept, I suspected he was a werewolf. It would certainly explain the dark hair and skin. Whatever he was, whatever his intentions, he didn't like being left outside in the hallway. The minute Nikola opened the door the man jumped up and disappeared inside.

Nikola's door slammed shut at the same moment Gabriel arrived and escorted me out of the building.

"An odd man just walked into Nikola's office," I said. "His aura was dark, very damaged."

"Nikola often keeps grim company," Gabriel said. "It's a function of his time in the Balkan Wars. A lot of his associates are veterans. Serbs, I think. As a rule, they're very reticent people."

A black BMW sedan was waiting for us at the curb outside in front of the museum. Gabriel greeted his driver warmly as the man stepped out of the car and came around to open the door for the two of us.

"I am old-fashioned and prefer to let someone else do the driving. I hope you don't find it too ostentatious."

I laughed. "I don't mind at all," I said. "My mother also likes to use a car service, but with her I think it's safer for everyone if she doesn't operate a vehicle. She gets too distracted to watch the road."

"Too distracted?" Gabriel repeated.

"Oh, yes," I said. "She can never look at the scenery as a driver, she has to look as an artist, which is not very safe for anyone. By the way," I asked, changing the discussion abruptly. "Where are we going for dinner?"

"You must know that to a Frenchman this is a question of paramount importance and must be considered carefully," he said, a faux graveness in his voice.

"*Oui, monsieur,*" I said, my hand over heart. "*Mais j'ai très faim!*"

I could tell our banter delighted him, a thought I said very clearly to myself.

"I am delighted," he said, "It's a pleasure to meet someone who enjoys the French language and culture."

Our exchange reminded me that for some reason both he and William seemed to read my thoughts very clearly. I made a note to ask him about it later.

"I was thinking we would have dinner at an old favorite of mine called Bix," Gabriel said. "Do you know it?"

Anyone involved in San Francisco politics knows Bix, a former speakeasy located on the lower lip of North Beach. It is a quintessential San Francisco watering hole that attracts the high-flying set. Once, while dining there, I had been asked to move from my table to make room for the actor Sean Penn.

I nodded back, replying in mock seriousness, *"Ç'est très cher!"*

"Olivia," Gabriel said, his dramatic voice returning, "How can you put a price on a good meal?"

After a few minutes, we arrived at the restaurant and I allowed him to lead the way as we walked inside. I assumed two things as we entered the ornate dining room: first, that Gabriel knew the owners, and second, that he must have called ahead, because he managed to walk in at 8:30 and secure a table immediately. As we were being shown to our seats, I had the terrible thought that the headwaiter might mistake me for Gabriel's mistress. Once again, Gabriel turned around quickly, having heard my thoughts; he wagged a finger at me as he scolded, "You worry too much. Relax."

It should have been spooky to be read so easily, but with Gabriel, for some reason, I did not mind. I knew he was shielding some emotion from me, but I also knew instinctively that he did not intend to harm me, or harbor any romantic intentions.

Once seated, we quickly ordered. "Two Champagnes," Gabriel said. "And I will have the oysters." I wrinkled my nose at the thought, and asked for the steak tartar. Our server tilted his head slightly in approval of my choice and then took our order for salads for the next course.

After taking a sip of my drink, I decided to ask Gabriel about something that had been bothering me. "You know," I said. "The one topic we didn't discuss tonight is the connection between Stoner Halbert and Lacy Smith. Does his demon work for her now?"

Gabriel shook his head. "I don't think so, at least not in the way you suggest. She is a fiercely religious woman, so I don't think she would be comfortable with it out in the open. But Stoner and his demon, they would be quite attracted to her and the kind of extreme energy her conviction gives off."

"It doesn't make sense to me that Halbert—a lifelong Democrat—would work for a conservative candidate," I said.

Before either of us could speak again, our waiter appeared with a platter of oysters for Gabriel, picked fresh 50 miles up the coast in Tomales Bay. He left and returned a few minutes later, pushing a wooden cart toward us with a small metal bowl fixed into its center. In the bowl was the beginning of my steak tartar.

Around the edges of the mixing bowl were other small containers with various ingredients: minced shallots, capers, salt, pepper, and mustard. I watched intently; I enjoyed the attention to detail that the dish required and the briny smell of the capers. As the server pointed to each ingredient, I nodded slightly. Once all of the ingredients had been placed in the bowl, he took an egg from inside a small drawer and cracked it over the mixture. Then he gently tossed it all together, forming a small mound, which he served to me on a plate, along with several small warm toasts.

When I looked up from my dish, I found Gabriel watching me. "I know," I said. "Sometimes I feel as if I am secretly part French."

For a moment, Gabriel's eyes reflected a shadow of melancholy, but then very quickly it was gone. "Eat up," he said. "You want to enjoy it while it is fresh."

We ate in silence for a few moments until I steered us back to our conversation.

"Please finish telling me why Halbert is working for Lacy."

Gabriel took a sip from his second glass of champagne. "That was his old life, Olivia," he said. "He made a deal with the devil. Now, he has no alliances, no allegiance to anything. His goal is to win and to be powerful."

I was beginning to see the logic, but I wasn't quite sold. "I understand the part about Stoner," I said. "But why would the dark forces want to elect a God-fearing Christian woman to office? Her whole purpose in life is to root out the devil."

Gabriel let out a burst of laughter, "Yes, yes, *bien sûr*! And how delicious to be the devil and be sitting right under her nose; even he has a sense of humor, you see. How satisfying to work to elect a candidate that appeals to the worst in human beings, eliciting their fear, their paranoia and insecurity. To help a candidate who excuses the shortcomings of their supporters by blaming their misery on some other religion or culture."

"Are you saying that the devil likes to elect conservative Christians to office?" I asked.

Gabriel shook his head. "No, not at all. You look at it too literally," he said as the waiter removed our dishes and placed our salads on the table. "The devil has no political agenda in a Republican or Democratic way. He cares nothing for elections. What he enjoys is watching humans reap what they sow."

"But you don't want that to happen," I said.

"*We* don't want that to happen," he corrected, pointing his salad fork across the table. "You are a part of this now."

"I've never placed that level of monumental importance on my campaigns," I said earnestly. "I can't function under that kind of pressure, the kind where the world ends if my candidate loses. Now the stakes feel so much higher. No one knows about Stoner Halbert but me. No one knows that he is only running the campaign to cause trouble."

Gabriel smiled back with a glint in his eye. "It only takes one person to change the course of something," he said, pausing to ask for a dessert menu. "Besides, no one knows about you either. *Ç'est la même chose*"

"Do you really think I will make a difference in this race?"

"Yes, I do," Gabriel said. "Campaigns are unpredictable things. Your intuition and ability to read people will be invaluable."

I nodded, feeling more confident. It was getting late, but

I had one more question I needed to ask. I waited until our sorbet arrived and then I pounced.

"What are you?" I asked, taking a spoonful of chocolate sorbet.

"You already know, but you didn't ask me if I am a witch," he said.

"How do you do that," I asked, "read my thoughts so quickly?"

Gabriel took a spoonful of lemon sorbet and paused for a moment. "I am a witch," he said. "One of many from a family that can trace its roots back to the dawn of France. More recently, the Laurent family hails from Aix-en-Provence, where we settled in the sixteenth century."

"Do you mind if I ask how old are you?" I asked, watching Gabriel's bemused expression. "*Pardon*, what I mean is, are you actually aging, or are you like Elsa?"

Gabriel smiled at me, a slight sadness in his voice. "Regrettably, I am aging," he said. "Even I do not possess the ability to stop time."

"Can you walk through time like Elsa?"

He nodded, but turned to the waiter to ask for two glasses of calvados before he said. "I can, but it's not my main skill. My skill is telepathy."

Now it all made sense. "So can you read all my thoughts," I asked, an image of William popping into my head. I wondered if he had the skill too.

Gabriel let out a snort. "Olivia, when you push them to the front like that, then, yes, I can hear everything. Curiously, there are times when I feel like you are trying to send me your thoughts directly. Is it possible you are also telepathic?"

"I don't think so," I said. "I believe my mother would have told me if she thought the trait ran in the family."

"Hmm, it's something for you to think about," Gabriel said, signaling for the check.

We sat in amicable silence for a moment or two as he looked over the bill and placed his credit card on the table. "By the way, about this man you're seeing...what does he do…*C'est ton ami? Qu'est-ce qu'il fait?*" Gabriel asked. "You know you are driving Elsa crazy."

"I'm not sure yet," I said, as we walked out of the door to our waiting car. "It's a work in progress. What about you? Do you have anything to say about William?"

Gabriel raised his hands to his chest in surrender. "*Rien, mademoiselle!*" Not a thing.

From the restaurant the driver drove straight to my house. As I turned to walk to my doorway, Gabriel called out to me.

"Olivia, remember what I asked. Please do not go into the park alone."

"Yes, I promise," I said, and thanked him once again for dinner.

CHAPTER 22

When I awoke the next morning, my first thought was that I would be seeing William that evening. We had been texting each other every day, but tonight would be our first opportunity to be alone since I tracked him down at the nightclub. The days had passed quickly, the campaign occupying an ever-greater portion of my attention. Now that Lacy was entering the race, I knew the pace of the campaign would accelerate, as we were forced to respond to any criticisms she might level against Levi in the press.

In anticipation of the deluge, my day was booked solid with meetings with our opposition research team to comb through her records and our own. Clients are often shocked that I ask them to pay for the privilege to dig up their own dirty laundry, but it is always better to know what your opponent will find *before* they find it.

I pondered these details for a few more moments as I got dressed and walked downstairs. When I reached the foot of the stairs, I caught a glimpse of Elsa in the living room in the middle of her usual morning ritual of yoga and stretching.

"Good morning," I said softly, as I padded into the kitchen for espresso. I made her a cup of tea before walking back to the living room. "Do you want to come into the office today to listen in on these briefings?" I asked. "There may be something that turns up that interests you about Halbert and his demon." Elsa was bent in a sun salutation and did not respond immediately. I set her mug of tea on the coffee table and waited patiently. There was no rushing a time-walker. Finally she came out of her pose and looked at me, grabbing the tea I'd made for her.

"I would like to get a good look at the demon if he comes around again," she said.

I nodded. "You're welcome to come with me wherever I go," I said, pausing. I was about to say, "Except when I'm with William," but I decided we were having too cordial a conversation to muddy the waters. "I mean, you can come with me whenever it interests you."

"You were going to mention him," she said, not bothering to use his name.

I smirked.

"Look, I wouldn't ask to come on a date with you either," I said, trying to make light of the situation.

Elsa made a quick sound of exasperation. "As if that is ever going to happen," she said. "Besides, I often think I prefer the company of women to men," she said.

"Are you saying that you're a lesbian?" I asked, not really caring one way or another about her answer.

Elsa shook her head. "No, I bed men, but I am saying that after I'm finished, I prefer the company of women."

I laughed. "Elsa, that is a very common sentiment among women, regardless of the century."

We both finished getting ready and left the house together for the day. Elsa stayed with me for the majority of the briefings, but then left after receiving a call from Aidan. The two of them were spending an ever-increasing amount of time with each other. I began to wonder whether he was interested in Elsa for more than her experience with weapons. Given her lack of ability to read the bigger picture, I was certain she would never have a date in this century without some serious intervention on my part. I resolved to ask her more about it when I saw her next.

As I had predicted, the day flew by and I was able to make it back to my house to shower and change before the doorbell rang. I stood upstairs listening to the chimes. There was a vampire ringing my doorbell, something I could not have imagined a few short months ago. I quickly ran downstairs to open the door, delighted by the sight waiting for me. William was wearing faded Levi's, a navy t-shirt and a brown cord jacket with a lamb's wool lining. He wore a brown wool ski hat sat on top of his head, pulling his red hair close to his face. I didn't imagine for a moment he was cold. I assumed he did it to fit in, since the night air was growing increasingly chilled as we approached winter.

"Come in," I said as I opened the door wider. When he was inside, I shut the door and turned to kiss him. He pulled me into an embrace and kissed me deeply on the lips.

"Now that is much better than a text message," he said, keeping me close to his body.

"Mmmm, I agree," I said, enjoying his touch. We stayed in our embrace for a moment and then I pulled back and asked him if he would like a drink.

"No, thanks," he said. "I thought would we take a detour someplace first before we start our official date, if that's OK."

"Sure," I said. "What did you have in mind?"

"A friend of mine is having a jewelry show at a gallery on Polk Street," he said. "I thought we might go and take a look."

"OK," I said. "Then are we going to the lake?"

William had a playful smile on his face. "Actually, I'd like to take a rain check on the lake. I have someplace else in mind I'd like to take you, if you're up for a surprise."

I didn't really care about the destination as long as I was with him. "I'm game for a surprise," I said, and opened the door to leave.

Hooks and Catches made its name as a gallery by featuring one of a kind handmade jewelry. Open since the 1970's, it caters to women who do not want to run into their friends at social gatherings wearing the same necklaces and rings. Tonight they were debuting an exhibition entitled "Carbon Spot," a term used to describe a black mark often found on copper coins. It was a play on words, since the exhibit featured several artists working with copper and gold, but there were no black smudges to be found.

We stopped at a table for a glass of wine, then began our tour of the gallery.

The first artist we encountered was William's friend. She made necklaces featuring colored beads, cut glass, turquoise and copper charms. They were striking pieces, very primitive and provocative. One necklace in particular caught my attention. It was a mix of elements: a series of copper feathers, several strands of gray, smoky glass beads, and a small turquoise teardrop charm hanging from a ribbon of copper and brown leather woven together. I signaled to the owner of the gallery and asked if I could try on the necklace. He walked over to the case and pulled a small black velvet tray from a shelf underneath the counter. He carefully laid the piece on the tray, then placed a small handheld mirror in front of me. I glanced at the price tag. At $300, it was one of the more expensive *objets d'art* I had looked at in a while, but I had no reason to worry about money.

I tried on the necklace and stared at myself in the mirror. It was an unusual piece, and dressed in my current outfit, lent me a sort of a rebel image. I was trying to imagine wearing it with a suit and realized I probably would never have to worry about presenting myself that way again. I worked for the Council now. I wasn't going to have to wear that conformist uniform. I must have drifted off in my thoughts because when I turned to ask William what he thought of the necklace, he was gone. I scanned the room and found him at the cash register handing the cashier his credit card.

He walked back toward me a satisfied smile on his face. "That necklace was made for you, darlin," he said.

"You didn't have to do that," I said, feeling a little awkward at receiving such an expensive gift on a first date. "I can afford to buy it for myself."

"I know that," William said, fingering the necklace. "But my friend made the necklace and it suits you. It seems right that I would buy it for you. Besides, I am of the opinion that women should never buy their own jewelry. That is the purview of husbands, boyfriends and lovers."

Before I could ask which category he fell into, William moved me along to the next set of glass cases, which were located in the main room of the gallery. There were three cases in the middle of the floor, all housing copper and gold bands that were embedded with sapphires, rubies and diamonds. As we circled the glass cases, I realized they looked suspiciously like wedding rings and I tried not to glance at any one ring too intently. Still, I couldn't help myself when I came upon a set of three thin bands made of copper. The middle of the trio featured several sapphires. It was a beautiful piece, very romantic and old-fashioned, a bit like a sepia-tinged photograph. I concentrated on relaxing my facial features and clearing my mind. I didn't want William to think I was getting ahead of myself.

Thankfully, as we approached the end of the cases, he said he was ready to leave. "OK, so now it's on to my surprise," I said, fingering the necklace hanging from my neck as we walked out of the gallery.

William did not reply immediately. He seemed to be looking for something. "There is a liquor store near here," he said. "It's called the Jug Shop, do you know it?"

"I do," I said. "It's one block up."

We stopped by the store and picked up a bottle of wine. As we walked toward his car, we passed a cheese shop and William encouraged me to go inside and buy something for dinner. I didn't like the idea of eating alone, but my stomach was grumbling. It had been hours since I'd had lunch, so I ordered a ham sandwich with butter on a baguette and grabbed an apple from a bowl near the cash register. William paid for my dinner and asked the clerk if he could have a small bag to carry the food. Soon we were back on the sidewalk, William carrying a petite brown paper bag with handles that said CHEESE DEPOT in one hand, while holding my hand with the other.

"I want to take you someplace special," he said, glancing at me as he spoke. "Time is running out to see it, so we have to go tonight."

"I'm all yours," I said. "Let's go."

I glanced out the car window as we left Polk Street and crisscrossed the city, leaving downtown behind us in the rear view mirror. William drove the length of Valencia Street to Caesar Chavez and then on to Bayshore Boulevard. We were moving southeast toward the old Hunter's Point Shipyards, where the Navy had once maintained a thriving base during World War II.

"Where are we going?" I asked, finally unable to control my curiosity.

"I'm taking you to a castle," William said nonchalantly.

"A castle," I said, "Here in San Francisco?"

"Yep, in fact, here we are."

True to his word, we pulled up in front of a large compound that was hidden behind a massive stone wall. The wall was partially obscured in places by a number of very old oak trees. William leaned in front of me to open the glove box. He pulled out a set of keys and a small black flashlight. He kept the keys and handed me the Maglite.

"This is for you," he said. "I can see in the dark, but you might need some help."

I looked around, regarding the city's skyline in the distance. We were in the middle of nowhere, with nothing but the pale light of a quarter moon to guide us. As we left the car, I focused my flashlight on the path ahead of us. It led to a gate shut tight with an enormous padlock. I shined the beam of the light on the lock, while William flipped through a set of keys and unlocked the gate.

"Welcome to Albion Castle," he said, as we walked through the gate. "You're now entering an official historic landmark. It was built in 1870 by a man named John Burnell, a Londoner who came to San Francisco to start his own brewery."

"Why here? This is the middle of nowhere."

"Good question. He wasn't motivated by the landscape, he was compelled by something lurking beneath," William said ominously, guiding us through the grounds toward the front door. When I shined the light on him, I saw that his face was animated in mock horror for good effect.

"Sounds spooky," I said, giggling. "Maybe we should go in so you can give me the tour."

The set of keys jangled in William's fingers as we stood in front of a massive wooden door with its ornate metal fixtures. He quickly opened the door and led me inside. I ran a beam of light around the perimeter and caught a glimpse of an enormous main hall with vaulted ceilings and wooden crossbeams. A scattering of furniture had been left behind in the room, an old couch with a sheet draped over it, a few rickety chairs and an large oval mirror, still hanging on a wall.

"Don't move," William pleaded, disappearing into the dark. I heard his footsteps, then a drawer opening and the strike of a match against its igniter strip. He returned, illuminated by the light of a large candle. He looked every inch the vampire tonight, pale and shimmering in the light of the taper. He had taken off his hat in the car and now his red hair gave off an amber glow from the lit flame. For the moment, I felt utterly human, and was struck by the difference in our situation. He could walk through the dark without assistance. It made me uneasy, and though I tried to brush it aside, my throat tightened with a feeling of doubt. What was I doing here alone with a vampire?

William must have sensed my uneasiness because he quickly handed me the candle and left to retrieve several more. Soon we were sitting on the floor, a sea of candles of various sizes illuminating the room. "Don't be alarmed," he said, gently. "I know it's weird that I can see in the dark, but we'll hardly ever be in these kinds of situations. I'm not so different from you, really."

With the room half-lit with candles and my sandwich and the wine laid out on the floor, my survival instincts retreated. It seemed silly to have been so alarmed and I tried to put it behind me. "I'm fine," said. "For a moment in the dark, it was a little unsettling." We sat for a few minutes and had a glass of wine. I wasn't feeling all that hungry, so I asked if we could take a tour. William smiled, clearly happy to oblige.

"I read in a real estate blog today that the castle has been sold," he told me as we walked into the gardens. "I know the caretaker for the property, so I asked if we could pay a visit tonight before the new owner takes possession."

We crossed the grounds, coming to a small gate that opened on to a set of steps. The steps led to an underground passage, which in turn, led into a series of caverns, some of which were filled with water. "What's with all the water?" I asked, feeling slightly claustrophobic underground.

"It's the reason Burnell came. The castle sits on an underground spring. It has its own source of water," William said, clearly delighted to be sharing this with me.

I raised my flashlight and let the beam of light skim the top of the pools of water. Burnell had carved deep stone pools hundreds of feet beneath the castle to collect water from the springs. Each pool was adorned with a lion's head, its mouth slightly open. It was a gothic spectacle and although certainly a noteworthy feat of engineering, I couldn't see how it could ever be anything but unsettling down here, trapped beneath the surface. The room was damp, the air thick and rank smelling. I shuddered, overcome again with an unaccountable feeling of discomfort, perhaps a reaction to the energy trapped beneath in this long-forgotten place.

William gently took my hand and pulled me away. "Come on," he said, a tinge of disappointment in is voice. "This place is bothering you. I can feel it."

It didn't take us long to retrace our steps and return to the main room. We sat down once again at our makeshift picnic, me with my sandwich and apple and he with a glass of wine.

"Well, this did not turn out to be the best first date ever," William said, as we sipped our wine. "Sorry, darlin, I generally try not to alarm my companions within the first few minutes of our outing. I'll try harder next time."

I let out a long breath and laughed. "It's OK, I'm fine," I said, touching his hand with mine. "Why did you decide to bring me here?"

"This castle is almost as old as I am," he said. "I have visited here a few times over the decades, invited to parties by various artists who have owned the property. Now though, an anonymous buyer has purchased it out of probate court. Who knows what the new owner will do."

"Why did they stop selling beer," I asked.

"Prohibition. All of the breweries in San Francisco shut down," he said. "After that, it sort of languished. It was also the site of a spring water company, but the main house and grounds were neglected. As I said, a few artists have owned it through the years, but mostly it's been abandoned, a relic out of sync with the times."

"Maybe you should buy it," I said. "Then you could fix it up."

"I wish I had known it was on the market. I might have. Then I could have built you a castle."

I took a sip of my wine. "I'm not sure I'm regal enough to live in a castle," I said. "I might be more of a barn or bungalow kind of gal."

"I don't see it that way at all," he said and then stood up abruptly grabbing my hand. In his other hand he held a candle as he led me to the mirror that had been left hanging on the wall.

"Look at your reflection," he said, gently cupping my chin in his palm. "I have scanned thousands of faces in my time, Olivia. You were meant to be a leader. It's etched in every line of your face."

We were inches apart from each other as he spoke. No one had ever said anything like that to me. I wasn't sure how to respond. As usual, my emotions around William were a mess. I was worried about how vulnerable I'd felt earlier. I was agitated by the energy of the building, and yet so desperate to feel his touch. In the end, I decided to say nothing. Instead, I stood up on my top toes and kissed him gently on the lips.

"Thank you," I whispered, bringing my lips back for a second kiss.

This time though, he was ready and kissed me back passionately.

We were combustible elements, alone in a 140-year-old castle with nothing but a bottle of Côtes du Rhône and some lit candles for company. Once we began kissing, neither of us wanted to break the connection, sinking onto the floor where we had been standing. My doubts quickly disappeared, replaced instead by unbridled lust.

William had managed to quickly remove my jacket and t-shirt, leaving only my bra covering my upper body. The cold air hit me and caused me to shudder. He ran his kisses down my neck and across my collarbone. He used his fingers to explore, eventually arriving at my breast and moving aside the lace of my bra. We both gasped as his fingers made contact with my nipple. The differences in temperature made the experience both excruciating and delicious. I was overheated, and William's mouth and the air around us were cool as he explored my body. The sting of the cold was both unbearable and pleasurable. I shivered and moaned, bucked and arched. I felt inconsolable and insatiable. Our kisses were long, luxurious affairs. Cradled in his arms, my body felt strangely like one of his guitars, being played fret-by-fret, note-by-note, transformed into a beautiful song.

Somehow we'd managed to overcome the awkwardness of the evening and recover our connection to one another. I should have been content to stay that way for a long while, but for some reason a practical thought popped into my head. I hadn't told William of my work with the Council. As much as I wanted this to turn into something more, I didn't want to get too much farther in our *entanglements* without telling him. I had a nagging feeling that he would want to know. With regret, I broke our kiss and placed my hand between us.

William looked down at my hand and smiled.

"Am I going to fast for *you* this time?" he asked.

I shook my head. "No, but I think I need to tell you something before we get more, um, involved—it was the only euphemism I could think of at that moment. We separated and I grabbed my shirt, suddenly chilled by his absence.

"OK," he said, cautiously. "You have my attention."

"Do you remember when you told me that Elsa's arrival was unusual, and that it probably meant I was about to do something important?" He nodded, an inscrutable look set on his face.

"You were right. She introduced me to an organization called the Council. Do you know it?"

William nodded, his face registering a hint of surprise. "I do, but finish your story first."

"Not long after I started training with her, Elsa introduced me to Gabriel Laurent, the current director. He told me that it was rare for a human to have such acute skills and offered me a job. I told you I'm running a political campaign, but I didn't tell you that it was Gabriel who helped me get the job." His silence caused me to ramble on a bit. "Anyway, it seemed important to tell you about my connection. You say you know about them? I don't know much about how life works for Others. Is the Council something everyone knows about?"

"You must be the first human to ever work for the Council, or at the very least, one of the few ever asked," he said. "Congratulations, Olivia. It's quite an honor."

It didn't sound as if he was thrilled. "Why don't you like the Council?"

William did not reply immediately; he seemed to be choosing his words carefully. "I suppose we could offer each other the same apology," he said. "I also once worked for the Council."

"Once, as in past tense," I said. "You don't now?"

"I haven't been in contact for some time," he said. "It never occurred to me that Elsa would lead you to them. I didn't see that connection coming. It's funny, I didn't think that part of my past would come up for some time."

"And now?" I asked, sensing that he was holding something back.

"Now, I suppose I should tell you a little bit more about myself," he said. "But first, let's get out of here. We can talk on the way back to your house."

I'd always heard the advice that couples should not discuss work in bed, and now I could see why. Reluctantly I got up from the floor, dressed and followed William to his car. Once we were inside, he started to speak.

"I know the Council. Remember, darlin, my father was a U.S. Army officer. He had a deep sense of honor and patriotism that did not die when he became a vampire. I was no different; perhaps it's why he and I lived so easily together over the decades. As I've told you, after I was reborn we left for Paris. We arrived in 1863, long after cholera, the Revolution and even the Prussian Army had ravaged its citizens. We managed to live in relative peace for many years, watching the Eiffel Tower rise along the way as a part of the World's Fair. Finally though, the whims of humans caught up with us.

"When World War I began," he continued. "My father wanted us to join the Allied forces—France and Britain—against Germany. He felt a deep loyalty to the French for their assistance in the Revolution. He convinced me to become involved, to support France. I was not a full-fledged French citizen. I had no papers to enlist. I found the perfect solution in the American Ambulance Corps. The United States had not yet joined the war in 1916, but money was pouring in to support the Allies.

A group of men founded a volunteer ambulance service to help reduce the distance injured soldiers had to travel from the Western Front. My father went back to America to see what he could do to hasten their entry into the war, but the United States had little appetite for getting involved," William said, pausing for a moment. "How much do you know about the war?"

"The obvious details," I admitted.

"It was horrific, I can tell you," he said. "Humans are so fragile. These men were living in enormous trenches that were damp and filled with the blood of the dead. I could smell the rotting bodies for miles."

"You must have realized the value of your work," I said. "You were able to withstand things a human couldn't."

"I might have seen the value, if I had witnessed a shred of common sense from the generals. It was so similar to the Civil War; man upon man massacred, as if humans could be reproduced indefinitely. On any given day, France easily sacrificed 60,000 men. Russia lost more than one million solders. Over and over the generals sent their men to slaughter, often never moving their lines more than a foot or two in the process. And here I was, racing to drive these mangled young men, many younger than myself, to a hospital so they could be patched up and sent back out on a fool's errand."

"I don't understand, William. How does the Council fit into this?"

"One evening I was out in the forest near Lille hunting for something to eat when I came across a group of men traveling in the cover of darkness. They were like me. There was another vampire, a werewolf and a powerful witch. His name was Pierre Laurent; Gabriel's great-grandfather. Pierre recognized what I was immediately, and asked me what I was doing in the area. I told him about the ambulance corps. He in turn told me he would find more drivers to assist.

"The next day he arrived with additional drivers, including himself. Over those days and weeks, he slowly introduced me to the Council and its mission. The war was not supposed to be the Council's main focus, but no one wanted to sit by while the human leadership of the world worked to slowly kill off an entire generation of young men."

"And then what happened?" I asked. "Did you continue to work for them?"

William didn't reply immediately. He was looking out the window and at first I thought he would not answer me.

"I did," he said after a while. "I spent many years working for them, traveling back and forth between the United States and Europe. Eventually I quit."

"Why? Why did you stop?"

"I stopped because I began to feel that humans deserved their own fates. I started to believe that our intervention was a wasted effort."

By now we had reached my house and William had pulled into the driveway, letting the car idle while we spoke. I thought of inviting him in, but didn't think he would accept the invitation. I knew I had to choose my next words carefully.

"Look, I'm not sure yet what this is all about, but it sounds like you made a difference during the war. We don't always have a choice in the bigger decisions that are made, but you helped save lives and reduce suffering. My job isn't nearly as important, but I am trying to do something helpful. I am trying to ensure that good people get elected. People who will work toward fewer wars, and more opportunities for stability and prosperity."

William shook his head. "I'm sorry, I don't see it that way. The Council gives your candidate an advantage. I know the Laurent family; they are powerful witches who can bend people to their will. You are highly empathic and probably a little telepathic, you know what the crowd wants and you can help make sure they get it. As far as I'm concerned, you are changing the fate of another human being. Maybe he isn't meant to be elected to office, maybe humans deserve to live with electing the wrong person."

Now it was my turn to object. "I don't see it that way," I said, repeating his words to me. "Levi is a good person, I can't make him *into* that. I'm not deceiving voters. I'm making sure Levi communicates to the best of his ability."

"And what if the voters want a war monger or a racist?" William asked sharply.

"Then I can't help them," I said, confused about our discussion. "What is it you really object to, William? I'm not controlling the minds of voters. I am listening to them and helping Levi win by really connecting with people. Not by making up catchy slogans or sowing fears about far-off dangers that may never happen."

"I object because I don't think we should meddle in the lives of humans, period," he said. "They are incapable of learning from history. They are incapable of resisting their worst urges for power. They should be left alone to their own devices."

Our conversation had certainly hit a wall. I needed to put some distance between us. "One thing about humans you should probably remember," I said as I reached for the car door to get out, "is that I am one, and I don't have such a poor vision of our collective destiny as you do. So I'll say good night. I'd say thanks for a lovely evening, but I wouldn't want to say something trite because I think that's what you want to hear." I slammed his car door and turned to walk away. I was barely up the walkway when he reached me, his quick vampire reflexes giving him the advantage of speed.

"Olivia, I'm sorry," he said. "That was a lot to drop at your feet."

"I can see you have strong feelings about the Council," I said. "The question is whether they are stronger than your feelings for me."

William frowned. "I thought we were having a discussion, Olivia. Can't I express my opinion?"

"I don't know. Can you do it without making me feel like a carny sideshow?"

William let out a sigh. "I am sorry. Years of living alone can do that to you," he said. "I will try to be more careful with my opinions." He walked me the rest of the way to my door and kissed me good night.

I went inside, tossing my keys and purse on the floor. As I laid my head against the door, I wondered how it could be that after everything I had experienced recently I could still be so naïve. What did I think William had done with all of the years of his life? He had died as a soldier in America's bloodiest conflict, and been reborn a vampire. The tattooed angel on his back made more sense now. It was astonishing to think I had been sitting in the car with someone who walked the fields of Belgium in 1916. I had a connection to the world's history...the only problem was, he didn't seem to have emerged with a very good opinion of the human race.

I decided I would try not to take it personally.

CHAPTER 23

I woke up the next morning knowing I needed to hit the books if I was going to have a meaningful relationship with William. My degree was in American history, not world history, and my education felt incomplete. The man I wanted to be with had walked across the Western Front and watched the dawn of Prohibition. While my education may have been extensive, to truly understand William, I would need to delve deeper.

Luckily for me, my best friend ran the library system. With one stroke of a computer keyboard, Lily could locate any book I needed. I had texted her on the way over to make sure she was free.

When I arrived at her office, she was sitting at her desk, reading her email. I noticed she was wearing new eyeglasses, a pair of thick black rectangular frames that had become a fashion statement for the elite nerds of cities everywhere.

"I like your glasses," I said as a way to catch her attention. "You look like a very sexy East German spy."

"Why thank you," Lily said, fingering the frames. "I know they're a bit of a fashion cliché, but I like how they look." She turned away from her computer monitor and looked up at me. "What brings you to the Main Library today?" she asked. "I thought you were off to Palo Alto."

I slumped on the edge of her desk and hid my face in my arms. "I am going to try to head down there for a few hours," I said, "But Levi is out of town and after last night, I've decided I need a quick research assignment."

"Hmmm," Lily said. "What happened last night?"

"If you must know, the main thing is that I have been acting like a silly, moonstruck child," I said. "William is vastly more complex than I ever imagined."

Lily stood up from her desk and walked to my side. "I don't want to say 'we told you so,' but that is what Elsa and I were trying to tell you," she said.

I didn't reply. I was too busy sulking, my head still buried in the crook of my elbow. "What did you find out last night?" Lily continued, the alarm audible in her voice.

Her concern caused me to laugh. "It's not what you're imagining," I said. "In fact, you'll be quite surprised to learn it's the opposite. I'm the one with the dark secret *he* didn't approve of."

"What?" Lily said. "Listen, let's get out of here and have a cup of coffee. When we're done, I will help you find whatever books you're interested in, or drop them off at your house while you're on your way to Palo Alto." I followed Lily out and we walked up Van Ness to a nearby coffee shop to order cappuccinos.

"OK, now tell me everything," she said, "and start at the beginning."

I sighed. "William's life is much richer and more complicated than I gave him credit for," I said, sipping my espresso drink. "I saw a handsome man in faded jeans who played in a band and gave him a one-dimensional biography. But he's not human. Maybe I could have taken a human man at face value, but William was born in 1830. It turns out those 181 years make quite a difference."

"That makes sense," Lily said. "What did you learn?"

I tilted my head back and closed my eyes for a moment. I was trying to think about where to begin. "He is a former confederate soldier reborn in Baton Rouge as a vampire, a citizen of Paris at the time of the World's Fair, and a volunteer ambulance driver during World War I …and that gets us to only about 1917."

Lily was obviously delighted at my predicament. "Yes, I can see what you mean."

"Wait," I said, holding up my hand. "I haven't told you the best part yet."

She raised an eyebrow, but did not speak.

"He was a member of the Council. He ended his involvement at some point, but we didn't get that far in our conversation." Lily's eyes were wide with surprise. "Yes, I think you may be starting to appreciate the situation," I said. "But here is the real kicker: I found out about his work for the Council when I told him what I was doing. And you know what? He didn't like it at all."

"I'm confused," Lily said. "Why not?"

"He said that humans deserve to live out their fates and that intervention is wasted on them," I said, again growing anxious about my situation with William.

"And then what?" she asked. "Did he ask you to stop working?"

I shook my head. "He didn't ask me to do anything," I said. "I'm not sure he had to, though. I mean, it's clear that he disapproves."

Lily shifted around in her armchair. "I wouldn't jump to any conclusions," she said, patting my hand. "As you said, this isn't some regular guy from the Mission who plays in a band. He is much more complicated than that. I think you need to discuss this with him further before you can understand what he wants. It's possible he will ask you to do nothing."

"Why do you say that?" I asked, wondering how Lily could be so sure.

"For a number of reasons," she said. "First, he is not the first Other to feel strongly against intervening in human events. This is a frequent topic of discussion in my own family. It is a common theme, and one that *you* will encounter more often as you wade deeper into the Council's affairs. Second, William has lived a long life and may have seen what ultimatums do to relationships. It's possible he will never ask you to change your life, but he is certainly entitled to question what you're doing."

"Why is there opposition to the Council's work?" I asked, realizing I probably should have known these things before I allowed myself to be tattooed by a witch.

Lily walked over to a window and regarded the passersby on the sidewalk, before she spoke. "They are the watchers, the invisible hand. The work of the Council is hidden from view," she said. "It goes unnoticed by humans and, in the opinion of some, doesn't always make much of a difference in the long-term."

"But, if you know you are going to live forever, why wouldn't you try to ensure the world is a pleasant place to live?" I asked, some of the bewilderment of my situation showing.

"I'm not William, Olivia," she said. "I think you need to ask him why he left the Council. That is an important part of his story that may tell you a lot about why he feels the way he does. But one theory may be that after many years he came to realize his actions were only a drop in the bucket."

"Yes, but if you get enough drops, the bucket will slowly fill up," I said, feeling slightly defeated.

Lily took my hand in hers. "Olivia, are you falling in love with William?"

I nodded.

"I think I have been in love since the moment I first encountered him in the tunnel, even before I knew who he was. I know it's silly."

Lily smiled. "No, it's not," she said. "But I do think it's time you introduced him to your friends. If you love him, then he needs to know the people in your life."

"He is playing at a club tonight. I was planning on going after I get back from Palo Alto. Do you want to come?"

Lily nodded. "I'll text Elsa and ask her to come too," she said, smiling. "You might as well expose him to everything at once."

"OK," I said with a laugh. "You're right."

Lily grabbed my hand once again. "If you love William, you must try to accept his perspective of the world. It may always be less optimistic than yours; he's been around longer and has had more time to be disappointed by humans."

I knew that this was good advice, but the human in me was itching for a rebuttal. "You know, Lily," I said as we were gathering our things to leave, "It's possible that one day an Other will do something to disappoint a human."

Out on the street, we went our separate ways, Lily promising to choose a few books for me about the Civil War and European history. I walked to my office and picked up a few files and then got in my car to drive to Palo Alto.

It was an easy day of reviewing website text, editing fundraising appeal letters and creating a schedule for house parties through a network of volunteers. I left feeling that I had put in a good days' work in Levi's absence. During the afternoon I texted with Lily who confirmed she had found several books I would enjoy reading, and that she and Elsa would be joining me at the Treasure Chest for William's performance. My stomach tightened at the prospect of assembling the whole group, but Lily was right. I couldn't separate him from the rest of my life. It was time I brought everyone together.

Once again, I got home in enough time to shower and change. Elsa and Lily were in the kitchen having a drink when I arrived. Lily was educating Elsa in the ways of mixing a dry martini, and she had assembled the shaker and other tools of the craft. Just as I was finishing upstairs, I heard the doorbell ring. Elsa answered the door and I was surprised to hear not one, but two men's voices coming from downstairs. As I descended, I found both William and Aidan in the entryway.

"Hello there," I said, amused at the picture before me. "I assume you two met on the sidewalk?"

"Something like that," Aidan said quickly, turning his attention toward Elsa. "Is that a martini you're holding?"

She smiled and nodded. "Lily has been trying to convince me that this is a good drink, but I don't care for the gin. Would you like it?"

"Don't mind if I do," he said, his Irish lilt more on display than usual.

I looked over at William. "Follow me and I will get you a drink," I said, wiggling my eyebrows. William came along, and as soon as we were alone in the dark of my dining room where I kept a small bar, he grabbed me and pulled me toward him.

"You smell good," he said, burying his face in my hair and then he kissed me. "And you taste good."

"Thanks for being such a good sport," I whispered. "I hope you don't mind being with all of these people."

"I have been waiting to see if you would introduce me," he said. "I wasn't sure you wanted them to know about us."

"I wasn't sure either," I admitted. "It's less complicated when we're alone."

William kissed me again. "Darlin, complicated is my middle name. Now come on, or your friends will think we've run off."

We walked back into the kitchen, everyone suitably outfitted with cocktails. After a round of drinks, Aidan said he would take Elsa and Lily with him in his car. I tried to look over at Elsa and gauge her response, but she wouldn't let me catch her gaze. Even hard-as-nails time-walkers need a boyfriend, I mused, and I was happy she had found someone who suited her so well. As we walked to our cars, I gave Aidan directions to the club.

William opened the door to his car and helped me in. "Aidan and I know each other," he said, moments after pulling away from the curb. "I don't think he wanted to be the one to tell you, to surprise you, so he sort of changed the subject back at your house. I didn't realize that he was Gabriel's deputy, otherwise I would have said something last night."

I wasn't surprised. After everything I'd been through in the last few weeks, I was prepared to hear anything.

"How do you know each other?"

"Occasionally I have worked for the Council unofficially

to help them locate things," he said. "Aidan has been my contact for some of the assignments in Europe."

His connection to Aidan struck me as too close for comfort. "Did you know about me from Aidan before we met?"

"I knew you would ask me that," he said. "Honestly, I didn't. It's a coincidence, call it fate, but I swear I had no idea of your involvement with the Council. I've never even met Gabriel."

It was obvious he was being honest from the moment he began to speak. I also knew he was aware I would pick up on any deceit in a minute.

"You're right," he said. "I know you can read me and I can often hear your thoughts, too. Makes for an interesting relationship, don't you think?"

"How easy is it for you to hear my thoughts?" I asked, as we pulled up in front of the club.

"It varies. Sometimes it's so clear, it's as if you're in my head. Other times, it's more of a vague whispering. Why?"

"I'm taking a survey," I said, climbing out of the car. "You'll find out later."

We walked into the club together, but split up inside. He went backstage to find Cat and John, while I scanned the room for my friends.

I spotted Aidan standing near a booth in the corner of the club with a clear view the stage. As I walked over, he slid in, inserting himself between Elsa and Lily. I slid in next to Lily, arriving at the same time as our waitress, who came to take our drink orders.

"I recommend we start with Champagne, or in this case, sparkling wine," Aidan said, frowning at the wine list. His dismay made me laugh. The Treasure Chest was definitely a beer kind of nightclub; any wine on their list would need to be drunk with caution.

"OK," I said enthusiastically. "I'll let you lead tonight."

This caused Elsa to snort into her drink. "Won't that be nice for a change?" she said, drawing laughter from all of us. I did have a tendency to take the lead. Maybe tonight was a sign that I was ready to let go a bit.

A bottle of sparkling wine was delivered to the table, just as William's band came out to play the opening set. He took his place on stage, picked up a guitar and gave me a wink as he began to play. Not surprisingly, given the group I was with, everyone noticed our interaction.

"Are you and William quite serious?" Aidan asked.

"You know William," I said. "He told me the two of you have worked together before. What do you think? Is he serious?"

Aidan glanced at Elsa, and then back at me. "I think anytime a man with William's background decides to share his life with a human, it's serious."

"What about his background?" I asked. "Do you mean because he's a vampire?"

Aidan looked over at William playing and stared at him for a few moments before he said, "It's really not for me to say, but William is a tracker, Olivia. He has a long history of finding objects and people that have gone missing. When the Council needs help locating something, he is one of a handful of individuals we've called over the years. Has he told you anything about his life?"

"A little," I said, "We've barely made it past the 1800's."

Aidan nodded. "I'm sure he will tell you the rest by and by. Now in the meantime, let's drink to our friend William," he said, raising his glass. After our toast, we sat together watching the band, our conversation kept to a minimum because of the music.

When William's set ended, he walked directly from the stage to sit with us. I made room at my end of the booth and he slid in, pressing snugly against me. He glanced over at the glass of sparkling wine in front of me.

"I'll remember that," he said. "You see, I was right about you and castles."

I called the waitress over and ordered William a Jack Daniel's, neat. William gave me a tip of his cowboy hat, a gesture that reminded me of the day I first saw him in the battery tunnel above the Golden Gate Bridge.

"You're sure that day in the tunnel was a coincidence?" I asked, hating myself for still doubting him. William crossed his fingers over his chest where his heart had once beaten.

"Scout's honor," he said. "I go up there sometimes to play my music and get away from the city. I never expected to run into someone like you, much less see you again at the Bluegrass Festival."

"OK, I believe you," I said, turning to face the other three pairs of eyes watching our conversation. "It's just that it's an incredible coincidence."

Aidan sipped his drink, contemplating a reply. I could see him formulating a response; his eyes gave him away. Elsa was leaning in against him, watching him intently as he began to speak.

"The world is a smaller place than you realize. We all share common interests and similar talents," he said. "Our paths, while different, have led us all to the same place. I, for one, am glad. After all, the best breeds travel in small packs."

"That sounds suspiciously like another toast," I said, cajoling the group to clink glasses for a second time.

Afterward, Lily got up from the booth to stand at the bar with William's band mate John. The first time we met, I was so nervous that I had not studied him closely. Now, upon further inspection, I realized that he was quite striking. He was as tall as Lily, with long brown hair and green eyes. Dressed in skinny black jeans and a gray T-shirt, he was handsomely disheveled. Lily must have liked what she saw, because she was leaning quite close to him, hanging on his every word.

"Is John single?" I asked William, who had been following my gaze.

He laughed. "Darlin, John is in a band in San Francisco. Need I say more?"

I looked over at my best friend, a fairy hiding in plain site of humans, and decided she could take care of herself.

"Olivia," Elsa said, breaking into our conversation, "Aidan and I are going to leave. We're going to look for a place to grab a bite."

I remembered that it was a full moon tonight and wondered if Elsa would go running with her boyfriend in the park. It was sort of a romantic vision, the two of them frolicking in the moonlight.

"You should go to Stow Lake. It's a good place to swim at night," I said. "Just don't try to get on the small island, it's covered with sharp blackberry bushes."

Aidan laughed, "Do you know this from experience?"

I nodded. "Elsa gave me peyote tea when we first met. I spent an entire evening running through the park, seeing colors and hearing voices. Lily thinks I disappeared."

"We all agreed I made the tea too strong," Elsa said. "But it worked. She regained her sixth sense."

"It was extraordinary. All except the part where I woke up in the lily pond next door to the de Young."

"You spent the night sleeping at the pond?" William asked.

"I was drawn by a voice in my head," I said. "What I thought was a voice, anyway. It was a hallucination."

I noticed Elsa gently place a hand on Aidan's leg and I assumed she was anxious to leave, so I signaled for our waitress to come over so we could settle our bar tab. William waved her off, telling us that the drinks were on him tonight. Aidan slapped William on the back.

"If I had known that, I would have stayed for another round," he joked, and bade us good night.

Not long after Elsa and Aidan left, we gathered up our belongings to leave. I looked up to find Lily, and saw she was still standing at the bar.

"Do you think Lily will be OK with John?"

"I think Lily can take care of herself, Olivia. She isn't some naïve human woman. I suspect it will be harder on John when it's over."

I glanced one more time at the bar as we were leaving. I caught Lily's eye. She turned to me and waved, clearly delighted to have a playmate for the night. We exited the club and walked along Divisadero Street for a few blocks until we reached William's car. It didn't take long to load his Subaru, and soon we were on the road to my house.

"I'm sorry I can't invite you in," I said, as he pulled into my driveway. "I have a busy day tomorrow and need some rest."

"Not a problem," he said, walking me to my door. We agreed that we would see each other soon, but I was hesitant to make plans with all of the work I had coming in the next few weeks.

William kissed me deeply on the lips.

"Remember," he said, "I don't sleep. You can call me anytime."

CHAPTER 24

Although the campaign office was in Palo Alto, I continued to spend a few days a week in San Francisco, or at least part of the day. Most of the members of the campaign team, including the pollster, had offices in the city. R.J. Klein ran his company out of a small suite on Sutter Street near Union Square.

As was my usual routine during campaign season, I met with R.J. alone to map out the contents of a poll. In politics, nothing is left to chance, even with skills like mine. Polling is one tool consultants use to learn what voters want, so they can win their support on Election Day. After asking a voter's opinion on a certain issue, we ask questions about their age, income and even their education. With those kinds of demographic details, I can ensure that Levi's messages are targeted to various audiences. It's a backbreaking business, one that takes hours of work to plan, analyze and execute. Our collaboration that morning was successful, and by early afternoon, when I left his office in search of lunch, I had a draft poll in my briefcase.

After grabbing a lentil and bean salad at a French café next door, I headed back to my car, which was parked in a nearby garage. It was a pleasant, sunny day in San Francisco, and I enjoyed a stroll past some of the country's most prestigious boutiques and jewelry stores.

After living with my new skills for several weeks, I'd decided that being an empath is a lot like a bad acid trip. All of the colors and sensations that come zooming at you can be a shock to your nervous system. Early on, there were moments when I was barely able to enter a busy street without feeling overwhelmed by the totality of people's emotions and feelings. Now, thanks to hours of training and focus, I have learned to shield myself from most of the chatter of everyday life.

Today, however, it felt as though I was a novice all over again. There was a terrible buzzing in my ears, and it was growing worse as I neared Post Street. It took me a moment to make sense of the sensation in my head: something very powerful was nearby. As I approached Post Street, I could feel the force of the energy vibrating through me. Behind the energy was a wall of emotion: fear, anxiety, and excitement.

As I approached the corner of Post and Grant, I carefully looked around for the source of the disturbance. I did not want to meet whatever was throwing off such intense energy until I had a chance to see it first. I pushed myself to pick up the direction of the forces I was feeling. I did a visual scan of all four corners of the intersection, but didn't detect anything, or anyone, out of the ordinary. The fact that I could not see them, however, did nothing to diminish the sensation.

In addition to the vibration resonating through my sternum, there also was a feeling of pressure building behind my eyes. I realized I needed to redouble my focus on shielding myself before it overwhelmed me. As I worked to get my defenses in place, a sound in the road caught my attention. I looked up to see a black sedan speeding toward me. The darkness of the emotions traveling inside the car, which was careening down the one-way street, left no doubt that its passengers were not human. Despite the pressure on my skull, I felt drawn to the energy, and began to walk toward the oncoming car. I had to get a peek at the passengers inside.

Before I could glimpse so much as an eyebrow, however, the sedan turned abruptly and jumped the curb, crashing through the majestic gold-trimmed doors of a Peabody Jewelers store. I missed being hit by the car, but collided with a man on the street, throwing us both down onto the sidewalk with a horrible thud. I felt the full force of the impact on my right shoulder as I hit the pavement. As we lay there trying to untangle ourselves, my shoulder throbbing, the car pressed its way further into the store, sending shards of the glass picture windows and two stone planters that had been smashed to bits onto the sidewalk.

Finally I was able to extricate myself. I stood up off the ground and approached one of the store's windows to get a better look at what was happening inside. Peabody Jewelers has occupied the corner of Post and Grant Streets since the Gold Rush. Through all that time, it seemed safe to say their sales people had never watched an automobile plow through their main entrance. I'm also fairly sure they'd never witnessed four men exit a vehicle parked in their showroom, fire off several rounds of ammunition from semi-automatic weapons, and then smash the glass display cases containing millions of dollars in rare jewelry and timepieces.

As I peered through the window, another thought was rapidly forming in my mind: the beings inside were hoping to keep my experience limited. Someone inside the store, a member of the robbery gang, had sensed me and was trying to blind me. I couldn't tell whether they were aiming for a temporary condition or something more permanent, but the pain behind my eyes now was excruciating. I tried as best I could to ignore the pressure in my head, and continued to watch from the window.

The men were brazen. They wore no masks or disguises, a detail that only reinforced my conviction that they were Others, supremely confident they would never be found. The thieves used small rock hammers, the kind geologists favor, to shatter the glass cases and scoop the jewels into generic black backpacks. It seemed to me that they could walk out of the store—or maybe into a waiting car—and disappear into the crowd without a single identifying mark. Each of the thieves was young, fit and well coordinated. Four tall beings, each with olive skin; they didn't speak to one another, nor to the frightened salespeople and customers cowering below the gold-plated display cases. And yet I knew they were communicating, the same way I knew they were trying to blind me.

I continued to squint through the window, my right arm hanging awkwardly at my side. Maybe a minute or two had passed since the crash. I could hear sirens coming, and decided it was time to leave the area. My efforts to block the force against my eyes was proving feeble: the pressure in my head continued to build, my vision growing dimmer every second.

I felt the unmistakable warm trickle of blood run down from my nose to my upper lip. I tried to wipe it away and caught site of my hands, which were also covered in blood from the fall. I searched around in my purse for some tissues. Having none, I wiped the blood off my face with my fingers, and then cleaned my hands on my pant legs. I knew I wouldn't be able to drive with my vision diminished; I was going to have to make it to the Chinatown gate and use the portal. It seemed risky to walk the three blocks covered in blood, but if I moved quickly, perhaps no one would mistake me for more than the usual disheveled homeless person wandering nearby.

I willed myself, despite the acute pain in my head, to start walking toward the gate. I felt a bit like Richard III, limping up the street, hurling one side of my body as if it were a deadened limb. I could feel my heart beginning to speed up, my adrenaline finally kicking in. Whoever was in that bank did not want me to see them, and I was worried that if they had their way, I would never look upon anything again.

What a mad sight I must have been for the tourists as I approached the stone lions at the foot of the green tile gate on Grant Street. I managed to bump into a man, mumbling a hasty "sorry" as I approached the lion's mouth. I knew I was making a bit of a scene with my appearance, and now I was going to disappear from plain sight, but I had little choice. I had to get away from the thieves.

I walked up to the statue and placed my fingers inside the beast's open mouth. This was my maiden voyage using a portal. Elsa had practiced with me, but I had never traveled alone. I managed to remember the instructions, despite being rattled. I visualized the doorstep of my house and then uttered one word: *Apĕrio!*

The moment the word left my mouth I was transported into darkness, then light. I felt a gentle pull as I dropped out of thin air onto my doorstep. I lay on the landing in a crumpled heap, disoriented and unable to see. I wanted to scream for help, but I was afraid to attract the attention of anyone on the street. I didn't need the police coming to my doorstep. I would never be able to explain how I managed to leave the scene of a robbery, injured and blinded, without the aide of a taxi or a companion. Instead, I lay still, pushing my anxiety out to my friends with all my might.

"Help!" I exclaimed at the top of my inner voice, "I need help."

Those were my last thoughts, before I lost consciousness.

When I woke up, I was afraid to open my eyes. The memory of the pain I'd experienced returned and I began to cry, tears streaming down my face from my tightly closed eyelids. The first voice I heard was Gabriel's.

"Olivia, please try to open your eyes," he said. "We're all here with you, you needn't be afraid."

I shook my head. "Too painful," I murmured. I felt someone sit down next to me on what must have been my bed, a familiar set of fingers taking my hand.

"I heard you, darlin," William whispered in my ear. "I heard you call to me. So whatever happens, I am here. You can open your eyes."

I began by blinking to get myself ready; slowly I opened and closed my lids until my pupils would accept the light. The light! I thought to myself, thank God, I can see the light. Eventually I opened my eyes and found myself staring into the faces of William, Gabriel, Lily, Aidan and Elsa.

It seemed they were destined to be my permanent entourage.

"Hello," I said feebly. "I see you got my message."

Elsa exhaled the breath she'd been holding. "I was inside the house. I heard you loud and clear, so did Gabriel and William. By the time I pulled you inside, they were practically at our doorstep. How did you manage to do that?"

"I pushed the words out," I said. "I was afraid to make a sound. I couldn't see and didn't want any strangers calling the police and connecting me with the robbery."

"Robbery?" Aidan asked.

To tell my story properly, I needed to sit up. As soon as I tried to use my hands to prop myself up however, the sharp pain in my injured shoulder caused me to wince.

"Careful," William said soothingly.

With William's assistance, I pushed myself upright on the bed before I began to speak. "I went downtown early to work on a poll with R.J. When I was finished, I intended to drive to Palo Alto. I stopped for a quick lunch before getting in my car. As I was walking to the parking garage, I noticed something, a sort of buzzing in my ears. I felt like I was walking toward an energy field. I was curious, so I followed the sensation until I got to the corner of Post and Grant, in Union Square. As soon as I made it to the corner, a black Audi sedan came careening toward me. It jumped the curb and crashed into Peabody Jewelers."

"Was it an accident?" William asked.

I shook my head. "No, they meant to crash into the store." I said. "When the car stopped, four men with guns got out and smashed every display case inside to bits and took the jewelry."

The three men exchanged grim glances at each other.

"Did the men see you, Olivia?" Aidan asked.

I shrugged. "I don't know. I was knocked down by the force of the car crash, that's how I cut my hands and hurt my shoulder. I managed to crawl up to a side window to peek in. I wanted to see who was inside. It all happened quickly…the whole robbery was probably completed in less than three minutes. I don't know if they noticed me. I pushed out toward the energy, and that's when my head began to ache and it got hard to see."

"Can you see now?" Gabriel asked, stepping into my line of sight.

I nodded. "Yes, but my eyes feel sore and scratchy." At that moment Elsa, who must have slipped out of the room earlier, returned carrying a tray with a mug of something warm and a small mirror. She handed the mirror to William who turned to face me.

"Don't be alarmed, but you look a bit like a zombie," he said holding the mirror up to my face. I gasped at my reflection, startled to see two red dots staring back at me; whatever had been tracking me used enough force to burst the tiny blood vessels in my eyes so that the pupils were barely visible through pools of crimson.

"They were trying to blind me," I said, "Will this heal?"

"I think so, to both things," Aidan said. "Someone in the robbery party was an Other and knew there was a empath nearby. My guess is they never actually saw you, they only felt your presence, the same way you could feel theirs. That would explain the nature of their attack."

"Are you saying that if they had seen her, they would have attacked her physically?" William asked.

Aidan raised his hands in frustration. "I am merely speculating," he said. "I cannot say for certain what would have happened if they'd actually seen her, but I think we can all guess it wouldn't have been pleasant."

"Who were they, the guys who drove into the jewelry store?" I asked.

"From what you have described, it sounds like the Serbian mafia," Gabriel said.

"The Serbian mafia? Here?" William asked. "Isn't this a bit far afield, even for them?"

Aidan shook his head. "I'm afraid not. Since the war, they have branched out far beyond Europe. This kind of robbery has become a signature of their work."

William's face was grim as he faced Aidan and Gabriel. He regarded them both, a deep look of frustration upon his face. "We need to make sure she doesn't show up on any video. Someone needs to begin searching now. I know a person that can help us delete any footage without leaving a mark." His response caught my attention, if only because it sounded so tactical, as if he had done something similar before. I wanted to ask him, but I knew better than to bring it up in front of everyone.

"Can I have some eyes drops?" I asked interjecting myself into the conversation. "My eyes feel like someone ran a rake over them. And maybe some ice for my shoulder."

My remark caused Lily to wince, and she quickly came over to my bed and handed me a small bottle of eye drops. "These will help take the sting out," she said. "I'll go get an ice pack from the kitchen."

I examined the green glass bottle closely before she left the room. It had no label or markings of any kind. "What is this?"

"Nadia made it," she said. "She said it would help speed the healing. She also said to remember your fortune and not to be afraid."

"Who is Nadia?" William asked, his curiosity peaked.

"An old witch who lives in the park," said Elsa said, as Lily left the room. "She is a healer."

"What did she tell you, Olivia?" he asked. "Does it have anything to do with this?"

It was a good question. *Ni oui, ni non.* Yes and no, she never mentioned a robbery or being blinded, but she did mention adventure and a great love; I didn't think this was the time to explain.

"It was nothing," I said. "She read my palm and told me I would have a long life. Listen, if you don't mind, I would like to get back to the robbery. I think we should check the videos, maybe there will be something there…a clue," I said.

"Good God, darlin, what do you mean, a clue? Do you

see the damage these men are capable of, even from afar? Why would you go looking for trouble?" William asked, clearly agitated.

"They are criminals, supernatural ones at that," I said. "Don't you think we should find out who they are?"

I'd crossed a line somehow. William looked at the two other men in the room with a pleading look that spoke of exasperation at my remarks.

"No, I don't think you need to go looking for anything," he said.

Before I could reply, Gabriel intervened. "Olivia, it's late. We should be going. You need some time to recover from this attack. We have a lot of work to do with the upcoming poll and our first major house party in Carmel," he said. "Elsa and Aidan will search for images of the robbery and if there is any footage, I will arrange for a screening at our offices *after* the party. They will also make sure you don't show up in any video that is floating around out there on the Internet. The last thing we want is for the mafia to track you down. In the meantime, you must rest. I think we can leave you in William's capable hands."

I was being shut down, at least for the time being. "OK, I see where this is going," I said, sounding mildly petulant. I managed to say goodnight in a civil tone to the group before William walked them to the door. I heard the door shut and the deadbolt lock in place. William returned a short time later with more tea, placing the warm mug in my hands.

"I'm going to get a cool cloth for you," he said wandering off to the bathroom. He brought a wet cloth and insisted I lay back with it over my eyes. "The cold will soothe your eyes and help them heal faster."

"You seem to know a lot about what is going on," I said, ignoring his first aid. "Are you going to fill me in?"

Silence followed as I lay there, my eyes pressed shut under the weight of the cloth. Finally, he spoke.

"I've told you about my time as an ambulance driver and how I came to know the Council," he said. "I didn't linger in

Europe after World War I ended. In 1920, I took a ship to New York and from there spent considerable time traveling across the United States. My father was living in Wyoming, of all places. He had purchased a small plot of land in a remote area near the Snake River. It was very beautiful and full of good game to hunt. We lived there for a time, but missed Europe and decided to return to France. There was an apartment for sale in Paris, near Place de la République at a decent price, so we purchased it and settled in."

I felt William rise from my bed, gently lift the cloth from my face, and leave the room. As I blinked to test how my eyes were recovering, he returned and once again placed the cloth, freshly rinsed with cool water, over my eyelids.

"So, as I said, we went to Paris and we enjoyed ourselves for several years. But then, as you know, things in France turned very dark by 1940. We found ourselves with a choice: leave France or live in occupied territory. Of course, slipping out of the country wasn't a problem for us, but I decided to stay behind in Paris. My father traveled to England to offer his services. Then, after the Germans invaded, it became clear I would need to join the Resistance. In France they were called *Les Maquis*, do you know that name?"

Indeed I did. All over the country there are memorials in tribute to the men and women who fought courageously against the Nazis and lost their lives. I had once visited the War Memorial Museum in Caen, with exhibits that went on in great detail about the brutal deaths resistance fighters faced. "Yes, of course," I said. "They were heroes. You were a part of the Resistance?"

"Yes, and so was the Council," he said, pausing. "The Nazis were the most evil people on earth, Olivia. They despised everything that failed to meet their vision of racial purity, including vampires, witches, and werewolves. They were happy to torture and kill anything they could not control or use to advance Hitler's cause."

Somewhere in the last few minutes, this had become a conversation that required eye contact. But when I tried to remove the cloth so I could see William, he stopped me. "No, leave it on," he said. "It will help you heal and I prefer to tell my story without you watching me."

I nodded, the heavy, wet cloth sliding slightly off my eyes. "What did you do during that time?"

"Everything and sometimes, it seemed, nothing. The goal was to hobble the Nazis and make it impossible to move men and supplies. I blew up train tracks, killed German soldiers, and helped free captured Allied men," he said. "I infiltrated the highest levels of Parisian society, *bien sûr*, and fed the intelligence back to my father in England."

"I was a perfect operative," he continued. "No need to eat or sleep. I could travel great distances in the dark of night, and with my reflexes, I was able to sneak up on German troops without them hearing a sound."

"Did anyone suspect you weren't human?"

"Perhaps," he said, "But it was war. It was better not to look too long at anything or ask too many questions. To be ignorant was safer. Those who were betrayed faced unimaginable torture."

I realized that this was the second story I had heard about William's father in the past, but I had never heard him mentioned as part of his life currently.

"William, where is your father now?"

"He's dead, murdered in a village in Normandy," he said. "There was an informant; the Nazis knew we were set to receive radio operators and their guides by parachute. It was a moonless night, perfect for Others to make a jump. They were watching and waiting. Before I could even get to the field, the Germans ran in and beheaded him, along with his colleagues. It was a well-planned ambush, right down to the silver bullets in their guns."

"How did they know?" I asked.

"I never found out, but I have always suspected it was one of our own," he said. "Who else would have known? It was 1943, no human had set foot inside the Council."

This time I did remove the cloth from my face and sat up. I reached for William's hand and brought his palm to my lips.

"I am sorry about your father," I said.

He pulled me close and kissed my forehead. "Thank you. The worst part was watching and not being able to do anything," he said. "To do so would have put the whole operation at risk."

"And after?"

"I waited until the bastards had left and then I collected my father. His head had been severed from his body, and he had been shot clean through the heart with a silver bullet. I couldn't risk a fire or a lantern, so I dug a grave in the darkness and buried him. I've returned to the area many times, but I've never located his grave. Finally, I gave up. After the war, I purchased a plot in a cemetery outside Caen and bought a proper tombstone for him."

"Is that why you left the Council?"

"No. If anything, his death inspired me to work harder to create as much mayhem as possible," he said. "My reasons for quitting were more complicated. It was the cumulative effects of the Nazis and their concentration camps, the Americans and the atomic bomb…and then there was Stalin," he said. "When I think of all the blood that ran through the fields of Europe, not once, but twice, and in the end, it changed nothing. The result was more bad human behavior."

"I don't mean to be disrespectful, but you're being unfair," I said. "The United States' use of the bomb, however cruel, doesn't compare to the horrors unleashed by the Nazis and Stalin. The argument could be made that some humans *did try* to make a difference. The U.S. helped end the war, however brutal the means. The Resistance was also full of humans trying to stop fascism."

"You weren't there to see the lapses in judgment, the betrayal, the bottom feeders living off the misery of others," he said bitterly.

"That is the essence of being human," I said. "We don't have the luxury of watching from hundred-year old seats. We make a choice in the moment. Some of us make poor choices; some of us rise to the occasion. Life is the struggle we all face to eke out a meaningful existence." I had no idea where my impassioned speech had come from. I'm generally not that philosophical.

"You've proved my point," he said, his voice rising. "Humans are incapable of change."

It was my turn to get angry. His bias bordered on the ridiculous. "OK, I get your point, although I fundamentally disagree with your perspective," I said. "Let's move on. Tell me what happened after the war."

"Nineteen forty-six marked the end of my formal connection with the Council. I didn't have the heart for it anymore," he said. "Eventually, though, the Council began to contact me to work on small projects. My years in the resistance were fruitful. I had connections across Europe. I was discreet and could assimilate into any environment. I agreed to search for things that had disappeared."

"Disappeared?' I said. "What kinds of things disappear?"

"When an Other wants to hide from this world," he said, "they can do it quite successfully. I helped track them down."

I laid my head back down on my pillow and closed my eyes. I was relieved to finally learn more about William's life, but his view of humans was bringing me down. I hoped I could restore some of his faith in humanity.

"Have you ever been asked to track one of these Serbian mobsters?"

"I have, which is why I am asking you not to go looking for trouble," he said. "Hopefully no one saw you and you can just forget the robbery ever took place."

As far as he was concerned, I was an interventionist and he was the isolationist.

"I'm not looking for trouble," I said. "But I would like to know more about the people who tried to blind me. Don't you think I am entitled to know?"

"You know what they say about curiosity," he retorted. "Why are you so stubborn? Why can't you take my word for it and agree not to search for them?"

Here we were again, facing William's lack of confidence in human decision-making, only this time it was the merits of this human and *her judgment*. I'd had enough. My eyes no longer ached, but the rest of me did, chiefly my heart.

"Listen, I don't think I can discuss this with you anymore," I said. "I'm feeling better so I'd like to ask you to leave so I can go to sleep."

"You're kicking me out?" William asked incredulously. "I thought I would spend the night and look after you."

"I appreciate the offer," I said, trying to keep a brave face. "I think I would rather be alone."

William stared at me. "Olivia, again, I'm sorry. I think I may have said too much," he said. "I'll try to be more open to your point of view."

I patted his hand. "I'm exhausted and I really need to be alone," I repeated. Begrudgingly, he rose from the bed.

"Come down and lock the door behind me," he said as he left my room. When we were at the front door, he turned to me, "Promise me you won't do anything until we can talk again?"

I nodded, allowing him to kiss me goodnight. Shutting the door, I could feel the tears forming at the corners of my eyes. I didn't see how we could continue. It seemed impossible that I could have a relationship with a man who had such a low opinion of humankind, and who was so opposed to the things I wanted to do.

CHAPTER 25

Despite my injuries, I managed to get out of bed the following morning to work. I booted up my laptop, pulled out the draft of the poll and completed it by phone with my staff. A final version of the document had been sent to a call center in Omaha and now, almost two days later, we had the first results, which were promising: Levi was ahead in the race.

It was welcome news as I started to recover from my injuries over the following days. My eyes remained a shade of pink, but at least I no longer looked like a wandering zombie. Elsa was my constant companion, watching my every move, under the guise of needing to apply more of Nadia's healing remedies to my shoulder.

Although I had no proof, I suspected William had contacted Gabriel and Aidan to tell them I'd kicked him out. If they knew, then Elsa did too, but she didn't mention William, and neither did I. The last time I'd seen him or been in contact had been at my front door, when we said goodbye.

Thoughts of our last conversation continued to churn my stomach. It felt futile to try to convince him of my views, so I kept my distance. The fact that my heart was broken was irrelevant. There was no room for prolonged conflict in my life. Thanks to my walk-on role as an accidental witness to a jewelry heist, I'd already lost precious time I needed for the campaign. I was determined to focus on my work and set thoughts of William aside, at least until I could figure out how to deal with him.

By the third morning, thanks to Nadia's magic drops, my eyes were clear. My shoulder was tender, but not terribly bruised. Inspecting myself in the mirror, I decided I looked "safe" enough to make an appearance in Palo Alto.

It felt good to be back at work, and for the next several days I spent long hours at the campaign headquarters writing direct mail pieces, and running impromptu meetings with the Campaign Committee, which consisted of me, Levi, Gabriel, and Richard Lyon, a close friend of Levi's and the founder of a hugely successful venture capital fund. Lyon's seaside home in Carmel was scheduled to be the site of our first house party, a meet-and-greet with potential donors and friends in an informal setting.

The party, which was about a week away, was being organized by Richard's office, which was managing the catering and event staff. A separate fundraising firm had been hired to send the invitations and identify major donors. All that was left for me was to manage the press and escort the candidate—easy tasks I was more than prepared to do. It all would have been simple, if my phone were not buzzing every few seconds, signaling I had a text.

Olivia
Finish what you start
Please don't walk away
… Again.
William.

I ignored him. By the following day, the texts had turned to phone calls, which I ignored. The missed calls turned into voicemail. Each message caused the phone to beep and vibrate. After the fifth or sixth call, Gabriel, who'd come to help me work on the party, reached across the table and grabbed my phone, holding it up for me to see.

"I assume this is William," he said. "Aren't you going to answer his calls?"

"No, he doesn't approve of my work," I said. "What's the point?"

"*Ce n'est pas bon*, Olivia," he said. "*Il n'est pas un vautour.*"

"He's not a vulture? Can you explain that?"

"You know what I mean. A vulture is always buzzing around looking for an opportunity. William is the opposite; he's a good man."

"He's too complicated."

"And you?" Gabriel asked. "Aren't you a bit complicated, too?"

I dodged the question, changing the subject. "How are the videos of the robbery coming? Any luck?"

"You must wait until after the party," Gabriel said. "Then, and only then, will I show you what we found."

Grudgingly, I agreed to wait, and Gabriel headed back to San Francisco.

Later that day, JP walked into the headquarters and asked to see me. We'd been emailing regularly, but this was the first time I'd seen him in person for a while. The campaign sent out press releases weekly, sometimes daily, announcing key milestones, such as a notable endorsement. JP contacted me after every release for a formal comment, and then we would chat amicably for a few minutes. He hadn't asked me out on a date again. Now, today, for some reason, he was here in the flesh, carrying a whole lot of nervousness.

Earlier that morning, the campaign had sent out a release announcing Levi's position regarding raising income taxes for billionaires, a popular topic of conversation since the 99% movement had taken root in San Francisco and there had been riots at UC Berkeley and UC Davis.

JP, it seemed, had decided to come in person for his quote, asking if Levi would agree to tax himself at a higher rate.

"Absolutely," I said. "Like Warren Buffett, Levi Barnes believes the wealthy have an obligation to pay higher taxes."

"Yes, but can a billionaire ever really relate to the average American?"

I leaned back in my chair, ready to play press secretary. "It's not wealth that defines a person, but their actions," I said. "Levi Barnes wasn't born into wealth. He acquired it by living the American Dream. He was a university professor who used his education to start companies that created technologies embraced by consumers and the business community. Any entrepreneur can follow in that path."

I watched as JP furiously scribbled in his pad. I'd grown used to the long silences while reporters tried to capture their dictation. I used to feel compelled to fill the silence with more talking, but I had learned over the years to be patient. I knew Levi has gotten his quote.

"Did you get what you needed?"

JP nodded, as he closed his notebook.

"OK, then if you don't mind, I have some work to get back to."

"Wait," he said, his nervousness reaching a peak. "I was wondering if you had reconsidered having a coffee with me, or maybe dinner. I thought perhaps after Lyon's party next week."

"That's a private event," I said in my haughtiest voice. " I don't recall the media being invited."

JP laughed. "Wow, that was excellent campaign spokesperson reprimand voice," he said. "But you'll have to stand down, because Richard Lyon invited me."

Not good, I thought to myself. Overconfident FOC— friend of candidate—invites reporter to lavish party in Carmel full of Silicon Valley insiders. I had to wonder who benefitted from that kind of exposure. "If Richard invited you, then we're done here," I said. "I assume you'll keep everything off the record?"

More laughter. "Yeah, right. Now about dinner, do we have a date?"

"OK," I said, "But let's keep it light. This is more of a casual meal than a date. Deal? "

"Deal" he said, and collected his notebook and left.

The next few days whirled by. There were plenty of preparations to make and our tax policy release had managed to get Levi a space on Nightline and CNN. I had been swamped with calls from producers seeking Levi for television interviews. Levi was thrilled with the exposure and Gabriel was excited to see the campaign going so smoothly.

Gabriel had managed to keep Elsa and Aidan out of my reach, knowing that I wanted to speak with them about what they had found in their search of the videos and media coverage of the robbery. The minute the party in Carmel was over, I had big plans to install myself at the Council's offices. Meanwhile, I had simply locked my cell phone in a drawer at home to avoid seeing more of William's texts.

All of the activity kept me busy, and very quickly I found myself standing in the living room of Richard Lyon's home, watching the sunset. After all of the buildup and anticipation, I was relieved that the house party was going well. The view from his floor-to-ceiling windows of the Carmel shoreline had never looked more beautiful. Even more glorious, the home was full of Levi's supporters; the most wealthy and influential families from the region had sent at least one person to attend. The 1950's ranch-style home was basking in the last rays of the sun and Levi was basking in the acceptance and encouragement of his peers. I was loving the energy buzzing in the room, for these people were truly hopeful that Levi would make a difference, that the government could make a difference. Maybe it was all the wine and sunshine, but the vibe in the room felt right. It felt hopeful. It felt like…victory.

Out of the corner of my eye I caught JP interviewing some of the guests and sighed. In the days that had passed, I'd grown increasingly uncomfortable with Richard's decision to invite him, and for that matter, my acceptance of his dinner invitation. He was a thorough, competent reporter, but whether he was suitable as anything more remained to be seen. JP was certainly interested in me, but I was missing in action. It was true that he and I had something in common …we were human, but there was no spark there. I was deeply in love with someone else. Of course, that someone didn't seem to approve of my choices in life, so from my viewpoint, there was no hope for the three of us.

Fortunately, I was too busy working the room to reflect more on the futility of the situation. Moving through the dining room, shaking hands and trading business cards, I was relishing being part of a well-funded campaign. I caught Levi's eye and began to make my way across the room. I gestured with my hands to ask if he would like a drink, and he answered with a subtle nod while holding conversation with someone. I stopped and began to backtrack toward the deck where the bar had been set up. I took a few steps, but ran into JP before I reached the bar.

"Where would you like to go for dinner?" he asked quietly under his breath.

"I don't know," I said, "Maybe Il Fornaio? It's sort of old school, but they have a nice deck."

JP nodded, "Sounds good. There's also a café nearby, it's named after a bicycle in French, I thought maybe you would like that."

I nodded. "La Bicyclette. Sounds good," I said, suddenly distracted by an uncomfortable feeling of pressure against my skull. I turned my head in the direction of the source of my discomfort and saw something I did not expect: standing next to Gabriel in the living room was William. Were it not for his red hair, I might not have recognized him. I had never seen him wear anything but jeans and a T-shirt, but tonight he was dressed in an expensive Italian khaki linen suit that been altered perfectly to fit his frame. He had paired the suit with a striped shirt and a yellow tie bathed in the pale color of the sun at high noon. He looked wealthy, successful and above all, *invited*.

Although I was dismayed at his presence, William's cleverness tickled me. For him, fitting in here this evening was likely no different than infiltrating one of the Vichy cocktail parties he'd described. He understood the dynamics of political theater well, and had managed to stroll into the room as if he had been on the guest list to begin with. There was not a single woman in the room whose gaze wasn't fixed on him. I felt a deep twinge of regret for refusing to speak with him, for avoiding him. But really, what choice did I have in the matter?

At the moment, however, he was impossible to ignore. I smiled at JP, trying to find a way to make a graceful exit.

"I'm sorry to run out, but I see someone over there I need to speak with."

JP turned his gaze to William and locked on. It was just my luck to have an intrepid reporter and a stubborn vampire sharing the same room. What were the odds?

"Who is that?" he asked, no doubt noticing William was an unfamiliar face in a sea of insiders.

"No one," I answered casually, "A friend of a friend. But I do need to go and say hello."

I walked across the room, trying to keep my face as blank as possible, my body relaxed, my head held high. I acted as though I didn't have a care in the world. JP's curiosity was burning a hole in my back, his uncertainty about my truthfulness palpable.

"Gabriel," I said, offering a relaxed smile for the room to observe.

"Olivia," Gabriel said. "As you can see, that is to say, I invited William. I believe the two of you need to speak," he said, raising his eyebrows in a sympathetic expression.

I looked at Gabriel and then back at William. He had the advantage, as they say, of the element of surprise. I was on the clock, being watched by a prominent reporter and a room full of wealthy donors. While I was tempted to be petulant, I couldn't afford to make a scene or express even the slightest emotion in front of this audience. William was the one who had made my life sound so unworkable. But here, there was no opportunity to rebuke him, and to be honest, I'd missed him.

"I don't believe there is anything to discuss," I said lightly. "We seem to have reached an impasse."

Gabriel smiled nervously, "*Pas grave.* I think I may have softened the beaches in that area."

I was on alert now. "*Vraiment?* I hope you didn't promise

anything on my behalf, Gabriel," I said in hushed tones. "I must be free to make my own decisions."

"I only promised that the Council would not let you do anything alone," Gabriel said, sounding a tad defensive. "And we won't. The robbery is a matter of concern for the organization. There is no need for you to investigate this by yourself, or take any unnecessary risks."

I looked at Gabriel and then at William, who had been standing silently during this exchange. My focus had been about managing my emotions, so much so that I had failed to read his. He was quite angry. Apparently, looking on silently while I restated my position was not what he had in mind.

"Gabriel," William said crisply. "Olivia is leaving with me. Can you please make her excuses?"

Kidnapping may not have been what Gabriel expected as the outcome of the evening, but the French are never vexed for long.

"I suppose that will be OK. The event is almost over, and has been a tremendous success. I will tell Levi that you caught a ride with a friend."

I let the two men enjoy plotting my exit for a moment, before I made it clear I would not be cutting out early unless it was on my own terms.

"If you fellows don't mind, I will make my own exit from the party." I glanced at my watch. It was 7:30. The event was set to end in a half hour. I didn't think it would harm things too much if I left in the next ten minutes. But first I had to think of how I was going to break my dinner date with JP.

"William," I said, a terse smile on my face. "I am going to make another pass through the room and check in with Levi, then I will be ready to leave. I will meet you at the front door in ten minutes."

He nodded, fixing me with a stare that was unfamiliar. His eyes revealed a look of profound exasperation. Clearly, I had pushed my luck by avoiding him for so long.

I came up behind Levi, his long-ago requested drink in my hand.

"I am going to leave in the next ten minutes," I whispered into his ear. "A mutual friend of Gabriel's has offered to give me a lift back to San Francisco."

"Tonight has been fantastic," Levi said, beaming. "This thing is in the bag."

His remark spooked me. Even without the supernatural connection, campaign consultants are a superstitious lot. We don't believe in tempting the gods by calling a race too soon.

"Shhh," I said. "You'll jinx us. You have to knock on wood and hope for the best."

Levi laughed. "Next thing I know, you'll be reading my horoscope. Now go on, I'll touch base with you tomorrow."

I smiled and walked away, tapping a wooden chair as I passed, hoping the gods would accept the gesture. Moments later JP caught my eye and walked over. I was working furiously to maintain a neutral expression as I tried to concoct a story that would sound even vaguely convincing.

"Listen," I said, trying to sound serious, but not too grave. "I hate to do this, but it turns out I need to return to San Francisco to deal with a few things this evening. I'm really sorry. Can I take a rain check?"

JP didn't believe a word I was saying. I could feel his skepticism as he gripped his reporter's notepad.

"What could be so pressing that he would ask his campaign manager to leave a fundraiser early?"

Ouch, it looked like we might not be able to be friends after all. Again, I strived to keep my face relaxed. I managed to laugh and placed my hand on his arm. "He didn't ask me to leave," I said. "I remembered something I need to work on before tomorrow. That's the nature of campaigns, I'm afraid. Things like this happen. But I don't have to tell you that, right?"

JP was debating. He was scanning the room for William. William, meanwhile, was waiting in the corner, his eyes locked onto me. My excuse seemed thinner in the harsh light of the living room, and for a moment I thought JP was going to take another pass at breaking me down, but he didn't.

"Rain check, then," he said smiling.

"Rain check," I agreed, and headed for the door.

CHAPTER 26

William and I walked out of the house in silence. I don't think either of us knew where to begin. I'd been ignoring his texts and emails for more than two weeks. After our last conversation, it was apparent we had no way to break our impasse. For now though, Gabriel seemed to have smoothed things over. I wondered why he cared if William and I were together; then again, it was hard to know what Gabriel's motivations were when it came to me.

William opened the door to his car for me and I slid inside. He closed the door wordlessly and then walked to the driver's side to get in. Once inside, he slowly fastened his seat belt and started the engine, all without saying a word. The silence was oppressive. Our anger and hurt feelings were rising up inside the car until it was difficult to breath.

"Where are we going?"

"I thought we would take a drive to a friend's house," he said, offering nothing more. I leaned back against the car's leather seat and looked out the window. There was no use in forcing him to speak. He would say something when he was good and ready. I'm not sure if it was the intense silence, or the fact that I had been working long hours, but within minutes I fell into a deep sleep. Sometime later I awoke, propelling myself forward toward the dashboard as I came out of my stupor.

"Oh my God," I said, rubbing my eyes. "I am sorry."

William smiled, his normal happy demeanor back in place. "It's OK," he said. "It gave me time to calm down."

I looked out my window but didn't recognize the

landscape. "Where are we?" I asked, rubbing my eyes again.

"We're about to enter Hearst Castle," he said calmly.

"This is an old friend's house?" We were nearly a hundred miles from Carmel, heading in the opposite direction from home. "Now you're going to tell me that you knew William Randolph Hearst?"

"We were acquainted," he said. "But it's his grounds keeper that I'm close with. Frank is a vampire and a former ambulance driver; he took this job after the war. Over the years, he's taught me every inch of this place. I thought you might like to go for a swim."

"You thought I might like to go for a swim? We haven't spoken in two weeks, and the first idea out of the gate is to kidnap me and take me to another castle?"

"I told you…you belong in a castle," William said, as he pulled the car into a darkened spot along an entrance road and turned off the ignition. "Besides, you needed a nap and I needed a private place to speak with you. You've been avoiding me, Olivia, and that won't do at all. I was willing to wait only so long before I came for you."

As I was about to give him my opinion of the situation, he took my hand and admonished me to stay silent until we were inside the castle.

Hearst Castle is not just any castle. Conceived and built during an almost 30-year period beginning in 1919, the sprawling complex was designed by architect Julia Morgan for newspaper magnate William Randolph Hearst. The Hearst family donated the property to the state and it's been run as a historic park since the late 1950's. Hearst had an appetite for big things and he spared no expense for his so-called country house, which by my calculations was about 250 miles from San Francisco, give or take a mile.

William led me along a darkened path to a small cottage at the end of the service road we'd parked on. He fished in his pocket for a key and opened the door. It swung open into a hallway. The hallway became a long tunnel that led to the main complex of the castle. Once inside, we walked along the well-lit interior of a secret passageway that crisscrossed the property.

As we walked, I tried to stay calm, overcome by a series of emotions. I was angry with William for showing up at the party, but also happy that he came. I was nervous about trespassing in the middle of the night, but secretly pleased that this time he had found a way to keep me out of the darkness. Using the hidden system of tunnels beneath the castle that Hearst had built so his guests could swap lovers discreetly, William and I made our way slowly to a subterranean pool built at the east end of the castle.

I stood in awe as we entered. William bowed at the waist and waved his arms in a sweeping gesture.

"Welcome to the Roman Pool," he said.

I scanned the room, watching the light bounce off of what seemed to be one million small, square blue glass tiles. The blue seemed a shade deeper juxtaposed against similar sized gold tiles that formed a border on the walls. The tiles shimmered in the dim light of the lamps that illuminated the room. The blue also made the water of the pool look deep, endless.

As I walked further into the room, I noticed a tray sitting in one corner; it held a small bowl of fruit, a bottle of Champagne and two glasses.

"Would you like a drink?" he asked, stepping in close to whisper in my ear. I nodded and soon had a flute of Champagne in my hands.

"What did you mean about waiting for me?" I asked. "The last time we spoke you made it clear you didn't approve of what I was doing."

William crossed the room, returning the champagne bottle to the tray.

"I may have mixed feeling about you chasing after gangsters and meddling in the affairs of humans, but that doesn't mean I don't want to be with you. You were injured in the robbery, almost blinded. Did you really think I wouldn't have an opinion?" he asked, taking a bottle of Jack

Daniel's from a small backpack he had carried into the castle with him. "You seem to think I'm not entitled to have a view on things, and then, as usual, before we could really discuss it, you just gave up and threw me out."

"I didn't see the point," I said, trying to hold my quivering chin up high. "How can I be with a man who won't support my work?"

"Darlin, that is overly dramatic, even for you," he said, laughing. "And of course untrue. But I am curious, is that why you were planning to have dinner with that reporter?"

William, it seemed, knew more about my activities then I realized.

"Why not?" I said, but with half the defiance I intended. "He's human. He likes politics. Seemed like a good start to me."

If a rulebook existed for how to deal with vampires, the first piece of advice would probably be not to provoke one when they're feeling possessive. William quickly came to stand in front of me and grabbed my chin in his hand.

"Yes, but does he know you and Gabriel like to fix the races?" he asked, his voice low and angry. "Were you going to tell him what you do for a living, or would you have him believe you are especially lucky in your career?"

He was right, of course. I would not have shared my secrets with JP, at least not right away. The truth was that I had no interest in having a relationship with him. I wanted to say as much, but found myself mute, unable to reply.

"Were you planning on leaving with him tonight?"

I nodded.

"Did you plan on sleeping with him?"

Without thinking, my hand came around and slapped William square in the face.

"You bastard," I said. "Why would you ask me something so insulting?"

William rubbed his cheek, a look of satisfaction on his face.

"I warned you about friendships with vampires. Did you

really think that I would let you into my life, my inner circle, and then let some human man come in and walk away with you?"

I didn't reply. Instead I scanned the room for a ladder to get into the pool. I needed to cool down. Unfortunately, Hearst's pool was ten feet deep everywhere but at the far end, where a small wading area had been created. I turned toward the shallow end.

"Let's swim," I said, walking toward the water.

William blocked my path. "Let me help you out of your dress," he said, reaching around to unzip the back of my black sheath, then letting it fall to the floor.

Very suddenly I was wearing nothing but black lace boy shorts, a matching bra and heels. William came around and ran a finger under one bra strap pulling it down around my arm.

"There you go, walking away again, but I want to finish our discussion. I saw the way he was looking at you, Olivia," he purred, and then he slipped his finger under the other strap and pulled it down, exposing my breast. Slowly, he ran his thumb across my nipple and then leaned in closer. "There is no man alive who wouldn't want you, the way you were dressed tonight."

I grabbed his hand where it rested on my breast and brought his thumb to my lips. "You fool," I said, as I slipped his finger into my mouth and gently bit it. "I'm not interested in any man alive. I'm in love with you. Only you. But if you want me to stay, you're going to have to accept me for who I am… my work… my ideas, all of it…or this night will be nothing but a waste of time."

William brought me into his arms and held me. We stood there for some time, until finally he lifted his head and began to speak.

"It's been more than a decade since I've had a mate," he said. "In fact, for almost all my nearly two hundred years I have lived my life alone. Then one day, you walked into that tunnel, throwing all my plans to the wind."

I smiled, squeezing his hand.

"What I'm trying to say is, yes. I agree," he said. "I will change. I will learn to be more flexible."

I kissed him then, thinking it was the most economical way to express my thoughts. It was hopelessly impractical to bind myself to a vampire, but I was in love for the first time in my life, and had no wish to sacrifice my happiness for practical purposes. I had been that person who jettisoned her emotions in exchange for a well-ordered life, and it had nearly killed me. I was ready for a change, damn the complications. I wanted a lover who understood me, maybe better than I understood myself. So I kissed him again, and threw my fate into the hands of the supernatural, just as my ancestors had done.

We undressed and climbed into the pool, bringing our bodies together. I kissed his face, his eyelids. He pressed his lips into the small of my neck and nibbled on my earlobe. We floated in the warm pool for some time before he spoke.

"Would you have slept with that reporter?"

I shifted in his arms so I could look at him more directly. "No," I said. "In fact, I'd been dreading the date since the moment I'd agreed to it. If you hadn't kidnapped me, I'm certain the evening would have ended badly."

"I didn't really kidnap you," William said smiling. "I knew you'd come with me."

"How can you be so sure of yourself?"

"I'm not sure of myself, far from it," William said. "But, I'm sure about *us*. I know we're meant to be together."

"I don't know if I would have come for you," I admitted. "I was convinced you'd never be comfortable with my work with the Council."

William nodded, pulling me closer. "Darlin, I'm certain you and I are destined to get under each other's skin. But that doesn't mean we shouldn't be together."

Before I could reply, William kissed me again. Our kisses quickly turned heated, as we pressed our bodies together in the warm, salt water. Finally, he picked me up and sat me on the edge of the pool, parted my legs and asked me to lie back, leaving me exposed to him. He started at my ankle, placing feathery kisses along my leg. Eventually he reached my center, kissing me deeply at my core. Then he moved his lips back to the tender skin on the inside of my thigh, where without warning, he bit me. At the same moment his teeth pierced my skin, he used his fingers to the same effect. This is what being hit with a Taser must feel like, I thought, as my body bucked and rocked against his mouth. I screamed at the shock of the pain and the pleasure.

Hard to believe, but I had forgotten for a moment that I was making love with a vampire. Your imagination only goes so far when it comes to day dreams of moments like these. Imagining being bit is nothing like the real thing. It's shocking, but perhaps not as scary as one might think. This wasn't an attack, at least not the lethal kind. He was a gentle lover and true to his word that night at his house, seemed to take only a sip before he raised his head to gauge my reaction. I sat up and smiled, beckoning him to join me. William climbed out of the pool, standing above me, his long red hair matted against his shoulders, glistening from the water. He was beautiful and menacing to behold, pale and thin, his body marked with tattoos and ancient scars he must have received on the battlefield before he died. He sat down next to me.

"Dar-lin," he said, his twang more pronounced tonight. "Are you ready? Cause this is the point of no return."

"Which point?" I asked playfully. "The trespassing on state property, or the part where you make love to me?"

"Both," he said, smiling as he slipped inside me, "Both."

Our first time together was slow and languorous.

"This is why you belong in a castle," he whispered. "Good things happen to you."

The second time, after he had fed me strawberries and Champagne, was different, rougher. William approached me from behind, and ran his hands down my back and bent me over at the waist as a ballet dancer would with his partner. I could feel his sharp nails, the ones he used to play guitar, as he ran them along my spine to the top of my neck. Then he ran his sharpened teeth along the same path, reaching the top of my neck and grazing my skin at my nape, a place that would be covered by my hair in the morning. The rest of his body followed as he penetrated me. My senses were overloaded, overcome by his sensual nature and my own lust and desire pouring through my body. Sex had never been this good, or this intense, before and I wondered for a moment if it was because I allowed myself to feel so greatly now, or because I was with someone who made me feel so much.

When we were finished, I slumped over onto the pool floor. "My God," I said, deciding to leave it at just that. I looked over at William and knew he was thinking the same thing. We had truly given ourselves to each other tonight. Our emotions had been as exposed as our bodies, but neither of us had any regrets. I could feel it.

We dressed and walked hand in hand back to the car. My body began to ache as soon as I slid into the seat. I was sore in places I knew many women would never be. I smiled, amazed at what I had done with William and how badly I wanted to do it again.

"You tasted my blood," I said, as he pulled his car back onto Highway 1.

"I promised myself I wouldn't," he said, his voice drifting off a bit. "In the end, I had to take a small taste. Did I hurt you?"

I yawned, overcome with fatigue before I said, "I'm fine," I said. "It was magnificent, but I have to tell you I don't think I can stay awake much longer."

"Go to sleep then," he said. "I'll wake you when we're home."

As I drifted off, I wondered which home he meant.

It was disorienting to wake up in bed and feel another body next to mine. It wasn't something I'd done very often, and at first my mind could not reconcile the facts. A moment of panic set in as I tried to retrace my steps from the night before. A horrible image of JP jumped into view for a moment. Then, slowly, my body began to register the sensation of the cool mass beside me. A tumble of memories came flooding in, causing me to blush, and I realized that it was William next to me.

What confused me at first, too, was the bed, which had not existed in his house when I'd first visited. Made of a dark wood, the queen-sized frame sat in the middle of his bedroom against one of the walls. I knew instantly that he had made the bed for us. I was touched at his thoughtfulness, but also chagrined at his expectation of success.

I sat up to get a better sense of things. As I placed my hands down on the sheets to push up, I became aware of something else that was new and unexpected: the trio of copper bands with the sapphires I had admired at the jewelry gallery was sitting on my ring finger. I examined my hand, not sure what to do next. An image from a vintage horror movie popped into my head: the scene where the innocent, impoverished girl is lured from the village to a fate worse than death…to be the bride of a vampire.

But I knew that wasn't my story. I had walked into the castle as a willing participant. I was curious to know what significance the rings had for William. I looked over at the body next to mine. My suitor seemed to be asleep, or at least in a deep trance. Just as they do in fairy tales, I kissed my sleeping prince, gently biting his lower lip. I pulled the blanket away, running my tongue across his chest, savoring the cool, smooth skin. I found his nipple and bit it to see if I could wake the dead.

Instantly, I felt his senses alight, and once again I experienced the merging of our desire. I was hungry and impatient, my teeth suddenly set in a clench. My awareness was instantaneous to his, and quickly I was rolled underneath him as he slid into me. I would have howled at the sun had William not kissed me. My body was inexplicably ravenous and I bit down on William's lip, impatient for something I could not name. Despite my provocation, he did not drink from me.

After we'd finished making love, he wordlessly left our bed, put on a robe and walked out of the room. When he returned, he was carrying a tray with a glass of juice and whole-grain toast.

"Wow, a bed and food," I said. "You were certainly confident your campaign to kidnap me would be successful."

William looked mildly rebuked. "I was hoping," he said. "I figured I could always throw the food away."

"Yes, but the bed, that took some work," I said, sitting up to sip the juice. "What would you have done with the bed, if I'd refused?"

"I would have worked to get you in it, of course," he said, coming to sit next to me. "Eventually I would have worn you down."

I held up my hand and wiggled my finger with the ring. "You have a good memory," I said. "Usually, though, people ask before becoming engaged."

William took my hand, and stared at the rings. "My mother had a set very similar to these. When I saw you admiring the trio at the gallery, I knew I had to buy them for you."

"Are we married?" I asked, unsure if vampire courting rituals skipped some of the crucial steps humans found necessary. He shook his head as he squeezed my hand.

"That would be a little fast, darlin, even for a vampire. Think of it more as a set of commitment rings," he said. "A sign that we're together."

"Are we bound to each other?"

"No, I didn't drink enough of your blood, and you have not drunk from me, but after last night I would say that we are unquestionably *committed*."

I was more than fine with that, but I wondered how people would react when I appeared with what looked to be a set of wedding bands on my finger, with nary a mention of a man in my life.

"These are beautiful, but I think we need to ease into my wearing them in public; at least until the campaign is finished. I don't want to draw attention to myself, especially from JP. Please don't mistake me; I do want to wear them. But I can't show up overnight with three rings on my finger."

I was being scrutinized, but eventually the former Resistance fighter saw the elegance of my strategy.

"You're right," he said. "When you get home, take off two of the rings and leave the single plain copper band. That doesn't look like it has any significance and people won't notice." It was good advice from someone who'd managed to blend in for decades.

I would have been happy to sit in bed and chat all day about rings and commitment, but all of the discussion of JP had given me an uneasy feeling. I scanned the room for my purse, realizing that I hadn't heard my phone ring. I also had no idea what time it was. I assumed it was late, given what time we'd left Hearst Castle and because the sunshades had been drawn on the skylights in the bedroom.

"Where is my purse?" I asked. "I need my phone."

William walked over to one of the leather chairs and retrieved my purse. I dove in immediately looking for my iPhone. The ringer was off. "Did you turn off the ringer?"

"We didn't get home until dawn, I thought it better to let you sleep."

"Very sweet of you, but campaign managers have to hear their phone ring."

I would have said more, but my eyes fell upon the clock, which read 11 am, and the number 50 that appeared next to the telephone icon on my screen. "Shit, someone has been trying to get in touch with me." I looked at the texting icon, where the numeral 30 sat, unblinking. My email was similar; there were 250 outstanding messages waiting in my inbox, which was more than twice what I usually had for this time of the morning.

I knew without a shadow of a doubt that something had gone wrong with the campaign. My heart was in my throat as

I opened my email. I quickly began scanning the subject lines to see what I had in store. The first headline I saw sent my pulse racing.

"Candidate's Chief Fundraiser Rails Against 'Fat, Lazy Americans' In Secret Video Recording By Internet Journalist."

"Oh, fuck," I said, scanning the rest of the story. JP, it seemed, had managed to get lucky last night after all.

CHAPTER 27

There is an old French saying one of my teachers would use to scold us for misbehaving when she left the room. *Quand le chat n'est pas là, les souris dansent.* When the cat's away the mice will dance. In other words, leave the children alone, and they will get into mischief. The same holds true for campaigns. There is no rest until the end, no moment when you can let your guard down. Every word must be spoken with intent, and every action must be carefully vetted to weigh its potential impact. One step in the wrong direction can be the end. To be a good candidate requires discipline. As with all things in life, without discipline, you get chaos.

I let out a few more expletives as I scanned the emails.

"Darlin, you sound like some of the men I've heard in the trenches."

"I assure you I can do worse," I said. "Listen, something happened last night after we left. I need to get in touch with Gabriel. I will probably need to get out of here quickly and go back to my house. I need my laptop and my phone charger." I dreaded dialing his number. I knew he would be furious at me for being out of touch. *C'est la vie,* I thought. I can't take it back; I can only try to fix the mess.

"Olivia," Gabriel said, his French accent weighing down the first vowel of my name. "Call Levi, he will explain everything. There is a video; that damn reporter Richard invited took it. After you speak with Levi, call me back."

I pressed the number on my speed-dial for Levi. He picked up on the first ring.

"Where have you been?" was his only greeting. "I have

been trying to reach you for hours. The reporter, you know the one Richard invited, he videotaped us...Richard and me ...I don't know what happened. Last night I thought perhaps that he'd had too much to drink. He said...some unfortunate things."

"I know about the video," I said, scanning my email. "Let me take a look and I will call you back in five minutes."

William, who had walked out of the room, returned with what looked like a brand new MacBook. We sat at his desk, side by side, and called up YouTube to view the video. Even before watching the video, my heart sank. The clip had already been viewed 10,000 times. The video itself was shaky at best; JP had clearly filmed it with his phone at a distance so the two men would not see him.

They were standing on the deck at Richard's house, near the bar, illuminated by outside lights mounted to the side of the house. Levi and Richard clearly were already in the middle of a conversation. Richard looked agitated. He was holding a glass of wine in his hand, but didn't appear to be drunk.

"Come on, Levi. Do you honestly believe that woman has a chance? She thinks the Bible should be the basis for all of our laws, for the Supreme Court for Christ's sake. She is crazy and so are her few meager supporters. They're pathetic, the lot of them. Those fat, lazy high-school dropouts...Why on earth should they forever have jobs building houses, or making cheap American cars no one wants to buy? There is no room for them in this new economy. What person in their right mind would support someone who wants to 'ask for a sign from God' to fix immigration? This is Silicon Valley, not the Beverly Hillbillies. People are smart enough to know better."

I watched the video five times in succession, trying to memorize all of the words and gestures. The one thing that stood out immediately was that Levi never said a word. He never agreed with Richard. On the flip side, he didn't try to stop him either. At the end, when Richard had finished his tirade, Levi said, "OK, Richard. Let's go inside now. Let's let the voters make up their minds. I think they can be trusted to make good choices."

Levi's faith in voters was something I could use. It was a small thing, but it provided the foundation necessary to build a plan for responding. The bitter irony of the moment settled upon me as I prepared to conference in Gabriel and Levi. I had assumed Stoner Halbert would try to do something directed at me personally. Now, it appeared that either Halbert's demon had come in contact with Richard and egged on his outburst, or we'd been walking around with a ticking time bomb inside the campaign for weeks.

I'd warned Levi not to jinx us.

I pulled out my phone, which was beeping frantically, to see what the noise was about and ran smack into a set of Twitter feeds from Lacy Smith's campaign.

Barnes must quit campaign.
Intellectual elite have no place in government
It's of the people, by the people.

William leaned over my shoulder as I scanned the tweets. "I call it Constitutional haiku," I said. "It's a favorite of conservatives."

"Smart," William said. "They are striking while the news cycle is hot."

I nodded in agreement. I had to acknowledge their discipline, but I had no intention of letting Levi resign, at least not yet. I picked up the phone, resolved to put Humpty-Dumpty back together again. I dialed Levi and conferenced Gabriel in to the conversation.

"Levi, get Richard on the line," I said, as I rummaged around for a piece of paper in William's desk. I found a yellow legal pad and began to doodle as I spoke to relieve some of my nervous energy.

"Richard isn't answering his phone," Levi said, sounding apprehensive.

"I bet," I said. "Listen, I've reviewed the video, as well as the story JP wrote. I also reviewed Lacy's tweets calling for your resignation. It looks bad, but I think it can be fixed.

"Here's what we're going to do," I continued. "First, Richard is going to issue a big, fat apology for his thoughtless remarks, which I will write for him shortly. Next, we will hold a press conference in Palo Alto tomorrow to discuss what he said. We're going to make sure everybody knows this is about him at the moment and what Levi's response is going to be."

"That's it?" Levi asked.

"No, there's more. I will be leaving shortly for Palo Alto to begin on-the-street interviews with voters, to gauge what they really think about this situation. Patrick and Maggie from the campaign will conduct a quick phone survey, using some of the voters we identified in our poll.'

"While we do our work, Levi, you need to come up with a gesture, a donation of some kind that will unequivocally demonstrate your respect and belief that no one gets left behind in this new economy. Unemployment is still high with blue-collar voters; you must reassure them that you will help them find work. We need a donation to a major foundation that funds job training and career transition programs. Finally, both of you should plan on being in Palo Alto later this evening. We'll regroup then and put all of these pieces of the puzzle together. Is everything clear?"

"Sounds like a solid plan," said Levi. "What time is the conference tomorrow?"

"I'm recommending 3 pm; that way we can make the 5 pm news cycle."

"Will you let JP into the conference?" asked Gabriel.

"Of course," I said. "It won't do at all to shoot the messenger. I'm leaving now to pick up my gear and go. As ritzy as it sounds, I will be checking into the Four Seasons by the highway. I'll see you later this evening."

Time was ticking away… I was anxious to get started. I put my phone away and gathered my things to leave.

"You're as good as any general in the field," William said, standing in the doorway watching me.

"I don't know about that," I said. "I led our troops right into this mess, this is my fault."

"You think because you didn't go out to dinner, JP decided to write something negative?"

"Sure, isn't it obvious?"

"Darlin, you're a campaign manager, not an escort. If JP was basing his favorable coverage on your affections, then this was bound to happen, regardless. You were never going to end up in his bed; you said so yourself."

"I did. Shit. Why did Richard Lyon invite JP in the first place? Before I knew you, I would often tell people that reporters are a lot like vampires—you should never invite them into your house because you can't get them out."

William laughed as we walked downstairs to his garage. "That's a bunch of folktale nonsense," he said. "We can come and go anywhere we please."

William took me home and I quickly picked up my gear and left for Palo Alto. I phoned my staff from my car and asked them draw up a script to use in the phone interviews. My plan was to conduct in-person interviews at the Stanford Shopping Mall and among small businesses along University Avenue.

Being able to read people's emotions put me in a good position to conduct voter interviews. It's common knowledge in the industry that people often lie, or minimize things when they participate in surveys, especially on the phone. No one wants to tell a stranger they drink four cocktails a night, or eat red meat five days a week. It's the same with their views on candidates and political issues. Most people don't want to tell you they don't like someone when they have to look you in the eye. None of that would matter for me, though, because I would know their true emotions whether they shared them or not.

Thankfully, traffic was light and I made it to Palo Alto quickly. As I pulled into the parking lot of the shopping center, I readied myself for an afternoon of reading people.

After several hours of speaking with voters, I took refuge

in a café on University Avenue to rest my tired feet and type up my notes. I ordered a chai latte. Elsa's love of all things tea rubbing off on me. I sipped the frothy, fragrant milk feeling both exhausted and exhilarated after my conversations. I couldn't wait to relay the results of my discussion with the team.

I had been typing for about an hour when Stoner Halbert suddenly appeared in front of me. It was a shock to see him; we'd managed to sidestep each other for months. I'd avoided him when he was in the midst of stealing all of my clients. Later, when I joined the Council and had given up any work connected to him, I became too busy to care.

Halbert took the chair directly in front of me. A changed man stood before me. It was difficult to fathom this was the person who'd ruined so many of my days months ago. Now his aura was hollow, as if someone had stolen his very essence. The blue eyes peering into me were flat and dark.

Sitting in silence, regarding each another across the table, it struck me that I should have been more intimidated to face such a creature, this weasel that stole from the nests of others to feed himself. But I was no longer flying blind; I could read people's intentions, see their true colors. It hadn't been easy, but I'd come to trust my instincts and my intuition, two powerful forces that have served women for centuries. Elsa had prepared me for a moment like this, when I could sit face-to-face with an old nemesis and breathe a sigh of relief.

"Look what the cat dragged in," I said. "What brings you here?"

Halbert licked his lips and sat for a moment before replying. His gestures were human enough to keep people from noticing, but to me, his air of decay was unmistakable, as if he would peel open at any moment and allow some malevolent beast to come pouring out of his center.

"I came to discuss the terms of your surrender," he said. "You must have known I would be the one to take you down. I felt I should deliver the message in person."

As odd as it may sound, I was delighted by his remarks

because it showed that he didn't know what I knew: that the majority of local voters cared very little about Richard's comments. My interviews had revealed that most people were too busy living their lives to tune in to these kinds of petty clashes. And the few who had heard about the video were more interested in Levi's words and actions than those of his friends. Everyone, it turns out, can relate to being at a party where someone you know says something embarrassing. Halbert, meanwhile, had to stick with the media and their views on controversy—something that didn't necessarily indicate voter interest.

"Why should I surrender, as you put it?"

"To avoid humiliating yourself," he said, clearly enjoying the conversation.

"I see," I said, nodding as if it was the most logical thing in the world. "So you would like us to resign and let your boss run unopposed with six weeks to go in the election?"

"Exactly," he said with a sense of satisfaction.

His comments were designed to enrage me, but I knew that keeping my temper in check was crucial. Halbert had no gift to read thoughts or emotions. He was one-dimensional. If people looked like losers, then they were. Some in the press might already have made up their minds that our campaign was about to collapse under the weight of Richard's comments, but I knew better. Tomorrow we would put the campaign back on its rightful course, but I didn't want Halbert to know it. That secret was all mine, and for once I had something he couldn't steal. Now it was my turn to prolong the reply, and I sat back savoring the silence that stretched before us.

"I'll think about it," I said. "You had better ask Lacy to pray that I make the right decision."

Having failed to get the response he was expecting from me, Halbert's face twisted into a grimace. I was tempted to taunt him further, but realized it was time to end our discussion. His overt waves of hostility were starting to alarm the other café patrons.

"I think it's time for you to leave, Stoner. You've delivered your message," I said. "Now you can go back and report that you've done your job."

"Yes, but what is your response?" he asked tersely. "Will you quit the race?"

"I said we would think about it. You don't believe I would actually make that decision for Levi without discussing it with him," I said, feigning surprise. "I am a campaign manager, not a puppeteer."

He rose from his seat, his eyes full of malicious intent. He seemed poised to say something, maybe a threat. I decided to cut him off.

"Halbert, you mad, old stray dog," I said. "Look at you chained up at the post, waiting to attack. When you sold your soul to the devil, did you expect to become his pet? I'm through being your meal ticket, so you'll have to look elsewhere. Now, I think you had better leave before my boyfriend comes over and disembowels you right here at the table." That caused Halbert to look up and search his surroundings.

William had come into the café minutes earlier. I could feel his presence as he pressed gently to signal his arrival. As Halbert made for the doors to leave, I turned around and scanned the room until I spotted William sitting in the far corner, reading a book. I knew he would not approach me until we were outside. We had agreed on a plan to help protect the campaign. I would drive to Palo Alto alone. He would follow later by train, so there would be no second vehicle for the media to notice.

After Halbert exited, I rose slowly from my seat, giving my lower back a chance to catch up with the rest of my body. I grabbed my bag and left the café. William was already outside waiting for me.

"Miss Shepherd, my name is William. I'll be driving you back to the hotel," he said, his words intended for anybody who might be watching.

I nodded and stayed mute, as I was certain Halbert was

nearby watching. I handed William the car keys, and he slowly walked behind the car toward the driver's side, keeping vigilant along the way. One part lover, one part bodyguard, I thought to myself, although he picked right up on the sentiment.

"With me, they are one and the same, darlin, one and the same," he said. "How did the interviews go? Good news?"

I was almost too excited to speak. "Really well, and the phone surveys, too," I said. "As far as our research is concerned, voters don't hold Levi responsible for his friend's remarks. If Richard issues an apology and disappears for the rest of the campaign, we should be able to right this ship."

"Is that what you told Halbert?" William teased. "He looks awful, by the way."

"Wow, vampires have excellent hearing," I said. "What else did you hear?"

"Apart from threatening to have your boyfriend kill him, I think my favorite line was 'mad, old stray dog,' " he said. "I believe you could write your own bluegrass songs."

We both laughed and I slid back in my seat, relieved to have someone to talk to after such a grueling day. He took my hand in his as we drove, and within minutes we reached the circular driveway of the Four Seasons. William insisted we check in under his name and booked us into a suite on the 15th floor. It made sense. We needed a large room to work in, and didn't want anyone in the media to know our whereabouts while we prepared for the next day.

I scanned the suite as the bellman led us into the living room, checking for electrical outlets, the one thing hotel rooms always have too few of. This was to be our campaign's secret field office for the next several hours. Gabriel and Levi were set to arrive shortly. Maggie was on her way, bringing a portable wireless printer. We would need enough electricity to power a small city, when everyone in our group arrived with their phones and laptops.

When Maggie arrived, William left the main room, leaving us to set up my laptop and the printer. As was his way, he'd wandered off into one of the suite's two bedrooms to read and play guitar. Since we'd met, I found myself repeatedly taken with his ability to sit quietly and soothe himself. I hoped when the campaign was over, he would teach me how to adopt some of his methods, although I had serious doubts I had the personality to be so restful with my time.

Not long after we set up, there was a gentle knock at the door. William walked out of the bedroom to investigate.

"It's them," he said, peering through the peephole, and he quickly opened the door.

Gabriel and Levi walked in, looking exhausted. Twenty-four hours is a long time to be in the churn of the news cycle, and from the look of things, it had been rough on them. I could feel Levi's deep, deep sadness at the predicament he found himself in. Gabriel, on the other hand, was angry, with Richard, I presumed, or maybe even me.

He wanted to know what had happened today. The thought came into my head clearly and I sent one back just as fast. *All in good time*, I pushed back to him. *I will set your mind at ease.* He looked up and nodded, a thin smile on his face.

Levi and Gabriel went into the living room, sinking into a pair of plush library chairs that had been decorated in a jaunty brown and blue French sailor stripe. Now that they were both comfortable, I jumped at a chance to try to relieve Levi.

"As you know, I've spent the better part of today interviewing registered voters, while Maggie and Patrick from our campaign conducted about fifty phone interviews, using numbers we got when we ran our poll of the participants who had given permission to contact them again."

Levi listened, trying to be patient, but clearly wished I'd cut to the chase.

"The bottom line is that after dozens of interviews with voters, we believe that this will not harm your campaign permanently, so long as Richard apologizes and you indicate very concretely that you disagree with his views. If we do those two things, we should be able to pull out of this."

"The donation," Levi asked. "Is that still something we want to do?"

"Absolutely," I said. "Tell me what you have in mind."

Levi leaned back in his chair and closed his eyes as he spoke. "I have a friend who founded a charity in the Valley called Vocational Service Corps or VSC. It's a non-profit that helps people find employment and provides classes to improve skills, rewrite resumes, those kinds of things. I am prepared to donate $5 million over the next five years to help start a drop-in program for people who've been notified they'll lose their jobs. Studies show people who prepare are often better able to find work quickly. I'll place one hundred percent of the money in a trust for them and they can draw the funds annually."

"*Ç'est bon,*" Gabriel said.

"It's perfect, and very generous," I said.

Levi shook his head ruefully. "The sad thing is that I planned on doing something like this anyway, but now it will also look like a gesture forced under duress."

"Yes, *mon ami*, but it's an elegant gesture, and that is what will be remembered."

CHAPTER 28

Our game plan in place, I sat down to write Levi's speech. The words were swimming around in my head, and I was eager to get them down on paper. As I typed away, I raised one eye from of the computer screen to glance at the others in the room. Gabriel appeared to be introducing William to Levi, who glanced in my direction, a look of surprise on his face. William must have seemed like a man conjured up out of thin air, and I wondered how Gabriel was explaining my new paramour to his old friend. I decided not to guess. It was more important to work than to speculate at this point.

I wrote for a few more minutes and then glanced up again, amused to see the three men consulting what looked to be the room service menu. Another test, I thought. William would have to feign the absence of an appetite in front of Levi, or find another way to distract him from his lack of interest in food. Again, I opted to work, rather than worry. William had survived more than 100 years without me, so I was certain he would manage this evening. By the time the food was delivered, I had a decent first draft of a speech for the team to review.

Gabriel, it turned out, helped play a role in William's diversion. The meal he'd ordered consisted of raw fish. Sushi and sashimi are foods I knew William's system could tolerate in small doses.

"It's better not to eat a heavy meal when we need to be thinking on our toes," he said, as the waiter wheeled in a cart with assorted fish and a bottle of vodka on ice. "We can always order more if we're hungry later."

I watched William out of the corner of my eye as he picked up a pair of chopsticks and deftly nibbled on a piece of tuna. The shot of vodka went down more easily, his system long accustomed to hard alcohol. Still, his ability to blend in was admirable, and I concluded that vampires were the best chameleons I'd ever encountered.

I turned out to be the one without the appetite—too keyed up to eat. I managed a few bites and then took a shot of vodka for courage. It was difficult to believe as I surveyed the room that only the night before, I'd been floating in a ten-feet-deep, salt-water pool at Hearst Castle, making love and drinking Champagne.

Elections once again were proving to be a lot like a long drive on a narrow mountain road; one false move and you were in danger of swerving over the side. This speech was to be our way of getting back on course safely. I hoped we could do it without any more injuries.

After the meal, I handed out copies of the speech. Levi got out of his chair, walked over to a desk nearby and began making notes on his copy.

Gabriel handed his pages right back to me, saying, "This is his speech; I will let him make the first comments."

Levi returned to our circle of chairs, handing me his notes.

"You've always been a good writer, Olivia," he said. "But this has to come from my heart if it's going to be credible, so I've made a few modifications."

His changes were great. I nodded. "Let me update your remarks, and then we can rehearse."

By midnight, Levi had completed several practice runs of his speech, as we made minor tweaks to the language along the way. By 12:30 we disbanded, Levi and Gabriel going to their rooms in the hotel. Maggie was bunking in the spare room in our suite, and had long since retreated to get some rest after what had been one of the toughest days of her young political career. I stood in the window of the room massaging my neck, listening as William locked the door to the suite.

"I need to try to be more ergonomic," I said, as he took over pressing on the tender pressure points in my neck and back. "Political campaigns are hard on the human body."

"Seems that way," he said. "It feels like you have a rock embedded in your shoulder."

I laughed. "That's been there for a while, if you try to remove it, my arm will fall off."

"As soon as this campaign is over, we're going on a vacation," he said, continuing to knead my muscles. "Some place where you can relax and stop thinking about everyone else's problems."

"Hmmm, sounds lovely," I murmured as the muscles in my neck finally relented into a relaxed posture. "Let's get through tomorrow and then we can start thinking about vacations."

I watched the reflection of William's face in the window break into a smile. "I've been observing you since this all began this morning. You always do what's necessary first, regardless of your needs or wants. I understand now how Gabriel came to choose you for his team; you seem to have an abundance of something that is rare in humans."

"What's that?"

"Discipline," he said, as he walked us to our bedroom.

Once there, I quickly undressed and collapsed into bed, managing a feeble "good night" to William before I dozed off.

Discipline was definitely what I needed to get out of bed the next morning when my alarm went off. The first beeps of the small plastic box on the nightstand had gone unnoticed, but when my phone chimed in with the backup alarm, I opened my eyes. It took a few moments to remember where I was, having failed to sleep in my own bed the last two nights. Finally though, I brought myself up to speed and rolled over to look for William. I hadn't expected to see him, since sleeping wasn't a vampire's main form of leisure.

I didn't I mind though, since I don't like to snuggle when I sleep. Lying flat on my back with nothing, and no one, near me is my preferred way to slumber, so William was the perfect bedmate. Reluctantly, I got out of bed and went in search of the workout clothes I had hastily packed the day before.

As I pulled on my running tights and a fleece, I began to think about the day's schedule. I was grateful to get in some exercise before the day started. Fortunately for me, the Four Seasons had a world-class fitness center only a few floors away by elevator. After lacing up my shoes, I padded down the hallway in search of William. As expected, he was reading in the living room, a guitar propped against his chair.

"What are you reading?" I asked, knowing he heard me coming down the hallway.

"Come and give me a kiss and I will tell you," he said, setting his book on a side table. "You slept well? Feel OK?"

"Despite the utter chaos of yesterday, yes, I do," I said, as I settled into his lap. "I went to sleep feeling very optimistic; we'll see if my intuition holds true."

I received a kiss for my optimism, a very deep long kiss, and then a second more gentle kiss in the small of my neck near my shoulder. Such intimate, peaceful play was new to me, and it made my heart soar. It would have been wonderful to stay in his arms for the remainder of the day, but I was back to reality. "I need to go to the gym," I said rising from his lap. "I need to get some exercise in before the day grows too long."

"I'll go too," he said. "Give me a minute to change."

True to his word, he reappeared in a pair of black warm-up pants and a T-shirt, and we quickly set off for the elevators. I was not at all surprised to see Levi and Gabriel both jogging away on treadmills as we walked through the door of the gym. The only person missing was Maggie, who I assumed, at her tender young age, had decided sleep was more important than exercise.

There being no need for pleasantries at this hour, we all

jumped into our morning routines. I stepped on to the treadmill next to Gabriel and began what I hoped would be a three-mile run.

My three miles concluded forty minutes later, I lifted some weights and did some push-ups on the mat next to William, who was engrossed in his own routine.

We left the gym as a group, but went our separate ways, agreeing to meet at the campaign office at 2 pm, one hour before the press conference. William also left, saying he had some business to attend to and would see me at the press conference.

I stayed behind in the room, intent on working, hoping to call back reporters and review last minute details before the press conference. My plans were disrupted immediately, however, by a series of taunting texts from Stoner Halbert, all saying the same thing:

Resign.
It's not too late to avoid embarrassing yourself - SH

I picked up my phone, tempted to throw it out the window. The last time Halbert had texted me, months ago, I'd rolled up into a ball on my bed and cried. Now, I felt like punching him in the mouth. My days of running from my enemies were over, so I scrolled to the top of the messages section on my phone where Halbert's number was listed and pressed the call button, wondering if my nemesis would answer the phone.

"That was quick," Halbert sneered. "I had no idea you would fold so easily."

"I didn't call to resign, you idiot," I said. "I think all that black magic is rotting your brain."

"Then why did you call? Just wanted to hear my voice?"

"I called to tell you to knock it off," I said. "For someone with the devil on his side, you're behaving like a desperate loser. I want you to stop bothering me."

"Or what?" he asked. "What will you do?"

I was on the verge of saying something similar to my remarks in the café—threatening him with some painful retribution involving his limbs being separated from his body, but then I remembered that cell phones could record conversations.

"You don't think I would be stupid enough to threaten you on the phone on the eve of my press conference?" I asked.

Halbert was silent, and it occurred to me that perhaps he'd hoped for just that situation.

"Goodbye, Halbert," I said, "I'd tell you to go to hell, but then I'd only be encouraging you."

After I hung up, I tried my best to calm down and focus on my work. Halbert did not contact me again. A few hours later, I was stuffing my laptop into its bag when I heard my phone ring. I picked up the phone with trepidation, hoping it wasn't Halbert.

It wasn't. It was JP, so I pressed the talk button to hear what he had to say.

"Were you planning on inviting me to the press conference?" he asked, without offering so much as a hello. Even through the phone, I could feel his anger.

"Hi, JP." I said, trying to sound casual. "I believe your newsroom received an advisory from the campaign like every other news outlet."

"Yes, but were *you* going to call me?"

"You know, things have been a little busy these last twenty-four hours," I said. "I guess it slipped my mind."

"So you have no comment on the video," he pressed.

"We'll be commenting at 3 pm today," I said, trying hard not to show my anger.

"I'm asking if *you* have anything to say yourself about the video," he said, his voice tinged with sarcasm. "Or about the fact that I saw you leave with that man. I saw him with you again last night at the café."

Oh, but did I ever have words to say... none of which could ever be uttered on the record. "Any comment from me or this campaign will come at 3 pm. Now if you'll excuse me, I really have to go. I expect I'll see you shortly."

I pressed the red button to end the call and closed my eyes.

I'd been so busy trying to find a solution to our debacle that I hadn't had much time to consider his role in all of this. Was it fair to be angry with JP? Or was JP just doing his job? Had Halbert's demon provoked Richard? Or had those horrible sentiments been lurking inside him, just waiting to come out? Maybe that's what evil does; it brings our worst fears and prejudices to the surface, it strips away our ability to silence those voices in favor of patience, or compassion. I'd told William that I couldn't change a bad man into a good one using my skills, but maybe the devil worked differently. Perhaps he could take a good man and reduce him to his worst impulses.

In the end, I realized, it didn't matter. During the countless hours I'd spent talking with voters, it was clear that they didn't care about Richard Lyon. They cared about Levi Barnes. They wanted to see what he would do, whether he would take responsibility, if he would be accountable. If so, they were prepared to move on and not wallow in the scandal.

The press, on the other hand, would prefer the scandal to live on, for more details to emerge and for side players to continue their outrageous behavior. If we could deny the media of any further fuel—steal the oxygen for their fire—then the news cycle would close. The plan was for Richard to disappear. Levi would apologize, announce his donation and we would get back to talking about Lacy and her policies. That was what this election was supposed to be about in the first place.

CHAPTER 29

I turned my car onto University Avenue, but found that every parking space around the campaign office was already taken. I circled the block, finally finding a space around the corner and walked slowly toward the office. I was in no hurry to jump into the circus. I knew it would be tense until we got through the speeches. I stepped through the mob of reporters, promising we would begin promptly at 3, which was in less than an hour. As I walked past the press corps, I noticed JP standing off to the side looking at me. I raised my hand to wave; I didn't see any reason to ignore him. He saw my gesture, but did not wave back. As I turned to walk away, it struck me as ludicrous that I had ever contemplated a romance with someone capable of such pettiness.

I made my way to the conference room at the back of the suite of offices we'd rented. There inside, wearing tense expressions, were Levi, Gabriel, Maggie, Patrick, but no William, whom I assumed would show up when things got started. We took the few remaining minutes we had to get organized and then walked toward the front of our headquarters, where a table was set up to face the press.

"*Bonne chance,*" Gabriel said to me as we walked toward the media throng. "You have done a good job of taking control."

"Do you blame me for this mess?" I asked, knowing the walk was too short for such a conversation.

"No, no, not at all," he said quickly. "The fault of this lies with the man who let his tongue slip, and no one else."

I took comfort in his words as Levi and I took a seat at

the table, which was now covered with microphones from radio and television stations.

"OK, folks," I said, greeting the assembled group. "I think we'll get started, but first I want to give you a brief description of the format for today's conference. At this moment, Maggie and Patrick from the campaign are handing out a statement from Richard Lyon, in which he issues an apology for his outburst two nights ago. As you know, Richard made his remarks at a private party, where he was videotaped. Then, his remarks were distributed over the Internet, unbeknownst to him. This statement will be his only comment regarding the other night. He will not be giving interviews, and is not here today at the conference. In a few moments, Levi Barnes will make a statement, and when he is finished, we will take your questions."

I was relieved to see William slip into the back of the room, just as Levi prepared to address the crowd. Levi waited until everyone appeared to have a copy of Richard's statement in his hands, and then he rose from his chair. "I'd prefer to stand if you don't mind," he said to the assembled group of reporters.

"Let me begin by apologizing to the voters of congressional District 15 for this unnecessary detour from discussing the issues I know they want to talk about. I also want to apologize for Richard Lyon's remarks. He is one of my oldest friends, and yet here today, in this very public way, I must say that I strongly disagree with his statements, and I wish I had said so more forcefully the other evening. Of course, I didn't know the conversation was being recorded. But I want to make it clear today that I do not share Richard's sentiments. I believe they have no place in politics—certainly not as a part of the kind of campaign I am committed to running."

Levi looked up at the reporters for a moment before continuing. "The fact is that I *do believe* in the power of people to change their lives, to change careers, to reinvent themselves, because I did, and I know that many others in their lifetime will, too. I think that is the fundamental promise of our country, but that promise is predicated on a few things that I think are worth mentioning: hard work, honesty and civility. Without those things, there is very little that can be accomplished, which is why I have asked Richard to step down as chairman of my campaign's fundraising operation. His presence would distract from the real issues of this campaign, but also more fundamentally, I think that his views require me to sever my ties for the time being. I have an obligation to lead by example, and as much as it pains me, I have asked Richard to withdraw from campaigning and to refrain from speaking publicly again until the campaign is concluded. He is now out of the country on business and I do not expect him to return until the New Year."

Levi shifted the pages of his speech, bringing the few remaining words to the front of his pile.

"As I mentioned earlier, I do believe in the power of people to change their lives, and to ensure that everyone in Silicon Valley has that opportunity, today I am announcing my family's pledge of $5 million to the Vocational Service Corps, a leading job-training non-profit in the Valley. I was a member of VSC's board of directors for many years and I admire them tremendously for the work they still perform every day. The donation is intended to establish a drop-in center where clients can walk in and immediately begin to find the information and tools they need to find new employment, or transition to a new career. I hope that this will help to demonstrate my belief that all of us have the power to change our lives, even in adversity. I hope as well that this gesture will end discussion of the events of two nights ago and allow us to focus on the real issues of this campaign. And now, if any of you have questions, I'd be happy to answer them."

A row of hands shot up immediately.

"Can you confirm that you had no idea you were being recorded?"

I looked at Levi to signal I would answer the question.

"Yes, I can," I said addressing a reporter from a local TV station. "We only knew of the existence of the video after it had been uploaded to YouTube. We were not asked to comment prior to its publication."

"Did you know a member of the press was present at the party?"

Again, I indicated that I would reply. "Yes, we were aware that Mr. Lyon had invited a reporter to interview guests, but the conversations were supposed to be obvious, on the record interviews, not a private discussion between two old friends at the end of the evening when they believed they were alone. It's an unfortunate part of journalism today, but we acknowledge the comments were made and as you can see, we were prepared to respond."

"Did you make the $5 million gift out of guilt for your friend's remarks?" asked JP, clearly determined to draw blood before this campaign was through.

Levi looked over at me to let me know he was OK to respond.

"If you check with the Service Corps," he began, "you will find that I had been discussing some kind of gift with them for several weeks. It's unfortunate to have to do something like this under a cloud, but my donation is one that I intended to make all along. So, yes and no. I do take responsibility for Richard, and I want to make amends for his thoughtlessness, because I can."

"You said you want to get back to the campaign," JP said, asking a second question. "Do you have any comment on Lacy Smith's demand that you withdraw from this campaign?"

"I'm sure Ms. Smith would love to spend the next six weeks talking to herself," I said, generating laughter from the reporters. "But the fact is that Levi Barnes has done nothing wrong, and there is no reason for him to end his candidacy. In fact, our research indicates that voters continue to remain focused on the real issues, such as how unemployment, education and job creation will be managed by Congress.

At this moment, the approval rating of the federal government has never been lower. The voters want to see new leaders and they want to see this debate continue, and that is exactly what we intend to do until the election."

After that, the press seemed to calm down and the remaining questions from reporters all related to actual government policies—not the video. When the last cameraman had packed up his gear and left, we all breathed a sigh of relief. As soon as the door was locked, we returned to the back conference room. The moment we were away from prying eyes, Levi locked me in a forceful embrace that lifted me up off the floor.

"You were brilliant," he said. "We were brilliant. That could not have gone better."

"Oh, no! Please don't jinx us again," I said. "I do think we turned a corner, but let's not tempt the gods. We'll watch the news tonight and see what happens tomorrow."

No sooner than I finished my sentence, Gabriel burst through the door carrying a bottle of sparkling wine and a stack of plastic glasses. *"Très bien, excellent,"* he said. "I knew we were going to be fine, so as soon as I could, I went out to find something to celebrate with. They call this Champagne…but we will see," he said, waggling his eyebrows to indicate his skepticism.

We had beaten the devil, for the moment at least, at his own game. As the evening wound down, however, I began to have an uneasy feeling in the pit of my stomach. I knew that either Stoner or JP would be waiting for me outside. It didn't seem possible to escape without one more confrontation. William, sensing my anxiety, was quickly by my side.

"Are you expecting trouble outside?" he asked.

I nodded. "It feels inevitable."

"We'll go together," he said. "Whatever is there, we'll meet it together."

I suggested Levi and Gabriel use the back door of the offices to leave. It didn't seem necessary for either of them to deal with any more trouble tonight. But before Gabriel walked out, I asked for a minute of his time.

"Now that we're finished with this mess, I want to see that recording," I said.

"*Merde*, you are stubborn," he said, but without a trace of irritation. "*Bien sûr*, I will ask Aidan to have them ready tomorrow night."

Feeling victorious, I grabbed my bags, ready to walk outside with William to my car. Time was a marvelous thing, I mused, in its ability to speed up and slow down depending on your adrenaline. Two days had passed with almost no sensation of their conclusion. I wondered if time felt that quick for William, too.

"Sadly, no," he said, hearing my thoughts. "Not when it's centuries, instead of days."

"Does it make you weary?"

"Sometimes," he said. "I have learned to pass the time gracefully. Come on, let's go home."

Unfortunately, as anticipated, both JP and Stoner Halbert were waiting for me outside. I studied the two of them, noting their body language, and got the distinct impression that they had known each other prior to the campaign. They were standing too close to one another to be strangers. Men normally don't give their personal space away that easily, but these two were standing as close as brothers would. A light bulb went off in my head. Was Halbert so determined to humiliate me that he would ask his friend the reporter to play seducer? Perhaps that's where the video came in. JP had needed something for Halbert, having come up short in his quest to compromise me. William's trip to Hearst Castle, it seemed, had saved me on several levels.

"Gentlemen," William drawled, as he held my hand tightly. "Is there something we can help you with?"

Both men regarded William warily, now unsure of themselves.

"What you do want?" I asked. "The press conference is over."

"I have it on good authority that you were not even in

the house when Lyon made those comments to Levi," purred Halbert. "My sources tell me you walked out of the fundraiser, and off the job, early for a tryst with your lover. How professional do you think that would look to the world if it were broadcast?"

William started forward, but I put out my arm to stop him.

"I've got one better," I said. "How about I tell the press about your longstanding friendship with JP, a preeminent Silicon Valley reporter, and how you two conspired to have him lure me into his bed to gain confidential information, and when that failed, violated the privacy of two men by secretly videotaping them. What do you think the press will make of that? Shall we have a race to see who can pick up the phone faster? My instincts tell me my story will prove far more damaging to your boss, especially when I tell the press I am engaged to be married—that it had been a surprise proposal that caused me to leave early."

Two pairs of eyes stared back at me, unmoving. This they hadn't expected.

"Shall we get started? I'll start data mining and see if I can turn up any compromising photos of the two of you together on Facebook. You know, you can never really delete things from the Web."

"Bitch," Halbert said, taking a step towards us. "You think you can—"

"Shut up," JP said, pulling Halbert's arm. "For once, just shut up."

"I suggest you two leave here, *now*," William said, leaving little doubt about what would happen if they refused. Both men glared, but turned and walked away.

"Are you going to turn JP in to his editors?" William asked, opening my car door for me.

"No," I said, sinking into the seat with relish, my body finally realizing it was exhausted. "JP will live in fear that I will call his editors and that is punishment enough for him. As for Halbert, he's got one hell of a boss, how pleasant can that be? I am satisfied just to get on with my work."

"You surprise me," William said, as he turned the key in the ignition. "Most people would be ready for revenge by now."

"Oh, I do want revenge," I said, yawning. "But the best revenge will be for Levi to win the race. So I would rather focus on that. Besides, I feel foolish, having almost fallen into their trap. If you hadn't come for me, I might have done something far worse to harm Levi's campaign. I hope you don't mind that I lied and told them we were engaged. It seemed like the one thing that would take the wind out of their sails."

"I don't mind one bit," he said, giving me a provocative look that spelled hours of fun later. "I say we go back to my place and make it official."

CHAPTER 30

The sun, it seemed, was taking its time to set, driving me crazy as I waited for dusk to arrive. Only when it was dark could our group assemble at the Council's offices and review the videos of the robbery. Unlike the two days before, when time had passed at the speed of light, today had dragged on.

The only bright spot in my long, restless day was reviewing the positive media coverage we continued to receive following our press conference. My instincts and my ability to read people had paid off. Earlier in the day, our campaign pollster had phoned with news that Levi was widening his lead against Lacy. Even JP had surprised me. His story hadn't betrayed any of his venom; he'd played it straight.

Finally, as the foghorns began to wail and dusk crept into the city, I called upstairs to Elsa and asked her to walk with me to the museum. She had gone up to take a nap earlier, something I'd never seen her do before. She complained of being tired, which was understandable given that we'd all been working at a fast pace for weeks.

On the way to the museum, we spoke very little, too wrapped up in our own thoughts, I suppose. We walked around to the side door and I placed my palm on the copper, waiting for the sensors to recognize my fingerprints and open the door. Once inside, as we approached the main bay of cubicles, I saw William seated, speaking with Aidan. Their discussion, whatever the topic, looked serious and I sensed that I was being mentioned in some context. Gabriel was there too, nodding solemnly. Perhaps William was simply recounting last night's finale, which were details I had yet to tell the team.

"Hello," I said, breaking into their conversation. "How is everyone tonight?"

"Olivia," Gabriel said standing to take my hand in his for a moment. "William is telling us about Halbert's threat against you. He tells us you handled them well, but I am still concerned. This Halbert, he is about to enter a lost place, we have an expression *au diable vert*, a place that is inadvisable."

"It was his choice," I said. "He chose the dark side. But I wonder what will happen if he loses the election. How will he and his entourage take the loss?"

"Indeed, that's a good question," Gabriel said, a glint in his eyes. "You have come through all of this a changed woman, Olivia. You seem more...composed."

"My newfound responsibilities are growing on me," I said earnestly. "Thanks to Elsa and the rest of my training, I don't feel as vulnerable. I feel more in control of my destiny."

"From what I have been told, you're more than comfortable, Olivia," Aidan said, joining the conversation. "You're becoming a leader."

I blushed, feeling suddenly shy at the compliment. I looked over at Elsa to see if she was happy, but her face gave away no hint of any emotion. I found it curious, but let it pass. I knew she was tired and surmised that perhaps she was not feeling well.

"Can we watch the videos?" I asked, giving Gabriel an imploring look.

"The room is set up now; we can go in," Aidan said, gesturing toward the closed door of a nearby conference room—a structure whose size and shape seemed not at all to correspond to the actual footprint of the building.

Once again, I marveled at how the building always seemed to have a conference room available when we needed it. I hoped one day to be shown the spell required for making whole rooms out of nothing, but in the meantime, I enjoyed the trick, and the privacy it offered.

A large flat-screen television was mounted on the wall inside, and there was an iPad, a keyboard, and a tray with a pitcher of water and several glasses. Aidan and Elsa sat down in chairs at the head of the table and began speaking. Gabriel did not join us.

"We believe we've reviewed all of the videos that popped up on YouTube in the first two days after the robbery. Here is a montage of what's out there."

I cringed as I watched the first images of the car crashing into the building. I remembered how it felt to fall on my shoulder when the car jumped the curb, the pain in my eyes as I tried to peer through the windows of the jewelry store. I watched one video, then the next. My memory of the crime was so much different from the images I was looking at. My recollection was that there were very few people on the street, but as I watched now, I saw that there were actually dozens more than I remembered.

"Did you see me in any of these images?" I asked.

"Surprisingly, no," Elsa said. "There were smart phones filming the robbery from almost every angle, but so far, you have not shown up in a single frame. It's almost as if you became invisible."

"That's the second time I've seemed to become invisible," I said, remembering Lily's comments at dinner. "Obviously, that's impossible, so there must be another explanation."

The images on the TV continued to whirl by, when suddenly something caught my eye.

"Wait, stop, hold that frame for a moment," I said, squinting at the face of a man I recognized. "I know him."

"What do you mean, you know him?" Aidan asked.

I pointed at the screen. "I don't know him, but I recognize him. I saw him, here, in this building."

A shot of dread ran up my spine and it wasn't my own. The collective reaction of the group was grim.

"Where did you see him?" Aidan asked, walking briskly to close the door to the conference room. Elsa followed him, closing the metal blinds in the room completely. I shut my eyes to get the memory straight, so much having happened in the last few days.

"It was here," I said slowly. "Gabriel and I were having dinner together that night, and I was waiting for him to get his coat. This man was pacing outside Nikola's office. I remembered him because I thought at the time he looked like a soldier, or an athlete of some kind. He was very tense. He was waiting, and pacing, and then the door opened and he went inside. I mentioned it to Gabriel."

"What did he say?" Aidan asked, coming to sit next to me.

I massaged my finger against my forehead for a moment as I thought back to our conversation. "He said something like, 'Yes, Nikola knows a lot of Serbs from the Balkan war and some do look quite grim.' "

William, who had been lingering in the back corner of the room, came to stand next to me, placing his hand on my shoulder.

"This man?" he asked. "Did he see you watching him?"

I thought for a moment. "No, I don't think so. I was standing in the shadows, waiting for Gabriel. It was only when he arrived that I stepped into the light to greet him and by then, this man had gone inside Nicola's office."

The group's concern was growing more palpable by the second, so I said to no one in particular, "You know, I can feel your worry. Is someone going to tell me what they think this means? Do you think Nikola had something to do with the robbery?"

"We don't have enough information to make that connection," Aidan said quickly, ever the cautious diplomat. "It could be nothing but a coincidence. The Serbian community is very small in San Francisco. His visit could have been about something totally unrelated."

"Are we going to check it out?"

William and Aidan exchanged glances that told me all I needed to know. This was off limits to me.

"Olivia, I will look into this," Aidan said sternly. "The Council is a fragile organization, made up of many competing interests. Certain protocols must be maintained. It would not be appropriate for you to ask Nikola about this."

Elsa peered out through the blinds, checking, I guessed, to see who was working in the main bay. "We can't discuss this outside of our group," she said.

"What about Gabriel?" I asked, unsure if she included him in this discussion.

"Yes, of course," Aidan said, "But always in private, never in open rooms, hallways or elevators. Understood?"

His question was posed to all of us, but I got the feeling his directive was mostly aimed at me. "Understood," I said, nodding my head.

The meeting ended on a somewhat subdued tone, with Aidan clearly distressed about this new wrinkle. I knew from our previous conversations that he was no fan of the Eastern bloc delegation. Now he would have to seek them out to discuss something uncomfortable, possibly illegal.

William and I remained silent as we stepped into the elevator to leave. As the doors opened on the main floor, we ran straight into Nikola. I couldn't have imagined worse luck, considering Aidan's last words to us.

"Olivia," Nikola said. "How are you? We heard that you were injured recently."

William squeezed my hand, a subtle warning not to pick a fight. I nodded, smiling warmly. "Yes, but I am feeling better. How did you find out?"

"Gabriel, of course," he said. "It's standard for the Council to issue a report when a staff member is injured under unusual circumstances. In our line of work, that kind of information can be important."

"Well, I'm fine now," I said. "I'm not sure what happened. One minute I was walking down the street, the next I was knocked down by a piercing pain in my head."

"What a shame," he said, although I knew he was not

even remotely sorry. "Do you know anything about the robbers?"

"I heard they might be Serbian," I said.

Nikola smiled, his perfect vampire teeth gleaming back at me. "Yes, of course I have seen the news reports, but who knows what the truth is? Western media love to blame everything on Serbs. We are the perfect villains for the twenty-first century."

"You would know better than I about these sorts of things," I said innocently. "I've been so busy with my campaign work that I haven't given the robbery a thought."

Nikola doubted me; I could feel it. But I knew I had gone as far as I could with this conversation, so I changed the subject. "Nikola, I apologize for my poor manners. Let me introduce my close friend, William."

They eyed one another coolly, vampire to vampire. I suspected this was not the first time they had met.

"You are full of surprises, Olivia," Nikola purred. "You become the first human to work for the Council, and then you take a vampire for a lover. You certainly like to live dangerously."

"Indeed, Nikola, I've surprised myself sometimes with my choices," I said. "I hardly know what I will do next." At that William dug his finger into my palm.

Nikola tossed back his head and laughed, clearly amused at my insolence. "How exciting," he said. "I must remember to keep a closer eye on you in the future."

With that, Nikola nodded curtly at the two of us, and walked into an open elevator. After the elevator doors had closed and we were alone, William regarded me with a look that was one part amusement, two parts fury.

"You can't do that, darlin. You're not prepared physically or mentally to pick a fight with a thousand-year-old vampire." he said. "He is more cunning and far more ruthless than you."

"Maybe I will surprise you," I said, feeling prickly, but William stopped me from speaking further.

"If you want to pick a fight, then you need to be prepared to see it through. Now let's get out of here before we get ourselves into trouble."

We walked through the park toward my house in silence. I was feeling sullen, like a small child told to mind her manners. I wasn't allowed to ask questions, I mustn't speak in the hallways, and I couldn't pick fights with vampires who were older than me. It was petty, but I felt chided and hemmed in, so I walked in silence, feeling a bit sorry for myself. William strolled beside me, listening, I knew, to my thoughts as they whizzed by. Wisely, he stayed out of the conversation.

Despite my grey mood, I turned to William to ask if he would come in. It was Friday night and the next two days were clear, the campaign staff on duty more than able to manage the few volunteer events we had scheduled during the weekend.

"You're not going to kick me out in the middle of the night again, are you?"

I thought back to the night of the robbery and about how different things were now. Our lives were linked, and by more than the copper bands he'd placed on my finger.

"Are you kidding me?" I said. "I may never let you leave."

CHAPTER 31

Aidan watched Olivia and William walk into the elevator. He waited until the doors closed before turning to speak with Elsa.

"Why do you think she doesn't show up in any of the videos of the robbery?" Elsa asked, simultaneously sending a text to summon Gabriel to join them. "We watched footage of every angle of the building, at the exact time she is supposed to be there, but she doesn't register in any of the images."

Aidan put his fingers to his lips to signal someone was coming. The door opened and Gabriel stepped into the room, followed by Madeline Kline. Their faces were grim; it couldn't be good news if their presence was required.

Everyone took as seat as Aidan began to speak.

"We have two pieces of information to report," Aidan said. "First, Olivia appears to have the ability to disappear, or at least *appear* to be invisible when she's hurt or when she experiences acute distress. We've reviewed several short videos of the robbery filmed by bystanders and there isn't a single image of Olivia outside the building at the time the car jumped the curb and smashed through the storefront."

Madeline grimaced. "That's absurd," she said. "She's human. It's impossible for a human to have such a gift. Maybe she'd already left the area when the video was taken." Her remark sent an almost imperceptible shudder through Aidan and Elsa. If someone in the room had been looking carefully for a response, it would have been seen as a telltale sign of a body reacting to a lie. But no one was watching, so it went unnoticed.

"Not exactly," said Elsa.

"What do you mean not exactly?" Madeline asked. "Either she's human, or she isn't. Can she be tracked with the homing device when she's invisible?"

"Yes, we did track her," Aidan said. "That's how, in addition to her own pleas for help, we knew she was in trouble after the robbery. We don't know if she actually was invisible to those around her—we have to assume she was—but it would explain why the thieves locked on to her mentally and tried to blind her instead of shooting her dead in the street."

And with that, a hush came over the room. Gabriel had remained silent all this time, his lips pinched shut. Aidan looked over at him, his eyebrows raised.

"Later," he said curtly. "What's your other piece of news?"

Aidan looked down at his hands for a moment before speaking. "Olivia recognized someone from the footage we cataloged of the robbery. She saw him pacing outside Nikola's office a few weeks ago, while she was waiting for you."

"*Merde*," Gabriel said. "She was certain?"

Elsa nodded. "Yes, quite. In fact she was prepared to go off herself and ask Nikola directly. Aidan stopped her."

"Those damned Serbs," Gabriel said. "The whole country is crawling with the undead, and they all love to fight in wars and steal jewels."

"Calm yourself, Gabriel, it's not only the Serbs," Aidan answered. "Much of eastern and central Europe is full of Others with criminal records that stretch back to the Balkan wars and beyond."

Gabriel wagged his finger at Aidan. "I have asked Nikola and Zoran to remember their responsibilities to this organization," he said. "They smile at me and then go and do whatever the hell they want. They couldn't care less if the human race perished tomorrow.

"Oh, I don't know about that," Madeline said. "Both Serbia and Croatia have applied to become members of the European Union. As head of the Croatian National Bank, Zoran must maintain some semblance of respectability and ensure stability in his country. Croatia's acceptance into the EU depends on it."

"I'm not sure Zoran even knows what's happening," Aidan said. "He's been in Brussels for weeks now in his capacity as head of the bank. It's possible Nikola is doing this all on his own."

"Alone, together or with one thousand of his comrades, it doesn't matter," Gabriel said. "There can be no connection between the Council and a band of jewel thieves."

"My friend," Aidan said, coming to place his arm on Gabriel's shoulder. "These thieves no doubt are all members of the Serbian Mafia. And half, if not all, of the mafia are Others, mostly werewolves and vampires that have survived for centuries, outliving the Nazis, Stalin, even Tito. Why would they care if their presence disturbs the Council?"

Gabriel stood up, a thin, brittle smile on his face. "I'm not a fool," he said. "I know they don't care. And I know that many of them have little regard for humans. But we must find out whether Nikola has compromised the Council and its operations to help a crime ring. Our organization has existed for centuries to help in subtle and not so subtle ways to ensure the survival of our kind. Acting as a home base to a ring of international jewelry thieves falls outside the parameters of our mission."

Elsa and the rest of the group wore pained expressions.

"Nikola is shrewd and ruthless. He will not like us looking into his affairs," she said.

"Then I shall have to do it with the utmost care," Aidan said. "The utmost care."

CHAPTER 32

"Wake up, sleepy head," William said, as he opened the shutters on the windows in my bedroom. It took me a few moments to remember where I was, thanks to my recent vagabond status. When I finally opened my eyes and focused, I found William standing over me, a steaming mug in his hands.

"You brought me espresso? Now I really am serious; you can never leave," I said, gratefully.

He was smiling, but said nothing as he handed me the cup. I sipped the coffee, savoring its warmth as I slowly awakened. Not long after, my stomach growled, reminding me that I was overdue to eat. It had been a late night and dinner had been an early affair—mainly snacks inside the Council as we watched the videos.

"I'm going downstairs for a bowl of cereal," I said. "Care to join me in the kitchen?"

William nodded and we descended to the kitchen. Once there, I quickly got the impression that there was something he wanted to talk about.

"What's on our agenda today?" I asked, pouring some shredded wheat into my bowl. "I can tell you have something in mind."

"As a matter of fact, I do," William said. "I'd like to take you to meet someone. He owns a school that teaches fencing and other forms of self-defense. Interested?"

The prospect of meeting a new person from William's world was intriguing. He was my lover and my confidant. But other than seeing his band mates, I knew very little about where he went, what he did or with whom, when we were separated. I was eager to change that and here was a chance to do so.

"I'm game," I said. "What should I wear?"

"Workout clothes would be a good idea," he said with a smile.

"What are we waiting for?" I said. "Let's go."

An hour after our conversation, we pulled up in front of a nondescript brick warehouse in a part of San Francisco known as Dogpatch, an eastern neighborhood near the waterfront. There was a small sign painted on the door of the building that read San Francisco School of Fencing, in large black cursive letters. William walked up to the door and knocked three times. A man opened the door, looked me over and then embraced William. They began to converse in a language I didn't recognize. I stood there awkwardly, wondering when I would be introduced. Finally, the two of them turned to face me.

"Olivia, this is my brother, Josef," he said. "Josef, this is Olivia."

A petite, wiry man with short black hair and intriguing dark eyes peered back at me. He looked nothing like William and then it dawned on me that he wasn't his brother by blood—at least not in the human sense.

"Your father," I said, knowing I didn't have to finish my sentence.

"Josef is Czech," William explained. "My father saved him from dying alone in a field after the Nazis had wounded him."

"I was a member of the Resistance," Josef said. "I was caught outside after curfew and chased into a field, where they shot me in the back, and left me for dead. William and his father had been waiting on the other side of the field to receive my message. That night, I left the human world, but I gained a brother."

"It's a pleasure to meet you," I said. "William, why didn't you tell me you had a brother?"

Josef threw an arm around William protectively. "Vampires are like onions, Olivia. It takes many peels of the layers before you know all of our secrets."

"I see," I said. "Are there any other brothers I should know about?"

William shook his head. "No, there were only the three of us, now just the two of us."

"William convinced me to move to San Francisco some years ago," Josef said. "The weather here is very agreeable. And I enjoy teaching people how to defend themselves."

Josef led us inside and shut the door. Following him, we walked down a short hallway that led to a large workout room. A few smaller offices lined the perimeter of the larger space. A set of lockers occupied one corner of the larger room, and in another corner, a dozen or more hooks were attached to the wall. Several fencing uniforms hung from the hooks, as well as a brown leather jacket and wool cap. A portable punching bag made of red and blue leather had been placed in the center of the room, but was designed to be rolled away when not in use.

While I was examining my surroundings, I heard the front door open again and a set of footsteps came down the hallway toward us. Within seconds I sensed it was Elsa. William met Elsa in the hallway and shook her hand.

"I asked her to come," he said, turning to face me. "I meant what I told you last night, darlin. If you want to pick fights with the likes of Nikola, then you need to be prepared to defend yourself. "

"What do you have in mind?" I asked, feeling a little uneasy. I'd never raised my hand against another person in my life. I wasn't sure I could.

"I want you to train with Josef," William said. "Elsa is here because I thought you would feel more comfortable doing the work with her."

Elsa tossed her gym bag down in the corner of the room. "This will be good," she said. "I need to brush up on my skills a bit, too. It's been ages since I had to engage in hand-to-hand combat."

"Hand-to-hand combat?" I repeated. "When did you do that?"

"I've been alive since the sixteenth century," she said. "There were times when I had to defend myself. Often I guarded my tribe while the men were off hunting. And then there is also the fact that time-walkers are not always welcome in villages when they appear...*suddenly*."

Josef, who had been standing slightly apart from us in the middle of the studio, was listening to our conversation. He rubbed his hands together and clapped twice. "A human and a time-walker," he said. "This should be interesting."

"Wait," I said. "Can you clarify what you mean by train?" I asked William.

"He means that you will come and work at my studio a few days a week until you are sufficiently ready," Josef said.

"Ready for what?" I asked, feeling yet again as if I was entering another phase of my life where I jumped in with both feet before looking.

"What you least expect, of course," he said. "What you least expect. Now please, let's get started. In my school, I teach a combination of fencing, Krav Maga and *savate*, or French kickboxing.

"Why fencing?" Elsa asked.

"For stamina and to build fast reflexes," Josef answered. "You have to be ready to defend yourself, and to be able to quickly get away from someone who attacks you. I will not teach you to pick a fight, but I will teach you how to end one."

As I watched William in the corner of the room, I felt a mixture of both anger and admiration. I knew what he was doing was necessary. I did have a taste to pick a fight with the Serbs who robbed the bank, and at the moment, chances were good that I would be injured if they or their minions came after me. But I didn't like surprises or mandates, and I felt as if I had been given both in the span of minutes: a brother I hadn't known existed, and an obligation to work with Josef. What would happen, I wondered, if I refused to undergo the training?

Reservations aside, I decided to give it a try. I was in good physical shape, thanks to Elsa. Surely I could at least hold my own for one afternoon.

Of course, I was mistaken.

We began to spar, jogging around one another. The first time Elsa took a swing at me, I fell down immediately. I simply had no will to hit back. My body rebelled against the very act; my arm felt as if it were pinned to my side. Fortunately, we were wearing a mountain of padding, so the only thing hurt so far was my pride.

"Come on. Attack, Olivia!" Josef said to me, and so I gave Elsa a slight push with my hands.

"Not good enough," he said. "Come on. William tells me you taunted Nikola Pajović. What prompted you to do that?"

"I didn't like his attitude," I said.

"Try to find that energy again. When Elsa comes forward to strike you, raise one arm to block her, and with the other palm, hit her with all your strength." We went through the exercise again and again, and though I always managed to block her, I didn't have the constitution to hit her.

After a few more unsuccessful bouts, Josef brushed Elsa away and leaned in next to me, his lips just inches from my ear.

"Where is your energy, your passion, Olivia?" he whispered. "Perhaps you have not been properly schooled in the ways of passion? You are human after all. Maybe you need someone other than my brother to teach you. Maybe another vampire, who won't be so gentle."

At the sound of his voice, my body betrayed me. My cheeks turned pink, and I felt my pulse quicken at his taunt. But his jeering worked. With one hand, I took a swing straight at him, my palm stiff and flat, and caught him hard across the face. With my other hand, I pushed against him, using all the force I could muster, causing him to take a step backwards. The slap made a loud noise, and my stomach lurched.

Josef, however, was thrilled. "Yes! You see, you found it...your anger," he said rubbing his cheek. "Don't lose it... Nikola is ruthless! If you want to hunt him, you will need to maintain that edge."

I looked over at William to gauge his reaction. He peeled himself off the wall and came over to me; putting both hands on my face as he pulled me toward him.

"Josef knows you are with me, Olivia."

"He goaded me into hitting him," I said, tears lurking at the corner of my eyes. "I don't want to do this. I don't want to fight."

William wiped a tear away with his thumb. "You can't have it both ways. You want to pursue Nikola. You want to work for Gabriel. No one wants to fight, Olivia, but when the time comes, you've got to be able to defend yourself," he said. "You asked me to accept your life, your work. The only way I will be able to relax is if I know Josef has taught you to take care of yourself."

Josef was standing in the corner, dark and brooding. I knew what he was thinking, because I felt it too. There was an attraction between us. I could feel his desire. As usual, my thoughts came through loud and clear.

"Vampires are competitive and covet what others have," William said, with a gentle laugh. "It's in our nature, though some of us can ignore our impulses. But you will be safe with Josef, he is my brother."

I didn't doubt William's sincerity, but I wasn't so sure about Josef, who at the moment, seemed to hold my fate in his hands.

"OK, I said, warily. "I will do the training."

From then on, training, reading and campaigning became the three activities that consumed my days. I rose at dawn to meet Josef at his studio—sometimes with Elsa, sometimes alone. Then, after ninety minutes of sparring, I would return home, shower and drive to Palo Alto. My days were filled with political luncheons, walking neighborhood shopping districts, visiting the editorial boards of newspapers and writing last-minute direct-mail pieces.

Flush with additional funds from generous donors, we created targeted direct mail to send to voters, along with radio and television commercials. In the last few days, I had been on location for hours as Levi was filmed taking walks with firefighters, police officers and small-business owners. Our field operations were relentless. We worked every angle, pressing to locate as many hidden pockets of voters as we could before the campaign came to a close.

I reported to the Council weekly, meeting Gabriel in the evenings at their offices to brief him and the rest of the team. He was pleased with the progress in our race, especially since many other campaigns across the country were faltering. It's a volatile time in U.S. politics, with the economy sluggish and so many people out of work in many parts of the nation. Incumbents of both political parties are facing tough races. For many, their only shortcoming is being the current office holder, but when mass-group dynamics take over in a race, it can be very difficult to win.

In the midst of this frenetic schedule, Elsa moved out, taking with her the few possessions she had from my guest room. She gave no explanation, but I didn't need one. It was obvious she and Aidan had become inseparable. After so many years of walking the planet alone, it was lovely to see that Elsa had found a mate. I didn't pretend to understand how her penance worked or how much time she had left to fulfill her debt, but I assumed she knew. Or perhaps she and Aidan were simply happy to enjoy the time they had together.

By comparison, my love life was tepid most of the time, thanks to the campaign. Periodically, William accompanied me to my appointments for the day, but he had his own businesses to attend to. He continued to perform with his band at night, though I wasn't often able to watch him play. JP and Halbert, meanwhile, kept their distance. I saw them both lurking together at a debate between Lacy and Levi sponsored by the San Jose Chamber of Commerce, but neither of them approached me. JP limited his stories to current campaign events and seemed to prefer to call my staff to obtain a schedule or request a quote.

When William wasn't spending the night, I would crawl into bed and pore through a stack of books I'd requested from the library. Lily, who delivered the books personally, would stay for a quick drink or meet me for dinner. She also was very busy at work, but we texted one another everyday, staying in touch as best we could.

When I was alone, I read for hours, reviewing the historical events leading up to the two world wars. It was both fascinating and frightening to see how the stage was set for World War II. Absorbed by the narratives of how world leaders had let Hitler get so far ahead of them, my curiosity kept me awake till dawn some nights. I read about the unbridled lust for power by Germany, the great ambivalence of other powers when Poland and Czechoslovakia were invaded; and then finally, the world's horror as France, too, was occupied and divided.

William and Josef were my connection to this history. Through my readings, I also began to understand why members of the Council seemed so deeply skeptical that society could manage its own affairs. The opportunity to upset the balance of power remains a constant, no matter the century. Even today, newspapers carry headlines of governments suspending constitutions or eliminating their judiciary. And too often the inexplicable fringe candidate surges suddenly to the forefront, running on a platform of paranoia and hatred.

And yet, as absorbed as I was with history, my training with Josef also became a source of fascination. William didn't always accompany me, leaving me to work without his scrutiny, and perhaps also so that I might ask questions to feed my inquisitiveness. I made the most of my time when we were alone. Josef was intensely handsome, more so than

William in some ways. Where one was fair, the other was swarthy. I had to remind myself that they were brothers through a vampire bond; two very different men bound to one another through a man, not a woman.

Unlike William, Josef was provocative, his motives complicated. I had no doubt of his loyalty to his brother, but I remembered what William said about "vampires coveting what the others have." When Josef took my body through its paces, knocking me to the ground, using his arms and legs to block me, lust was left hanging in the air. I would be lying if I didn't acknowledge some desire for him, too. I wondered if this, too, was a ploy by William to gauge the strength of my own fidelity.

Perhaps William had reason to test me. After a particularly intense sparring session, as we were catching our breath on the mats, I made the mistake of telling Josef that I could read him, that I could see his aura, and pick up on his emotions. William would have had a fit, reminding me to be more discreet. I don't know what caused me to push the limits like that. But when I did, Josef fixed on me the fiercest of gazes.

"Do not let other vampires know," he admonished me. "We are a private sort, and do not like to be so transparent to others."

He stared intently, his dark-brown eyes scrutinizing me. "It is curious that you can read vampires. Humans don't usually have the skills. It is no wonder William wants you to be able to defend yourself."

"Why didn't William mention you right away?"

"If you know a vampire's family, you know where they sleep," he said. "We protect our privacy."

"So the fact that William introduced us is significant." It was half question, half statement.

Josef eyed me warily. "Yes, but please don't ask me if he *really* loves you," he said in a mocking tone. "Vampires are not like a grade-school crush. My brother has survived close to two hundred years by limiting his exposure to humans.

If he has brought you to see me, it's because he has found his mate. He trusts you with his survival."

"Apparently, he entrusts *my survival to you*," was my comeback with a twist. I shot my right foot in the air to try to knock him down and my timing was right. Josef was too distracted by my comment to move out of the way and I managed to get him partially to the floor.

"Very good, sister," he said.

"Sister," I repeated, continuing to spar. "Don't I have to be married to William, to become your sister?"

"You are as good as married to William now," Josef said. "He has left you alone with me for days…if he hadn't made it clear you were his mate, I would have taken you for myself. Immediately."

Ever so briefly, an image popped into mind. I shook it away, ashamed that I had entertained it at all, but Josef caught a whiff of what my imagination evoked. He sensed my slip and let out a loud laugh as he knocked me to the ground. He came down to the floor, hovering directly over me.

"Olivia, I believe you have a bit of vampire in you," he said. "*Now* who is coveting what she may not have?"

I laid still for a minute, feeling the outline of his body on mine. He smelled of cinnamon and cumin, like some exotic spice out of the East. I suppose I was testing his mettle as much as my own, but I could sense he was merely playing with me. He had no intention of betraying his brother. We both stayed silent apart from the sound of my deep breathing, and then I pushed him aside and got up to leave the studio.

"*Au revoir, mon frère.*"

"*A bientôt,*" he said, with a mock salute. "I will see you again, yes, and soon."

Twenty minutes later, as I walked into my house, I heard the phone ringing. The caller ID told me it was my mother. I hesitated to pick up, cognizant of being only intermittently in touch these last few weeks. I hadn't been avoiding her exactly, but there were so many events, so many revelations, that I wasn't feeling up to telling her everything. Learning of my injuries from the robbery alone would have been enough to send her over the edge.

She sounded happy when I answered, though I gave off the vibe that I was very much on the move yet again. "Are you coming or going? Do you have a minute to speak?"

"I'm just walking in from working out," I said, "What's up?"

"My trip to Paris is coming up," she said. "I'm leaving in two days. I think I may have mentioned that I was invited to show my paintings at the Left Bank gallery. It's down the way from the Musée d'Orsay on the Quai Malaquais."

"Two days?" I said. "Is someone already in Paris helping set up?"

"Yes, darling, you know me well enough to know I would never agree to an exhibition on such short notice. I chose the paintings weeks ago and an assistant flew ahead to get started. The show doesn't actually begin for two more weeks, but I would like some time with my work to decide its final arrangement."

I was happy for her. Paris was her refuge, a place she felt welcome and safe. The customs of the French and their rituals were second nature, and I knew she would spend the next few months at peace.

"Wonderful, I am so thrilled for you," I said, wanting to emphasize how I felt as she was heading out of the country.

"You sound good too," she said.

"I am," I said. "The campaign is keeping me very busy, but I'm enjoying myself. Gabriel is very pleased with how things are going. I will have to mention your show. He keeps an apartment in Paris; perhaps he will get a chance to see it after the election is over."

I felt a deep pang of alarm from my mother across the phone line. "Mom, what is it?"

"Olivia, how old is Gabriel?" she asked. "What does he look like?"

"I don't know, I'm terrible at guessing, but I would say he is in his mid-fifties," I said, amused. "He has salt-and-pepper gray hair, dresses like a Frenchman and has an obsession with ordering everyone's food and wine for them. Why?"

"I'm curious about this man who has so changed your life," she said, trying to mask her anxiety. "I've been meaning to ask you more about him, but it never came up." The worry she had so clearly transmitted was gone, but I sensed she was still concerned about something.

"You needn't worry, Mom. He has given me the freedom to do great things."

"I'm your mother. It's my job to worry, and to lobby. Would you consider coming to Paris when your work allows? It would be nice to spend a few days with you."

I thought about for it moment and knew that it was the perfect place to escape to with William when the campaign was finished. "Sure, I'd love to come," I said. "Let me look at my schedule and I will call you when I figure out the dates."

"Will you be coming alone?" my mother asked, the tinge of concern back in her voice.

"No," I said. "I will probably bring a friend."

"OK. I've taken a suite at the Ritz. Extravagant, I know, but at my age I need the pampering. There will be an extra room for you if you want it."

"*Merci, maman, je t'aime.*"

"Love you too," she said.

After the conversation, I began to daydream about walking the streets of Paris with William. It was romantic and thrilling—except the part where I explained to my mother that I have a vampire for a companion. I wasn't sure how much she would pick up, or how much I should tell her. I needed to discuss the situation with William and see what he wanted to do. Meanwhile, my conversation had thrown me off schedule, leaving me little time to clean up. I raced upstairs, excited at the prospect of Paris in the autumn, strolling carefree through the city's magnificent *arrondissements*.

CHAPTER 33

Election Day is always a strange day for campaign consultants. After weeks and weeks of nonstop work, there is nothing to do now but wait. When a race is in play, it can feel like the longest day of the year. The polls in California don't close until 8 pm and the results don't begin to trickle in until an hour or so later. That means that from the minute I wake up, and then for another ten hours or more, I have to find a way to occupy myself, hoping that in the end, all of my hard work pays off. Every consultant has a different way of coping. I know some who arrange long, extravagant lunches with friends. Others go into the office and busy themselves with other projects. For me, it's a rare day to get in plenty of exercise.

On this Election Day I got up early, as I had for the last several weeks. But instead of heading to Josef's studio, I had another idea in mind as I stared at William in my bed. With a little prodding, he agreed to join me for a run in Golden Gate Park.

"Let's run to the beach and back," I said, as we stretched at dawn on the sidewalk in front of the house.

We jogged through the Music Concourse, its rows of sycamores fading with autumn. A dozen Chinese senior citizens were doing their *tai chi* exercises, accompanied by traditional music coming from an old cassette player. We passed the de Young and then quickly turned behind the museum and headed west toward Ocean Beach. I looked up at the now-empty floors of the tower, where we normally met with our colleagues. Still dark outside, the copper skin of the building was illuminated by the white glow of interior office lights, giving the building an odd, artificial color.

"It's amazing to realize this building leads two lives," I said as we jogged past.

"Sort of like you," William said.

"I guess so," I said. "All of us, really."

"A necessary evil," he said. "Because in this case, the truth is more complicated than the fiction."

As we continued to run, I picked up on the distinctive caw of a raven somewhere behind us. I stopped for a moment to stretch and casually turned toward the noise, and there atop a streetlight was a trio of the black birds. William, who'd run a few paces ahead of me, realized I'd stopped and circled back.

"Why'd you stop?"

"I was distracted by the ravens," I said, pointing. "I've never known them to be so bold, so early in the morning."

He eyed the enormous creatures with disdain.

"Get out of here, you three!" he said, facing in their direction. "Tell your master you've been discovered."

The ravens didn't move, nor did they make another sound either. We were locked in a staring contest, making me feel like a character in a Hitchcock film.

"They can understand you?" I asked quietly under my breath.

"I'm guessing," he said, never taking his eyes off the trio. "You said it yourself, these birds are normally not this active so early in the morning. I think they're spies, shape-shifters that report to someone, perhaps Nikola."

"That's odd. I don't sense anything. How can you be sure?"

"I can't," he said. "All I have is my instinct, but their presence is odd."

"Let's ignore them," I said. "You might be right, but what can they tell him anyway?"

"OK," William said. "But don't say anything you don't want him to hear."

"You mean Nikola?"

William nodded.

"Oh, but I should like to send him a message," I said.

"That's exactly what I was afraid of," he said. "Say nothing, love. Let him know nothing of what you're thinking."

Reluctantly, I agreed.

"Come on," I said, turning my back on the birds. "I feel like going over to Strawberry Hill instead of the beach. We can run up the hill and look out at the Golden Gate."

A few minutes later we turned onto the access road that climbs up to Stow Lake, and followed the pavement until we reached the opening for the trails that lead to the top of the hill. Morning was in full swing for the creatures of the lake, the ducks and geese quacking and honking, waddling back and forth as they searched for their morning meals. Small pink crayfish were crawling out of the muck onto the grass, creeping slowly toward a point unknown. I marveled at the activity as we slowly zigzagged up the dirt path, climbing up the hill, the city panorama coming into view. Our climb finished, I paused with my hands on my knees to catch my breath. I looked around for the gathering of fallen tree trunks we'd first sat on months ago after the bluegrass festival and pointed them out to William.

"Do you remember when we sat on those logs?" I asked. "I told you my story and then you disappeared."

"That's not exactly how I remember it," he said.

"How do you remember it?"

"I kissed you," he said. "I kissed you, and then I disappeared."

"That's right," I said. "I was so disappointed. When I opened my eyes you were gone."

"I was disappointed, too, darlin," he said. "But I thought it better to leave."

"Did you know I would find you?"

"I hoped you would try."

"I didn't know what I was doing," I said, surprised at my

admission. "I mean, I wanted you so badly, but I didn't realize…"

"I know," he said. "That is why I decided to leave that day."

"And now?"

"Now," he said, pulling me into his arms. "Now I know that you *know* exactly what I'm thinking."

What he was thinking is that he wanted to kiss, so I obliged, several times over. And this time, when I opened my eyes, he was still there, right by my side. The moment wasn't lost on me and I decided to make my long-term intentions clear by mentioning Paris.

"My mother has invited me to visit her in Paris," I said. "She has an exhibition there. I told her I would come for a few days to visit after the election. I thought maybe we would go together."

"You want me to meet your mother?" he asked.

"Isn't that normally what people do before they get married?" I asked, hoping my proposal would make him happy. "But I need some help. What should we tell her? Will she be able to sense you're a vampire…the way I can?"

"I'm not sure," he said. "We'll have to see when we get there. I have an apartment in Paris, the one my father bought before the war. It's near the Canal St. Martin. We can stay there."

"You still own an apartment in Paris…from the war?" I asked.

William nodded. "After we're married, I'll tell you more about our holdings. We've been very fortunate over the years."

"Can we have a ceremony?" I asked.

"If you can live with a judge instead of a priest, then yes," he said. "We can have a ceremony in Paris if you like, or wait until we're back home."

I was already imagining a small café on the Left Bank, or maybe inside the Hôtel de Ville, City Hall. And then by chance I got to the part in my daydream where they say "till death do you part," and I caught myself wondering what life will be like watching myself grow old, when he would not.

"I can hear your thoughts. Don't worry about that now. We have many years together before that is an issue. Let's enjoy our fortune in finding each other. Even human couples have no guarantee that they will grow old together, Olivia."

"You're right," I said, taking his hand in mind. "Let's take it one day at a time."

We jogged back through the park and returned home, no ravens in sight. By the time we showered and changed, it was time for me to leave for Palo Alto. William said goodbye, promising to meet me at the campaign offices later in the evening. We would monitor things for a while from there, and then move to a restaurant nearby that Levi had rented for the evening.

After I arrived at the office, I passed the last few hours until the polls closed packing up boxes of confidential documents and organizing the equipment and other supplies we'd rented so they could be returned.

By 7 pm I was ready to check in with the local news outlets and see what they had to say about election results. I managed to stay calm most of the day, reminding myself that our own internal polling had shown Levi ahead in the race by a solid ten points for several weeks. The numbers for undecided voters, however had not moved, making it possible we could still lose the race if those votes went to Lacy.

Levi had texted me earlier, letting me know he would see me at the bistro at 8 pm. I didn't see any reason for him to arrive sooner. Gabriel was also coming around that time, and I suspected William, Lily and perhaps even Josef would follow. At the last minute, I'd sent Josef a text inviting him to the dinner, figuring I should include my future brother-in-law in our plans.

Just as I turned on the local news a reporter began discussing the station's process of exit polling. It is *possible* to predict the outcome of a race using exit polling, although not always. Exit polls, they said, showed Levi Barnes as the winner. I could only hope they were right, I mused, as I tried to stay busy for the final hour of voting.

At 8 pm we all assembled and indulged in a light dinner and plenty of wine as the first results arrived. Each update revealed a slight lead, until finally at 10 pm, with most of the precincts reporting, Levi had jumped twelve points ahead. It was astonishing, a better win than we could have hoped for.

As we were regarding the computer screen, watching the Department of Elections update the results, my phone vibrated in my pocket. I pulled it out to glance at the caller ID, curious since most members of the press and campaign team were already standing within a few feet of me. The number was blocked, but I answered anyway, putting the phone to my ear to say hello.

"Are you going to claim the seat?" said a voice that was familiar for its unique salty brusqueness. Paul Levant, head of the California Democratic Party, went straight to the question, skipping any greeting, as usual.

"I'm thinking about it," I said. Claiming the seat meant having us declare ourselves the winner...before Lacy had conceded losing. It was a bold statement.

"*Christ Almighty,* you've got it in the bag, kid," Levant said. "Our own number-crunchers are calling you the winner, with fifteen points to spare."

"Shit, really?" I was dumfounded. Fifteen points was a hugely comfortable margin. It afforded a candidate the kind of maneuvering room that freed him from having to glance over his shoulder at the opposition too often. Candidates who win by two points can never say their ideas have a mandate. But win by fifteen points, and the world is yours.

"There are still a few precincts outstanding," I told Levant, unable to overcome my superstitious nature.

"Suit yourself, kid," he said. "But I am telling you Levi Barnes will shortly be Congressman Barnes. I'll expect a sizable donation from him to the party *toot sweet!*" The line went dead, his words ringing in my ears, my pulse in my throat.

"Who was that?" Levi asked.

"It was Levant," I said. "He says the seat is ours by a margin of fifteen points, and we should call the race." Silence followed as everyone looked up at the television above the bar, which was now, in fact, posting election results confirming our fifteen-point lead, with two precincts left to report.

Victory chants cropped up around the restaurant. "Levi! Levi! Levi!"

"OK, let's call it," I yelled over the din. I hugged Levi, "Congratulations, Congressman Barnes, I think you should address your supporters."

Levi smiled and embraced me tightly. "Amazing. Amazing work, Olivia," he said. "The way you took control and stayed calm. I've never seen anyone with better instincts and courage. Thank you."

"My pleasure," I said, smiling. "It's easy to run a race for someone like you. Promise me you'll call when it's time for re-election."

"Aren't you coming back to Washington with me?" Levi looked puzzled.

"No, not this time. I hope you'll take Maggie and Peter with you; they will make great legislative aides."

Levi squeezed my hand. "You're not the same person anymore," he said. "There is something, a certainty in you that didn't exist before."

"I suppose I know more about what I want now. Perhaps with not so much certainty, but confidence in my own decisions," I said, "which is really about growing older and knowing oneself."

"Ah, but they are all *cousins*," said Gabriel, who had come up behind us while we were talking. "You cannot be certain without confidence."

Richard Lyon was with him. They both urged Levi toward the front of the room to give his victory speech. I nodded in agreement and promised to follow in a moment. As they departed, I stopped and exhaled deeply, releasing much of the pent up stress and anxiety I had been harboring for weeks. It was over. We'd won. A weight that had been pressing on my chest lifted and a feeling of lightness returned to my body. I was about to turn and make my way to the front when an arm wrapped around my waist holding me in place. It was William.

"Well done, darlin," he said, pulling me to his side. "Now that you're officially unemployed, can we kiss in public?"

"Yes, definitely," I said.

We did, quickly, and then walked forward to the main area of the bistro's dining room in time to watch Levi climbing onto a chair to speak to the crowd. I glanced over at Patrick, giving him a nod to grab a glass and a piece of silverware to signal to the crowd to quiet down. After a few whistles and clinks on a beer mug, everyone fell silent and looked toward Levi as he stood above them. Flush and happy, his blue oxford shirt rolled up at his sleeves, here was the newest member of Congress from the great state of California, alone, with no entourage, no driver, not even a microphone. Remember this moment, I silently urged Levi; as a consultant I knew it was fleeting, irreplaceable.

"We did it," he said to a sea of cheers. "Can you believe it? We won by fifteen points! I'm not prepared to say much more except that I want to thank all of you, my supporters, for believing in me. I want to thank the voters who made me their choice; I promise to work hard on your behalf. Finally, I want to tip my hat to Lacy…"

A chorus of boos rang out from the crowd.

"Now, now," Levi admonished his supporters, but with a smile. "I do want to thank Lacy Smith. I may not agree with her on just about *anything*, but I respect her for raising the issues."

More applause. More cheers.

I smiled, squeezing William's hand. When you're a

winner on election night, *anything* seems possible. Fly to the moon? Sure. Balance the budget? Immediately! It's like getting into your new car at the dealership and driving off into a brilliant orange sunset. Tonight, at this moment, these people were ready to follow Levi on a great journey. Would they feel the same way in sixty or one hundred days? Who knew? And that is the essence of politics. I really hoped Levi would enjoy the evening, because tomorrow the real work would begin.

After speaking, Levi stepped off the chair and disappeared into a crowd of well-wishers. Champagne corks were popping, the volume on the music rose and the group prepared to party into the night. It was, after all, officially a victory party and in politics, there is no better place to be.

My thoughts drifted to Lacy and whether she would concede. I wondered too, if Halbert would have the courage to dial my number. My answer came across a television screen, as a tearful Lacy climbed the stage at her campaign party and spoke into a microphone to say she "had called Levi Barnes to congratulate him."

"This was not our moment," she said, tears streaming down her cheeks, her mascara following in streaks. "God works in mysterious ways and I'm sure he has a purpose for us beyond tonight's defeat. This is not the end. We will continue to fight for the things we believe in."

I closed my eyes for a moment, savoring her words. I had no doubt she would live to fight another day, but for now, she was no longer my concern, nor were her advisers. Still, I wondered where Halbert was, knowing he would be furious at his loss. When I opened I eyes, I noticed reporters entering the restaurant. My job was to lead each one of them to Levi for an interview. I made sure he gave them each a quote, but I wouldn't let him speculate about what he would do next. For now, it was enough to declare victory and thank his supporters.

I sent word through William to ask Richard Lyon to stay in the back of the room while the press was around. I couldn't ask the man who'd raised hundreds of thousands of dollars for the campaign to leave, but I felt no compunction at asking him to make himself scarce for a few moments.

Levi seemed about finished with his interviews when I realized there was one major player missing from the room. JP had not been in the building all night. It didn't seem possible that the valley's biggest online journalist would skip the party, but I knew better than to assume anything. His relationship with Halbert had been a revelation, one that had taught me to assume nothing.

Finally, about a half hour after most of his colleagues had departed, JP appeared in the doorway. He looked timid, as if he expected to be stoned by the crowd. If anyone had been sober enough to care, there might have been trouble. In general, drunken winners are a magnanimous group, and JP was able to walk inside unscathed. I stood still, waiting for him to notice me. When he caught my eye, I waved him over.

I began by giving him my most professional greeting, a gracious winner's smile. "Would you like some time with the congressman?" He nodded, a notebook and pen clasped in his hands. "Will you be videotaping this?" I added, unable to resist.

"Yes" he said tersely. "But…"

"This is on the record?"

"Yes," he said. "Exactly."

"That's certainly a much better way to do things," I said, my heart not really much into scolding him further.

I caught sight of Patrick from across the room and signaled that he should join us. Since the two men knew each other, I didn't make introductions. Instead, I simply asked him to find a quiet place where Levi and JP could do an interview. As they were leaving, I pulled Patrick aside and whispered in his ear to keep the interview short and not to allow any questions about the fundraiser that was the scene of the controversial recording.

"If he dredges up the past even for a second," I said, "stop the interview."

Patrick nodded and escorted JP out of the main dining room.

"That was very magnanimous of you," William said, coming to stand beside me again. "You could have been much harder on him."

"I haven't any energy left to be that petty. I could sense his shame the minute he walked in, and besides, he doesn't know it, but I already promised an exclusive interview to a rival publication when Levi arrives in Washington. JP will be furious, but it will make us even as far as I'm concerned."

I closed my eyes again, this time feeling weary as I thought back to JP's video and the damage it had caused.

"Let me take you home, love," William said, pulling me close. "You look exhausted."

I was completely spent, and serious fatigue was creeping into the corners of my body now that the adrenaline had finally receded.

"Let me say goodbye and then we can leave," I agreed, making my way through the crowd. On my way out, I promised to meet Gabriel and our small inner circle for dinner the following evening. I scanned the room, waving to a few acquaintances and noted with pleasure that Josef and Lily were out on the dance floor, dancing cheek to cheek.

"Does he know she is a fairy?" I asked William as we were leaving.

"Yes," he said. "Everything is always more complicated when you mix species, but they'll be fine. They both live very openly in the human world, so it probably gives them something in common."

"Is he giving her a lift home?"

"Don't worry, darlin," William said. "All of your baby chicks will get back to the nest safely."

"I'm a worrier, I know," I said, smiling. "I'll stand down for the evening."

As we departed, I turned back, savoring the image of celebration. Victory was finally mine again. I had overcome my demons, helped a good man win a seat in the United

States Congress, and I had recovered my sense of identity along the way. I leaned into William, as I peered through the glass, enjoying the sensation of a partner at my side.

"Not a bad day's work, darlin," William said. "What's next? The Senate? Maybe the presidency?"

"For now…Paris," I said, feeling content. "I've been thinking about places we should visit," I continued. "Maybe we can take a trip to Normandy, see the coastline. I'd like to visit the memorials and maybe visit your father's grave."

I continued rattling off potential destinations, blissfully unaware that Stoner Halbert was approaching. It was only when William gave my hand a painful squeeze and I looked up to chide him, that I noticed the teetering figure coming toward us. Halbert was drunk, almost to the point of incapacitation. Fifteen points is a bitter loss to swallow, especially when you're supposed to have the advantage. William made a noise next to me that sounded almost like a growl.

"Halbert," I said. "What brings you here? Did you come to congratulate me?"

"You would like that, wouldn't you," he slurred. "Shall I get down on my knees and tell you how magnificent you are? You're all the same—not happy until the man has been ruined and humiliated."

"I think you have the wrong person," William said. "Olivia has never done a thing to you."

"She's never done a thing for me," he said, almost incoherently.

"Halbert, what is this about? First you steal my clients, then you try to ruin my reputation as a consultant, and now you're here to what…hurl insults at me? You need to call a cab and go home. It's one election, sleep it off and get a life."

"You made an ass out of me," he said, coming to stand directly in front of me. "Lacy threw me out of her campaign office."

"No," I said, shaking my head. "You did that all by yourself. Now go home."

Halbert swayed back and forth, clearly trying to formulate a response, but no words escaped his lips.

Finally, after a few awkward seconds, I turned my back on Halbert, grabbed William's hand and walked away.

For a moment, I felt sorry for him. The pain and disappointment of his life hung about him like a cloak. It permeated the air, giving him a rank and bitter scent. This, I mused, was an example of human betrayal left festering, and I felt some compassion for the man whose life had been so disturbed by his wife's ambitions and dishonesty.

And yet, everything that transpired from that moment on had been his choice. He chose to align himself with the darkest of paths, but had no better angel to come to his aide. Now, he was left with nothing but his own reproach, a reprobate saddled with a growing paranoia that all women were out to humiliate him. Even if he won his next campaign, or the next, I doubted he'd ever find happiness again. Halbert seemed either incapable or unwilling to move, so we left him standing alone on the sidewalk, backlit by the halogen glow of a streetlight.

"I doubt you'll ever see him again," William said, as he unlocked my car door.

"You never know," I said earnestly. "Fate is a funny thing, and the world of political consultants is so small."

CHAPTER 34

William heard the front door open and listened as Josef climbed the stairs to the second floor. It was early evening and they were both expected at the post-election dinner at The Moss Room in one hour. Gabriel had arranged for a celebration, a private meal for the Council and associates. He'd extended an invitation to Josef as a courtesy for his work with Olivia. But William would have recognized his brother's presence on the stairs regardless of the time, or a pending social obligation. Thanks to their father, whose blood coursed through their veins, he could feel Josef's proximity deep in his bones.

"You built her a bed?" Josef asked, as he strolled into the room. "By God, you are besotted. Are you sure it's worth it? She is human, after all."

William stayed seated in his chair, a guitar in his hands, his fingers slowly picking a tune as he regarded his brother.

"Don't be so provocative. You had a human lover for years, Josef," he remarked. "Why so dismissive now? Unless of course, you would like Olivia for yourself?"

Josef laughed, picking up another guitar from a stand nearby. "I prefer fairies, it turns out," he said. "They're delicious. By the way, your work is flawless. This guitar is magnificent."

"Thank you," William said. "Can we get back to Olivia?"

"You know, for a vampire, you worry too much," Josef said, pulling the soundtrack to the movie *Cabaret,* off the shelf. "Mind if I put this on?" Josef asked. "I'm in the mood."

William nodded as Josef set the vinyl album on the turntable.

"I'll admit she has a certain allure," Josef continued, "but I have not laid a finger on her, except to train. For a woman, she has incredible endurance, far more than I would expect from a human. I will admit there is something about that, that is alluring."

William set his guitar down against the chair and stood up to face his brother. "You don't have to tell me," he said. "I remember the first moment I sensed her. She is captivating in a way that escapes her notice. But I brought her to you because I wanted someone to teach her to fight for her life, if it comes down to it. Can I trust you?"

Josef bared his teeth and hissed. "You must truly be in love if you would question my loyalty after all that we have been through."

"I intend to make her my wife, Josef. I'm counting on you to help me protect her."

Josef carefully positioned the tone arm of the turntable onto the record and "Mein Herr" began to play. "Why are you so certain she is in danger? I mean no disrespect, but she's a human female, after all, why would an ancient vampire like Nikola care about her?"

William walked over to a small side table where a bottle of Jack Daniel's and two tumblers rested on a tray. He grabbed the bottle, poured two fingers' worth in the glasses and handed one to his brother.

"Several reasons," he said. "One, she is an agent of the Council aligned with Gabriel Laurent. That alone makes her vulnerable, since Nikola has little love for the Westerners and their zeal to help humans. He could harm her just to strike at Gabriel. Laurent's term is ending. Nikola is deputy to Zoran Mikić, a Croatian central banker who is too much of a bureaucrat to really sense what is going on around him. Aidan told me the two of them are to be installed as directors next year.

"Reason No. 2, and more importantly, I don't think she is human, or at least I don't think she is one hundred percent human."

Josef raised his eyebrows as he took a sip of the whisky.

"Come on, I know you sense it too," William said. "She's mildly telepathic, a skill few humans possess. And she can read vampires, something a normal empath woman shouldn't be able to do."

Josef downed what was left in his glass and poured another.

"She told me," he said. "She told me she could read my thoughts."

"I see," William said grimly. "And what did you say in reply?"

"I told her to never let another vampire know she could do such a thing."

"You must see what I mean. She possesses skills that don't belong to a human and that is bound to attract the wrong sort of attention," William said. "Olivia is curious, outspoken and above all, determined. It's inevitable that she will run into trouble."

Josef snorted into his glass. "I can understand why you had to have her," he said. "Must be a delightful change of pace from your monkish existence these last few years. Still, I am surprised you would choose to step back into the Council's affairs. You were determined to leave humans to their own devices."

"Yes, I was. And like all men, I was drawn back in because of a woman."

"Understood," Josef said, refilling their glasses. "But there is one thing I don't understand. Just what do you suspect she is, if she isn't altogether human? Witch? Fairy?"

"Possibly," William said thoughtfully. "I expect we'll learn the truth very soon."

CHAPTER 35

I woke up early the day after the election and decided to do nothing for the first few hours. I didn't meet Josef at the studio. I didn't read my email, or make any telephone calls. Instead I went downstairs in search of William, who had spent the night. I managed to lure him away from a copy of E.E. Cumming's poetry and into the shower, then back to my bed for several hours of lovemaking. Afterwards he left me lying in bed, returning a few minutes later with a cappuccino. The morning left me deeply satisfied. My body felt spent, worn out by my lover. My house felt like a home, the aroma of warm espresso and sex filling the air.

Of course, given my habit of worrying, I immediately began to wonder what would happen after we married. I didn't want to leave my little house, but I was inclined to let my vampire husband stay in his home, which was better designed for his survival. Perhaps we would rent mine and keep it in the family until we could find a use for it. I had no idea where Josef slept; I suspected it might be inside his school. Perhaps he would enjoy living here. There would be no children to inherit my home—not unless a miracle of science occurred.

It seemed best not to dwell on those kinds of details. There was no assurance I would have either longevity or a child with a human man, so I counted my blessings for having found someone to love, someone who returned my feelings, for that, too, was not something anyone could be assured of in this world.

I said goodbye to William around noon and went directly upstairs to throw on my workout gear and take a leisurely run to Ocean Beach. At the shoreline, I lingered briefly despite the cold to stretch under a clear, blue sky.

When I returned home, I returned the phone calls and emails that had been pilling up all day. I spoke with Levi several times, helping tie up loose ends and organize next steps. Patrick and Maggie were his staff members now, and I was eager to give them some responsibility to help arrange his move to Congress.

Fortunately, Levi had been a member of the House of Representatives once already, so his transition was not as disorganized as it might have been for a genuine freshman. When I hung up the phone for the last time early that evening, I felt confident that things would go smoothly.

My work concluded, I drew a bath and gave myself a facial, listening to a new playlist I'd made on my iPod. Without the pressures of a campaign, I was free to indulge in the little rituals that women enjoy, scrubbing and buffing until the skin on my body felt smooth and taut. Slowly, I began to feel human again. I dressed, pulling on a pair of wool capris along with a sequined tank top and leopard-print ballet flats. To stay warm, I planned to wear a wool pea coat over my clothing for the walk to The Moss Room, where Gabriel had arranged for our celebration.

Lily showed up at my house at 6 pm, about an hour before we had to leave for the victory party. She walked through the door wearing a similar outfit, but her pants were wide-legged and silk, a fitting style for a woman of her height. She sailed into my living room all smiles and it didn't take much for me to guess why she felt elated.

"Watch out, I think he bites," I said, needing no further explanation.

"Nothing I can't manage," Lily said confidently.

I opened a delicious bottle of white Bordeaux I'd picked up at a wine store nearby and poured us each a glass, hoping to talk to Lily about something that had been on my mind.

'What is it?" she asked, noticing I'd grown quiet.

"We spend so much time talking about the Council and William, but we never really talk about you."

"Me? You did ask about me the night I met Elsa," she said.

"I didn't really ask," I said. "I made some flip remarks."

Lily smiled. "Don't be too hard on yourself. You were given quite a shock that night."

"Yes," I said, nodding in agreement. "At that moment, all I could think was that everything I thought I knew was false. That maybe you'd never been my friend, not in the way I'd imagined."

"And now?"

"I guess I'm just curious about your life. Are you my age or older? Do you like being a fairy? Are you happy?"

Lily grabbed my hand and held it. "Things get confusing when you live in the world of Others," she said. "Let me put your mind at ease."

"No, don't you see? That is what I want to do. I want to put *your* mind at ease. Let me make you happy. Let me do you a favor, or find you a book that you would like to read."

Lily's eyes grew wide. "Are you worried that I'm unhappy?"

"I'm worried I don't really know anything about your feelings. I have been too preoccupied with my own saga to ask, and you never seem to offer up a single complaint or regret that would distract me from my own woes."

"Fairies don't complain," she said. "We do not live our lives in a state of expectation. We don't experience disappointment, at least not the way humans do. But since you asked, let me try to answer your questions."

"I am aging at roughly the same pace as you," she continued. "If I'm lucky, I will live to be about one hundred and fifty years old, which means I will start to show signs of aging a little later that most human females. In my heart, I feel like I am living the same life as you, that of a thirty-something woman. Fairies can have babies, just like humans.

We carry them for about ten months, give or take."

"As for happiness, that's more difficult to answer. Fairies are born to a purpose: service to others. We don't wonder what to do when we grow up. We don't rebel against our parents and ask for a different occupation. It's just not in our DNA. We were born to help move the world forward. Some fairies help the salmon move upstream, others remind bears when to hibernate. Others are police officers or librarians. We are a part of the fabric of nature, a critical piece of the framework of humanity."

"Fairies remind bears to hibernate," I repeated, inexplicably fixated on that detail.

"They are very absent-minded creatures," she said.

"Are there fairies on the Council?" I asked.

"There might have been a few over the years, but it's probably a rare occurrence. We help people regardless. Our work comes with no political purpose or ideology attached."

"Is our friendship out of duty or ..." I wanted to say love, but I was too nervous to give what I felt a name.

"Maybe it's out of character for a fairy to be friends with a human, but what we have is real," Lily said. "You're not a project, you're my friend. My best friend."

I let out a breath I didn't know I was holding. Feeling confident, I decided to broach my engagement.

"I'm hoping to leave for Paris in a few days," I said casually. "My mother is having a show and invited me to come and visit. I'm bringing William to meet her."

Lily smiled wistfully. "I would love to come to Paris in the winter; it's so romantic," she said. "Maybe I should take some vacation days and join you."

"I wish you would," I said. "It will make it easier for you to be my maid of honor at my wedding."

"Oh, my," Lily said. "Married. Olivia, that is a big commitment."

It wasn't the kind of ringing endorsement you normally get from your best friend hearing such news, but I wasn't surprised. I hadn't said I was marrying a pediatrician I'd been dating for three years. This was William, a vampire, a man I'd known for only a few months.

"I can sense you're worried, maybe even a little surprised."

"Both," she confirmed. "I'm happy for you. Your life was bound to be unconventional once you started work for the Council. But I'm concerned about what happens if you want out of this relationship."

"Are you saying vampires don't grant divorces?"

"That is exactly what I am saying," Lily said.

"I doubt a piece of paper from a judge would make a difference anyway," I said. "As far as William is concerned, we are already a couple permanently. The ceremony is a formality for me."

Lily ran her finger over the rim of her wine glass, averting her eyes for a moment. She was anxious to ask me something.

"Has he asked you to drink his blood?"

"No," I said, shaking my head. "He hasn't really drank from me either...there were a few nips at Hearst Castle, but since then nothing. I had been hoping..."

"Olivia, you *want* to drink his blood?" Lily asked, incredulous. "Once you do that it will be impossible to separate from him. He's already tasted you; you will carry his blood in your veins. You will be linked together and able to *feel* one another's emotions, share thoughts. It is an ancient kind of magic that should not be entered into lightly."

This was the second time in recent weeks that it was made clear to me that reading a vampire's thoughts was not only a skill unheard of in humans, it was also frowned upon. I wondered what Lily would do if I told her the extent of my abilities, and then quickly I ruled out doing so. Keeping my own counsel was becoming ever more important. As much as I wanted to confide everything to her, I knew now that some things were better left unsaid.

"I didn't say I wanted to," I said sheepishly. "But I am curious. When we're together, I feel this overwhelming hunger to taste him. We both do, and I would be lying if I didn't wonder what it would be like."

"If I were you, I would put off making such a decision until you've spent more time with him," Lily said. "There's no rush."

True, I thought to myself, uninterested in drawing out such unhappy issues. Then I maneuvered the conversation back to more pleasant topics, such as what kind of dress I should wear for the ceremony, and whether we should visit certain landmarks. Our time quickly evaporated, and in short order we left the house to walk to the restaurant.

I hadn't been back to The Moss Room since the night I first met Gabriel. The newspapers had posted a story announcing the restaurant was closing to remodel, and yet somehow our French host had been able to reserve the entire space for our private dining pleasure. It was the kind of grandiose gesture he was known for. Gabriel was unselfish in his lavishness, always ensuring that others benefitted from the extravagance.

We walked down the staircase into the main dining room, which had been festooned with dozens of candles and small vases filled with tulips and peonies. Most of Gabriel's top staff people were present, but I did not see Nikola or Zoran in the crowd.

"*Bonsoir,*" I said, greeting Gabriel with a traditional kiss on both cheeks. Lily leaned in and gave him a kiss on one cheek, grasping his hand in one of hers for a gentle squeeze.

"Good evening, ladies," he said, as a server passed by us with a tray of Champagne-filled flutes.

"This all can't be for one election," I remarked, hoping that there was more to celebrate than me.

"Yes, yes of course," Gabriel said. "We won many elections across the country. Not as many as we would have hoped for, but overall our results were positive. This also is to celebrate you, the first human ever to be employed by the Council, and for you to meet a few more of the members of the organization."

It was a version of the truth, but again, I knew Gabriel was once again holding something back. Invariably, these inconsistencies occurred when we were standing amidst a crowd of people, with no way for me to press further. I hoped that if he traveled to Paris to see my mother's show, we would have an opportunity to talk privately about whatever it was he was hiding from me.

Not long after I took a glass of champagne, I felt William's presence. I turned as he and Josef descended the staircase. They wore black suits, narrowly tailored and made, no doubt, to order. William had paired a black tie against a crisp white shirt, Josef a silver tie against a shirt of light gray. Chic, elegant, timeless; they were easily the two most handsome men in the room, immortal and potentially lethal.

Lily's warning played in my head, her plea to delay any efforts to bind myself to him. And yet, as I watched him tonight, I could think of little else. He looked up at me and smiled, revealing in his glance that he understood the depths of my desire. There was no separation between us, no veil of mystery that new couples enjoy. Perhaps that was why we were so eager to be married.

Elsa walked in next, followed by Aidan. They stood side-by-side on the staircase, clearly inseparable. I hugged Elsa, asking her how she was doing.

"I'm fine, enjoying all of my free time now that I don't have to look after you," she said, with a wink. "Aidan and I are hoping to leave on a trip shortly to Scotland."

Another marriage? I wondered, but kept my thoughts muted.

"I'm hoping to be in Paris in the next week or so," I said. "To visit my mother."

"Your grandmother would be happy to know that," Elsa said. "When she was alive, she feared you two would always be estranged."

I didn't reply immediately, suddenly feeling wistful at the loss of my grandmother. She had acted as a buffer between my mother and me. Her death had resulted in an almost total withdrawal from my mother's life.

"Yes, she would have," I said thoughtfully. "She seemed to know a lot about my future; perhaps she saw that one day we would work through our differences."

Now it was Elsa's turn to shade her response. "She did see your future quite clearly. She loved you a great deal, and of course, she sent me to help you."

"Yes, and I will always be grateful, to her and to you."

The unsentimental Elsa I'd grown to know returned.

"I don't want your gratitude," she snapped. "I want you to use your instincts to continue to help people. What you did for Levi after that video was posted was amazing. There is no trace of the person I had to pull off the floor so many months ago."

"All thanks to you," I said. "I will never forget what you did for me, Elsa."

"You owe me no debt."

"Maybe not," I said, "But I hope that one day, if there is anything I can do for you, that you will ask."

Elsa nodded. We ended our conversation and went in search of our dinner companions. As I weaved in and out of the crowd, Gabriel picked up a knife and tapped it against his Champagne flute to catch the attention of the guests.

"Everyone, please… If I might have your attention," he said, grinning broadly. "We are here tonight to celebrate a good season for the Council." Applause filled the room briefly before he continued. "Our election portfolio was quite good, winning a little more than half of the U.S. races we chose to be involved in. And abroad, we helped ensure peaceful elections in several countries. All in all, it was a victory for democracy, and for religious and ethnic tolerance." More applause.

"In addition to our electoral victories, we successfully managed to integrate someone special into our ranks, a first for a human associate. I am speaking, of course, of Olivia Shepherd, our newest campaign specialist," he said, gesturing in my direction.

"As you all know, Olivia managed a win in a congressional race that was a high priority for us, despite a serious gaffe on the part of someone inside the campaign's inner circle. We're very proud of this historic alliance and look forward to assigning her even more ambitious projects."

In the spotlight, I smiled and raised my glass in salute to Gabriel.

"Thank you," I said, first to him, and then pivoted in a circle to thank those who were clapping. Gabriel beamed, fixing me with a stare for a moment, before informing the crowd that dinner would begin momentarily.

William was standing at my side, his arm gently draped across my back. Once my moment was over, I turned to him to see how he was faring.

"OK, now I can focus on you for the rest of the evening."

"Darlin, this is your night to mingle," he said. "Besides, we'll have plenty of time alone in Paris. Do you know when you want to leave?"

"As soon as possible," I said. "I need to check the airfares. I'm sure it's outrageous unless we book ahead."

"Don't worry about the cost; it's my treat," he said. "Consider it a honeymoon gift. One among many," he said. "Just decide when you want to leave."

"Let's leave at the end of the week," I said. "That gives me a few days to pack and shop."

"I thought the point of visiting Paris was to do the shopping there," he said, pulling a fresh glass off a tray for me. "Pack light and buy all new things when you're there."

I sipped my drink and savored the bubbles as they ran down my throat. "I guess it's good to know ahead of time that my husband has an extravagant side."

"All vampires are extravagant after a certain age," he said. "It makes life bearable.

As the dinner bell rang we moved to take our seats, searching the tables for our name cards.

"Gabriel could have done the seating at Versailles,"

Aidan said with some exasperation as he passed us in search of his own chair. "He excels at social management."

The first course arrived, a mixture of Vietnamese-inspired rolls, hot and cold, stuffed with combinations of shrimp, pork, cilantro and cellophane noodles. The rolls were followed by a series of clay pots that had been simmering for hours. They were filled with sauces in every color of the rainbow: yellow curry with potatoes, green curry with shrimp and green onions, red curry with chicken. Next came bowls of noodles tossed with Dungeness crab meat. Platters bearing whole steamed sea bass followed the noodles. It was a feast, paired expertly with sweetly crisp Rieslings to keep pace with the spicy food on the table. For dessert, *pot de crème*—chocolate pudding—was offered, but made the French way with more egg yolks and cream than one person should eat. It was a decadent, but satisfying, way to end a rich, spicy meal.

I glanced around the room, watching people under the sway of good food and wine. Aidan's remarks about Versailles struck me as prophetic, for we seemed perfectly suited, our small band of like-minded comrades, now sated, savoring our hard-fought victories.

After the luxurious meal, we all walked out of the Moss Room together, climbing the restaurant's steps in pairs and exiting through a steel gate located at what would normally have been the "backyard" of the Academy of Sciences. In the evening, the gate is unlocked so that guests can enter the restaurant when the museum is closed. We walked through the gate one by one, full of laughter and heady from multiple bottles of wine. We all walked slowly, lingering in the warmth of a good meal, made better by good company.

As we approached the street, something shiny and black caught my eye. I was not the only one; the group turned its collective head in unison. There, a few hundred feet ahead, sat a row of black Lexus SUVs. Clearly, Gabriel had arranged yet another luxury for his guests.

William and I stopped for a moment to admire the front of the Academy. It was early November, but the museum had already decorated its façade with Christmas wreaths and red bows. One of the largest natural history museums in the world, the front of the building was a mix of old and new, consisting of a set of massive, glass walls affixed atop the historic stone shell of the original building, built in the early 1900's. Steel beams run in a grid through the glass. The panels create a feeling of transparency, a fitting metaphor for the goals of an institution devoted to science and learning. Dozens of solar panels above the entryway serve as an awning in inclement weather, and provide electricity to the building.

Aidan was the first to approach his car, a smile on his face as he regarded Elsa from a distance. For some reason, she was trailing far behind him, deep in conversation with Madeline, who'd come late to the meal. Strangely, there was no driver standing outside his vehicle, or any of them, for that matter. The absence of drivers should have made us question the arrangements, but we were too much in the afterglow of our meal to notice the details.

The moment Aidan opened his door, the car exploded.

CHAPTER 36

The detonation of the first SUV set off a chain reaction, causing each car to explode and burst into flames, followed by the next, and then the next. I toppled over, dazed. Thick, black smoke filled the air around us, making it impossible to breath. Seared by the intense heat, the steel of the museum's façade began to whine as it twisted and bent against the inferno. The force of the explosions blew out the building's glass entrance so that the solar-panel awnings, having nothing further to rest on, collapsed to the ground.

It all happened so quickly. One minute we'd been standing together laughing, the next we were trapped—on one side by a wall of fire, on the other by a cascade of jagged glass shards falling to earth. There seemed no way to escape. Confused, disoriented from the deafening noise and blinding smoke, I lay on the pavement panting, listening to the chaos around me. At one point, I thought I heard Elsa screaming, but I couldn't be sure. I felt the heat of the fire on my skin, but could not see beyond where I lay.

William, who had been standing next to me, was gone. I didn't know when he had vanished and felt a pang of desperation to find him. The commotion all around me was disorienting and I had no idea where to look. I needed to move, but it was impossible to tell what direction to go as the cars continued to explode, sending pieces of metal everywhere. Finally, I realized that I had to get up immediately, and find my friends so we could escape the inferno.

I pushed myself up, only to nearly collapse from a sharp pain in the back of my leg. I made an awkward pivot to my left and immediately collided with Josef, who seized me tightly and started to shout. Despite the volume, it was hard to tell what he was saying over the ringing in my ears.

"I have her!" Josef yelled. "William, I have her!"

"How do we get out of here?" I asked, worried the fire would kill the vampires before they could escape the flames.

"We run," he said. "Now that we've found you, we run like hell." Josef grabbed my hand and started to pull me through the smoke. I resisted. It felt as if we were heading straight for the inferno.

"What about Elsa? And Gabriel? We have to find them too," I yelled, struggling against him. I could sense the immense fear my friends were feeling, but I could not see them through the smoke and ash of the fire.

"Don't stop," he growled. "Not for anything, not for anyone."

I obeyed, hearing the sound of fear in his voice, something I would have thought impossible a few weeks ago.

"Where is William?" I asked, wishing it was his hand dragging me through the curtain of smoke.

"He's moving the wounded to the fountain," he said quickly. "We're going to make a jump." He meant the portal; the fountain Elsa had called the Guardian. I realized we were only a few hundred yards away. Josef's mention of the wounded brought my thoughts back to Aidan.

"Aidan?" I asked, choking back a sob as I remembered that last moment when he had turned to smile at Elsa before reaching for the door handle.

"Dead, I presume," Josef said quickly, yelling over the noise. "We couldn't get close enough to see. We were looking for you. The force of the blast threw you backwards, away from the car, but then you seemed to disappear. Until you bumped into me, William and I couldn't see you through the smoke."

Although I tried, I wasn't able to pay attention to his words. I could barely hear. There was a tremendous buzzing in my ears. I was suddenly aware that my leg was throbbing, and it was difficult to walk. Josef was forced to drag me toward the fountain, my shredded leg trailing behind. I leaned down, trying to locate the pain, running my hand quickly along the back of my left thigh. My fingers returned, crimson, covered in my own blood. Josef saw my hand, but wouldn't let me stop.

"Later!" he said. "We need to get out of here before the police arrive. All of us; there can be no trace."

I nodded, trying to keep up with him, but it was a losing battle. The pain overwhelmed my mobility. My leg began to feel chilled in the night air thanks to all of the blood collecting in the fabric of my pant leg. When I caught a glimpse of Josef, I opened my mouth to tell him to leave me, that I was too injured to move, but I never had the chance. Darkness closed in and I felt a faint sensation of falling, and the sound of my name being called from far away.

I'm not sure how much time passed, but sometime later I awoke to "Drink, Olivia. Drink!" Those were the only words echoing in my head, and I struggled to respond, unable to awaken from a deep sleep. Someone was pushing me, imploring me to wake up, but I didn't want to. I was very tired, so I resisted. The person on the other end of my dream, though, was relentless and persisted, shaking me and rattling my bones until I regained consciousness.

I blinked several times, trying to make sense of the chaos and bloodshed before me. People were leaning against the walls of the room, some slumped on the floor, bodies wounded, bloodied, bandaged and disoriented. I scanned the faces, trying to piece it all together. Elsa was on her knees, hovering over a body under a sheet. Why, I wondered, were we all here? Then, as if to make the answer obvious, the searing pain returned, passing through my leg and shooting up my spine until it caught in my throat, forcing me to choke back the agony. Now, I was present, in the moment. My eyes opened wide and quickly recognized Josef's face directly in front of me.

"Drink, Olivia, you must drink from William," he implored me. William was also kneeling inches away from me. He was holding his arm in front of me, revealing an open cut, his blood pooling at the edges of the incision.

Despite my injuries, I managed to recall Lily's warning about drinking a vampire's blood.

"Why?" I managed to ask, my tongue rough and swollen in my mouth. "Is it safe? What will happen to me?"

"It's safe enough. Besides, you won't survive unless we stop the bleeding right away," Josef said. "You've lost a lot of blood. Drinking from William will help close the wound at the back of your leg more quickly."

William, stone-faced, nodded softly in agreement. He held my gaze, and I could hear him clearly inside my head pleading with me to hurry up before I bled to death.

I was in no position to doubt them, so I nodded.

William brought his arm to my lips and I opened my mouth. His blood was warm and sweet, quenching a terrible thirst I wasn't aware of until the liquid ran down my throat. After a few seconds of timid sipping, my body's survival instinct kicked in and I began to drink more robustly. Feverishly I drank from him until finally he pulled away. I mewed like a kitten whose milk bowl had been removed, but William soothed me.

"That's enough for now, darlin," he said softly. I heard him from a faraway place, his voice slightly muffled. I felt drowsy, maybe from his blood, and once again, I succumbed to sleep.

My rest was short-lived. I awoke a few minutes later to witness something I could hardly believe. William was stitching up the back of my leg. I came back to life with a start, just as he pulled a stitch through my skin.

"Olivia, love, stay still," William urged me. "Someone come over and hold her down."

"This hurts like hell," I said, to no one in particular, tears springing from my eyes.

I was rewarded with a sharp prick in my arm, and looked up to see Elsa holding a needle.

"You're a nurse too?" I asked, my words slurring as the painkiller dulled my senses.

"Try to rest, Olivia," Josef whispered. "This will help with the pain."

I did as I was told, and when I awoke the third time, I found myself in bed at William's house. This time I knew where I was, and sat up quickly, desperate to see William, to know that he was OK. I rose and saw that he was sitting in a chair across from the bed, a guitar on his lap, great sadness written on his face.

"I thought you were going to die," he said quietly. "You lost so much blood. The glass from the museum. You wouldn't wake up."

I began to recall the events at the concourse, the injury to my leg, Josef dragging me to the fountain to make the jump. I remembered drinking William's blood in a strange room I didn't recognize.

"I did wake up though," I said. "We were in a room with lots of people and you put your arm out. I did drink from you, right?"

William looked down at his guitar. "I didn't want this to be the way it happened," he said. "I wanted you to do it freely, to want to bind yourself to me."

"You saved my life," I said earnestly. "I would have died without your help."

"I know, but," he said, and then paused.

"But what?" I asked.

"You drank a lot of my blood," he said. "Once I drink from you, our bond will be very strong.

"Go ahead," I said, holding my arm out, wrist up. "Let's finish this so we can stop worrying."

"No," William said. "You're too weak. We'll have to wait until you are better to even consider it."

I was fully aware of the depths of his anguish. His feelings were strong inside me, almost parallel sensations to my own. I wondered if it would wear off eventually, but for now, I had another question.

"My leg," I asked. "Will I be able to walk again?"

"That depends," said a surly voice from the opposite corner of the room. It was Josef, walking into the room carrying a serving tray carrying a glass of water, a bowl of broth, a bottle of Jack Daniel's and two tumblers.

"Do you promise to listen to your nurses and follow their instructions?" Josef asked, setting the tray on my bedside table.

"Maybe," I grumbled. "What do I have to do?"

"Your leg will be fine," William said. "I asked Nadia to come over and examine it. You needed a lot of stitches. You sustained a pretty severe cut in the back of your thigh. It will heal, but you will be stiff for several days.

"What did Nadia do?" I asked, curious to know the extent of her healing powers.

"She made a salve that she rubbed over the wound. It was already healing rapidly because of my blood, but she says her salve will help keep the swelling down and prevent too much scarring."

I ran my hands along the bandages, admiring the tightness of the wrappings. "Did you learn how to do this when you were an ambulance driver?"

"A bit," William said. "But mostly later in the Resistance. We couldn't be sure there would be a doctor around so we had to learn to care for our own. Being the least squeamish about blood, I learned how to stitch wounds."

I paused for a moment, steeling my courage. "Did you have a lot of wounds to sew today?"

"It was yesterday, actually," Josef said, finishing his bourbon in one gulp. "You've been asleep for almost a day."

His words made me feel even more separated from my friends. People I'd seen last lying against a wall, covered in

EVETTE DAVIS

blood, perhaps their own, perhaps not. I had no idea who'd survived.

"You must tell me everything," I said. "I need to know."

William and Josef grimaced, but nodded in agreement.

"Aidan is dead," William said. "He was killed instantly when he opened the door of the car. We left his body at the scene when we first made the jump, but Elsa went back to search for his remains. She brought back what was left."

I buried my head in my hands, trying to banish the ghastly images William had described.

"Everyone else is alive," Josef added, pulling me out of my thoughts. "I was burned pretty badly on one arm. Gabriel suffered a series of cuts on his face from the glass."

"What about Elsa, and Lily?"

"Lily broke her arm," explained Josef. "It was a compound fracture which made for a lot of blood. She is in the next room resting. She wouldn't leave until she knew you were OK."

"Elsa was not harmed physically," William said. "She was the furthest away from the blasts when they happened, but…"

"But she saw the man she loved blown to pieces in front of her eyes," I said, tears streaming down my face. William came to sit on the bed with me, holding me gently in his arms.

"Yes. She's not said a word since it happened. She helped hold you down so I could sew your wound, gave you the shot that knocked you out, and stayed to see that you were stable. Then she left. I warned her not to go to Aidan's house, that it might also be booby-trapped. She nodded, but left anyway."

"Where's Gabriel?" I asked.

"He made a call and asked a security team to meet him at his apartment," Josef said. "He's expected back here tomorrow morning."

"Were you hurt?" I asked William.

"Miraculously, no," he said. "A piece of shrapnel hit me

306

in the leg, but it was minor. Josef and I took turns feeding after we treated your wound. Both of us are fine."

"Where were we? When I drank from you? I didn't recognize the place," I said.

"Vampire safe house," Josef said. "You know, vampires and our privacy. Occasionally we need a place to rest or to heal after an altercation. We have a spare house. We use it for those kinds of moments. It contains an infirmary of sorts and a doctor who's on call. She set Lily's bone in her arm. When you were all stabilized, we brought you and Lily back here. She was given a very powerful painkiller to ease her pain for the next few hours. Fortunately, fairies have rapid healing capability."

The three of us sat quietly for a moment, absorbing the details of the conversation we'd shared. Car bombs, vampire safe houses, security teams—so much for ghost stories and fairy tales. The real version was infinitely more lethal than the fables parents sent their children to bed with.

"Someone tried to kill us all last night," I said, wiping my eyes. "It wasn't some fluke accident or a case of mistaken identity, was it?"

"Car bombs are a specialty of the Serbian mafia," Josef said. "The door detonator is one of their signatures."

"Let's finish this conversation when Gabriel arrives tomorrow morning," William said abruptly. "Olivia needs to rest."

Josef bade us goodnight, saying he was going to look in on Lily. I wasn't sure how much I could rest thinking about my role in Aidan's death. If I hadn't pressed him to investigate, if I hadn't taunted Nikola in the lobby, maybe Aidan would still be alive.

"This is my doing," I murmured.

"No," William said. "Aidan was a grown man with years of experience. He wasn't sloppy. He wasn't emotional. He wouldn't have done anything simply because you asked him. He was killed because he either uncovered something, or confronted Nikola directly."

"That doesn't make me feel any better," I said, lying back on the pillows. My leg was beginning to throb and suddenly I felt exhausted. "Can I have something for my pain?"

William nodded and brought me a bottle. "Gabriel sent it over, it seems he has a pharmacist that fills prescriptions on demand. Take one, it's a Tylenol with codeine."

I swallowed a pill and laid my head back to wait for sleep. William came and stretched out beside me on the bed, our faces a few inches apart. Despite the pain in my leg, I leaned in to kiss him, yearning to be close to him. He returned my kiss, gently touching his lips to mine.

"That was close, Olivia," he said. "Too close. We have got to be careful until this is resolved." I nodded, sliding my body closer to his. As the codeine began to take effect, it registered with me that we still were in grave danger.

CHAPTER 37

My name was being uttered in harsh tones in a room nearby. I struggled to regain consciousness, my head still fuzzy from all the painkillers. I looked down to find my boiled wool slippers, the pair from home. William must have brought them for me. Sliding my feet into their comforting softness, I set off toward the voices.

My body felt awkward as I tried to move without putting pressure on my wounded thigh. It was a slow process; even my uninjured leg was stiff from lack of activity. I nearly screamed in triumph after I reached the foot of the stairs without falling or knocking anything over. From the top of the staircase, I could hear the voices clearly.

"There is no evidence at the blast site, nothing to tie us to the bombing." Gabriel said. "The police will learn nothing from the crime scene."

"If you're right, then Nikola will feel empowered to strike again," William said. "He has zero risk of being linked to the bombing. And if you're wrong, and we left something behind, a trace of clothing, a drop of blood, then it would be wise for us to leave town immediately."

"We don't know that it was Nikola," Gabriel said, exasperation in his voice. "Aidan never had a chance to tell me about his investigation. We have no idea what he uncovered."

"Even worse," Josef said, inserting himself into the discussion. "Our enemies have no idea what we have, but whatever it is they fear we know, they were willing to incinerate all of us to keep it from being revealed."

"It doesn't make sense," Gabriel said. "We don't conduct criminal investigations at the Council. Whatever information Aidan found would only have come to me."

"All the more reason for us to leave town," William said. "Do you have access to a private jet? We'll be more difficult to locate if we stay out of public terminals."

I'd been slowly descending the stairs even as I eavesdropped on their conversation. By the time William asked about a private plane, I was standing in the doorway of his living room.

"So I gather we're all going to Paris then," I said, catching the three men by surprise.

"Olivia," Gabriel said, jumping up to greet me. "*Ça va? Are you OK? Je me suis inquiété de ton santé.*"

"I'm OK," I answered, reaching out to touch Gabriel's face. His handsome lines had temporarily given way to dozens of small cuts. A small bandage crossed over one of his eyebrows, and a faint bruise clung to the side of his jaw. "How are you?"

"This?" he said, touching his face. "It is nothing, it will heal. It's you I'm worried about, and your friend Lily, her arm."

"Where is Lily?" I asked, directing my question to Josef.

"She left a few hours ago at daybreak," he said. "She said she wanted to see her family. I expect you will hear from her when she is feeling better."

When had Lily ever left without saying goodbye? She was no doubt horrified that I had nearly gotten her killed, thanks to my escapades. I hung my head for a moment, trying to absorb the magnitude of what had happened.

"I blame myself for all of this," I blurted out. "Aidan's death...if I hadn't pressed him, pressed you about the robbery, none of this would have happened. Where is Elsa? I have to apologize."

"Elsa's gone," Gabriel said. "I assume she jumped back into another time to escape all of this. If she were here, she would have shown up by now."

"I think she and Aidan were in love," I said, my voice very low. It was difficult to find the air to speak. My chest felt tight. "She told me they were going to Scotland. I thought maybe they would be married there."

"Olivia," Gabriel said sternly. "You must not blame yourself. Aidan was *my* deputy. I asked him to investigate; he acted on my orders. I have always regarded Nikola and Zoran as buffoons. That was my mistake. I was a fool to be so cavalier and now I have lost one of my greatest friends as punishment for my stupidity, and I put you in harm's way. Please forgive me."

"There is nothing to forgive," I said, feeling too drained to say anything more.

I hobbled over to a chair and gently lowered myself into the seat. William came over and sat on the edge.

"I do have a question," I said, addressing the three men in the room. "Was this about Aidan, or will Nikola try again? Are we in danger?"

"At this point, we don't really know," William said, placing his hand on mine. "We need a safe place where we can investigate and to decide what to do next."

"Then I was right," I said. "We need to go to Paris. It's easy to disappear there. And besides, my mother is expecting me. If Nikola does find out, he'll think I left to be with her."

"We have a small office in Paris," Gabriel said. "It will not look suspicious if I move my team there for a week or so. We have plenty of issues overseas to justify the trip."

"How much time do you need to arrange for our transportation?" William asked.

"Not long, a few hours at the most. I will be back in touch shortly. In the meantime, keep Olivia in your sight at all times. She must not be left alone."

William and Josef both nodded and I got the distinct impression that the conversation had started much the same way before I had entered the room.

CHAPTER 38

Later that evening, five of us—Josef, William, Gabriel, Madeline and I—set out for Paris. Gabriel sent a car for us at 10 pm, and by midnight we were in the air, traveling on Levi's private plane, with one stop in New York for refueling. Levi was only too happy to send us on what he thought was a celebratory trip after a successful election.

The flight crew brought several newspapers onboard, giving me a chance to read about the bombing. The police, the news accounts said, were baffled by the explosions, which at this point they were labeling an act of terrorism against the museum. One journalist theorized that an animal rights group opposed to the Academy's collection of reptiles and amphibians had set off the car bombs in protest. A special team had been brought in from the FBI. But so far, no human remains had been found, leading investigators to believe the bombs were detonated as a warning, a threat of further violence.

Did Aidan know what was coming, I wondered? Did he see the threat lurking? We'd never know. Hastily, I folded the newspaper against my chest and sat for a moment, my head down, contemplating the weight of what had transpired.

"Don't, Olivia," Gabriel said, as he sat down beside me. "This is my responsibility, you understand? Aidan was not an amateur. He didn't put himself in harm's way because of you."

I nodded, trying hard to swallow his logic. I opened the paper back up and pointed to a story. "I lost a lot of blood at the scene," I said. "Did you go back and bewitch the site?"

Gabriel nodded. *"Bien sûr.* Indeed, there was a lot of blood, and much of it was *not* human," he said. "I cast a spell to hide the evidence. The police will look and look, but never find a trace of DNA."

"How did you manage to get back there without being caught?"

"Magic, of course." He said. "The fog came in thick that night, but you know how this works, why are you asking?"

"I guess I needed to hear you say it," I said. "Since the moment we met, I've felt as if I've entered a world that seems to *defy* logic, or perhaps bend it a bit. I'm still absorbing it all. I should have died in the explosion. Instead I'm on a plane to Paris, my leg almost healed. The force of the car bombs collapsed the front of a major American museum, but the police will never know why it happened. We, the Council, are a heavy, but invisible, set of hands."

Gabriel regarded me for a moment after I finished speaking. He seemed poised to say something, but then merely put his hand on my knee, gave it a gentle squeeze and then got up and walked away. I watched him make his way to the other end of the plane, take a seat and close his eyes. Exactly, I thought. Cheating death, misleading a police investigation, the disappearance of Elsa and Lily. It was difficult to imagine more dramatic circumstances. It was enough to leave anyone speechless.

Hours later, the plane landed at a private terminal at Charles de Gaulle International Airport. Madeline was the first to depart, promising to quickly open the bureau and settle the staff. She wasn't seriously injured in the blast, but her wounds were painful all the same. The rest of us walked off the plane a few minutes later in somber silence. As we descended the stairway, I picked up on the group's feelings that we were missing part of our team. No Elsa, no Aidan, and no Lily. Their absence was palpable, but we had no choice but move forward.

I could think of little but justice, of catching Aidan's murderer. I had intended to pressure Gabriel to develop a plan, but still feeling shell-shocked and grieving, I couldn't find the courage to press him while we were in the air. Later, after a day or so had passed, I would ask what he intended to do to punish Nikola. All of my instincts told me he was the person responsible for this calamity.

Revenge fantasies occupied my thoughts during the drive into Paris. After making our way through the usual maze of landmarks, we arrived at the 10th arrondissement and the Rue du Faubourg Saint Martin, where William's apartment is located. The driver removed our bags from the car, and we bade Gabriel á bientôt, promising to see him later that evening, perhaps for drinks.

While I marveled at the stark elegance of the nineteenth century buildings, Josef stepped under the building's awning to punch in the security code. William and Josef's apartment was just steps away from the Canal Saint Martin and the Quai de Valmy, an up-and-coming neighborhood where many of the city's fashionable boutiques set up shop.

"Remind me again." I asked. "What year did your father buy this apartment?"

"Nineteen thirty," William said. "A broker, another vampire, found it for us. This neighborhood was not always so chic. We needed a place out of the spotlight."

"Do you visit often?"

"I was here last spring," he said. "I usually come in April and leave at the end of June before it gets too hot. Despite my Southern roots, I don't care much for the heat. Explains why I like San Francisco. I've also visited in November and stayed through winter. The time I spend here hinges on where else I need to be."

"Where else do you need to be?" I asked, curious, as we loaded some of our luggage into the tiny elevator inside the building. Josef had decided to take the stairs. The elevator door closed and William continued. "I own property in Paris, Zagreb, New Orleans and San Francisco," he said. "Some are long-term rentals, others I advertise as short-term vacation places."

"And this apartment?" I asked, as we stepped into the elevator.

"This is our family home," he said. "No one else stays here."

The family home occupied the top floor of a six-story building. I counted four bedrooms and three bathrooms on my tour, as well as a kitchen, a living room, a formal dining room and a terrace that wrapped around most of the apartment, giving each of the bedrooms a small veranda. Clearly, a caretaker or concierge helped maintain the apartment. Trees and plants on the deck were healthy and lush. The apartment itself was immaculate, free of any lingering odor that usually accompanies a home that has been abandoned or closed up for long periods of time. Freshly cut flowers had been placed in vases in every room.

The shell of the apartment maintained its nineteenth century bones through original moldings and wood floors. Beyond that, the space had recently been remodeled to include modern appliances and conveniences. A dizzying array of art lined the walls—paintings, sketches, and propaganda posters—all of it documenting the decades marking the dawn of modern Europe. Antiques and modern pieces of furniture were paired together in great harmony, achieving the perfect Parisian salon.

"It's a magnificent home," I said, standing in the living room. "I can see why you keep it private."

William glanced over at Josef, who'd walked in with our remaining bags.

"It's the last link we have to our father," William said quietly. "We've maintained and updated the property as necessary to avoid attention from my neighbors. "This *arrondissement* wasn't always so fashionable. But we wanted to be away from the center of the city to attend to our needs in private."

"It's beautiful," I repeated.

"We can live here if you like," William said, taking my

hand. "At least part of the year. That is, if you don't mind Josef popping in and out."

"I would love to live here," I said. "I'll have to ask Gabriel. Since there is an office here, perhaps he won't mind."

"You don't have to work," he said. "Once we're married, I mean. I have plenty of money and so do you. We could disappear and enjoy the surroundings."

"Are you being romantic, or trying to protect me?"

"A little of both."

I confess, it sounded splendid. Paris is a city of infinite diversions, not to mention a fabulous access point to the rest of Europe. Wouldn't it be magical, I thought, to explore the world with William, lingering here and there as the mood struck us. It was an attractive offer, and I was giving it serious thought. That is, until current circumstances brought me back to reality in the form of a sore, tired leg. I shifted my weight off the wounded limb, leaning back and forth to reduce the discomfort. It seemed our long flight was finally catching up with me.

"I need a bath," I said, fluttering my eyelashes. "Care to join me?"

"Darlin, it would be my pleasure," William said. "But you go without me. I should pay a visit to our concierge to let her know we're settled. I phoned her before we left, which is why we arrived to find things so civilized. When you're finished, meet us on the deck for a drink."

Before leaving, he walked me into the master bedroom. Spacious, its walls painted in royal blue, a wooden four-poster bed dominated the room, with a chandelier hanging above it. If Lily were here, she'd have said the room was something straight out of a romance novel. Too true, I agreed, as I gazed around at the antique chests along the wall, and then slowly I ran my fingers along the chocolate brown linen duvet and matching pillows that covered the bed. I was no stranger to money or elegance, but living for centuries seemed to provide an advantage when it came to meaningful, timeless décor.

I entered the bathroom and studied the porcelain knobs on the bath as I ran the hot water. While the tub was filling, I decided to call my mother's hotel and let her know I was in town. Explanations would be in order for arriving early, but as I dialed her number at the Ritz, I decided that sticking with the truth—that we'd had an opportunity to come earlier by private plane—was the best idea. Any deviation, however small, and she would certainly detect it. I was spared putting my theory to the test, however, when I was informed that my mother was out at her gallery for the afternoon, so I left word with the front desk.

Near the tub was a large glass jar with bath salts. I removed the lid and inhaled, delighted by the scents of geranium and rose oil. I sent a generous scoop cascading into the steaming water and prepared to settle in. Once submerged, I let out a grateful sigh as the heat soaked through my bones and muscles, dissolving the stiffness brought on by travel and fatigue. I closed my eyes and let my mind wander, lulled by the quiet. I drifted away, pulled into a dreamlike state as I inhaled the perfumed oils. I would have gladly stayed that way were it not for Josef's voice breaking the spell.

"Be careful now… you might drown," he said, regarding me lazily from the doorway.

"Go away," I said, sending him my fiercest gaze. "I would never have pegged you as a peeping tom. How long have you been standing there?"

"Long enough," he said, waggling his eyebrows. "I came in to check on you, it was so quiet. I feared you were about to fall asleep."

"Unlikely, but thank you, mission accomplished," I said. "It seems your work is done here."

Josef didn't budge. Instead he regarded me, and I mean all of me, silently, the two of us staring at each other. Locked in his gaze, it occurred to me that this was a test; it was always a test with him. For my part I refused to play the prude; showing any discomfort would only bring him pleasure.

"Out with you," I said, my voice made of sterner stuff this time, while flicking water at him from the tub. "You may go and let your brother know I'll join you both for drinks shortly."

Josef grinned, amused at my firm rebuke. "As you wish, my lady," he said bending at the waist, before turning out of the bathroom.

After he'd gone, I rose from the tub and wrapped a towel around myself. I dried off and returned to the bedroom to find my suitcase. As I crossed the room to get my things, I noticed that my leg felt much better, most of the stiffness gone. It was amazing that I could walk at all, and I marveled at how William's blood had saved my life. My life was becoming more interesting than any science fiction novel I'd ever read.

I pulled on a black woolen sweater-dress and paired it with suede boots and a brown-and-black leopard print pashmina shawl. I'd vacillated about whether to bring the boots. Being in a hurry usually means packing light. But this was Paris, and I was loath to arrive underdressed for the most elegant city in the world.

I gave myself one last look in a small mirror on a table and went in search of William and Josef. As I progressed down the hallway I popped my head into each of the apartment's rooms again, admiring the décor along the way. I found the two brothers seated outside on the terrace, a bottle of red wine decanting in a glass vessel on a table next to them. Next to the wine, apple slices, bread and a small selection of cheeses had been arranged on a wooden tray. Heaters were set up around the furniture, making the outside temperature comfortable. I looked up at William, who winked at me, "*Bon appétit, ma chère.*"

"*Merci pour l'aperitif. C'est très charmant,*" I said, thanking him for a lovely meal. I was famished, having eaten little in the days prior to our trip. It felt good to sit and eat, to drink French wine, and gaze across the rooftops. For a few moments, I pretended that none of the memories I was carrying existed. No danger pending, no death, no mourning, no loss. It was a selfish thing, burying them away. But for a few seconds, I wanted to feel happy, not be obligated to carry the lost and the dead with me in my heart.

"Did you reach your mother?" William inquired, pulling me back to earth.

I looked over and gazed at my future husband, pale and lovely in the dusk. My heart did a little flip in my chest watching him; he was mine and I was his, our blood mingled in our veins. William smiled at me, clearly hearing my thoughts. His smile was small and private, and I knew that he understood.

"I didn't reach her but left a message," I said. "She's out at her gallery, so I don't expect to hear back from her until tomorrow. She'll work until very late and then go to bed. I was planning on inviting her to meet us tomorrow for drinks at a café nearby."

"Do I get to meet your mother?" Josef asked, a petulant tone attached to the question. "Are you introducing the whole family?"

Good question, I mused. *Hello, Mom, meet your new sons-in-law, they're vampire brothers.* But how could I not? In for a penny, in for a pound, I decided. "Yes, of course. After everything we've been through, I'm not hiding anything from my mother."

That brought a rare, joyful smile from Josef. We passed the next hour amicably, making small talk while I nibbled away at the bread and cheese. Not long afterwards, it was decided that we needed to experience Paris nightlife. William suggested an old jazz club in the Latin Quarter, where he knew a full bar and reliable musicians could be found. There was a taxi stand near the apartment and within minutes we'd secured a cab. Josef slid in first, giving the driver directions in impeccable French.

"Did you speak French before the war?" I asked.

Josef looked over at William, a private memory shared between them. "No," he said. "I spoke Czech primarily, a bit of Hungarian…a little German and English. French is something I acquired in my second life."

The cab made its way toward the Latin Quarter. We were heading to a club located underground that didn't open until 10 pm, wouldn't really be in full swing until midnight, and closed only when the sun began to rise. The doorman greeted William and Josef by name, sending us inside with a hearty *bonne soirée* and a pat on the back. A helpful but flirtatious woman brought us to a table in the rear of the club. Drinks were promptly served and we sat back to enjoy the music.

A lone pianist under a spotlight began to play a sad, crisp lament that seemed to pay tribute to some far off place. Soon, a man appeared with a bass, then another with a trumpet, and *voila*, we were treated to a blues trio.

A few numbers into their set, William excused himself from the table and disappeared. He did not return again until he appeared on stage, a guitar in his hand. I watched, amused, as he and the pianist opened up a spirited rendition of "St. James Infirmary," the piano grinding out the notes against an upright bass and guitar. I closed my eyes, listening as William played. He remained on the stage for a few more numbers and then finally set his guitar against the wall and returned to our table.

"Play here often?" I teased.

"A bit," he said. "I know most these guys, a few of them are vampires, so it's always easy to ask if I can sit in when I'm in town."

Good music and an abundant list of drinks helped the night pass quickly. Eventually, I grew weary, jet lag finally catching up with me, and I asked if we could make our way back home. Josef scowled at first, clearly intent on staying until dawn.

"Feel free to stay," I said. "I don't want to be responsible for killing your fun."

"I'll see you both home and then go on from there," he said, picking up my wrap and handing it to me.

CHAPTER 39

Josef proved as skillful at hailing a cab to get us home, as he was in jumpstarting our evening. I was beyond exhausted and allowed myself to be led out of the taxi and into the building.

Soon, I found myself squeezed into the elevator with both of them. It might have been fatigue, the tight space, the dim light of the *ascenseur*, perhaps even the vast amount of Champagne I'd drunk, but whatever the cause, I leaned back on both men, pressing my body against them as we rode to the top floor. I turned my head to rest on William's shoulder, taking in his scent. Josef meanwhile began to do the same, leaning in to inhale me at the place where my pulse beat strong in my neck. I could feel the electricity of his lips hovering above my skin. He pressed himself against me, so that I was folded neatly between them.

I felt the question in my bones before it was asked, but I wasn't sure of the answer. I briefly thought of Lily and wondered whether Josef meant something to her. I picked my head up to face William. He kissed me deeply, his thoughts clear that it would be my decision. I turned toward Josef, knowing what he desired. I leaned in and kissed him as well, too curious not to have a taste. He raised his hand to cup my face as our lips met. His hands were as cold as William's, but did not feel the same upon my skin. William, meanwhile, was holding my hand, a reminder that he was by my side.

The elevator door opened as, absorbed in our own world, we spilled out into the entryway, an unruly threesome.

Composure regained, we strode out and approached the door, silent, focused on what would happen next. William reached into his pocket for the key and opened the door to the apartment. We stepped inside and I turned to William and kissed him again. Josef stood behind me running his hand along my spine. Together they removed my dress so that I was standing between them in little more than my suede boots. William slowly began to caress my arms, moving his hands along my shoulders, then down my back and along the curve of my backside. Josef, ever impatient and hungry, bypassed the niceties and slid his hand between my legs. His hand grew wet within seconds, my body eagerly responding. He easily tempted my body, and he knew it. Like a hungry cat playing with its prey, Josef fixed me with a ravenous stare.

It was the ferocity of his gaze that brought me out of my trance. Two vampires and one woman, not to mention a best friend back home...I recognized it as the recipe for a melodrama I didn't want to partake in. I smiled at Josef and placed my lips gently against his before speaking.

"I can't do this," I said. "I am attracted to you, I won't deny it, but..."

"But you love my brother," Josef said gruffly.

"Please don't paint me so provincial," I scolded. "You know I want you, but I am not ready for that kind of life."

"Another time then, perhaps," Josef said, kissing me again on the lips. I let him, drinking in his lust. There was a part of me that regretted sending him away, but I knew I'd made the right decision.

Not long afterwards, Josef left the apartment, no doubt in search of someone to relieve his tension. William and I quickly fell into bed, making furious love to each other. Later, as I was on the edge of sleep I asked him, "Did you expect me to refuse him?"

"I hoped," he whispered in my ear, spooned up against me.

"It wasn't a hard decision," I said, and drifted away.

The next afternoon, the aroma of freshly baked *pain au*

chocolat lulled me out of a deep sleep. I turned over to find William's side of the bed empty, but I hadn't expected him to stay the night.

Too much Champagne, combined with jet lag, made my exit from bed a slow affair. Eventually I tumbled out and threw on a beautiful grey cashmere robe that had been left nearby on a chair. It was a lovely gift, made sweeter because I hadn't asked for it. I tied the robe at my waist and walked into the hallway, on alert for the prowling brother. I was hoping he had gotten what he wanted the night before. I strolled into the kitchen and found the plate of *patisserie*. William had set a note on the platter, along with an apartment key, letting me know he was out for the day to run some errands. There was no sign of Josef. I grabbed the key and a croissant and went back to our room to dress.

It was time, I decided, for me to find Gabriel, return to work, and locate Aidan's killer.

Museums, it seemed, were the location of choice for the Council. The satellite office, as Gabriel had called it, was located inside the Musée de l'Orangerie, a small, but remarkable impressionist gallery located in the Jardin des Tuileries. It is a memorable destination for a number of reasons, but for me it is because it is home to the "*Nymphéas*," the eight legendary murals featuring water lilies by Monet. As I strolled out of the Concorde metro station adjacent to the Tuileries at dusk, I was looking forward to seeing the muted tones of the paintings again, set as they are in twin oval-shaped rooms with nothing to distract you from their peaceful views.

Following the directions that had been emailed to me, I approached the front door of the museum and flashed a badge that had been sent by courier to the apartment. Ingenious in its design, it appeared to be a kind of temporary badge issued to visiting scholars and professionals. The guard briefly looked at the badge and waved me in. I used my skills to locate Gabriel, pressing hard for him to send word about where they were gathered.

"Come to the bookstore," was his crisp reply inside my head, and I walked down a set of stairs to the second level, where a large gift shop occupied most of the space.

Gabriel appeared through the crowd, his ID clipped to his shirt pocket. He could have been any diligent docent, a retired teacher or accountant giving his time to the public. He smiled and beckoned silently to me to follow him. He walked toward the rear of the shop and opened a door that was almost hidden in the corner between two sets of bookshelves. Once we passed through the door, a familiar-looking scene revealed itself, very similar to the Council offices in San Francisco. Another array of desks and touchscreens occupied the space, only this time the faces of people staring into them appeared graver and more serious than they had been back home.

We continued to a small conference room. Gabriel waved me in and followed, shutting the door before he turned to face me.

"*Ça va?*" he asked, as we stood regarding one another.

"*Comme si, comme ça,*" I said. "I mean, I'm as good as I can be. You?"

"The same," he said, "I have not slept well since we arrived."

I experienced a tinge of guilt as I thought of my rooftop meal, the late night at the jazz club, and my encounter with the brothers. It was all I could do to stay awake as dawn approached. But I realized for Gabriel, his mind still stuck on the loss of Aidan, peace would not return for some time.

"What have you learned?" I asked, pushing the image of my abruptly halted threesome from my mind.

"Nothing, everything," he said, distracted. The door to the room opened, and Madeline walked in.

"*Bon après-midi,*" I said, grasping her hand. I was impatient, and regarded her for only a moment, before pressing Gabriel with the question at hand.

"When can we confront Nikola?"

"We must be careful, Olivia," Gabriel said. "Nikola is a

member of the Council and next in line as deputy."

"Careful? He killed Aidan, he almost killed us."

"Perhaps, but we have no proof," Madeline said. "At least not enough yet to ask Zoran to dismiss him as deputy."

"And what if Zoran is in on this too?"

"Olivia," Gabriel said, "Aidan's phone shows a half-dozen texts and calls exchanged with Nikola earlier in the day before the bombing. The day before, there are another six-to-ten calls recorded on his phone. There is no communication between Aidan and Zoran. No emails, no phone calls and no texts. If Aidan suspected Zoran was involved, he would have contacted him."

"Well at least we know more than we did before we left for Paris," I said. "What else?"

"Aidan's laptop had a series of files with Interpol notices containing information about Serbian mafia figures who are wanted across the globe," Peter said. "The man you saw visiting Nikola is listed on one of the bulletins."

"Nikola had to have known his friend was a wanted man," I said. "Perhaps that's why they tried to blind me that day during the robbery, so I couldn't see what they looked like."

Gabriel began to pace the room, his hands buried deep inside his chinos. "These are only theories," he said. "But it's not evidence that he killed Aidan. There is nothing to tie him to the bombings... *rien!*"

"We need to find something," I said. "It's out there, we just need to look. Gabriel, you must ask William to help the Council. You must ask him to investigate this for us."

Gabriel's unspoken reply was clear inside my head. *He will have to leave you. You will not see him again for some time. Is that what you want?*

"It doesn't matter what I want," I said aloud. "What matters is finding out who killed Aidan. You must ask him tonight. Come meet us for drinks so we can discuss what needs to happen next."

For the next hour, Gabriel and Madeline shared a more

detailed timeline of Aidan's last days, reconstructing what he had researched, and whom he had contacted. His search had taken him to Interpol's most-wanted lists, Scotland Yard and the FBI. He had contacted Nikola, too, and it was obvious they'd been having a conversation, although what they had said was not a part of our records.

I remembered my run-in with the cagey Serb—it was possible they spoke of nothing related to Aidan's inquiry. It was also possible they had been quite direct with one another. Only Nikola knew, and for the moment we had no intention of asking him. Our briefing completed, I excused myself from the offices and made my way down to the galleries that that display Monet's water lillies. I walked into the first oval gallery, its lights low and pale to encourage serene reflection. I lowered myself onto a bench in the middle of the room, stretched out my legs and leaned back to regard the paintings.

"It's amazing that these were created during World War I, don't you think?" Madeline asked, as she sat down next to me. "To be in the middle of war and create something of such lasting beauty."

"He brought them here to this museum to ease the suffering of the French," I said. "To give them something to help them heal after the war."

"Exactly," she said. "As a diplomat, I have always been struck by his gesture. As a witch, I have marveled that a human could create such a treasure with no help from magic. He felt a higher calling, when no obligation existed."

We were not, I decided, having a discussion about the paintings.

"Why are you telling me this?" I asked.

"Because you are capable of great things, but revenge should not be first on the list," she said. "I sense that you are struggling with your role in all of this. You must push yourself to see the bigger picture."

"I see a friend who has been murdered and no way to hold his killer accountable," I said quietly.

"Exactly," she said, a sad smile on her face as she walked

away. "Try, if you can, to see more of the landscape."

Enveloped in the violet light of the paintings, I lingered, forcing myself to see the landscape as Madeleine suggested. I sat on the bench ruminating. Aidan's death was a blow to the Council, robbing the organization of one of its best. This was no mere chink in the armor. He had been Gabriel's top lieutenant, murdered in front of his eyes, and it had been a close call for Gabriel himself. Who would risk such a thing? What could motivate someone to be so audacious?

I began to understand what Madeline had meant: My anger had narrowed my view of the situation. My obligation should be to protect the Council, not avenge my friends. A vibration coming from inside my purse rousted me out of my thoughts. I quickly made my way upstairs and back into the hidden offices where I could return the call without the scrutiny of the museum's security.

"Hello, Mom," I said. "Or should I say, *Bonjour, maman*?"

"Either's fine, *ma chère*," she said. "Where are you?"

"With Gabriel, at our offices," I said. "I was hoping you would join us all at a bar near the Canal Saint Martin at seven tonight. I have so much I want to tell you, a lot has happened in the last few days. Can you come?"

I could feel her concern through the phone.

"Mom, everything is OK," I said. "I promise. Come enjoy a nice evening with me."

"Of course I'll come," she said.

"Great," I said. "I don't remember the name, except it's got the word bar in it and a bright blue awning. The address is sixty-eight Quai de la Loire."

We hung up and then I texted William to check in. He responded and said he would meet me at the apartment. I collected my things and looked around for Gabriel. One of the staff said he'd already left for the day, so I texted him the address of the bar. As I walked back to the metro, I began readying myself for an evening I knew would be full of proverbial bombshells.

CHAPTER 40

William, Josef and I arrived at the bar and grabbed two tables outside facing the canal. The night air was crisp but clear and so, with a good hat and coat, it was bearable to sit outside. William and Josef volunteered to go up to the bar and place an order. That left me sitting next to Gabriel. I leaned in closer to him to better hear our conversation over the din of traffic on the street. I hadn't mentioned my mother was meeting us until we arrived at the bar. His face, upon hearing the news, took on an odd expression.

"You mustn't worry," I said, watching the traffic pass by. "My mother is a bit of an eccentric, but harmless. I promise."

Gabriel smiled, but said little. He seemed a bit nervous. I could feel his tension, but could not detect the cause of his distress. It didn't concern me. It seemed natural that he would be anxious, given the last few days. As I leaned in once more to speak to Gabriel, the sound of my mother's voice caught my attention.

"Olivia, Olivia," she said, pleading for my attention as she crossed the street to join us.

I stood up as she reached our table. "Mom, hello," I said. Suddenly I was overwhelmed with dread; icy cold and creeping slowly up my spine. I shrugged off the sensation, hoping to understand everyone's feelings better as the evening progressed. Since Gabriel was directly next to me, I decided to begin introductions with him.

"Mom, let me introduce…"

"I don't need an introduction," my mother said, cutting

me off. "I know who your boyfriend is and you must stop immediately."

I couldn't fathom how she knew about William and I glanced at the bar where he stood placing our drink order. "Mom, why would you say such a thing? I asked. "You've only just arrived and…"

"For God's sake, Olivia, the man is your father."

"My father, what on earth are you talking about?" I was baffled.

Now it was her turn to be silent. Her gaze was fixed on Gabriel, and to my surprise, he was staring back at her.

"Hello, India," he said, sorrowfully.

"You two know each other?" I asked, feeling their collective dread freezing the blood in my veins. It was obvious they had not planned on seeing one another again in their lifetimes. William and Josef arrived, drinks in hand, but paused as they read our body language. I held out my hand and drew William to my side.

"Mom, *this* is my boyfriend," I said.

India Rose narrowed her gaze, and I held my breath waiting for her to discover he was a vampire.

"I don't understand," she said.

"What do you mean?" I asked.

"All of the travel you two have been doing, the last-minute trip to Paris…I assumed that he was preparing to make you his lover," she said, waving her hands frantically in the air toward Gabriel. "When I finally realized who he was, I had to come to warn you to stay away."

"You know Gabriel?" I asked again, realizing that neither of them had answered that question.

"Olivia," Gabriel said, remorse in his eyes.

In those few seconds, my mother's ranting became crystal clear.

"Wait," I said. "She means *you?* You are my father," I half-asked, half-declared.

"I was going to tell you," he said. "Please, I came to Paris with the intention—"

"But my mother beat you to it," I said, cutting him off as the blood rushed into my ears.

Then I spun around to confront my mother.

"Mom, you knew where my father was all of these years, but you never told me?"

I was staring at my mother and Gabriel, trying to see them clearly—these two people I thought I knew suddenly transformed by their lies. I turned back to Gabriel.

"Why now? I have been working with you ... for how many months?"

A long, cold silence unraveled before us.

"I never told Gabriel I was pregnant," my mother blurted out, breaking the silence. "I didn't want him to take you away from me."

"Take me away?"

"Olivia," Gabriel said, "I am from a powerful family of witches. My relatives would have wanted to raise you in France."

"But I...I'm not a witch," I said, shocked by the facial expressions of the four people before me. I was in the minority opinion in this argument. I looked over at William, whose face wore the grim mask of someone who had inadvertently gotten trapped in the middle of a major betrayal.

"You knew?" I asked, quietly.

"I suspected," he said.

"Mom?"

"I didn't want him to take you away," she said, "His family wouldn't let him marry a human. So I never told him that I was pregnant."

"Are you telling me that you knew he was a witch?" I asked. "You must have known I would have some of his traits. Were you ever going to tell me?"

"I didn't think that far ahead," she answered. "I wanted to keep you with me, with your grandmother. I knew one day I would have to tell you, but then you refused to use your powers, and I thought maybe it wouldn't matter. Then your grandmother died and I didn't know what to do."

"Grandmother," I repeated. "She's the one who caused all of this. She is the one who summoned Elsa."

"Who is Elsa?" my mother asked, confused.

"I'm not really sure," I said under my breath.

"Elsa didn't realize who you were at first," Gabriel said. "I was the one who figured it out. She wanted to tell you. She wanted me to tell you."

"She didn't though. And you didn't," I said. "All of you knew, but you didn't tell me. How dare you play with my life like that? How dare you lie to me?"

"Olivia," Gabriel pleaded. "You must listen. You are my daughter, my only heir."

"You can go to hell," I said. "Both of you. I never want to see either of you again."

"Olivia," Gabriel said, "You cannot walk away. There is too much to discuss."

"That is exactly what I am doing," I said, barely aware of my surroundings, my pulse in my throat.

"What did you think would happen when I found out that you both had lied to me?" I continued. I grabbed my purse and began to walk away. "Did you really think this would end happily?"

I turned my back on the only mother I'd ever known, my newly discovered father, and walked away. I did not look back, my forehead burning with anger and humiliation. All the years I had wondered and asked about my father and my mother had known who he was. And then there was the Council. There had never been a real opportunity for me there. It was a setup from the start, from the minute Gabriel knew of my existence.

Looking back, it seemed even worse than that, for he must have known I had skills—like becoming invisible, or the telepathy—that I could not even imagine possessing. And he sat back and watched them unfold, an owner watching his pedigreed animal prance and kick to the pace of its trainer.

I felt sick, wondering if anything or anyone I'd come to rely on could be trusted.

William and Josef trailed alongside me, saying nothing while they raced to open the door to the apartment. They were right to treat me gingerly. I was infuriated, horrified at being betrayed and unsure of whom to trust. Once we were inside the apartment, I turned to face William, my hands clenched at my sides.

"Did you know Gabriel was my father?" I asked. "Did he set this whole thing up so we would meet? Are you my compensation for him dragging me into his intrigue? Did he promise me to you in exchange for being my bodyguard?"

William glared at me and then picked up one of the nineteenth-century vases in the room and threw it against the wall. I winced at its impact, exploding into a thousand pieces.

"Give me some credit, Olivia," he said. "I am 181 years old. Do you really think I would agree to an arranged marriage to a human?"

"*Ohhh,* but I'm not human, not one hundred percent anyway. I'm part witch, a fact you seem to have figured out some time ago."

"I only suspected, but I wasn't certain," he said. "Gabriel told me you were his daughter the night Aidan died. He intended to tell you everything in Paris, but your mother got there first. He swore me to secrecy. He wanted to be the one to tell you. As usual, you fled the scene before you gave him a chance to explain."

"Explain what?" I barked. "How he tricked me into joining the Council? How he lured me into his convoluted schemes, putting my life in danger, while failing to let me know he was my father? How can he possibly provide a satisfactory explanation for any of this?

Josef walked into the room, a furious look on his face. As he approached I thought he might strike me, his body was coiled so tightly.

"That's enough, Olivia! Calm yourself. No vampire would bind himself, give his blood, *risk his life,* unless he was truly in love," he said. "If you want to be angry at your mother and father, fine, be angry. But don't take it out on William, or me, for that matter. We're your allies… maybe the only people you can trust."

Josef words snapped me out of my hysterics and I hung my head for a moment, feeling deflated. He was right, of course. I looked up at William, transmitting my deep regret through every fiber of my body.

"I am sorry," I said. "This is all so shocking."

William came to stand next to me, holding my hand and running his fingers across the copper bands on my finger.

"I'm sorry, too," he said. "I should have told you my suspicions."

"Listen up," Josef said. "We have bigger issues to consider. First there is the fact that as Gabriel's heir, Olivia is technically eligible one day to assume his seat on the Council. If Nikola and his allies find out, it will give them another reason to harm her. Second, she is next in line to head one of the most powerful witchcraft families in Europe, not to mention one of perhaps a handful of children ever produced from a human and witch union. Rare, powerful and in line for the throne, that is a potent trio of considerations."

I was shocked to hear myself laughing at Josef's remarks, perhaps out of distress, perhaps out of fear. "Forgive me. I think you are making too much of it," I said. "I'm not nearly that important. I was running one tiny campaign in Silicon Valley."

"Yes," Josef agreed, "because that is what Gabriel wanted. He wanted to keep your profile low, until he could assess your abilities, but then you stumbled onto the robbery and began to reveal your skills—telepathy, invisibility. He knew he was running out of time."

I stood silent, unable to think of a response.

"Olivia, darlin, stop thinking like a human," William said. "You're an Other, at least partially, and that part, however big or small, is what counts now. The rules in our world are different and, I'm afraid, less forgiving."

I was too bewildered to speak. Lily was thousands of miles way. Elsa was missing. I was estranged from my parents and far from San Francisco, and yet I knew I could not go home again. Nothing I knew, or remembered, made sense.

"We need to get out of here," I said finally. "I want to disappear for a while, until I can figure this out."

William nodded. "I'm ready to go now," he said, clasping my hand. "But you know you can't stay hidden forever."

"I know," I said. "I just want a little time to think about all of this. Someplace where Nikola won't find us, or at least might not try to kill us."

Josef regarded us both for a moment before speaking, a knowing smile slowly appearing in his face.

"Pack your bags," he said. "I know just the place."

THE END

ACKNOWLEDGEMENTS

I'm blessed to be part of a circle of extremely intelligent, talented women who have all helped in some way with the publication of this novel. I want to thank Sara Hillman, my friend and neighbor who created my web site, and Leah Hefner, the gifted graphic designer who created the artwork for *Woman King.*

I also would like to acknowledge Marcia Schneider for her unwavering friendship and editing skills that helped shape this book, and Donna Bero, whose confidence has helped me to accomplish great things.

ABOUT THE AUTHOR

Evette Davis is co-owner of a San Francisco-based public affairs firm. She also serves on the board of Litquake, founders of San Francisco's iconic literary festival.

Prior to founding her firm, Davis worked in Washington as a press secretary for a member of Congress, and as a reporter for daily newspapers in the San Francisco Bay Area. She earned her bachelor's degree in communications from Mills College in Oakland, California.

For more information visit www.evettedavis.com, or follow her on Twitter, @SFEvette.

Made in the USA
San Bernardino, CA
09 May 2013